KISSING THE EARL

"Is something wrong, Sophie?" Simon's voice—an unfamiliar husky growl—made her legs tremble with a delicious weakness.

"No, Simon," she breathed. "Not a thing."

"I'm glad."

His lips moved over her cheekbone and down her jawline, trailing fire all the way. She clutched at the collar of his coat, trying to pull him to her mouth.

"Simon." Her voice whispered the plea.

The next moment he swooped, covering her lips in a kiss so devouring that she almost swooned from the sheer joy of it. . . .

Books by Vanessa Kelly

MASTERING THE MARQUESS

SEX AND THE SINGLE EARL

Published by Kensington Publishing Corporation

Sex And The

SINGLE EARL

VANESSA KELLY

ZEBRA BOOKS
KENSINGTON PUBLISHING CORP.
http://www.kensingtonbooks.com

ZEBRA BOOKS are published by

Kensington Publishing Corp.
119 West 40th Street
New York, NY 10018

All Kensington titles, imprints and distributed lines are available at special quantity discounts for bulk purchases for sales promotion, premiums, fund-raising, educational or institutional use.

Special book excerpts or customized printings can also be created to fit specific needs. For details, write or phone the office of the Kensington Special Sales Manager: Attn.: Special Sales Department. Kensington Publishing Corp., 119 West 40th Street, New York, NY 10018. Phone: 1-800-221-2647.

Zebra and the Z logo Reg. U.S. Pat. & TM Off.

ISBN-13: 978-1-4201-0655-8
ISBN-10: 1-4201-0655-4

First Printing: May 2010

10 9 8 7 6 5 4 3 2 1

Printed in the United States of America

ACKNOWLEDGMENTS

This book is dedicated to my friend, Beryl CoteJohnson, and to my critique partner, Teresa Wilde.

With love and gratitude, many heartfelt thanks to my husband, Randy.

Many thanks to Liz Sykes, for all her kind support this past year.

And to my friends in the romance writing community, Debbie Mazzuca, Manda Collins, and Kris Kennedy, who always give me insightful feedback and incredible support. You gals really make it fun!

A special thanks to Janga, for her perceptive and sensitive reading of this book when I really needed it.

Finally, I want to thank my editor, John Scognamiglio, for his generous support.

Prologue

Sophie would kill him if she ever discovered what he planned to do. But the benefits surely outweighed the risks.

Simon St. James, Fifth Earl of Trask, leaned over his horse's neck and surveyed the rolling, gorse-covered hills of the Yorkshire landscape. Satisfaction surged through his body, tightening muscles in the familiar response that always came to him before the next challenge.

His business agent, Henry Soames, huddled miserably on top of the serviceable mare standing beside Simon's big bay. He glanced at Simon before returning his gaze to the wind-scoured horizon.

"The surveyor would appear to be correct, my lord."

A gale-force wind, surprisingly cold even for the dales of Yorkshire in the late summer, snatched away his agent's words. Simon nudged Romulus with his knees, moving his horse closer to the mare so he wouldn't have to shout over the buffeting gusts.

"You interviewed the man yourself." He made it a statement,

not a question. Soames would never leave something this important to chance. He knew Simon too well to risk otherwise.

"Aye, my lord. Mr. Bedford came highly recommend by The Royal Society of Engineers. There are at least three major coal seams running through these hills, and large deposits of other minerals, as well."

Simon nodded. "Excellent. This land should provide all the coal required for the new mills in Leeds."

He flexed his hands within the soft leather of his riding gloves, no longer bothering to stem the sense of triumph that came with the knowledge he had been right. Now he could place the last stone in the path—the final piece that would bring to fruition his plan to dominate Britain's wool industry. Soon, he would exert an overwhelming influence over every aspect of the trade, from the production of the raw materials to sale of the finished goods in the shops of every city in the country.

Of course, he would have to retain an iron grip over these final steps, and make sure that Sophie's uncanny ability to cause scandal didn't blow all his careful work to perdition.

"Will General Stanton sell or lease these lands to you?" asked Soames.

"He might have a few months ago, but he recently promised to add the estate to his granddaughter's dowry." Simon could feel a cynical smile pulling at his mouth. "To sweeten the pot, as it were."

Soames's long face took on the puzzled demeanor of a basset hound. "How then will you acquire . . . oh. Are congratulations in order, my lord?"

Simon sighed. "Eventually."

He shifted in his saddle, irritated by the other man's barely concealed masculine pity. As Romulus sidled under the movement, he reached a soothing hand along the bay's powerful neck.

Soames returned his gaze to the chalk downs. "I'll contact Mr. Russell to begin negotiations immediately."

As always, Soames had read his mood and shifted the discussion accordingly. Simon had no desire to talk about Sophie now, or even think about the monumental changes that lay ahead for both of them—not until he had figured out in his own mind just how much his feelings for her had changed.

And then there was Bathsheba, another difficult situation waiting for him in London.

One problem at a time.

Simon gave Soames a brusque nod of approval. Jedediah Russell had built and run the most successful textile mills in Bristol. The industry was moving north now, to be near the coal, and Russell intended to move with it. And Simon fully intended to be his partner in building a series of wool mills in Leeds, even though other investors were already courting Russell.

"Do that, Soames. I can meet Russell in Bath before I travel on to Somerset. I might as well pay a visit to my aunts while I'm in that part of the country."

In a week Simon would be standing up at the wedding of his best friend, the Marquess of Silverton. The bride's estate was only twelve miles as the crow flew from Bath, and the elegant townhouse of his aunt, Lady Eleanor St. James, and her younger sister, Lady Jane. He hadn't seen them since Michaelmas, and he was due for a visit, though he would rather walk through Whitechapel in his nightshirt than spend even a day in the most boring city in England. But if he could meet with Russell, at least the trip would be productive.

"I will write to him immediately, my lord."

Simon took one last, lingering look over the rolling hills that would soon be his, then wheeled around to head back to the small hunting box on the estate parallel to the Stanton acreage. St. James land had marched side by side with Stanton land for generations, as had the families, through times of both war and peace.

Soames's mare cantered gently beside Simon's bay. "Lord Trask?"

Simon threw his secretary a glance. The man's lugubrious face looked even longer than usual.

"Well?"

"Mr. Russell will want some assurances that you can provide the necessary resources for this venture. The coal from the Stanton estate is vital to your plans. How do you . . . ?" He let the question hang uncomfortably between them.

Simon gave a harsh snort of laughter and tapped his crop against the flanks of his horse. Romulus exploded over the muddy earth, spraying large clots of dirt in his wake.

"I'll do whatever I have to, Soames," he flung back over his shoulder.

London

The women in his life would surely drive him to Bedlam, starting with his soon to be ex-mistress. Simon realized he should be feeling at least some modicum of guilt about ending their affair, but, oddly enough, he didn't. It had really run its course some months ago, and they hadn't slept together. . . . Well, he couldn't even remember the last time they had.

In any event, Bathsheba wasn't the type of woman to invite a man's pity.

Better known to the ton as the dowager Countess of Randolph, Bathsheba was a lushly beautiful woman in her late twenties, small of stature, but with full, round breasts and generously curving hips. A riot of titian hair had been ruthlessly tamed into the most fashionable style of the day, framing a face that had the serene beauty of an angel painted by, well, not Titian, but some other Renaissance painter whose name he couldn't remember.

Unlike an angel's, though, her eyes glittered like cracked ice, and the edges of what should have been enticingly full lips had a narrow sharpness that boded ill for anyone who crossed her. Bathsheba knew her own worth and, since the death of her husband in a carriage race two years ago, made sure every one of her acquaintances knew it as well.

She stood before him in the center of her French-inspired boudoir, her small fists clenched against hips barely covered by a wisp of a silk dressing gown, her green gaze hard as the emeralds he had bestowed upon her last month.

He, on the other hand, perched comfortably on the back of her chaise, grimly confident he had made the right decision.

"So, this is how it ends." Her melodious voice sounded high and thin, as if the muscles of her throat were constricted. "I should like to know, Simon, why you have decided to cast me aside so abruptly, when I have done nothing to merit such an insult. What do you imagine this will do to my reputation, when you have courted me so assiduously? What in God's name will all our friends think?"

Simon choked back an astonished laugh. Courting her? Bathsheba knew full well what had gone on between them. They had used each other, and used each other well. To suggest anything else was absurd. She knew it, and all their friends knew it too. Bathsheba Randolph was the furthest thing from an injured maiden he had ever met in his life.

There were things he would miss, of course. The nights spent in hot passion, leavened with lethally witty conversation as they dissected the foibles of the ton. But Bathsheba had become possessive and grasping, as if she expected something more than he could give. Even without the changes that Sophie would bring into his life, his time with the voluptuous countess was over.

He pushed away from the chaise and strolled across the soft pile of the Savonnerie carpet, coming to a stop before her. The gleaming leather of his hessians almost touched the tips of her gaily painted bare toes. She was forced to tilt her head back to meet his gaze.

"Come now, Bathsheba. Don't be dramatic. You know it had to end between us sooner or later." He smiled down into her beautiful features. Strange that he had never noticed before how the bones of her face seemed to grow knife-edged when she became angry.

"I don't see why," she flashed back. "Have I done anything to displease you? Embarrassed you in any way?"

"Now you're being deliberately obtuse, my dear. In fact, your reaction tells me that to continue as lovers would surely jeopardize what has been—and I hope will continue to be— a most enjoyable friendship."

She jerked away as if he had slapped her. An ugly flush of crimson swept up her throat and into her cheeks, clashing with her bright auburn hair. Her eyes narrowed to pinpoints of sooty rage.

"You call what happened between us friendship? How dare you! When I have given so much of myself to you . . . expecting nothing in return but . . ." She gasped and bit her lip, perhaps in response to the astonishment that must be evident on his face.

"My dear Countess Randolph," he began, deliberately using her title in the hopes she would make an attempt to reclaim her dignity. "I have never been anything but honest with you. We agreed when we started that there was no future beyond friendship. No future beyond our mutual enjoyment. I'm saddened to discover you thought otherwise."

She glared at him, but the anger had begun to fade from her eyes, replaced by a sullen wariness. He waited for her to see reason. After all, Bathsheba was hardly a creature of excessive sensibilities.

After a few moments she gave a reluctant bob of her head.

"Good." He smiled his approval. "You know you can always

be assured of my friendship. You must continue to come to me when you need financial advice, or have a desire to discuss your investments. I will always consider your best interests as my own."

God, now he sounded like a politician, not a lover. Not even an ex-lover.

"Thank you, my lord." Bathsheba nodded her head a second time, her voice scrupulously polite. Her face had resumed its usual mask of alabaster beauty.

Simon ruthlessly suppressed the nibble of guilt that finally gnawed at the edges of his mind. He had little reason to feel that way. Bathsheba had gained much from him, both in the generous gifts he had bestowed upon her, and in the financial guidance that had seen her fortune double in the two years she had been his mistress. *She* had nothing to complain about, and *he* should have no regrets.

"Capital, my dear."

He winced inwardly at his inane response. *Idiot.* He extracted a little velvet bag from his waistcoat pocket and tipped the contents into his palm. A spill of glittering emeralds draped over his fingers.

"Bathsheba, I would be grateful if you would accept this as a small token of my esteem and gratitude. I wish you to know how sincere I am when I say I shall always value our friendship."

Her face went as blank as a newly stretched canvas. She reached out, carefully extracted the bracelet from his fingers, and returned her hand to her side, clenching the expensive and delicate piece of jewelry in her fist.

"Thank you, my lord."

He stared for a long moment into her opaque gaze, then turned on his heel and strode to the door of her boudoir.

"Will I see you in town, my lord?" Her soft voice drifted

across the room and slid like a cool silk scarf over the nape of his neck.

He repressed the urge to hunch his shoulders. Instead he glanced back, smiling. "No. I'm off to Bath this afternoon, then into Somerset."

Her eyes blazed to life with razorlike curiosity. "Bath? You never go to Bath at this time of year. You never go to Bath at all, if you can avoid it."

"Nonetheless, I am going to Bath." Simon made his voice deliberately cool. She had to realize it was over between them.

She took one step, then another, toward him. He reached out and grasped the handle on the door.

"This has something to do with business, doesn't it? I know you, Simon, better than you know yourself. You're planning something, and you don't want me involved. You think I'll get in the way."

His hand froze on the knob. Just how much had he revealed to Bathsheba whilst in the throes of passion? They rarely talked about his ventures in trade, but she had a knack for wheedling information out of a man, especially when it had something to do with money.

He looked back over his shoulder at her, painfully aware of both her beauty and her grasping nature. A cold weight of frustration—with her, but mostly with himself—settled in his chest.

"I'm sorry, Bathsheba, but my business is no longer any of your concern. It would be best if you remember that," he said softly, trying to keep the sting from his voice.

Her breath gently hissed out from between clenched teeth, but her eyes blazed forth an answer that struck him like a blow. He turned away, pulled the door shut behind him, and strode down the hall of his former mistress's townhouse.

No regrets.

After all, business always came first.

Chapter One

Bath, October 1815

Sophie Stanton felt a sharp tug on her wrist, the beaded chain of her reticule digging painfully into her skin before snapping free. She spun around to make a grab for the dirty little urchin who slipped just beyond her reach.

"Stop! Thief!" she yelled.

Heads turned. The fashionable shoppers on Milsom Street craned their necks as Sophie hitched up her cambric skirts and dashed after the boy as fast as she could.

Blast and damn!

Racing down the street, she dodged startled pedestrians as she tried to keep the boy in sight. He was fast as a whip, but so was she. She couldn't let him escape or she'd never see her gold bracelet again. It was nestled in the bottom of her reticule, stowed for a trip to the jeweler's shop for cleaning and a minor repair. But instead of going straightaway to the shop, she had lingered in front of the display window of Barratt's and made a perfect target for an enterprising thief.

Sophie dashed up the long promenade running through the center of Bath, ignoring the startled exclamations of three soberly dressed matrons as she flashed by them. If she had the breath to spare she would have groaned. One of them was Lady Connaught, who would no doubt report her latest misadventure to Lady Eleanor before the day was out.

But panic drove her on. Dodging and weaving up the street, she pushed to catch up with the boy. Her heart, already pounding from exertion, beat faster at the thought of losing him—and of losing her mother's much-loved and valuable heirloom bracelet.

Just ahead, the boy slipped into an alleyway next to a coffee shop. She put on a burst of speed and rounded the corner of the shop, skidding to a precarious halt beside a pile of refuse partly blocking the entrance to the alley.

The boy had come to a stop in front of a high wall that cut off the lane from the street behind it. He was scanning it, obviously looking for toeholds in the rough brick, when Sophie came up behind him.

"Stop, boy," she gasped, bending over to catch her breath. Her voice sounded little stronger than a squeak, so she had no hope he would pay her any heed. But the lad froze in position, and then slowly turned as if confronting the devil himself.

They eyed each other across the back of the dingy laneway. The smell of garbage wafting out from dirt-encrusted baskets shoved up against the wall made Sophie wish she hadn't eaten quite such a large breakfast. The stones under her feet were slick with moisture, dotted here and there with a sticky brown substance that had splashed up to her ankles. She didn't even want to think about what that substance might be, but she suspected her new and expensive kid boots were ruined.

Repressing her irritation over the likely destruction of her footwear, Sophie drew herself up to her full height—which wasn't very considerable—and stepped firmly through the muck toward the boy.

And stopped in her tracks at the look of sheer terror on his pinched little face.

She drew in a startled breath, forcing herself to remain still as she studied the urchin before her.

He was small, as small as a child of five or six, but his face looked a few years older—almost the age she had been when her father died. A coarsely woven shirt several sizes too large gaped open at the strings that looped across his bony chest. The legs of his burlap pants ended in ragged hems trailing around his ankles, and his bare feet were so encrusted with grime they barely looked human.

Her chest squeezed with sympathy as she studied his emaciated limbs. But then she gazed into his small, terrified face and gasped, stunned by what she saw.

He was beautiful, with features so delicate and so perfectly symmetrical that she imagined she was gazing at the face of an angel.

An angel who had been abandoned by his Maker to the depths of hell.

His huge blue eyes blinked back tears.

"Don't be frightened, lad," she said, keeping her voice soft. "I won't hurt you." She struggled to force a smile to her lips, heartsick at the look of fear stamped on the boy's face. "You can keep the money and the purse, but there is a bracelet inside my father gave to my mother many years ago. I would be very sad to lose it. Do you think you could take it out and give it to me?"

A bit of color returned to the boy's ghostly complexion, and his terror seemed to recede under the soothing influence of her voice. He cast a quick glance past her, as if trying to assess his ability to get by and out into the street. Sophie shifted slightly to the center of the alley, making it plain she would block any attempt to escape. The boy skittered back against the wall, a look of panic returning to his face.

She frowned. For a street thief, the child seemed remarkably timid, but Sophie had spent enough time trailing behind her mother as she did charity work in London to know that most urchins hid their fear behind a mask of bravado.

"I won't hurt you, I promise," she repeated. "And I won't turn you over to the constable." She smiled and took a small step forward, offering her hand palm up in a gesture of reassurance. "In fact, I'd like to help you—if you'll let me."

The boy shrank back against the wall, almost disappearing inside his oversized garments. Her heart wrenched, and she stepped forward again, determined now to help this frightened child.

"My name is Sophie Stanton. What's yours?"

He hesitated while he stared earnestly into her face. What he saw there must have encouraged him, for he straightened his little body and opened his mouth to speak.

"My n-name is T—"

His stuttering reply was interrupted by a noisy bang, as a door in the wall beside them swung open and crashed into the bricks. A scullery maid—obviously from the coffeehouse— suddenly stepped out, throwing the contents of a large pail into the alley.

Sophie jumped, biting off a startled shriek as the rancid contents of the slop bucket splattered across the front of her dress. In the same instant the little boy took flight. Leaping forward, she caught the edge of his sleeve as he found a toehold on the wall, hoisting himself away from her. For a moment she had him, but the material of his shirt shredded between her fingers. He pulled away, scrambled to the top of the wall, and disappeared in the blink of an eye.

"Lord, miss, but you gave me a fright! Whatever can you be doing out 'ere in this nasty alley?" cried the scullery maid.

"Damn and blast!" This time, Sophie didn't bother to hold in the curse. The scared boy had started to trust her, and now she would probably never see him again.

Or the priceless bracelet that had been in her family for generations, and that she had worn almost every day since Mamma had given it to her on her seventeenth birthday.

The gloom she had been trying to fend off ever since her brother's wedding finally settled over her like a dank London mist. How could she have allowed this to happen? Mamma would be devastated, and the rest of the family would see it as yet another example of her careless regard for what really mattered. She was making a muddle of things these days, and disappointing her family no end. They only wished to see her happy and settled, but, for some reason, she just couldn't seem to comply. And she didn't know how to fix it.

"Lord, miss, let me help you." The scullery maid pulled a dirty rag from the waist of her apron and rubbed it vigorously down the front of Sophie's skirt. The rank drippings smeared into a streaky mess across the bodice and waist of the apple green fabric.

"Thank you, but that won't be necessary," Sophie choked out. "It's really a very old dress. I only wear it when I'm running errands." She backed away, wondering why she felt the need to explain herself to the gap-toothed maid.

In fact, the dress—like her boots—was new, recently arrived from her favorite modiste in London. She very much doubted even a long soak in vinegar would remove the revolting stain from the delicate cambric.

Waving a vague good-bye to the woman, Sophie turned and hurried from the laneway. She rushed out into the street, not bothering in her haste to look either right or left.

And proceeded to crash into a very hard, very broad male chest.

"What in the hell?"

A deep voice rumbled the question somewhere above her head. Sophie sucked in a breath, every nerve ending in her body coming to a sharp, almost painful awareness. Then she heard an exasperated, all-too-familiar growl.

"I thought that was you. Sophie, you are wearing your spectacles. Presumably they keep you from blundering about like a bull in a china shop. What in God's name were you doing in that alley?"

Even though her glasses had been knocked askew, Sophie would have recognized that gravelly voice and the smell of expensive tobacco anywhere.

Simon, Earl of Trask.

The man she had been madly in love with since the age of twelve. The same man who aggravated her so much at times she could barely think. That particular note of censure in his voice always set her teeth on edge, so it took a brief struggle to resist the urge to punch him in the arm. She had found out long ago that punching the earl had the same effect as punching a rock.

Adjusting her spectacles, Sophie drew herself up to her full height, just below his chin. She had been called many things by her tiny coterie of devoted admirers—angel divine, fairy, wood sprite. Only Simon would call her a bull in a china shop.

"A thief ran off with my reticule. I was simply trying to retrieve it," she replied with as much dignity as she could muster.

His dark eyes sharpened with concern. "Are you injured?" He took her arm and pulled her toward him for a better look. "Did you fall?"

She shook her head. "No, I'm fine. The thief was just a little boy."

A strange expression crossed his face as he took a large sniff. *Just like a retriever*, Sophie thought crossly.

"What is that smell?"

She began to bristle under his critical gaze, but then sighed with resignation. "It's me. A scullery maid came out into the alley and threw a bucket of slop all over me."

He snorted. "That's typical. Well, you can't go walking through the streets of Bath smelling like this. I have to get you home before anyone sees you."

The chances of that happening were nonexistent, since several people she knew had already passed by in the last few minutes, inspecting her with avid curiosity. She had no desire to tell Simon about all the others who had seen her running through the streets of the town like a madwoman.

"Yes, Lord Trask."

Simon waved at a hackney that approached from the other side of the street.

"Oh, don't get so starchy, Sophie. You know your mother would hate it if you went parading through the streets looking like this."

Lord. There was no point in trying to maintain her dignity around the blasted man. He simply knew her too well.

"Yes, Simon," she replied, biting back the grumpy tone that threatened to creep into her voice.

He ushered her across the street to the waiting hackney. She saw him cast a quick glance up the street and then wince when Nigel Dash, one of his oldest friends, waved tentatively at them from the door of a linen draper's shop. Simon practically threw her inside the carriage. He hated gossip and scandal, and her escapade today would generate both.

He gave a few terse directions to the driver before climbing in after her. He sat as far from her as he could, jammed against the side of the carriage and practically sticking his head out the window. The smell *was* bad, but it annoyed her nonetheless that he made such a show out of it.

This incident, sadly, was entirely typical of her. Simon had known her since she was a child, and clearly still regarded her as little better than a grubby twelve-year-old, forever tumbling out of trees and falling into lakes. Lately, whenever he spoke to her it seemed to be to deliver a reprimand or scolding. He refused to understand that she was a woman grown—after all, she had been out now for almost four years.

Not that it really mattered, since he would never look at her as anything more than an annoying female relation. More like a sister than anything else. Simon's tastes ran to voluptuous and sophisticated young matrons and widows of the ton, not to skinny misses who wore glasses and obviously didn't know how to behave. The only thing she had in common with his established flirts was that she adored him too.

Fortunately for her pride, however, not as openly as they did.

She slid her gaze sideways, covertly studying the man who always made her skin prickle with heat. Simon was only a few inches above average height, but he had the hard, muscular body of an avid sportsman. His broad shoulders and powerful arms strained the cloth of his beautifully tailored coat, while his sinewy legs, sheathed in breeches and riding boots, took up most of the space in the small carriage.

Those who were jealous of the earl's prowess both in the field and, she suspected, in the bedchamber sneered that he looked like a blacksmith, with his coal-dark hair, fierce black eyes, and brawny physique. But Sophie thought he looked absolutely perfect, and if he hadn't such a knack for annoying her, she would likely spend all her time in his company fluttering about like a schoolgirl with a mad crush.

"Sophie."

His deep voice made her jump in her seat.

"Yes?"

"Why did you chase the boy? You could have been hurt, not to mention the gossip that could result from your actions. Proper young women don't go about chasing thieves."

Sophie froze, casting desperately about in her mind for some reason to explain her rash behavior. She simply couldn't bear to reveal she had lost her gold bracelet, not yet, anyway. And especially not to him.

She opened her eyes wide, hoping she looked both distraught and innocent. "I know, Simon. But my, ah, coral bracelet was inside. The one Robert gave me after Papa died."

Please, God. Don't strike me dead for telling such an awful lie.

He twisted in his seat to look at her, his handsome face softening in sympathy. That made things even worse.

"I'm sorry, Puck. That was a bad piece of business." He took her hand and gently rubbed a smudge of dirt from the inside of her wrist, his calloused fingers sending a throb of sensation over her pulse.

"Don't call me Puck." Her reply was automatic. He had taken to calling her that many years ago, likening her to the mischievous sprite from her least favorite of the Bard's works.

"I'm sure Robert could find you another bracelet just like it," he said in an excruciatingly kind and patronizing voice.

"I don't want another one! I want that one."

A muscle in his jaw twitched, as if he struggled to tamp down his impatience.

"Sweetheart, you can't go off on a wild-goose chase through the streets of Bath as if you were a child in the woods at your grandfather's estates. I know we're not in London, but there are unsavory elements in this town who wouldn't think twice of harming a gently bred lady. You must learn to control your impulses."

Sophie retreated into a stony silence, aware she was acting like a child but unable to help herself. The last thing she needed on this day—of all days—was another lecture from him.

Simon turned his head to gaze out the window, seemingly unperturbed by her attempt to ignore him. After several useless minutes spent trying to regain her dignity, Sophie realized she might as well climb down from her high horse. Nothing could ever pierce Simon's implacable reserve.

"When did you arrive in town?" she asked.

"This morning. I had only just left my rooms in Milsom

Street when I saw you dashing down the street like a mad-woman."

Sophie ignored the last part of his answer. "You're not stay-ing with your aunts?"

Normally when Simon came to Bath he stayed with his elderly aunts, Lady Eleanor and Lady Jane, at their elegant townhouse in St. James's Square. The two women were also Sophie's godmothers. After Robert and Annabel's wedding, they had asked her to come for an extended visit in Bath. Sophie had leapt at the opportunity, hoping the change in scenery would ease the restlessness bedeviling her.

"No," Simon replied. "I thought it best to take lodgings of my own, since you are staying with them for the next month. I do not wish to intrude on your privacy."

Her gloom deepened. No doubt he wished to take his own rooms so he could see his latest mistress while in town. Or else he found her so irritating he had no desire to reside in the same house with her.

The hackney pulled to a stop in St. James's Square. Simon handed her out, escorting her up the honey-colored terrace steps to the front entrance of his aunts' house. Sophie made a halfhearted attempt to smooth down the front of her demol-ished skirt as he knocked on the door.

"You will want to come in, I assume, to call upon your aunts," she said.

"Not right now. Please tell Aunt Eleanor I'll wait on her first thing tomorrow. I have some urgent business to conduct in town. I was on my way there when you accosted me."

"'Accosted you?'" she snapped, irritated by the gratuitous poke. She drew in a breath, preparing to unleash her standard lecture on his lack of familial devotion, when the door behind them swung open.

"Good afternoon, my lord, Miss Stanton. Would you care to step inside?" asked Lady Eleanor's butler.

"No, thank you, Yates. I was just leaving," Simon informed him. Yates, though, was perusing Sophie's dress with an expression of barely repressed alarm.

"My lord, your aunts long to see you," Sophie insisted. "It's been ages since you've been to Bath. Now that you are here, why cannot you step inside for a few minutes?"

Simon's eyebrows drew together in a heavy scowl. He reacted like that whenever she lectured him, especially in front of the servants. He thought it yet another example of her lamentably unladylike behavior.

"As I explained a moment ago," he said in that same patronizing voice, "I have an urgent appointment in town. Now go inside, Sophie, and get cleaned up. You look like something dragged you backward through a bush."

Her temper finally broke free. "Oh, go to the blazes, you pompous ass!" Spinning on her heel, Sophie stalked past a stunned Yates. Glancing over her shoulder, she felt a surge of satisfaction at Simon's outraged look.

Well, he deserved to feel her temper. And at least this time, she had truly gotten the last word.

Simon made a point of always knowing what he wanted, and what he wanted right now was to haul Sophie into his aunt's drawing room, pull her across his lap, and paddle her round little bottom. Naturally, being the disciplined man that he was, he controlled the impulse.

After a brusque nod to Yates, Simon strode back to the waiting hackney and directed the driver to take him to his bank in High Street. Perhaps he could have taken a few minutes to call on his aunts, but he had no intention of facing them—or Sophie, for that matter—until his temper had regained its normal equilibrium.

He muttered under his breath, recalling the way she had

glared down her small, straight nose at him, spectacles askew across her flushed cheeks. How did the exasperating little thing always manage to make him lose his temper? She'd been doing it for years, and he found himself no closer to an answer. He must be insane for even contemplating what he was about to do.

But then he thought of her pretty eyes and the sadness in them when she told him about her bracelet, and the familiar, almost primitive urge to protect her swam up to the surface.

Sophie had wonderful eyes—amber, shot through with flecks of green—and they sparkled with whatever emotion she felt at the time. Spectacles usually hid their depths, but Simon had learned to ignore the gold frames long ago.

Her few suitors had called her an angel or, even more extravagantly, a fairy queen. For an angel, though, Sophie could be appallingly bad-tempered, a character flaw he'd been aware of since the day he had pulled her from the lake on General Stanton's estate.

She had been twelve at the time, rowing in a small boat near the shore with her brother Robert, giggling and shrieking with the annoying high spirits so often displayed by girls of her age. Simon had just returned from a hard ride across the downs, passing by the lake on his way back to the house. When Sophie stood up to call to him, the boat had rolled, tipping the girl and her brother into the lake. Robert had popped up immediately, but Sophie slipped under the surface of the water.

Simon's heart had seized with fear when he saw her bright mop of auburn hair disappear from view. But he threw himself into the lake and found her immediately, cradling her against him as he swam to the nearby shore.

After she had recovered, Sophie had been mortified. When he tried to cheer her up, telling her she looked like a drowned rat, she stared at him with red-rimmed, unblinking eyes. Then she lashed out and kicked him—actually kicked him—in the shins. It had hurt too, since he had pulled his boots off before diving in, and her sturdy half-boots were heavy with water. She pulled herself from his arms and stomped off to the house, her little stick figure rigid with fury.

Sophie was definitely more sprite than angel, and he'd acquired several bruises from her over the years to prove it.

The carriage came to a halt before his bank. He absently paid off the driver, his mind returning to the problem of Sophie and her bracelet. In spite of what she thought, he did understand what the loss of her trinket meant to her. After all, he had helped Robert pick the damn thing out not a month after her father died. But he wouldn't allow her to risk her safety or her reputation, for any reason. This latest episode provided ample evidence that she simply couldn't be trusted to take care of herself.

Sophie would balk at his interference, but she'd have to get used to it. He'd come all the way to Bath with the firm intention of wedding her, and even though he wanted—no, *needed*— her lands, that didn't mean they couldn't have an agreeable marriage. If it was the last thing he ever did, he'd mold her into a suitable and contented wife. For her own sake, as well as his.

Chapter Two

Lady Eleanor St. James looked up from her perusal of the *Bath Chronicle* and glowered at Sophie from across the drawing room.

"Don't be silly, my girl. No thief-taker in the world would be interested in such an insignificant trinket. Besides, this is Bath, not Bow Street. You really must try to rid yourself of these ridiculously romantic notions."

It took only an instant for her godmother to demolish Sophie's plans to recover her bracelet. Lady Eleanor had a knack for doing that, and was famous for a ruthless logic that had reduced many an unwary victim to quivering silence. Sophie had hoped to keep the knowledge of the theft from the old woman, but her dramatic entrance into the house yesterday had occurred just as Lady Eleanor stepped from the drawing room in search of her sister Jane. The ensuing interrogation had not been pleasant, but at least she had convinced her godmother that it was only her coral bracelet that had been stolen, not the Stanton family heirloom.

Sophie sighed, retrieving a dainty scrap of partially embroidered linen from the bottom of her sewing basket. She found herself sighing quite a lot these days, a melancholic habit she had always found annoying in other people. Her mother would say it was nerves, but that was absurd. Sophie never had the vapors or suffered from fits of the blue devils, except for that awful time after her father's death.

"Are you listening to me, Sophia? I insist you give up any idea of recovering your bracelet. I know Robert gave it to you, but it is not, after all, an heirloom, or even very valuable. What's that you said?"

"I didn't say anything, my lady," Sophie replied, cursing the gasp that had escaped her lips.

Lady Eleanor looked suspicious, but carried on. "You must not make such a fuss over something so insignificant. The Lord giveth, and the Lord taketh away. That has always been my motto in life, and it serves me well. You would do best to adopt it. In any event, how would one even go about recovering such a thing?"

That was exactly the question Sophie had been pondering for the last twenty-four hours. But a quick inspection of Lady Eleanor's jutting chin convinced her she best keep those thoughts to herself.

"I'm sure I don't know, ma'am. Can I cut you another slice of plum cake? It really is delicious." As she reached for the older woman's plate, Sophie tried desperately to think of a topic that would divert attention away from her cursed bracelet. "By the way, my lady, is there any particular book you would like me to pick up for you at Barratt's today? I understand there are some new volumes by the author of *Waverly*."

Lady Eleanor's sparse brows twitched together, her narrow but shrewd eyes staring back at her. But Sophie was spared any more lecturing by a light tap sounding on the drawing room door.

"Enter," Lady Eleanor bellowed.

Sophie rose and fluffed out her soft muslin skirt, preparing to greet the day's first visitors to St. James's Square. She loathed the idea of having to be social, but at least it would divert her godmother's attention from yesterday's fiasco.

"The Earl of Trask," intoned Yates.

Simon strode into the room, casting a glowering look her way before turning his attention to his aunt. He bowed gracefully, the fabric of his bottle green riding jacket clinging to his massive shoulders. Sophie ducked her head to hide the flush of heat climbing up her cheeks, silently lamenting—not for the first time—her ready response to his intense masculinity.

"Good morning, my dear aunt. It is a great pleasure to see you again."

"Well, if it's such a great pleasure, nevvy, I wonder why you don't avail yourself of it more often. It's a miracle I even remember what you look like."

Sophie grinned, relishing the look of discomfort that flashed across Simon's imperious features. But it vanished in an instant.

"Forgive me, aunt. Business in town has kept me much occupied."

Offering no other explanation for his behavior, he unleashed a charming smile on Lady Eleanor. Sophie felt a stab of irritation at his easy dismissal of his aunt's reproach. But even though his casual neglect of his aunts never failed to annoy her, she still had the insane urge to defend him from the stern old woman's impending reprimand.

But instead of ringing a peal over her wayward nephew, Lady Eleanor's grim expression softened into an affectionate smile as she invited Simon to join her by patting the overstuffed silk divan on which she sat. Irritation faded from her wrinkled face, replaced by an expression of doting fondness. As usual, all Simon had to do was walk into a room and every woman melted into a puddle of warm custard, including his crusty old aunt.

"What nonsense, my dear boy." Lady Eleanor trilled a surprisingly good imitation of a girlish laugh. "I have no doubt there were other things besides business that kept you in London. I suppose I should be grateful you found the time to visit your old aunties, especially now that the Little Season has commenced. Whatever will all those fine ladies of the ton do without you to squire them about?"

Lady Eleanor gave her nephew a knowing wink.

Sophie choked back a horrified laugh as Simon threw a glance her way. Although she returned his glare, she somehow managed to clamp down on the caustic remark that threatened to force its way past her lips.

"I hope I find you well, my lady," he replied, ignoring his aunt's outlandish gesture. "Indeed, you look to be in fine trim, in spite of all this damp weather. How is your gout?"

As Lady Eleanor launched into a detailed account of her various treatments at the baths, Sophie wandered to the window, wishing—as she had a thousand times before—that Simon would someday get the set-down he deserved.

She pushed back the heavy silk curtains draped across the tall, elegant windows, and gazed out into the quiet street. The golden limestone of the terraced houses reflected the gentle rays of the October sun. A matronly looking woman, dressed in last year's fashions, strolled down the pavement, trailed by a maid struggling with a bundle of parcels. Two men appeared at the top of the street, carrying a Bath chair. It disgorged its contents—an elderly man who limped up the steps of the townhouse opposite, leaning heavily on the arm of one of the chairmen as he nursed his gouty foot.

The whole scene was as tranquil and genteel as anyone could imagine. And utterly boring. As boring as it had been yesterday, and the day before, and the day before that.

Except for the theft of her bracelet, of course. But that hardly counted as an amusing diversion.

As she listened to Lady Eleanor drone on about her medical treatments, Sophie worried that it wasn't nerves she suffered from, but incipient madness brought on by boredom. Ever since Robert and Annabel's marriage three weeks ago, she had been consumed by a restless and vague emotion that grew worse with each passing day. The feelings that troubled her now were like nothing she had ever experienced before.

"Sophie, I failed to ask yesterday after Annabel and your brother. I hope you left them in good health." Simon's polite comment broke into her musings.

She pinned a smile on her face before turning back to respond. "I quite wonder why you forgot to ask me. Something must have distracted you, although I can't imagine what. Oh, wait. Perhaps it was the theft of my bracelet. Or the fact that I smelled like a slop bucket."

"Sophia, stop teasing the earl and answer the question," commanded Lady Eleanor. "Really, my dear, you must learn to curb your tongue around your elders. And don't think I have forgotten your actions of yesterday. We will conclude that discussion at a later time."

"Don't trouble yourself on my account, my dear aunt." Simon's handsome features took on a grim cast. "I, too, wish to discuss Sophie's behavior."

"Well, now that the topic has come up," Sophie replied, screwing up her courage, "I would actually like to discuss it with you as well. I need your help."

The grim look turned wary. "My help for what?"

"To get my bracelet back, of course." Sophie had decided last night, after many sleepless hours, that Simon was the only person in Bath who could help her. Whether he *would* was another question.

"And how do you propose we go about doing that?" He didn't even bother to mute the sarcasm in his voice, but she was used to that. At least he had asked the question.

"Well, Simon, I was hoping you could hire a thief-taker to find the boy for me. Not to turn him over to the magistrate," she added hastily when she noted the startled expression on his face. "Simply to track him down. I know the Bow Street Runners are very experienced with this sort of problem. Surely there's someone in Bath who could perform a similar office. Perhaps a local constable?"

"Sophia," Lady Eleanor's sharp voice interrupted. "I've already explained why that is impossible. Simon, perhaps you can make the foolish child see reason before she creates more scandal than she already has. Lady Connaught already sent me a note asking if that was Sophia running like a demented creature down Milsom Street yesterday."

Sophie set her jaw, meeting Simon's thoughtful look with a defiant stare. He rose slowly from the divan and crossed the room to stand before her. She tilted her chin, resisting the urge to lose herself in midnight eyes that contained a surprising amount of commiseration.

"Listen to me, Puck. I understand your loss. I know how much that bracelet means to you. But trust me when I say that you've set yourself an impossible task. There are too many street urchins and thieves in Bath to count, and your coral bracelet is not remarkable enough to excite any attention in the criminal underworld, or in the pawnshops of Holloway or Avon Street."

Sophie schooled her features to remain expressionless. Simon had no idea how much interest her bracelet would generate. But it wasn't only the loss of her bracelet—and how her family would react—that had kept her awake for most of the night.

"It's . . . it's not just the bracelet," she stammered, finally yielding to the nagging little voice in her head. "I'm worried about the boy, Simon. He was so small, so frightened. How could a child so young be a hardened thief? Something terrible must have happened to force him to steal from me."

"Good Lord, Sophia, you mustn't be so naïve," scoffed Lady Eleanor. "These children are bred to be thieves. They begin stealing at a very early age. I have no doubt they imbibe their wicked nature in their mothers' milk. Even if you were to find the boy in question I'm sure his character would be beyond redemption."

An image of the child's grease-smudged, terrified face leapt into her mind. Something terrible had hurt him—damaged his spirit. She was certain of it.

"I refuse to believe any child is inherently evil," she retorted. "It's too easy for us to blame the poor things. How can any child living in such poverty and despair be expected to act otherwise? How else could he survive? No, my lady, I won't accept that one so young is beyond salvation."

Lady Eleanor's taffeta skirts rustled with indignation, but Sophie refused to back down. She knew she was right about the boy. He was an innocent lost in a ghastly underworld, and something inside insisted she help him, even if Simon and Lady Eleanor were dead set against it.

Her ladyship's eyebrows started twitching again, a sure sign of an impending outburst. Sophie held her breath in preparation for the coming explosion.

"I'm sorry to disagree, Aunt Eleanor, but I think Sophie has the right of it," Simon broke in. "I've heard any number of reports to the Select Committee in the House. It's most unfair to blame these poor children, and I don't believe they have an innate propensity to crime. It's a failing of the government and magistrates that we can't seem to reduce the number of young criminals roaming our streets."

Sophie's mouth dropped open. Simon had actually agreed with her.

"Don't get too excited, Sophie," he said dryly after glancing her way. "I agree with Aunt Eleanor that there's nothing you can do. These boys go into the trade very young. There are hundreds of them in Bath. It has a very large population of thieves for a town of its size."

"It's all the wealthy visitors who come to the baths," interjected Lady Eleanor. "The thieves come down to the resorts from London—better pickings for them during the warmer months."

"Can't we at least try?" Sophie pleaded. "The slums aren't very big. We should be able to find one little boy without too much bother. I would know him again in an instant, I assure you."

Simon made an impatient sound under his breath. "Sophie, you're not thinking. The slums may be small, but they're very crowded. And Holloway is little better than a colony of beggars. I would no sooner risk taking you there than I would the stews in London."

She turned from him, staring blindly out the window into the street. Why couldn't he understand? She had to find the boy, as much for her own sake as for his. Sophie knew what it meant to be frightened and alone, and the boy's pinched face would haunt her until she could help him.

Taking a deep breath, she turned around to confront two disapproving faces. Nephew and aunt stared back at her, jaws set in identical lines of determination. She met Simon's eyes, cool and fathomless, and wondered again how she could love him as much as she did.

"I'm not naïve, in spite of what you might think," she said, trying to speak reasonably. "You know Mamma has worked with charitable associations and orphanages for years. I've been visiting them since I came out. I'm not afraid, and I've seen more than you can imagine."

"You've seen nothing," Simon replied in a stern voice. He covered the distance between them in two strides, took her wrist in a gentle but unyielding grip, and towed her over to an ornate walnut chair.

"It's not the same, Sophie," he said as she sank into the chair. "Your mother confines her charitable work to reputable institutions run by respectable churchmen. She never let you see anything that was not appropriate for you to see. You have no idea of the filth and depravation of the rookeries, the squalor. The inhabitants would sooner cut your throat and leave you bleeding on the pavement than speak to you. If you were ever to go down there by yourself . . ."

He broke off, eyes narrowing as he studied her. He loomed over her, obviously intent on intimidation. For a moment, she allowed herself to be distracted by the seductive closeness of his muscular physique.

"Don't even think about it, Sophie," he growled. "If I ever find that you go down to Avon Street by yourself . . ."

She opened her mouth, but he held up a hand to silence her. ". . . or with only a servant to accompany you, I'll make certain you won't be able to sit down for a week."

"Simon!" Sophie glared at him, stung to the quick, furious he would treat her as a child. He *always* treated her as a child.

On the other side of the room, Lady Eleanor gave a surprised snort of laughter at her nephew's threat. Sophie could feel the heat rise in her cheeks, and she pushed herself up from the chair to make for the door.

Simon expelled a frustrated breath and took her arm, silently urging her back into her seat. He dropped into the matching walnut chair opposite hers and took one of her hands between both of his own.

"Forgive me, Sophie. That was inexcusable. I'm a complete brute, and I give you leave to pinch me as hard as you can." A rueful expression lurked in his eyes, dispelling some of her anger. His eyes turned thoughtful as he studied her face.

"But don't forget I know you as well as you know yourself. Once you get an idea in your head you can't help acting on it. Since neither your mother nor Robert is in Bath, it's my responsibility to keep watch over you. You must promise me you won't go haring off into the rookeries by yourself."

She bit her lip, hating that she might have to lie to him again, but more determined than ever to find the boy. *And* her bracelet.

Simon's hard mouth twitched with a reluctant smile. "And you must promise me that you won't go down there even if you take a servant with you. It's simply too dangerous."

She blew out an exasperated huff of air. "Oh, all right. If you're going to be so stuffy about it, I promise I won't go down there by myself. Or," she said with a little growl, irrationally annoyed by his suspicion, "with only a servant to accompany me."

His smile curled into a grin that made her insides glow with a gentle heat.

"That's my good girl." He gave her hand a quick pat and stood, removing his watch from his waistcoat pocket to check the time.

"Aunt Eleanor," he said. "I have a meeting I must attend with my bankers. Is Aunt Jane receiving this morning? I'd like to see her before I take my leave."

"Of course. Sophia, please ring the bell for Yates."

Sophie rose and crossed slowly to the bellpull in the corner of the drawing room. Another idea popped into her mind.

"Simon?"

"Yes, Puck?" He had stowed his watch and extracted a Peacock's pocket repository from his coat, making notations in it with a small pencil. "What is it?" he asked without looking up.

"Do you think you could at least check the pawnshops for my reticule? It's a very nice one, and a broker might find it worth more than a few shillings."

She held her breath, hoping he would take the bait. If her reticule was found in one of Bath's pawnshops, she might be able to question the broker and acquire some information on the boy.

Simon's head came up from his notations. He stared at her, a slight frown creasing his forehead. After a moment he nodded, then closed his book and slipped it back inside his coat.

"All right, Sophie. It's likely a waste of time, but I suppose there's no harm done to look."

She gritted her teeth at his careless tone of dismissal, but held back the retort that sprang to her lips.

"But I have your promise that you will not go down to the slums," he added. "Is that clearly understood?"

He managed to look both arrogant and paternal as he inspected her. Sophie wondered if he ever looked at his paramours that way, but she suspected he saved that particular scowl just for her.

She leveled her sweetest smile at him, doing her best to look innocent. "I promise, Simon."

His eyes, alight with suspicion, followed her as she hurried over to the bellpull.

He was right to be suspicious, because she had no intention of keeping her promise. Not in such a dire situation. She had to find the boy, and she *had* to find her bracelet before anyone knew it was missing. Simon wouldn't help her, so she needed to find someone who would. Someone she could trust, and who would know where to look. Finding that person might prove to be a challenge, but not an insurmountable one. She just needed time to think about it, after any visitors that called today had departed.

Especially Simon. She always found it difficult to think rationally when he was about.

And think hard she must. After all, how exactly did one go about looking for a thief?

Chapter Three

Simon impatiently shuffled through the papers scattered before him, his mind refusing to focus on the business at hand.

The little minx will surely drive me insane.

Yesterday's call on Sophie had been another fiasco. He had fully intended to initiate the courtship of his future wife, and had lost his temper instead.

As she had lost her temper with him. Not that he could blame her for that. After all, he had threatened to put her over his knee and spank her. Aunt Eleanor's poorly timed amusement, along with her knowing jests about his rakish reputation, hadn't helped. He loved the old termagant, but she so often reminded him of his grandfather—loud, imperious, and unfortunately blunt.

Obviously, neither Sophie nor his aunt would make this courtship a tidy affair he could wrap up in a few days.

"I beg your pardon, my lord. Did you say something?" Soames asked.

"No. Please continue." Simon waved a hand at his business agent, who frowned at him from across the gateleg table crowded with documents and architectural drawings. Any thoughts about Sophie, or his erratic courtship, would have to wait for another time.

"As you wish, my lord." Soames resumed his detailed explanation of the resources needed to establish the new mills in Leeds.

Simon listened, all his instincts focused on the challenge. The timing was perfect. The bubble of 1814 had brought many investors to their knees, but not him. Steadily and quietly, he had been buying one mill after another. If he could establish a partnership with Russell, he would exercise control over the trade of wool throughout much of England and the Continent. And control—both in life and in business—was everything.

Of course, it was necessary to conceal the magnitude of his commercial dealings from all but a few of his friends and family. Most of them wouldn't understand his passion for making money, or his need to do something more than lead a life of noble indolence. His Aunt Eleanor, for one, would recoil in disgust at his crass talent for creating wealth, as would have his long-dead grandfather. Money was vulgar, and a St. James was never vulgar. That philosophy had been drummed into Simon's head by the old earl and by most every other member of the family from the moment he had been old enough to talk. The ancient ways were best, they said, a life tied to the land, and to the traditions that had stood fast for generations.

It set his teeth on edge just thinking about it—about the sheer, mind-numbing sameness of that aristocratic way of life. No. He needed the challenge of manipulating the numbers and playing the game. Feeling the thrill when one of his ships returned from the Orient or the Americas, loaded down with riches that would allow him to best his competitors. Without that stimulation he would go mad with boredom.

And the old ways were dying. He was certain of that. Any man with a brain realized that England's future lay not with the land, but with the wheels and engines of commerce.

Soames shoved a pile of ledgers to the end of the table, unrolling the architectural drawings for the mills.

"My lord, I'd like to draw your attention to a potential flaw in Mr. Russell's plans. I wonder if his architect miscalculated the amount of space required for the looms."

Simon squinted at the drawings. Light barely seeped through the rain-spattered windows of his rented lodgings in Milsom Street.

"What's the time, Soames?"

"Going on four o'clock, sir."

"Shouldn't Russell be here by now?"

"Any moment, my lord. He was riding in from Bristol this afternoon."

Simon retrieved a branch of candles from the polished mahogany sideboard and placed it in the center of the table. The tapers cast a soft nimbus of light over the architect's drawings, but the rest of the handsomely appointed room faded into shadows.

He immediately saw the problem.

"There's barely enough space for one man to pass between the machines—let alone thirty, moving from loom to loom." He tapped the drawing as he calculated the costs of the mistake. "Does the architect have the slightest idea what he's doing? These aren't plans for a pleasure garden or a lady's boudoir. There must be enough room for the weavers to move about, and for the bolts to be carried to the wagons."

"Perhaps Mr. Russell plans to use children to operate the looms."

Simon gave a low curse. "Then we'll have to disabuse him of that notion. These jobs must go to the men who need them, not children. Children have no place in a mill." He reached for a pencil and rule.

Soames let out a long-suffering sigh. "It is not necessary for you to correct the drawings, my lord. I will discuss the matter with Mr. Russell, and write to the architect this evening."

Simon ignored him, sliding the rule across the crackling parchment, visualizing the space as he methodically built an image of the factory in his mind. The discipline of the calculations took him to that familiar and welcome place where boredom and distracting emotion slipped away—replaced by stark, beautiful numbers whose clarity and precision never disappointed him. The ticking of the mantel clock, the swish of carriage wheels on the rain-washed cobblestones, even the other man's presence all but disappeared.

"My lord." Soames's voice held a barely repressed note of irritation.

Simon reluctantly tore himself away from the computations he had scratched on the parchment. He couldn't help grinning at the sour expression on his business agent's normally impassive face.

"Yes, Soames?"

"Please forgive my impertinence, your lordship, but may I remind you what happened the last time you became so closely involved with the architect's work?"

"That bloody bastard Anson quit, that's what happened, and a good thing it was. Every window bay in the terrace row would have been crooked if I hadn't intervened."

"You didn't exactly intervene, my lord. You threw him out of the library. And it took us two months to find another architect because Mr. Anson let it be known how difficult the investors were to work with. Which," he added sardonically, "everyone assumed included me."

Simon laughed. "I'm sorry about that, Soames, but those terraces sold like wildfire, and you were well compensated for your trouble. Forgive me if I don't share in your distress."

The other man threw him a dark look, then firmly rolled up the architectural plans and placed them out of reach on the sideboard. "Perhaps we will take these out again when Mr. Russell arrives."

Simon raised his eyebrows in mock astonishment. "You wound me, my dear fellow. You really do."

Normally, he wouldn't dream of allowing someone in his employ to treat him so cavalierly, but Soames was different. The youngest son of a baronet, they had met at Cambridge, drawn to each other by their shared love of mathematics and science. Several years later that bond had compelled Simon to offer his former classmate and friend a position as his business agent. The man had leapt at the chance, preferring a life of invigorating work to one of impecunious gentility. Simon had made full use of Soames's negotiating skills, which enabled him to maintain the convenient fiction that the Earl of Trask was no more than a bored aristocratic investor.

As his agent bustled around the room, stacking ledgers and clearing the table in preparation for their meeting, Simon allowed himself to remember those days at university. Back then, he had been able to convince himself that a life of pure science—even a position teaching mathematics at Cambridge—was possible. It was what he had always dreamed of, a life of intellect and study. But the death of his cousin Sebastian, heir to the earldom, had crushed that dream into dust.

"If I may be so bold, my lord." Soames's dry voice interrupted his musings.

Simon dropped onto the Sheraton settee by the window and pulled out his pocket repository. If he couldn't sketch, he might as well review the numbers he had gotten from his banker this morning.

"Yes?"

"Did you have a satisfactory visit with Miss Stanton yesterday?"

Sophie.

Simon threw down his book.

"No, my dear fellow, my visit did not go as planned. Instead of beginning my courtship, I found it necessary to persuade Miss Stanton that she was not to go haring off to the slums in search of a damned missing reticule and bracelet. Knowing Miss Stanton, however, she'll find some way to disobey my injunction—and try to convince me that her reasons for doing so were completely sound."

His agent frowned. "Mr. Russell will want assurances you'll be able to provide a steady supply of coal from the Stanton lands."

"Nothing is ever easy when it comes to Sophie Stanton, Soames."

"How unfortunate, my lord. Is there anything I can do to help?"

Simon rose from his chair and wandered over to the gateleg table, now rendered as neat as a column of figures by the other man's quiet industry.

"Yes, I believe you can. I told Miss Stanton I would search the pawnshops in Avon Street for her reticule and bracelet. She apparently thinks either one of them is valuable enough to attract a broker's attention. You might check in one or two shops to see if anything comes in. Likely nothing will come of it, but I promised her I'd look."

"I will see to it, my lord."

Simon nodded. Sophie expected him to conduct the search himself, and perhaps he should feel guilty about fobbing the task off onto his agent. But the bracelet would attract little interest from a receiver of stolen goods. In any event, Soames would do the job more thoroughly, and right now Simon didn't have the time to get involved in another one of her madcap schemes.

But it wasn't just Sophie's schemes that were distracting him, he acknowledged grudgingly. Everything about her distracted him. Her delicate face surrounded by a halo of auburn hair, her lithe body, her laughing voice. Even her mouth. Especially her mouth—sweet, bow-shaped, and pink as a rose petal.

He shook his head in disgust and began pacing the drawing room. He wasn't used to thinking of Sophie that way, wasn't used to feeling any kind of physical attraction for her. It didn't feel right, not after years of thinking of her as . . . well, not quite a sister, but something close to that. He supposed it was a relief he could feel that way about her at all, but it made him hellishly uncomfortable. Still, he had every intention of being faithful after their wedding. He owed her that much—the dignity of a stable marriage and a husband who would not seek his pleasure in another woman's bed.

Not that he wouldn't try to make her happy. He would. He was immensely fond of Puck and wanted the best for her—always had. But she could no longer be allowed to run wild, or their life together would be a series of disastrous episodes. He simply couldn't afford the damage that could pose to his work or their reputations.

A hand rapped firmly on the door to his apartments.

"That will be Mr. Russell, my lord. Are you ready to receive him?"

"Let him in."

Even as he sharpened his focus on the coming meeting, Simon allowed one more image of Sophie's face to drift across his mind.

He would approach the business of wooing her as he would any other financial or mathematical problem—logically, rationally, and with a minimum of fuss. He knew very well that she had loved him for years, and he suspected with the slightest encouragement she would tumble straight into his arms. And once he had her in his bed and flat on her back, his trouble-making elf would discover soon enough who her master was. After that, all would fall neatly into place.

Yes, Simon had no doubt whatsoever that Sophie would be one of the best investments he would ever make.

A stinging rain teemed down, mingling with the hot tears trickling over Sophie's cheeks. She rubbed the moisture away with an impatient hand, creating blurry smears on her spectacles. Plucking a lace-edged kerchief from the slit in her gown, she snatched the lenses from her face and wiped them dry.

She refused to cry. She had told Simon she had the strength of mind to endure this, and endure it she would. But he had been right, blast him. What she had seen today couldn't begin to compare with the genteel and carefully selected charitable work her mother did in London. The filth and disease of the place where Sophie now stood, the sorrow and despondency, were almost more than she could bear.

"Miss Stanton, please step under the porch. It will not do for you to catch a chill, especially in this place of contagion."

Mr. Crawford grasped her elbow and steered her gently into the shelter of a small overhanging portico. He peered at her from under the dripping brim of his cleric's hat, clearly unhappy she still insisted on searching the entire workhouse.

"Are you certain you wish to continue?" His eyes brimmed with concern, and she held on to their warmth as the one beacon of hope in this horrific place.

Sophie took a wavering breath and nodded, determined to push on. She carefully picked her way across the broken grey stones of the small courtyard separating the women's quarters from the rest of the workhouse. The rain should have washed the cobbles clean, but it only seemed to make them greasier. A thick sludge bled from the cracks to collect in brown pools of foul-smelling water.

She followed the cleric through a door half off its hinges into a narrow hall that seemed to run the entire length of the building. If not for Mr. Crawford's lantern, they would have been plunged into darkness, even though it was not yet five in the afternoon. The smell of human waste assaulted her senses once again, causing her stomach to pitch into her throat. Sophie pressed her kerchief over her nose and breathed through her mouth.

"At this time of day the children are still in the workrooms," the clergyman explained as he stopped by a door at the end of the hall. "They will continue in their work until six o'clock, at which time they will be served their evening meal."

Sophie had to swallow hard before she could speak.

"At what time of day do they begin working?"

"Seven, with one hour at noon for their dinner. Just the same as the adults."

"How can children work such long hours?" she protested. "Surely the parish cannot expect it of them."

Mr. Crawford's mouth twisted into a slash of dismay. "I'm sorry to say they can and do, Miss Stanton. The local authorities believe the conditions must be harsh, else the unworthy poor would surely overrun the very walls of the building."

He grasped the knob to open the door, but Sophie reached for his arm.

"Do you believe that, Mr. Crawford?"

"No, Miss Stanton, I do not. What man would choose to bring his family to such a place, when he could make a respectable day's wage by his own hand?"

The tightness in her chest eased ever so slightly. Both his words and his honest, open face reassured her that she had picked the right man to assist her in this task.

She had racked her brains most of last night trying to think of a practical way to find her street urchin. Then she remembered Mr. Crawford, the young curate of St. Michael's Church. Sophie had heard him preach on her last visit to Bath, and had been impressed with his efforts to raise funds for both the Refuge for the Destitute and the local orphanage. Both institutions seemed like a good place to start looking for the boy.

After breakfast, Sophie had told Lady Eleanor she would be visiting with friends in Laura Place for most of the day. Donning her sturdiest boots and oldest pelisse, she had then made her way to St. Michael's Church. Mr. Crawford had initially been vigorous in his refusal to accompany her to Avon Street, insisting it was no place for an innocent young woman. It was no place for any human being to step foot in, she had soon found out, but after much debate—and a promise on her part to make a generous contribution to his orphan's fund—he reluctantly agreed to assist her.

Their search of the small but well-kept orphanage tucked away in a quiet corner of the city yielded no information about the boy. After another short disagreement about the appropriateness of their mission, Sophie and Mr. Crawford took a hackney to the workhouse near Avon Street. A steady rain began falling the moment the coach stopped in front of the prisonlike building looming over the squat warehouses that lined the docks.

As they picked their way across a courtyard littered with refuse, Mr. Crawford tried to prepare her for what she would see. But no words could convey the horror of the place.

Women dressed in threadbare garments huddled against each other in rooms with only one or two smoking lamps and no heat. They stitched away on burlap sacks, their fingers shredded from the coarse material, gaunt faces pale and lifeless. When Mr. Crawford walked between their workbenches, murmuring words of consolation, most of the women didn't bother to look up.

Sophie had stumbled closely behind, too sick at heart to utter a sound.

"Are you certain you're ready, Miss Stanton?"

The cleric's gentle voice simultaneously recalled her to the present and warned her of what lay behind the door. She silently commanded her stomach to behave, and then nodded to the curate.

They stepped into a low, narrow room filled with benches and tables. Perhaps thirty children of various ages, from as young as four or five to as old as fifteen, hunched over the tables.

For a room full of children, the place was unnaturally quiet. A stern-faced matron garbed in pewter-grey bombazine rustled among the tables, a thick switch grasped tightly in her hand. When she passed between the rows, the tiniest ones shrank away from her, fear stamped on their scrawny features. But the older children never lifted their heads from their work.

The matron came to them and curtsied, greeting them in a flat but respectful voice. Sophie inhaled a deep breath to force out a reply and broke into a fit of coughing. An acid, powdery taste filled her mouth.

Mr. Crawford spoke quietly in her ear. "Take shallow breaths, or cover your mouth with your kerchief."

As she choked back another cough, Sophie noticed the air seemed to be filled with dust, a dust that drifted up from piles of white stones and pale-colored dirt on the worktables. The youngest children were sifting through the dirt for small stones, sorting and then placing them into little piles. The older children took the pebbles and, using larger stones, ground them down into dust. A white film blanketed everything—the children's faces, the rough clothing that covered their bodies, the cold stone floor. Even the wooden beams of the ceiling were covered in it. It looked like a sifting of dirty flour, bleaching everyone and everything in the room to the same dead color.

"What in heaven's name are they doing?" Her voice was suddenly raspy, her mouth dry. She dreaded the cleric's answer.

Mr. Crawford took one look at her face and hesitated.

Sophie shook her head impatiently, forcing herself to face it head-on. "I need to know."

"They are crushing bones to make fertilizer. The men grind the larger bones down, and the children sift through the dust for the smaller bones. You already saw the women stitching the sacks to hold the finished materials."

"Where . . . where do they get the bones?"

"Most of them are from slaughtered cattle or pigs, but some are human. . . ." He snapped his mouth shut, apparently thinking he had said enough.

She felt the room move away from her in an odd rush. Then, she remembered something she had overheard a few years ago—something her mother and a few of her charitable friends had talked about in revolted whispers. Sophie had forgotten it, perhaps because it was too horrifying to remember.

Human bones mixed with animal bones. Day after day the children ground away, breathing in the dust of men, women, and children, some of whom might have died in this workhouse. Some of them possibly members of their own families.

She stumbled back against a table, the sharp edge jabbing painfully into her hip. Black spots drifted across her eyes. She swayed as her vision began to blur.

A strong hand grabbed her elbow.

"Steady on, Miss Stanton." Mr. Crawford's calm voice penetrated the grey curtain threatening to envelope her. "Lean on my arm, and I'll take you out straight away."

Sophie took several deep swallows as she willed her vision to clear and her stomach to stay where it was meant to be. After a few moments she dared to shake her head.

"No, I'm fine. We must look first, before we can leave."

She began to walk between the rows, carefully inspecting the faces of the children. The curate kept his hand underneath her elbow, and she didn't move to pull it from his grip.

It took only a few minutes to ascertain her thief was not in the room. Sophie forced herself to take another long look before she turned toward the door, imprinting the children's faces, so void of life, into her memory. Someday, she would . . . no, someday she *must* find a way to help these children. They had been abandoned by the world, discarded as little better than refuse. And she—who had never been alone, even in the worst moments of her life—would never forget them.

Mr. Crawford led her across the courtyard and out through the iron gates into the street. Sophie peered out from under her drooping bonnet, grateful to see the hackney driver had obeyed the cleric's instructions to wait for them. She leaned her shoulder against the side of the coach, gulping in deep breaths. The stench from the docks smelled as clean as sea air compared to the horrid dust that befouled the rooms of the workhouse.

"Miss Stanton, are you certain you are well?" Mr. Crawford's brow furrowed in dismay. "Please, let me help you into the coach. We must get you home."

Sophie dabbed at her brow with the tips of her gloved fingers, suddenly aware of the sweat beading there despite the icy drizzle that slowly soaked through her pelisse. As she nodded, placing her foot on the step of the hackney, her eyes fell on a ramshackle public house across the way. The door stood ajar, and several small, ragged children darted in and out through the opening.

"Mr. Crawford, what place is that?" She gestured with her kerchief across the street.

A righteous anger darkened his pleasant features. "That, dear madam, is The Silver Oak, the most heinous flash house in Bath."

Sophie knew all about flash houses, as did anyone who lived in London. Notorious dens of gambling and prostitution, many a foolish young man had reason to regret a visit to their premises. Or at least that's what Robert had told her over their mother's vociferous objections.

"Are not the keepers of flash houses often receivers of stolen goods? And do they not often use small children as thieves?"

"I regret to say that is true, Miss Stanton. There are no schools here in the slums, and many of these children are left by their parents—if indeed they have parents—to their own devices. Even in Bath, these places exist, both here in Lower Town and across the river in Holloway."

He extended his hand, silently urging her to step into the hackney, clearly eager for them to be on their way.

Sophie ignored him, poised on the step as an idea took shape in her mind. Her spirits began to lift as she realized exactly what she must do next. Her street urchin was not in the orphanage or the workhouse, and, if Simon was right, he would not be found through a visit to pawnshops either. But The Silver Oak looked just like the sort of place where her little thief might work, perhaps even live.

She gave the cleric her hand. "I am ready to go now, Mr. Crawford."

As she settled onto the hard bench of the carriage, a welcoming flush of determination flowed through her veins, warming her frozen limbs. For the first time in weeks she had a purpose again, a reason to rise from her bed in the morning.

Simon could bluster and threaten all he wanted, but she was determined to keep up the search. Now that she had a place to look, Sophie knew she could find her slum angel and rescue him from the depths of hell.

Chapter Four

"Do forgive me, madam. I hope I didn't step on your foot."

Sophie twisted her grimace into a smile, directing it at the concerned and very large man who had just trod on her toes. Her kid dancing shoes were no match for the gentleman's sturdily shod feet.

"No indeed, sir, but I thank you for your kind inquiry," she reassured him.

The man opened his mouth to reply, but was swept away by the glittering mob that crowded the entrance hall of the Upper Assembly Rooms.

Lady Jane forged a determined path through the crowd, steadily making her way to the ballroom. "Sophie, my dear, don't fall behind in this crush. If you do I'll never find you again. I see Mrs. Heathcote and her daughters waiting for us," she said, glancing back. "We are quite late. I only hope we'll be able to find seats by the dance floor."

Their arrival at the Rooms had been delayed this evening. Lady Eleanor had not been well, her habitually troublesome chest aggravated by the October damp. Lady Jane had been reluctant to leave her sister, wanting to send for the doctor instead. With the images of the workhouse still fresh in her mind,

Sophie would have been more than content to spend a quiet evening at home. The last thing she wished to do was spend another night dancing on tired feet in a crowded room, listening to the inane chatter of impertinent bachelors.

Unfortunately, Lady Eleanor had insisted that her poor health not stand in the way of Sophie's fun.

"Besides, my girl, you're not getting any younger," the old woman had admonished. "If you don't find a husband this Season, I don't know that we'll ever fire you off. You don't want to end up an aging spinster like the two of us, do you?"

As Sophie had no good answer to that alarming question, she now found herself squeezing past turbaned matrons and portly gentlemen as she limped after Lady Jane.

"There you are, my dears." Mrs. Heathcote, an old friend of Lady Jane's family, waved frantically to them from inside the door. "If the girls hurry they might be able to find seats before the dancing starts. Miss Stanton, you remember my daughters, do you not? They have been excessively eager to see you again, I assure you!"

Mrs. Heathcote's two youngest daughters, both of them unmarried, barely gave her a glance. Matilda, the oldest daughter, who had wed just weeks ago, ran her narrow eyes over Sophie's amber-colored mull gown before giving her the briefest of nods.

"How nice to see you again, Miss Stanton. I suppose your gown is the latest from London, is it not? As you must know I am just this month married, and Mamma insisted that all my wedding clothes come from the finest modistes in London."

"Oh, quite," trilled Mrs. Heathcote. "My dear Matilda's husband, Mr. Tuddle, is nephew to the Earl of Rumsley. He couldn't possibly wish to see his bride dressed in anything but the latest fashions." Her voice dropped to a penetrating whisper. "He has an income of three thousand a year. What say you to that, Miss Stanton? And he was very generous in his settlements to my darling girl, I assure you. Her pin money is extravagance itself!"

Mrs. Heathcote's feathered headdress quivered madly, seemingly as excited by Mr. Tuddle's generosity as its owner.

Sophie murmured her congratulations, hoping she sounded more enthusiastic than she felt. She didn't want to lack Christian charity, but Matilda Heathcote was a pinch-faced, mean-spirited girl with little dowry. It surprised her to hear she had made so good a match.

"Matilda, my love, why don't you and the other girls try to find seats inside?" Mrs. Heathcote wriggled her fingers toward the front of the room. "Lady Jane and I mean to try our hands at a round of whist. We'll join you at the interval."

"Sophie, will you mind if Mrs. Heathcote and I take in a few hands of cards? If you'd rather I stay I certainly will, but the room is a trifle stuffy for my comfort." Lady Jane's thin, fine-boned face looked weary.

Sophie's heart sank at the thought of spending the evening with only the Heathcote girls for company. "No, of course not, my lady," she replied, smiling at her godmother. "We shall join you in the tea room during the interval."

She regretfully watched her chaperon exit the room, and then turned to push her way through the press of bodies.

On any given night the ballroom, huge even by London standards, could hold over a thousand guests, and this year the Season in Bath was very full indeed. Fortunately, the elegant space, painted in muted shades of green set off by white wooden pilasters and trim, had very high ceilings that allowed some ventilation on crowded nights such as this. Five massive chandeliers made of Whitefriars crystal hung from the ceiling, each of them holding dozens of candles. They threw a dazzling incandescence over the guests, who in their finery glittered like crystal shards themselves in the reflected light.

The Heathcote sisters jostled their way to the front, securing four seats—two before and two behind—right by the dance floor. Sophie brushed past two red-coated officers to reach them. Their insolent stares made her neck sting with heat before she could finally squeeze by and drop into the chair next to Matilda.

"Oh, Miss Stanton," cried the young woman, "have you ever seen such a delightful crush in your life? Mr. Tuddle says the balls in Bath are quite as mobbed as any he has ever seen in London." Maltida didn't wait for an answer, but twisted around to speak to her sisters, shouting to be heard over the appalling racket that surrounded them.

For once, Sophie agreed with Matilda. The balls and assemblies in London were as disagreeable as the balls and assemblies in Bath. She had attended so many over the last three Seasons she had lost count.

She thought that after all these years in the fishbowl of the marriage mart she would have grown used to daily inspections by eligible suitors and matchmaking mamas. If anything, though, she hated it more than ever. The constant need to be on her best behavior, the ever-present awareness that the eyes of judgment were upon her, grew more difficult to endure as time passed.

And always Sophie lived with the knowledge—as did every other unmarried woman—that she must avoid at all cost the grinding stones of the rumor mill.

She surreptitiously rubbed one tired foot with the other, growing gloomier by the minute. What was the point of it all, anyway? She would never be with the man she loved, and no matter how hard she tried, she couldn't bring herself to imagine marrying anyone but Simon. In truth, she had given up trying to fall in love with anyone else months ago.

"I say, Sophie, you look as crabbed as an old hen with gout. No one would ever know you were in the middle of such a bang-up ball."

"Robert!"

"Hallo, sis, how are you?"

Sophie leapt to her feet. "When did you get here?" she cried, throwing herself into her sibling's arms.

"Just this afternoon, and a bloody wet drive it was from Swallow Hill. If Annabel hadn't insisted, I don't know that we would've come until next week." Her tall, fair-haired brother gave her a grimace, but a smile lurked in his eyes.

"I'm so grateful you did." Sophie pushed by him to reach for Annabel. Her new sister-in-law enveloped her in a fierce hug.

"Sophie, darling, I'm so glad to see you." Annabel's porcelain complexion flushed pink with excitement. "I told Robert that if he didn't bring me today I wouldn't speak to him for a week."

"Aye, she did, and a pretty way for a bride to speak to her new lord and master."

Annabel rolled her eyes at Sophie, but reached over to squeeze Robert's hand. Her delicate features were alight with love and, for a moment, she seemed to forget her surroundings as she met her husband's adoring gaze.

Sophie fought back the jealous pang lancing through her chest. As much as she rejoiced in Robert and Annabel's happiness, she sometimes found it painful to be with them. Until Annabel had entered his life, Robert and Sophie had been as thick as thieves for as long as she could remember. That, quite naturally, had changed upon his marriage.

"Robert, you know you were just as eager to see your sister as I was," Annabel said. "Truly, Sophie, he wouldn't be satisfied with waiting till tomorrow to see you. Nothing would do but that we must drop our bags at our townhouse and rush to the Assembly Rooms to find you. He barely gave me time to change my dress. I'm sure I look a fright."

Sophie gave Robert another hug. "And I'm so happy you did."

"Well, old girl, you did seem to be suffering a case of the blue megrims when you left Swallow Hill. I'm not sure if spending the Little Season in Bath with a couple of crotchety old invalids instead of staying in London is really the way to go."

"Robert," Sophie hissed, "you must hush. Someone will hear you. In any event, how could I refuse when Lady Jane begged me to visit? Besides, she and Lady Eleanor have been kindness itself."

"Of course they have, dear," Annabel soothed, all the while frowning at her husband. "We've just been a bit concerned, that's all. Who's to say that a quieter Season in Bath isn't a good thing? You've done so much visiting with family and friends lately that perhaps the rest will do you good."

Sophie laughed. "You could hardly call this mad crush restful. It's worse than anything I've seen in London."

Robert winced as Matilda, standing right behind him, brayed something to her sisters. He turned his quizzing glass on the new Mrs. Tuddle, distaste writ large on his face, before swinging around to critically survey the dancers.

"You seem to have the right of it there, sis. What a mob. And a more ill-favoured set of mushrooms I've never seen in my life. I swear Bath gets worse every year. Doesn't look like there's one person worth knowing in the entire place."

Annabel shook her head at her husband, who returned the gesture with a sheepish grin.

"Well, it's true," he protested. "I don't see anyone we know."

"You sound just like Grandfather, Robert. And it's not true," Sophie said. "Lord Trask arrived just the other day." She did her best to keep her voice unconcerned. "Mr. Nigel Dash is in town as well, visiting his mother."

"Oh yes, you're right," replied Annabel, craning her neck to look at the dancers. "I see Lord Trask now, in a set with Lady Randolph."

"You do?" Sophie twisted in her seat. She couldn't help searching the dancers for a glimpse of Simon. "Where?"

"Over there. Just under the portrait of the king," Robert supplied helpfully.

There Simon was, looking magnificent as he always did when attired for a ball. The stark black of his beautifully cut tailcoat and trousers, set off by his frost-white waistcoat and cravat, suited his dark looks and powerful masculinity. She could have swooned at the sight of him, if not for the fact that his partner for the dance was the equally magnificent Lady Randolph.

Sophie's heart thumped painfully as she watched Simon's latest mistress—clad in the flimsiest gown imaginable—trail her silk-gloved hands down his muscular arms. She couldn't believe his paramour had actually lowered herself to come to Bath. Everyone knew Lady Randolph rarely left London, and certainly not for one of the provincial spas. Perhaps the rumors were true after all—that Simon intended to make her his wife.

Along with her thudding heart, Sophie's temples began to throb.

"Sophie, are you not feeling well?" Annabel's quiet voice reached her through the din. "You look terribly pale."

Sophie cleared her throat. "No, I'm fine. I'm just admiring Lady Randolph's unusual dress."

Annabel looked doubtful, but forbore from replying. Robert, unfortunately, did not share his wife's discretion.

"Well, I don't admire it. She looks like a demirep with her bosom hanging out like that. Never could understand what Simon saw in the woman."

A grudging laugh forced its way from Sophie's throat at the naiveté of her brother's response.

"Really, Robert. You've grown so stodgy since your marriage. Truly, Lady Randolph is a beautiful woman."

He grunted. "If you say so. She don't hold a candle to you and Annabel, though."

She smiled, grateful for her brother's loyalty. But there was no denying that Bathsheba, Lady Randolph, widow of one of the richest earls in England, was a fascinating and sensual creature.

Petite in stature, she had luxuriant hair styled in the latest fashion, almost the exact shade as Sophie's. In fact, now that she thought about it, the countess looked quite a bit like her—or at least she would have if Sophie had larger breasts and fuller hips, and wore her gowns practically falling to her waist. Even the woman's large, expressive eyes were the same clear hazel as hers, although Lady Randolph's were more green than brown. And, of course, she didn't have to hide her gaze behind spectacles.

The countess was just the kind of woman Sophie wished to be and, certain physical attributes aside, knew with a depressing certainty she never would be. Rich, charming, and beautiful, Lady Randolph held the world of the ton in her dainty grasp.

Including, it would appear, the Earl of Trask.

The flush of heat on the back of his neck came not from the closeness of the room or from Bathsheba's attempt to seduce him. Rather, it alerted Simon to Sophie's presence in the ballroom.

And to her eyes on him.

Some months ago he had become aware of his uncanny ability to sense whenever she came near him. Regardless of the size of the room or the crowd, he could feel her presence. It both mystified and annoyed him, and was responsible for the sudden death of more than one flirtation.

"A sixpence for your thoughts, dear Simon." Bathsheba's husky voice intruded on his reverie.

"Believe me, dear Countess, they aren't worth that much."

"But Simon, you know everything about you fascinates me.

There was a time, not long ago, when you were as interested in me as I am in you." Her purr held a faint trace of bitterness.

Fortunately for him, the movements of the dance separated them for several minutes.

Nothing this evening had transpired as planned. He had arrived early with the intention of claiming Sophie for the first dance, thus securing her to his side for the rest of the night. But there had been no sign of her, and the dancing began before she arrived. Then Bathsheba had unexpectedly appeared—dressed for battle in her flimsiest décolletage— and had practically dragged him onto the ballroom floor.

Bathsheba hated Bath, claiming no person of fashion ever set foot in the place. Simon had a grim, certain feeling she had followed him here with the firm intention of trying to seduce him back into her bed.

The violins scraped out the last chords of the dance, and Bathsheba dropped gracefully into a low curtsy before him. He took her arm and led her from the floor.

"Simon, why is that young man waving at you from across the room?" Bathsheba's voice was laced with boredom. "Does no one know how to behave in this benighted town?"

"It's only Robert Stanton. I assume he wants to make sure he attracts our notice."

"Good Lord, must we speak to him? Robert Stanton is such a silly boy. And his wife! A provincial nobody. She is fortunate indeed her grandparents even acknowledge her."

Simon ignored her comments, regretting he was forced to keep her by his side. He could already see Sophie, demure in her pretty muslin gown, inspecting Bathsheba's wisp of a bodice with disapproving eyes.

He ground his teeth—the last thing he needed was for Sophie to think him still engaged in an affair, discreet or otherwise.

"Well, at least Sophia Stanton is good ton." Bathsheba's light, disdainful chatter prattled on. "But I'm amazed to see the girl wearing her spectacles to a ball. Really, it will be a miracle if she doesn't end up on the shelf. She's perilously close to being an ape leader as it is."

Simon almost laughed out loud. By the ton's standards, Sophie was about to make the best match of the Season. And he, for one, felt nothing but relief that she had finally developed the good sense to wear her spectacles on social occasions. At more than one grand event—when her mother had insisted she remove them—Simon had been forced to rescue her from encounters with potted plants, or to pull her back from tumbling down a flight of stairs.

"Hallo, old fellow," exclaimed Robert, as Simon and Bathsheba joined the little group. "Didn't think to see you here in Bath."

"Indeed," murmured Bathsheba in a catty voice, "I think we all find ourselves surprised to be here."

Sophie stiffened. Annabel looked startled and moved to stand closer to her.

Simon quickly took Annabel's hand. "Mrs. Stanton, may I say what a great pleasure it is to see you again? I didn't expect to have the privilege of your company in Bath."

She returned his greeting with a heartfelt smile. "Lord Trask, it's always wonderful to see you. Robert and I thought we would spend a few weeks with Sophie since she was so close by, visiting your aunts."

"How are Lady Eleanor and Lady Jane, Simon?" Robert's voice expressed genuine concern. "Sophie tells me Lady Eleanor is troubled by the damp weather."

"It's a miracle only the weather troubles her," purred Bathsheba. "This town is so lifeless, so full of ennui and decay, it is a wonder she hasn't expired from boredom. What is there to do from day to day? Visit the Pump Room, walk about the Orange Grove, and drink so much weak tea that one feels almost drowning in the stuff. And the company! Such a combination of invalids and shabby genteels. I wonder, Lord Trask, how your relations, of all people, can bear to live here the year round."

Simon repressed a surge of anger. He hated the place as much as Bathsheba, but no friend of his had the right to criticize his aunts.

Sophie jumped in before he had a chance to deflect Bathsheba's vitriol. "I wonder, then, your ladyship, why *you* would choose to come here? It would, of course, be a great hardship for the citizens of Bath to be deprived of your presence, but I'm sure we'd manage to scrape along without you. When may we expect your departure?"

Robert choked back a laugh. An ugly scowl darkened Bathsheba's features, rendering her almost plain. The evening was going downhill, and fast.

Nigel Dash popped up at his side, breaking free of the herd around them. "Trask, I thought I'd finally catch up with you tonight. Where the devil have you been keeping yourself? Haven't seen you in the Pump Room all week."

Simon had never been so grateful to see his friend. The fellow might be a complete rattle, but he had impeccable timing.

Nigel executed a faultless bow. "Lady Randolph, Mrs. Stanton, Miss Stanton, charmed to see you all looking so splendid. Robert, you dog, no need to ask you how the married state agrees with you. You look in fine trim."

He chatted away in his usual, rapid-fire style. If Simon didn't know better, he'd think his friend had no idea he'd just averted a social disaster. But the other man's eyes darted back and forth between Sophie and Lady Randolph, clearly noting the flushed cheeks of the one, and the sneering countenance of the other.

"Lord Trask." Lady Randolph ruthlessly interrupted Nigel as he inquired after the health of Robert's grandparents, General and Lady Stanton.

Simon tore his gaze away from Sophie's tense face. "Yes, my lady?"

"Would you be so kind as to accompany me to the card room? We really should leave the children to their amusements." Bathsheba flashed her teeth at Sophie. "I'm sure we could find more adult diversions to beguile our time."

Her seductive tone suggested what those diversions might be, as did the slender hand stroking his arm. Simon's gut clenched as he saw the color leach from Sophie's face. He removed Bathsheba's hand, bowing over it before letting go.

"Your ladyship must forgive me, but I am promised to Miss Stanton for the next set."

He wasn't, but he suspected Sophie wouldn't object, especially if it meant escaping Bathsheba's wrath. Not that Sophie ever ran away from a fight.

Bathsheba's admittedly spectacular breasts heaved with indignation. She was, no doubt, about to administer him a verbal stab when Nigel intervened.

"I say, capital idea, Lady Randolph! Allow me the pleasure of escorting you to the Octagon Room. I've been longing to play a round of whist all evening." He gallantly offered his arm.

Bathsheba fixed her gaze on Simon, her breath coming more slowly now as she studied him. She must not have liked what she saw on his face, for she quickly wiped all traces of anger from her countenance.

"I would be delighted, Mr. Dash. Thank you for your kindness." She regally nodded her head to the others, before turning a seductive smile back on Simon. "Lord Trask, I look forward to seeing you again very soon." With that pointed innuendo, she turned and allowed Nigel to escort her from the room.

"Well, I can't say I'm sorry to see the back of that old harpy," muttered Robert.

"Lord Trask, how long do you intend to remain in Bath?"

Annabel said brightly. Simon didn't miss Robert's wince as his wife trod heavily on his foot.

"I can't really say," he replied, turning his attention back to Sophie. Her usual tea-rose complexion now looked as white as his cravat. The effect was stark, set off by the halo of her burnished curls and her amber gown.

"What's the matter, Sophie?" Worry sharpened his voice. "Are you ill?"

"No. I . . . I just have a touch of the headache, that's all."

Robert inspected his sister with concern. "You look like a piker, old girl. Best to get you out of these hot rooms. We'll take you home."

Her mouth, which she'd held in a tight line, loosened into a slight smile. "Thank you for the charming description, Robert. But I would indeed be grateful if you took me back to St. James's Square."

Simon grasped her elbow and pulled her gently to his side. "I'll take her."

Sophie gazed up at him, eyes wide and startled.

"Nonsense, Trask," Robert said. "You stay and enjoy yourself. We'll . . . ouch!" He yelped as Annabel again stepped on his foot.

"If you wouldn't mind, my lord," Annabel said, ignoring her husband, "I want to pay my respects to Lady Jane. We'll tell her you're taking Sophie home."

She gave Sophie a quick hug and dragged a protesting Robert off through the crowd.

Simon tucked Sophie's small hand into the crook of his arm and led her toward the door. He glanced down, surprised to see tears glittering on the end of her eyelashes.

"What's wrong, Puck? Is it the headache that bothers you so?"

"No," she said, rapidly blinking the tears away. "I'm fine. I just want to go home."

He steered her out into the hall, worry and frustration gnawing at his gut. Why wouldn't she tell him what troubled her? He would fix it—he always did.

Whatever it was, as soon as he got her alone he would worm it out of her. It wasn't too early for Sophie to learn that she might be able to keep secrets from others, but never, under any circumstances, from him.

Chapter Five

Sophie blinked back her foolish tears, silently chiding herself for being a watering pot. The last thing she needed was to draw Simon's attention. He had a certain look in his eyes—a look that said he wouldn't rest until he had discovered the cause of her tears. If he thought something was wrong, he would hound her until he got it out of her. She had never been able to say no to him, and she didn't suppose she could start now.

But how could she say anything about Lady Randolph, or ask him if he intended to marry her? She couldn't bear the humiliation of revealing her own feelings in such a petty manner.

She peeked at his handsome face as he guided her through the hot press of bodies crowding the entrance to the ballroom. He looked grim and not at all likely to be sympathetic. If only Robert and Annabel had taken her home tonight instead of Simon. She could have confided in them about him, and even about the workhouse. Robert always listened to her, and he always understood.

At the thought of her brother and how much she missed him, her eyes filled up again. She blinked harder, and prayed Simon wouldn't notice.

He noticed. Glancing down, brows knit with concern, he led

her toward the antechamber by the front entrance. She groaned inwardly, dreading the interrogation that surely would follow once they exited the Rooms.

"Miss Stanton. What a pleasure to meet you again, and so soon. I hardly expected to see you at the Assembly Rooms this evening."

Sophie tripped over her own feet, stunned to see Mr. Crawford's cheery countenance emerge from the crowd in front of her. If Simon hadn't snaked an arm around her waist she would have tumbled down to the floor.

"Mr. Crawford! Goodness me," she gasped, righting herself. "How do you do? I didn't expect to see you at the Rooms at all. But one is always running into everyone here, don't you find? Such a mad crush tonight! I'm sure my dress is ruined."

She heard the inane chatter pour from her lips, but she couldn't seem to help herself. Her heart began to thud with panic at the thought of what Mr. Crawford might reveal to Simon.

The cleric hesitated, his glance sliding from her face to her companion's.

Simon cut in. "Sophie, perhaps you would like to introduce me to your acquaintance?"

Oh, God. He had adopted what she had secretly long ago dubbed The Voice of the Imperious Earl.

"Oh, certainly. Mr. Crawford, allow me to introduce you to the Earl of Trask. My lord, this is Mr. Crawford, the curate of St. Michael's Church. I have heard him preach many times whilst visiting your aunts in Bath."

Simon looked down his patrician nose at the plainly dressed cleric, barely acknowledging the other man's respectful bow. Sophie had to repress the urge to pinch him. Sometimes his bloody lordship was such a snob she wondered he could even see the rest of them from his elevated perch.

The polite smile faded from Mr. Crawford's lips, no doubt

blighted by Simon's haughty expression. "My lord, it is an honor to meet you," he replied.

After an excruciatingly long pause, Mr. Crawford's gaze moved back to meet hers. His light brown eyes glowed with a surprising—and disconcerting—amount of warmth. In fact, he looked quite adoringly at her.

The muscles in Simon's arm transformed into iron beneath her hand.

"Miss Stanton, I hope you didn't suffer a chill from your time out in the rain today." Mr. Crawford ignored Simon's hostility, which Sophie thought a remarkable feat. "I would never forgive myself if you did."

"What were you doing out in the rain with Mr. Crawford?" Simon's glacial tone sent shivers up the length of her spine.

"Nothing, nothing really. We were simply talking out in the courtyard behind the church offices when it began to rain. The downpour was quite drenching, really, but I assure you I suffered no harm." She opened her eyes wide at the cleric, trying to signal her intentions.

Mr. Crawford frowned earnestly back. He stared at her for a few seconds before comprehension dawned on his features.

"Oh, yes, of course! We were discussing, ah, the parish orphanage when the skies opened up. A regular Noah's downpour, one might almost say. I tried to urge Miss Stanton to take a chair home, but she would have none of it." He beamed at her, clearly pleased he had understood her silent plea. For a clergyman, he seemed quite an accomplished liar.

Simon's hawklike gaze touched on Mr. Crawford before settling on her face. Suspicion narrowed his eyes.

"Mr. Crawford, do forgive us." Sophie winced when her voice cracked. Unlike the curate, she was an awful liar, at least in front of Simon. "The earl and I were just leaving. He suffers from terrible headaches, you know. The heat in the Rooms often triggers one."

She pulled Simon away, ignoring Mr. Crawford's kindly expressions of regret for the earl's uncertain health. If the situation hadn't been so appalling, she would have laughed at the outraged look on Simon's face.

"Wait here, my lord. I'll retrieve my cloak and be with you in a moment."

Sophie fled to the safety of the anteroom and leaned against the wall to catch her breath. After a few minutes, when her pulse had finally settled into something approaching a normal rhythm, she accepted her cloak from a serving girl and returned to Simon. His broad shoulders backed against a supporting column, his scowling gaze directed at his feet. He looked like Atlas in a greatcoat, holding the weight of the world on his powerful back.

She sighed, preparing herself for the lecture.

"I'm ready, my lord."

He plucked the heavy velvet cloak from her hands and draped it over her shoulders, drawing it with an oddly protective gesture around her throat. She lifted her eyes to his dark face, startled by the tenderness she saw there.

"You've been out in the rain already today. I don't want you to catch cold," he said gruffly.

He steered her out the entrance and onto the paved street. Once free of the press at the door, he signaled for a chairman as he wrapped a brawny arm around her shoulders.

Suddenly, Sophie had no wish to hurry home. The night had turned fine—bright with a full moon, sparkling clear after the rain-washed day.

"Oh, Simon, do let's walk back to St. James's Square. It's a beautiful night now, and it was so stuffy inside."

He hesitated, weighing her request. She waited patiently.

"Will you be warm enough?"

"Oh, yes. My cloak is very warm, and I'll put the hood up." She raised the satin-lined hood around her face as she spoke.

"Very well. The walk isn't long enough to harm you." He tucked her hand back in his arm and led the way up Bennet Street.

Her spirits began to lift. She loved it when they were alone like this, as they had so often been when she was a child, and before Simon had become such an important man. It seemed as if they were embarking on a grand adventure, even though they were only walking home through the quiet streets of Bath.

They strolled toward the Circus, not talking, simply enjoying the night and the peace that surrounded them.

"All right, Puck. It's time to cut line. What exactly is bothering you?"

Well, at least she *had* been enjoying the night. Simon obviously had other ideas.

"I'm sorry, Simon. I don't know what you're talking about."

"I'm not a fool, Sophie. You were in tears back in the ballroom, and I know very well it wasn't because Bathsheba was rude to you. Why are you so upset tonight, and what does the Reverend Crawford have to do with it?"

"Really, Simon, why can't you just enjoy the walk home? Why must you always assume something is wrong?"

"Because I know you, Sophie. Something is wrong. Does this have anything to do with your bracelet, or the thief who stole it?"

Her stomach lurched at the thought of having to lie—again. If she didn't find her bracelet soon, she'd have to confess everything. But not tonight. Tonight she'd take the coward's way out.

"Goodness, the Circus looks wonderful in the moonlight, doesn't it? Just like a fairyland."

Even through the layers of his clothing she felt his muscles bunch into frustrated knots.

But though Simon's mood grew worse by the second, she

couldn't resist the lure of the magical setting. She moved slowly away from him to stand in the center of the circling houses.

The pale stone of the Circus glowed under a bright harvest moon, highlighting the elegant arc of the vast open space between the graceful terraces. She loved it at night, and on sunny days too, when the three-tiered façade of the townhouses, with row upon row of gleaming windows, reminded her of a gigantic tea service.

"Sophie, don't try to change the subject. You were up to something with Crawford today, and it had nothing to do with the parish orphanage. Don't lie to me."

"I'm not lying," she cried, stung by the truth of his accusation. "I did go to the orphanage today, and I would never lie to you, at least not if I could help it."

Too late, she realized what she had just blurted out.

He crossed the ground to her side in two strides. Grasping her shoulders, he spun her around. Shadows hid his face, but she could hear the quiet menace in his voice.

"So, you went looking for the boy today, didn't you? What else don't you want me to know about? Where did Mr. Crawford take you? Tell me right now—the truth, Sophie."

Her heart began pounding again, but not from fear. Simon would never hurt her. But his words triggered a flood of images she had been trying to repress all night. A cold sweat gathered on her neck at the memory of what she had seen in the workhouse.

His hands tightened on her shoulders. "What did you do?"

"I went to the Refuge for the Destitute," she whispered.

He jerked back, as if she had slapped him. "You went to the workhouse?" His deep voice echoed like distant thunder around the terraces.

"Simon, hush! You'll wake everyone and bring the watch down on us."

He let loose a rapid string of curses, most of which she had never heard before, and certainly not from him. He released her shoulders and grabbed an elbow, towing her around the arch of the Circus. She hurried to keep up.

"I swear to God, Sophie, you won't be able to sit for a week by the time I'm through with you. And by the time I'm finished with that bastard Crawford he'll never set foot in a church again. What the hell were you thinking to expose yourself in a place like that, with its filth and disease? And what if someone saw you?"

She wrenched her arm out of his grasp, furious that she had been stupid enough to tell him. How could she have forgotten the Earl of Trask belonged to the most scandal-averse family in England?

"You will leave Mr. Crawford alone, Simon. I gave him very little choice in the matter, I assure you."

"That I can well believe," he flung back. "Someone needs to have the schooling of you, my girl, before you do yourself a real harm."

"You're not my brother or my father," she yelled, no longer caring if anyone heard them. "You have no right to lecture me or tell me what to do!"

"No, I'm not your father, thank God. But aside from Robert, I'm the closest thing you have to family in this town. Someone has to be responsible for you, and it might as well be me."

She turned her back on him and stomped off toward Brock Street. The ring of his heels on the pavement followed closely behind. His hand reached out and grabbed her shoulder, forcing her to a halt.

"What would your mother think, Sophie? To know you had been to a place like that? Can you even begin to imagine her dismay?"

"She would have felt as I did, I'm sure of it. Devastated, furious that human beings could be so ill used." She wiped angry tears from her eyes. "Do you have any idea what goes on in those places, Simon? You accused me the other day of naïveté. Well, perhaps it's true, but I think the whole country must be blind to turn its back on such things. You wouldn't treat your animals that way. Why do men allow such things to happen?"

She stopped as hot tears choked off the words.

He loomed over her, looking like a demon in the night, his greatcoat swirling about him like a cloud of ink. She should have been frightened, but right now what she most wanted to do was pummel some sense into him. But she'd tried that before—on more than one occasion—and it never worked.

She sighed as the fury suddenly drained away, overcome with a weary longing to crawl into bed and be done with this day.

"I can't fight with you anymore, Simon. It's been a terrible day, and I just want to go home."

He took her arm in silence and led her toward the Crescent. As they approached the open space at the top of the street, a gust of wind blew her hood back on her neck. Simon paused to draw the heavy material up around her face. His arm settled over her shoulders, pulling her against the side of his powerful body.

Sophie tensed, every nerve jumping at the intimacy of the gesture. But then she relaxed against him. Part of her wanted to push him away, but another part longed to burrow into his seductive warmth, the gentle embrace soothing the ache in her heart.

"Sweetheart, I do know what goes on in the workhouses. I've seen it." His voice had dropped to a quiet rumble. "They are slices of hell on this earth. But there's little that can be done, at least not without large-scale reforms. Most in government and the church believe the poor must be forced to seek employment. If the workhouses were not places to fear, to be avoided at all cost, most believe the parishes would be overwhelmed with paupers and their families."

"Mr. Crawford says no decent man would choose to take his family there," Sophie ventured.

Simon's voice grew hard. "We will leave Mr. Crawford out of this discussion, if you please."

They emerged from Brock Street onto the commanding heights of the Crescent. Lights burned in some of the houses, but all was still. Only the wind moaned quietly in the night, sending little dust devils playing about the hem of Sophie's cloak.

They stopped and gazed down the Crescent Field toward the Lower Town, the river, and Avon Street—and abject despair.

"I want to find my bracelet, Simon. It's important to me. But it's more than that. It's about that frightened little boy. I know I can help him. I may not be able to help those other children, but I can save him. I know it."

She had to. She had to find her precious bracelet *and* rescue that helpless, lonely child.

The wind swirled hard, tossing her hair out from under her hood and sending it whipping across her face. Simon pushed the strands back with a gentle hand.

"I agree there is much to be done to help the unfortunate, especially those men and their families who were affected by the wars on the Continent. Some of us are working to do just that. But you must give up trying to find this boy. Follow your mother's example instead. Confine your work to the appropriate charities. You can't change the workhouses, and you must promise me that you'll never go down to Avon Street again."

Disappointment weighed her down—heavy and sullen. "*You* could do something, Simon. You're a powerful man. Men like you and my cousin Silverton—you could make them change."

He fell silent. In the darkness she couldn't tell if her plea affected him at all.

"If only you could have seen the children," she whispered, unable to stop the flow of images. "They were grinding bones into dust. *Human* bones, Simon."

His arm tightened around her shoulder, but he remained silent.

"The dust . . . it was everywhere. On the walls, the floors, floating through the air. It coated the children's faces. It got in my hair, Simon. When I got home I scrubbed and scrubbed, but I feel like it will never come out."

She broke off, ashamed of her trembling voice. Simon growled something low in his throat, and his strong hands pulled her around in front of him. He tilted her chin up and searched her face.

"Don't cry, Puck. I'll see what I can do to find your boy."

She stared into his shadowed eyes, wishing she could read what was in them. He rubbed a single tear from her cheek, then brushed his gloved thumb across her lower lip. Her heart stuttered into a mad rhythm as electric prickles raced across her skin.

"You're so sweet, just like an angel," he murmured. "I can't bear to see you cry." He slowly lowered his face, brushing his warm lips across her wet skin. Sophie could swear she felt a spark leap out from the place where he kissed her.

Unbelievably, her hands crept of their own volition up the front of his coat and curled themselves into his collar. Any moment now he would push her away. But instead his hands slid around her waist, pulling her firmly into the sandalwood scent of his body. Despite their multiple layers of clothing, the heat between them felt scorching.

Sophie's mouth dropped open as his lips continued to feather over her cheeks. Her heart beat so erratically she thought she might drop to the ground in a dead faint. She took a deep breath, forcing her head to clear. She wasn't about to miss a second of this.

"Is something wrong, Sophie?" Simon's voice—an unfamiliar husky growl—made her legs tremble with a delicious weakness.

"No, Simon," she breathed. "Not a thing."

"I'm glad."

His lips moved over her cheekbone and down her jawline, trailing fire all the way. She clutched at the collar of his coat, trying to pull him to her mouth.

"Simon." Her voice whispered the plea.

The next moment he swooped, covering her lips in a kiss so devouring that she almost swooned from the sheer joy of it. There was nothing gentle about his mouth on hers. His tongue demanded—and she granted—entrance into her mouth. Its hot sweep filled her with a deep ache, an ache matched by a quiver low in her belly.

She hesitantly answered back, touching her tongue to his, then nipping his lower lip with her teeth.

He gasped and drew back. Even in the shadows she could see the look of shock on his face. Shame flooded every part of her being. How could she have been so bold as to bite him, actually bite him! Was she demented?

"Simon, I'm so sorry. I don't know . . ." Humiliation strangled her voice. She began to pull out of his embrace.

"Oh, no you don't," he growled. His steely arms yanked her hard against the massive wall of his chest. His mouth claimed her lips again, tongue stroking, lips nibbling, driving her to respond as she did before.

Sophie stretched up on her tiptoes, her cloak falling back from her shoulders. She tentatively rubbed her chest against the rough wool of his coat, trying desperately to understand the sensations flooding her body. How could an ache, especially an ache in her breasts, feel so wonderful?

Simon growled again, and a tiny part of her mind startled to the knowledge that he sounded like a wild beast of the forest. But a second later that alarming thought was blasted from her mind as his hands slid from her waist to grab her bottom, cupping in a hard grip.

She squeaked into his mouth, but he didn't let go. And

she didn't want him to. She wanted to feel his mouth on hers forever, his tongue stroking hot, wet caresses onto her tingling lips, and deep inside her mouth. It was like nothing she had ever felt before, and everything she had ever dreamed of.

She arched into him, desperate to bring every part of her body into alignment with his. Something wild began to grow inside her, as his hands cupped and kneaded her through the soft layers of her gown and chemise. The shocking thought flashed through her mind that she wished his long fingers were stroking her naked flesh.

Bang.

Behind them a door slammed open against a wall. They sprung apart, and Sophie almost tumbled to the ground at the sudden release from Simon's arms. He yanked her back on her feet, keeping a firm grip on her elbows.

Two fashionable young men, obviously in their cups, staggered down the steps of the townhouse across the way.

"Oh blast it, Freddie. It's too early to call it a night. I know the sweetest little hell this side of the Avon. The whores and the dice are both clean, so what's say we give it a go?"

"Lead on, dear fellow, lead on."

The young bucks swayed down the street, hollering and singing on their way to less appetizing parts of town.

"Damn it all to hell." Simon swore under his breath as he dragged her in the direction of St. James's Square.

"What's wrong, Simon?" Sophie had to skip to keep up with him.

"What's wrong? Are you mad?" He scowled straight ahead. "I was kissing you in the middle of the Crescent."

He hurried her along to the Marlborough Buildings, which stretched past the Circus and up the Commons like a long, elegant ribbon.

"I don't mind that you were kissing me. Really I don't." If

he didn't stop rushing her, she was bound to get a stitch in her side.

"Well, I mind. You will surely drive me to Bedlam one of these days, Sophie. You really will."

Sophie let out her own little growl. If she hadn't been working so hard to keep up with him, she would have kicked him in the shins for ruining the most wonderful moment of her life.

"Really, Simon, it can't have been that bad."

"It would have been, if someone we know had seen us. Put your hood up, Sophie. Your reputation is fragile enough as it is without something like this happening to you."

He towed her along to St. James's Square, lecturing her all the way. As she hurried to keep up, she listened with half an ear as the chill wind from the heights leached into her bones. The warmth of their embrace had fled, and only questions remained. Why had he kissed her in the first place? Was it only because he felt sorry for her?

"Hurry up, Sophie. It's late. After the day you've had, you should have been in bed hours ago." His tone was clipped, almost angry.

Sophie reached the depressing conclusion that when it came to Simon, no matter what happened between them, some things would always remain the same.

Chapter Six

Mr. Puddleford's monotone almost drowned out the boisterous chatter of the crowd in the stalls around them. Sophie directed a smile at the earnest widower, even as she strained to hear the latest gossip Lucy Whipple was imparting to Annabel.

". . . and that, Miss Stanton, is why one must only divide lilies in the late fall, and never in the spring."

". . . and so she told Mr. Courtney she never wanted to set eyes on him again!"

Both Mr. Puddleford and Lucy concluded on equally triumphant notes, but Sophie could give a hang about dividing lilies. She had, however, been dying to find out why Miss Geraldine Evans had broken her engagement to Mr. John Courtney. It was the talk of the town, but she seemed destined to be the only person who would never know the particulars.

Along with Mr. Puddleford, of course.

"I beg your pardon, Miss Stanton." The widower eyed her morosely. "I'm sure you must be finding all this talk about my garden exceedingly dull. But you seemed so interested in my lilies the last time we spoke."

"Oh, certainly not dull, my dear sir. Not dull, at all. Please tell me more," Sophie replied, mustering up her enthusiasm.

After all, Mr. Puddleford was a very nice man, and the last thing she wished to do was hurt his feelings.

Puffing out his already portly chest, he launched into a detailed explanation of experiments he was conducting in his greenhouse. He pulled his chair closer in his eagerness to explain the finer points of cross-pollination. In fact, he backed her right up against the railing of their box. If he got any closer, she would likely plummet into the pit of the Theater Royal.

The play tonight was *The Misanthrope*—never one of her favorites. But Annabel and Robert had insisted she join them in their outing with the Whipples, their friends from Kent who had chosen to spend the winter in Bath.

After several restless hours spent rattling around the house in St. James's Square, Sophie had been more than ready to be persuaded. Simon hadn't called all day. With a sinking heart, she finally admitted he wasn't likely to visit that evening either. The kiss that had meant so much to her had obviously meant very little to him. An outing with Robert and Annabel seemed the perfect antidote to her growing dissatisfaction with herself, and with England's most irritating earl.

Once Mr. Puddleford had spotted her, though, she had hardly been able to speak a word to anyone else. He hurried over to their box as soon as the interval began, ready to spend the rest of the night attached to her side.

She couldn't hold back a sigh as she smoothed her rose-colored silk gloves across the lap of her matching cambric gown. Fortunately, Mr. Puddleford didn't notice, as he was obviously enraptured with his own description of some newly arrived orchids to his estate in Yorkshire.

But Annabel noticed. Worry creasing her smooth brow, she studied Sophie before leaning over and whispering something in Robert's ear. He nodded politely, but continued listening to Lucy Whipple's recitation of the morning's events in the Pump Room.

Sophie focused her attention back on Mr. Puddleford, her most ardent and persistent suitor. She had met him two seasons ago, and he had asked her to marry him four times in the last year. He wouldn't take no for an answer. She wondered if he actually forgot her refusal from one month to the next—after all, he was very absent-minded—or if he simply intended to wait her out. The Lord only knew most of her other suitors had given up long ago.

Not that she'd had many to begin with. Sadly, they all tended to be like Mr. Puddleford, sedate middle-aged widowers mostly content to pass the evening discussing Roman history or dull botanical treatises. She liked Roman history rather a lot, but, generally speaking, not at balls or assemblies.

And certainly no man had ever tried to give her more than a chaste, stolen kiss on the cheek. Not until last night, anyway.

She shifted uncomfortably, flushing with heat as she recalled the taste of Simon's lips on hers, the feel of his hands on her bottom. All day, while waiting for him to call, she had worried how to act in his presence. She had succumbed so easily to his passion, responding, if truth were told, with a great deal of enthusiasm herself. God forbid he should think her a strumpet.

She bolted upright in her seat. Perhaps her enthusiasm had been so distasteful it had driven him away.

"Sophie, old girl, you're as red as a beet. Mr. Puddleford, what the devil are you talking to my sister about?" Robert had squeezed around the other side of Mr. Puddleford, inspecting both of them through the exaggerated lens of his quizzing glass. The older man's pale eyes widened in dismay.

"Miss Stanton and I were discussing the cross-pollination of orchids, sir. I can't imagine a more wholesome and invigorating topic for any young lady."

"Oh, my dear sir," exclaimed Annabel, abandoning her conversation with Lucy Whipple. "I have had such problems with my orchids. Won't you sit by me, and give me your expert opinion on what I should do?"

"Capital idea, my dear," enthused Robert, hauling Mr. Puddleford to his feet and shoving him into the chair next to his wife. "Mrs. Stanton hasn't been able to sleep for weeks, you know. She lies awake all night thinking about her blasted orchids. Lord knows it's enough to drive a man right around the twist."

Mr. Puddleford spluttered as Robert manhandled him away from Sophie.

"Indeed, dear sir, you can't imagine how my orchids have troubled me," Annabel exclaimed soulfully, even though her eyes brimmed with laughter. "You must help me, or I fear I might lose them all."

"Well, we can't have that." Mr. Puddleford's alarm finally overcame his gallantry. "Please calm yourself, madam. Once I have the facts in hand, I'm sure I can devise a sound plan to correct your problems."

Annabel launched into a lurid description of the afflictions of her nonexistent orchids, Mr. Puddleford nodding wisely all the while. Robert rolled his eyes and dropped onto the seat next to Sophie.

"Old poof," he muttered. "Can't think why you let him hang about so much, sis. You must be out of your mind."

"Oh, Robert, do be quiet," she hissed back, torn between laughter and irritation. "I can't seem to do anything to get rid of the poor man!"

"Well, Annabel will see to him. I wanted to speak to you alone, anyway."

Sophie glanced around the brightly lit, ornate theater, stuffed to the ceiling with noisy patrons. Only Robert would think they were alone in the middle of such a crowd.

"You really are looking rather flushed, Soph. Are you sure

you're all right? I hope you're not stewing about your bracelet. Get you another one, you know, if it bothers you."

Sophie clenched her fingers on the polished wood of the box's railing, then forced herself to relax her grip. She had told Robert earlier in the day about the theft of her bracelet—with certain modifications, of course—and what she had done to recover it. Unfortunately, he had reacted almost as badly as Simon had, ringing a peal over her head for a good half hour.

"It's not just the bracelet, Robert, although you know how much it means to me." She paused to control the little catch in her voice. She had never lied to her brother before today. Worst of all, she was getting quite good at it.

Robert squeezed her hand, thankfully misunderstanding her emotion. "I do know. It reminds you of Father. His death was horrible, especially since we didn't expect it. Worse for you, though, old girl. You two were always as thick as glue."

She swallowed against the familiar pain that lanced through her heart. Her father's death after a brief illness had been the great tragedy of her life. She loved her mother and brother with all her heart, but it had been Papa who had really understood her. He had encouraged her love of adventure, and turned a blind eye whenever she had thrown down her embroidery to join her brother in some grubby escapade.

"It's not only the bracelet," she said, pushing the sorrow back into the little mental box she had created long ago. "I truly feel I must do everything I can to help that boy. He was so sad and alone. I'm afraid he has no one at all to help him."

"No." Robert's voice was surprisingly stern. "Simon's right. The slums are no place for a lady like you. And who knows what that little ruffian was really up to? Playing on your sympathies, old girl. Trying to prevent you from turning him over to the constable. He's probably been thieving for years. As the head of the family, I absolutely forbid you to go looking for him. I mean it, Soph."

She felt her anger spike, her hand curling once more around the railing. If Robert didn't understand how much this meant to her, no one would.

All at once the gay tumult of her surroundings became unbearable. If she didn't escape now, she would probably say something she would come to regret a very short time later.

"Of course, Robert. Whatever you want." She stood and began to collect her things. "I'm really not feeling very well after all. It was a mistake for me to come out tonight."

Robert gazed up at her, confounded. "Sophie . . ."

"No, really," she interrupted him. "I think I best go home. I'll go in Lady Eleanor's coach, and perhaps Lucy can take you to Laura Place."

"Blast, Soph," Robert grumbled, jumping to his feet, "I'll take you home."

Sophie ignored him. "Mr. Puddleford, would you be so kind as to escort me to my carriage?"

"It would be my greatest honor," he exclaimed, springing to his feet with an alacrity that made her blink.

Annabel looked surprised, but after a quick inspection of Sophie's face she rose from her chair.

"Hush, Robert," she said, ruthlessly cutting off her husband's protests. "Of course you must go home, my love, if you are not well. Lucy will be happy to take us to Laura Place."

Sophie gave Annabel a quick hug, nodded to Lucy, and then rushed from the box. Mr. Puddleford hurried after her, puffing as he followed her down the stairs to the lobby.

She bolted through the lobby and out into the night, not caring who might see her furious dash into the street. A few stragglers lingering at the entrance to the theater raised disapproving eyebrows as she rushed by.

"Miss Stanton, please wait," gasped Mr. Puddleford as he clutched at his side. "You will surely do yourself a harm with

all this rushing about. It is neither seemly nor healthy for you
to do so."

"Forgive me, sir, but the air was so close inside. I really
couldn't bear it a moment longer."

"I understand, my dear Miss Stanton," the widower said,
struggling to catch his breath. "Please allow me to take you
home myself. Indeed, you must allow me to take care of you."

Mr. Puddleford's eyes held a certain gleam—the gleam they
got whenever he was about to solicit her hand in marriage.
Sophie couldn't bear yet another proposal, especially not now.

"Mr. Puddleford, I see Lady Eleanor's footman, James, just
over there. Could you please ask him to fetch the carriage?"

The widower hesitated and then bowed, moving down the
line of carriages to speak to the footman. Sophie exhaled a
huge sigh of relief and began counting stones in the pavement, determined to bring her temper under control before he
returned.

A flash of movement at the far edges of the torchlight
caught her attention. She glanced up and found herself looking straight into the eyes of her little street thief. Hovering just
out of reach, he looked as ragged and frightened as he had the
first time she had set eyes on him.

But he didn't retreat into the darkness. His pale, haunted
eyes fastened to where she stood frozen on the pavement.

A shiver of awareness ran across her skin.

Sensing that he looked for a sign, she gave him a wary smile
and gestured for him to wait. The boy nodded and drifted back
into the shadows.

"Your carriage awaits, my lady," Mr. Puddleford cried with
laborious gallantry as Lady Eleanor's coach and pair drew up
before her. "Allow me to escort you home."

"That will not be necessary, Mr. Puddleford. James will take
care of me." She grabbed his hand and briskly shook it, then

turned as if about to step into the coach. "I hear the gong for the interval. You will not wish to be late. Good night, sir."

In the face of so blighting a dismissal, the widower had no choice but to bow and murmur his good-byes. She felt a twinge of guilt at the hurt on his pudgy features, but knew he would forget the snub by tomorrow.

"Miss, will you step in?" James stood respectfully by to help her.

"In a minute, James." She waited until Mr. Puddleford disappeared into the theater. After a quick inspection of the street, she decided the few people milling about the steps of the building would likely not even notice her. In any event, she had to risk it.

"Stay here, James. I'll return in a moment."

The footman looked astonished, but bowed his compliance. After another swift glance around, Sophie hurried to the other side of the carriage, out of the direct light thrown by the torches.

"Little boy, are you there?" she called out in little more than a whisper.

The urchin appeared like an apparition from the darkness, moving cautiously toward her. Sophie's chest ached at the fear etched on his thin features.

"I won't hurt you, child. I promise." She held out her hand encouragingly.

"I've come to return your bracelet, miss." His voice shook. "My sister said it were wrong of me to take it, and I must give it back." He held out a trembling hand. The gold cuff nestled in his dirty palm, gleaming softly in the glow of the lamps from the coach.

Sophie sank to her knees, so powerful was the rush of relief and gratitude pouring through her veins. It took a moment to find her voice. "That was very good of you, my dear. How did you find me?"

"My sister said to watch all the places the swells went to. She said I must look until I find you." The boy drifted closer, but still remained just out of reach.

"Your sister must be very clever."

"Aye, my lady. The smartest and the prettiest that ever was. She takes care of me since my ma died. She said it was wrong to steal, even though my pa don't think so."

"Your fa . . . pa tells you to steal?"

"Aye. If I don't, he beats me."

Sophie clenched her teeth shut to prevent a very rude word from escaping her lips. It took her a moment to regain her self-control.

"And how long have you been stealing?"

"Ever since my ma died last spring. She would never let my pa put me on the street, even though sometimes he beat her fierce."

"Oh, God," she breathed. She couldn't imagine her own father lifting a hand against her—against anyone. He had been the kindest man she had ever known.

The boy shuffled from foot to foot, a portrait of abject misery. Sophie had not a lingering shred of doubt she must help him. But how?

The damp from the cobblestones began to penetrate both her cloak and her gown, and she could see the boy begin to shiver in the chill of the October night. She came to her feet slowly so as not to frighten him away.

"My name's Sophie. What's yours?"

"I remember, my lady." His beautifully shaped mouth trembled into a tentative smile. "Mine's Toby."

"Well, Toby, it's a pleasure to meet you. You are very good to return my bracelet, and I want to give you some money for your trouble. Won't you step into my carriage for a few minutes? It's much warmer in there."

He jerked away, his huge eyes growing even wider in alarm. "You be taking me to the constable!"

"I promise I only want to help you and your sister. Cross my heart and hope to die." She drew a cross over her chest, feeling her own heart racing with nervous anticipation.

Toby examined her doubtfully, but, after a few moments, crept back to her. She reached out her hand once more. Hesitantly, he put his grubby little fingers in hers, and Sophie exhaled an anxious breath, casting a silent prayer of thanks heavenward.

"Is anything wrong, miss?"

Both Sophie and Toby jumped as James rounded the side of the coach. If she hadn't been holding his hand so firmly, the boy would have bolted. She tightened her fingers in a reassuring grip.

"Everything is fine, James. This young man has found my— er—coral bracelet, and wished to return it to me."

The entire household knew Sophie's reticule and bracelet had been stolen, alerted to the fact by Lady Eleanor's talkative dresser.

"Come with me, Toby. We must get you out of this cold."

Under the startled gaze of both the footman and Lady Eleanor's coachman, Sophie towed the reluctant child round the other side of the carriage and led him to the steps.

"Good Lord, miss, surely you ain't . . ."

Sophie silenced the coachman's protest with a glare. Toby searched her face, his pointed little chin quivering in doubt. She brushed his matted blond hair back from his forehead.

"Don't worry, Toby. I won't let anyone hurt you."

Shaking her head at James's offer of help, she boosted the little boy into the carriage herself. As she turned to follow him, she caught the eye of a sleek, well-dressed man who must have just exited from the theater. He paused at the top of the marble stairs, astonishment written all over his sharp features as he gazed down at her.

Sophie bit her lip. He must have seen her assist Toby into the coach. The handsome equipage had no honors or crest on its body, but most in Bath knew it belonged to Lady Eleanor.

"Miss." James's voice held a note of warning.

Sophie took his hand and sprang up the steps, barely pulling her skirts out of the way before the footman slammed the door behind her. She dropped onto the padded bench across from Toby, who eyed her suspiciously in the dim light of the carriage lamp.

"Here, miss. You best take your bracelet and let me go. Becky will be wanting me to come home." He slipped the cuff into her hand. Sophie clutched it tightly for a second before sliding it into her reticule.

"Is Becky your sister?"

He nodded, then let his gaze drift over the richly upholstered interior of the coach. A grimy hand slowly reached out to trace the stitching in the velvet cushions.

"Why must you steal, Toby? Does your father have no money? Does he have no work?"

"Oh, no, miss. He works. We has a tavern down by the docks. Pa says we brings in more blunt than any other flash house in the town."

Sophie couldn't help but catch the queer note of pride in the child's voice. She felt a little stab of panic as her worst fears were confirmed. Simon and Robert were right—the boy was a professional thief. Was it already too late to help him?

"How old are you, Toby?"

"Eight, miss."

"Oh, Toby! You are much too young to be a thief."

"I know," he replied matter-of-factly. "Becky hates it, too. She says Ma wanted more for us. Ma was saving up to send me and Becky to London, to stay with my Aunt Sarah. She has a draper's shop." His voice sounded wistful, as if Aunt Sarah's shop might be the most magical place on earth.

"Does your father want you to go?"

"No, miss." Toby's voice turned hard and bitter, and, for a moment, he sounded much older than his years. "That's why I stole your bracelet. I has to get Becky away from here. I need the money to get her to London, away from Pa." His face turned dark with a hatred so intense it raised prickles on the nape of her neck.

Sophie had to swallow past the sudden constriction in her throat. "Why?"

"Because Becky's just turned thirteen. Now that she's a woman grown, Pa says he's going to make her a whore."

Chapter Seven

"I beg your pardon?" Sophie couldn't seem to get her brain to work. Surely she hadn't heard what she thought she did.

Toby blinked. "You knows what a whore is, don't you, miss?"

"Yes, of course," she replied hastily, forestalling any explanation. "What I meant is, does your father also run a . . . a brothel from his tavern?"

"No, miss. He says the whores bring too much trouble into the house."

Sophie stared at the boy, oddly dignified in his tattered clothing as he perched on the cushions opposite. She searched for the words to questions she hardly knew how to ask. Simon was right. She knew very little about life outside her own sheltered world—how terrifying and bleak it could be.

"How do you know he wants to make your sister a . . . a prostitute?"

"I heard him talking to Mrs. Delacourt. She keeps a whore-house on Corn Street. Becky's a real beauty, miss, just like my ma used to be. It was Mrs. Delacourt put the idea into Pa's head, to sell Becky at an act . . . an action?"

"A what?"

"You know, miss. It's like a bet. All the men will bet on who gets Becky first." Toby's voice broke.

Sophie took his small hand in hers. "Do you mean an auction, my dear?"

"Aye, miss, that's it. I knew you would get the proper word to call it." The boy smiled shyly, as if to thank her for knowing something so horrific. Her heart kicked with a sickening thud into her ribs, even as her mind struggled to reject the truth of what she saw on the boy's face.

But then Toby's brief smile faded. "I heard them, all right. They didn't think I was there, 'cause I hid behind the bar. Mrs. Delacourt said men would pay a lot of blunt for a girl as young as Becky. She said a virgin like her would be worth her weight in guineas." His thin features, so angelic in form, distorted with rage. "I'd kill Pa if I could, miss, I really would!"

He burst into tears, his narrow shoulders shaking with the force of his hatred and grief. Sophie reached over and pulled him into her arms, ignoring the stench of urine and soot that wafted up from his clothing.

"Hush, Toby." She gently rocked him against her chest. "I'll help you. I promise."

"How, miss?" He pulled away from her. She didn't try to stop him, knowing well the fierce pride of small boys.

"First, I must talk to Becky. Will you take me to her?"

He stopped knuckling the tears from his eyes and gazed at her with slack-jawed wonder. "Now?"

"Yes, now. Is your father's tavern on this side of the river? We're only a few blocks from Avon Street."

He nodded. "It's The Silver Oak, miss. Just across from the workhouse."

Sophie clicked her tongue against the roof of her mouth. How had she known the flash house would play a role in this child's life?

"We'll go immediately, Toby."

His pinched face registered alarm, but Sophie refused to be deterred, either by his fear or her promises to Simon and Robert. There was too much at stake—a young girl's life—to allow for empty proprieties.

She rapped on the window of the carriage. James swung the door open and stuck his head inside.

"Yes, Miss Stanton?"

"James, we are taking this boy home. Direct John to drive to The Silver Oak tavern, across from the Refuge for the Destitute. It's only a few blocks from here on Avon Street."

James froze in the doorway. Toby took advantage of the footman's paralysis to pipe in with further instructions.

"There's a lane that runs behind, off Milk Street. Best to pull up there, so Pa don't spy us."

"Lady Eleanor will have our heads, miss, if we take you down to Avon Street." James registered his protest in a faint but horrified voice.

"Well, we'll just have to make certain she doesn't find out."

Sophie wrested the door from the footman's hand and slammed it shut. She could hear James arguing with the coachman, but after a few moments the carriage jolted to a start.

"Miss, I don't know what Becky will say about this." The boy looked anxious, his body huddled against the squabs.

"Don't worry, Toby. I'll explain everything to her," she replied, with a great deal more confidence than she felt. She couldn't let Toby see the fear that rippled through her in tiny shivers.

Sophie did her best to distract the boy during the short trip by asking him about the magical draper's shop in London. He visibly relaxed, becoming almost animated as he described all the wondrous goods his Aunt Sarah surely had stocked on her shelves.

She listened with one ear, her attention fixed on the changing view outside her window. The prosperous world of Beaufort

Square was left behind in only a minute or two, replaced by increasingly dark and dirty streets. Groups of fashionable young men strolling along in twos and threes were replaced by roughly dressed day laborers and intoxicated bargemen.

Sophie shivered inside her warm cloak, fighting off a sickening wave of apprehension. It was one thing to come down to the docks in broad daylight, accompanied by a minister whose good name would protect her. But she had no such protection now. Only her own fading courage kept her company.

And if Simon and Robert ever found out about this, they would surely lock her in her bedroom for a month.

"Becky will be ever so surprised to see you, miss. We ain't never had someone like you come to visit. I bet Ma would have liked you a lot." Toby cautiously slipped his grubby hand into hers, and Sophie felt all her cold doubts vanish in the warmth of his trust.

The carriage jerked to a halt. She peered out the window, surprised at the amount of light shining out on the broken cobblestones of the street. Several of the buildings lining the way—taverns or gin houses, most likely—were brightly lit and seemed to be carrying on a boisterous trade.

James opened the door and let down the steps. He handed her out, his face set in grim lines, then turned to lift Toby to the ground.

The carriage had stopped close by the docks and near the entrance of the laneway the boy had spoken of. From where she stood, Sophie could see the iron gates of the workhouse. Directly across from it, a battered sign depicting an oak tree swung above the open door of the flash house she had seen yesterday.

A pair of men in the rugged garb of dockworkers stumbled out of the tavern, accompanied by two women dressed in gowns cut so low that even from this distance Sophie could see their rouged nipples. She flushed and cringed to think of Toby and his sister living in such degrading conditions.

"Down here, miss." The boy tugged once on her cloak and darted into the lane.

She took a deep breath, trying to quell the churning in her stomach. "Stay here, James. I'll return shortly."

"Nay, Miss Stanton. I should go with you."

"No. It's better if you remain here."

James opened his mouth to argue, but Sophie held up a hand.

"I don't want the children to be any more frightened than they are. Look." She pointed down the laneway. Toby had come to a halt by a door, clearly visible in the light filtering out from a window beside it.

"You can see me from here. It's best that you and John stay together. I'll call if I need you." She stepped firmly into the lane and then hesitated, glancing back over her shoulder.

"Will you be all right, James?"

"Aye, miss." A pistol materialized in his gloved hand. "John Coachman and I can take care of ourselves. Just be certain to call if you need help."

She nodded and hurried off down the lane, coming to a halt as Toby put a finger to his lips in a signal to remain silent. As he slipped through the door, she caught a brief glimpse of a dingy hallway and smelled the unmistakable odor of rancid mutton and something else. Something disgusting.

Sophie retreated against the dank brick of the building, pulling her thick velvet cloak around her. She hastily whispered a prayer that no one but Toby and his sister would emerge from the back door.

As the minutes crawled by, she became more aware of her surroundings. The river close by and the stench from the drains and sewers running into it, so potent she began to feel nauseous. She stepped cautiously away from the wall to the center of the lane, hoping to catch a breath of fresher air.

Something rustled in the heaps of refuse piled up beside the kitchen door. Whatever it was scuttled across her foot. She jumped, tasting blood as she bit back a startled yelp.

Fortunately for her rapidly fading courage, the door creaked open, and Toby slid through with a girl following closely behind. The girl—obviously Becky—crept forward to stand just inside the light cast from the window set in the wall. Even in the gloomy shadows of the alley, Sophie could see she was extraordinary.

Becky's eyes were a startling shade of cornflower blue, set off by a pale complexion and hair as black as midnight. Her full lips were a blushing pink, and her features were delicate and even. She had a surprisingly well-developed figure for a girl her age, amply displayed by an ill-fitting blouse and a coarse skirt cinched tightly around her waist. But she had the sweet face of an innocent child, not yet destroyed by the conditions of her terrible life. That aura of innocence and her astonishing beauty made a potent combination.

No wonder Mrs. Delacourt wanted to bring her into the trade.

Becky and Toby traded uneasy glances, both looking too frightened to utter a word.

Sophie took a small step forward into the light. "Hello, Becky. My name is Sophie. Your brother told me all about you, and I'd like to help you both if I can."

"What did Toby tell you?"

Sophie had to strain to hear the girl's whisper. "He . . . he told me about Mrs. Delacourt."

A spasm of fear flashed across the girl's features. She turned to her brother and gripped his shoulder. "You shouldn't be talking about such things! Pa would beat you if he found out."

"I don't care, Becky," her brother whispered fiercely. "She wants to help us. She'll give us money to go to London and live with Aunt Sarah."

"Indeed, Becky. I want to help you very much. If what your

brother told me is true, you can't possibly stay here. I could help you get away. You could come with me tonight, if you want." She swiftly crushed an alarming image of Lady Eleanor's reaction to such unexpected guests.

Hope seemed to flare in Becky's eyes. But a moment later she squeezed them shut. Her full lips trembled, then stilled.

"It ain't true, miss. What Toby said. I don't know where he got such an idea into his head."

"I told you," the boy cried. "I heard Pa and that evil old witch talking about it last week! They're going to do it, Becky, I swear they are."

"Hush, Toby." Becky cast a fearful glance at the back door of the tavern. "We can't leave. Pa wouldn't let us. He knows we would go to Aunt Sarah, and sure as anything he would fetch us back. He would beat you something awful if we tried to run away. I can't bear it when he beats you."

Toby's shoulders drooped under the force of his sister's unassailable logic. Becky hugged him, gazing at Sophie with a look of sad determination in her beautiful eyes.

"I'm sorry Toby put you to so much trouble, miss, but you mustn't mind what he says. Pa would never do that to me. It's just been so hard since Ma died, especially for Toby."

Sophie's confidence began to waver. Perhaps Toby had misunderstood what his father said—that was easy enough for a child to do—or mayhap the man had rejected the madam's idea. Even so, he must be a brute, as the children were obviously terrified. She had to do something to help them, but what?

The sound of masculine voices at the end of the laneway jerked her attention in that direction. A large form enveloped in a swirling coat moved rapidly their way, long strides eating up the distance between them.

Toby whimpered as Becky clutched him in her arms. Sophie's breath caught, then whooshed out of her body. She felt light-headed as fear took its place, but she stepped in front of the children, determined to shield them as best she could from the menacing intruder.

As the terrifying figure drew near, she parted her lips to cry out for James.

"Sophie, are you out of your feeble little mind? What the hell are you doing down here?" Simon's voice had never sounded so furious, and never had she been more thankful to hear it.

"Simon!"

She stumbled toward him on legs weak with relief. Strong arms reached out and pulled her into a tight embrace.

"Thank goodness it's you." She snuggled into the thick fabric of his coat, gratefully inhaling the scent of damp wool mingled with tobacco. He smelled of warmth and life and everything she had ever wanted.

"We'll see if you thank me when I'm through with you." His voice was a dark growl. Pushing her slightly away, he ran a swift gaze over her body. "Are you hurt?"

"I'm fine, but I want you to talk to Toby and his sister. We must do something to help them." She took one of his leather-gloved hands and tried to pull him over to the children.

"Sophie . . ."

She heard the warning in his voice.

"Simon, just talk to them for a minute. And don't scare them," she added when she heard him mutter a shocking curse under his breath.

He allowed her to tow him to the children, still huddled in the shadows.

"Toby, Becky, I'd like you to meet Lord Trask. He's my friend, and he can help us."

Toby's eyes popped wide. "You be a lord?" he squeaked.

"I am." Simon managed to make the answer sound like the crack of doom.

Becky crept forward into the light cast from the kitchen window. "What kind of lord are you?"

Simon drew in a sharp breath, obviously stunned by the girl's astonishing beauty.

"Ah . . . I am an earl."

Becky dropped into an awkward curtsy. "Pleased to meet you, m'lord." She elbowed her brother in the side. "Say hello to his lordship, Toby."

The boy ducked his head shyly. "M'lord." He retreated behind his sister.

A painful silence fell upon the little group. It suddenly occurred to Sophie how intimidating it would be for Becky to explain their situation to an earl.

Especially when that earl looked like a thundercloud about to burst over their heads.

Clearly, he meant to be difficult.

"Toby, are you the boy who took Miss Stanton's bracelet?" Simon's deep timbre sounded unexpectedly gentle.

Sophie almost jumped out of her kid slippers. She was sunk for sure if Toby described what the bracelet looked like. Someday she might tell Simon what really happened, but not here. Not like this. Not when there were more important issues at stake.

But Toby looked ready to bolt, too scared to utter a word. Becky gripped his arm to hold him by her side. "It were very wrong of him, m'lord. I told him he had to return it, and he did. Please don't tell Pa. He'll beat him something fierce if you do."

Simon's scowl turned even blacker, if that were possible. "Your father beats you?"

Toby nodded.

"Where is your mother?"

"She died six months ago," Sophie answered softly.

Simon threw her a brief, unreadable glance before returning his attention to the children. "I won't tell your father, Toby, but you must promise not to steal anymore from young ladies. Or old ones, for that matter," he added dryly, obviously noting the hopeful gleam on the boy's face.

Becky elbowed her brother again.

"I won't, m'lord, I promise."

"Good."

Simon extracted his purse from somewhere inside his greatcoat. He gently took Becky's hand and deposited several gold coins into her palm. She and her brother both gasped.

"Oh no, m'lord, it wouldn't be right," the girl exclaimed earnestly. "Ma always said we should never take charity from no one. She said we weren't no paupers, and we had to earn our bread good and honestlike."

Sophie took hold of Simon's arm, needing to feel his warmth in the face of so much hardship and courage. She felt the sinewy muscles ripple under his coat.

"I'm sure your mother wouldn't mind if you took the money, Becky. It's a reward for returning Miss Stanton's bracelet." He closed the girl's small fist over the coins. "You keep that for you and your brother. Don't tell anyone I gave it to you."

Becky's lips quivered into a heartbreaking smile. She dropped another curtsy before reaching to take her brother's arm.

"Thank you, m'lord. Thank you, miss, for bringing Toby home. We'll never forget your kindness." She began to pull Toby toward the door of the kitchen.

"Wait!" Sophie released Simon's arm and hurried forward to stop her. "Don't go yet, Becky. You must tell Lord Trask what Toby told me about Mrs. Delacourt."

Becky drew back in a panic. "No, miss. It weren't true what Toby said. We have to go now. Pa will come looking for us any minute."

She dragged her brother to the door. The boy looked over his shoulder at Sophie, his pointy features quivering with distress.

"Miss . . ."

"No, Toby!" Becky pulled the door open, yanked her brother through it, then slammed it shut.

Sophie scrambled after them, grabbing for the door handle. As her fingers closed around the cold metal, a powerful arm wrapped itself around her waist and pulled her away.

"Are you mad, Sophie? You will bring the wrath of God down upon those children if you follow them. You heard what the boy said about their father."

She struggled to escape, but he tugged her back hard against his brawny chest.

"Simon, we have to help them," she panted. "You have no idea of the trouble they're in."

"Well, you can't help them tonight, and I bloody well refuse to stand about in this pestilent hellhole chatting about it. You can tell me in the carriage, after you explain exactly how you came to be in this part of town." He placed his hands on her shoulders and began to steer her up the laneway. "Especially after I told you not to come down here again."

She tried to wriggle out from under his grip. "If you'd had the courtesy to take me to the theater tonight, instead of avoiding me, this wouldn't have happened." Sophie knew the accusation to be unfair, but she couldn't help flinging it at him. "In fact, you've been avoiding me all day, and I think you're very rude."

"I haven't been avoiding you, and I'm not being rude," he snapped, jerking her to a halt before him. "I called at Aunt Eleanor's this evening, but you had already left for the theater."

Sophie narrowed her eyes at him, refusing to be intimidated by the way he loomed over her or by his towering rage. She had been on the receiving end of his temper more than once over the years, and she had never let it stop her before.

"If you were visiting in St. James's Square, then why are you down in this part of town now?" All at once her throat went dry as a sickening thought popped into her head.

"You weren't visiting a brothel, were you?" she squeaked.

He stared at her with a look of utter disbelief. "Of course I wasn't visiting a brothel. What kind of bird-witted question is that?"

He grabbed her elbow and began pulling her back to the carriage. "I swear, Sophie, this kind of nonsense had better stop when we're married, or else we'll both end up in Bedlam."

The pavement suddenly tilted under her feet. "What?"

Simon winced. "Oh for God's sake, don't shriek."

She dug in her heels and skidded to a halt, forcing him to stop as well.

He blew out a long-suffering breath. "Now what?"

"What do you mean we're getting married? What are you talking about?"

He glowered down at her, looking positively demonic in the faint light of the alley.

"Don't be dense, Sophie. Of course I'm going to marry you. I wouldn't have kissed you in public—or in private, for that matter—if I didn't intend to make you my wife."

Chapter Eight

Sophie peered into Simon's obsidian eyes, staggered by his stunning disclosure. His lips twitched, and he tapped a long finger under her chin.

"Close your mouth, Puck. You'll catch a fly, especially in this neighborhood."

She snapped her lips shut, and then opened them again. "Why?"

"I beg your pardon?"

"Why do you want to marry me?"

She couldn't believe she was asking that question, but the distinct possibility existed that she hadn't heard him correctly. Her ears—and her head—felt stuffed with cotton batting.

His dark gaze moved slowly over her face. In typical Simon fashion, he took his time answering.

"I care for you, Sophie—quite a lot, as you know. And you're not silly like other girls your age. You're not romantic, and you don't make a fuss about things." His lips thinned into a dangerous line. "At least not generally."

Don't make a fuss about things? Hardly the declaration of passion one would have hoped for!

She opened her mouth to protest when he gently laid two

fingers across her lips. At the buttery touch of his leather glove on her mouth, all logic fled her brain.

"Besides, it will please our families," he added, as if he'd just thought of it. "Especially yours. You're going into your fourth Season next year, Puck, and your mother and Robert are beginning to worry about you. It's time you started your own family, and it might as well be with someone who knows you and will take care of you."

Her stomach felt as hollow as a broken old bell. She may not be romantic, but this had to be the most depressing marriage proposal a girl could imagine. How could Simon think she would ever agree? And how dare he ask her to marry him while standing in a disgusting alley behind a tavern populated by thieves and whores? Only he would think he could get away with this.

Her returning awareness of their surroundings reminded her of Toby and Becky's plight. Simon's outrageous proposal would just have to wait.

"Yes, well, that's all very flattering, my lord," she said through clenched teeth. "But I don't want to talk about that now. I haven't finished telling you about the children."

Even in the dim light of the alley she saw him roll his eyes.

"Tell me in the carriage." He wrapped a hand around her wrist. "We must be gone from this place before someone sees us and I'm forced to explain why I would allow my fiancée to wander around the slums of Bath."

Sophie practically had to run to keep up with his long strides.

"As to that particular subject," she panted, "I don't think the outcome has actually been decided."

Simon stopped in his tracks. Sophie skidded to a halt, her foot sliding into some grisly piece of refuse that squished over the top of her shoe.

Another pair of shoes ruined.

Simon's dark brows drew into a straight line of thunder

across his forehead. "Sophie, what possible objection could you have?"

"You have made me an offer, clearly under duress, and I have not accepted it." She did her best to keep any trace of resentment from her voice.

Simon drew in a deep breath, obviously preparing to unleash another blistering volley of sarcasm.

"At least not yet," she amended, giving him what she hoped was a placating smile. If they had an argument over this now, she would never get him to see reason about the children.

"As far as I'm concerned, you already have. I clearly remember how enthusiastically you responded to my kiss last night. Have you forgotten?"

Her cheeks flushed with a prickling heat, and she looked down to avoid his predatory gaze.

"I thought not," he murmured. He resumed his quick stride down the laneway, pulling her along behind him.

Her heart began to race. How dare he treat her in such a high-handed and mortifying fashion? She had dreamed of this impossible moment for so many years, and now that he actually had asked her to marry him, all she really felt was the familiar urge to kick him.

"Forgive me, Sophie. Did you say something?" He sounded preoccupied.

She glanced up, noting with irritation that he wasn't even looking at her. "Why does an offer of marriage from you sound like a punishment, rather than a consummation to be devoutly desired?" This time she couldn't manage to tamp down her resentment.

Simon halted, pulling her into a gentle but unbreakable grip. The sound of voices and the occasional snatches of song drifted in from the nearby street.

Simon eased her forward until the tips of her breasts pressed against his coat, and she had to tilt her head back to look at him. His heat and strength penetrated the multiple layers of her clothing, causing her nipples to harden with that strange, delicious ache.

Something shifted in his gaze, something dark and bewitching, pinning her like a butterfly on the head of a pin. He leaned down and brushed his mouth high on her cheekbone. She sighed, mesmerized by the velvet touch, succumbing all over again to the feel of his warm mouth.

"Why, Sophia, I thought you always wanted to marry me."

His voice washed over her—hot sugar syrup sliding along her veins. But the words themselves yanked her out of the enchantment beginning to steal over her.

"Why you . . . you bastard!" She had never used a word like that before in her life, but his insufferable arrogance drove her to it.

After a short and fruitless struggle to pull from his grip, Sophie finally stomped down hard on his foot. She had to swallow a yelp of pain, as her evening slippers were no match for his hessians. She wriggled madly in his arms, but Simon refused to let go. Instead, he slid a large hand down her back and captured her bottom in a firm grasp, pushing her hips against him. She froze, stunned by the feel of his rock-hard length against her stomach.

The stream of acid she had been about to unleash died on her lips. She looked up into eyes that glittered like black ice. Simon slowly lowered his face to hers, and his mouth—that perfect mouth she had coveted for so long—covered hers in a kiss that plunged her into a silken heat.

Sophie moaned at the waves of sensation coursing through her body. His hand closed convulsively around the globe of her bottom as he lifted her up to press her belly against his shockingly large masculinity. Her legs trembled, and a prickling at the top of her thighs seemed to reach deep inside to soft, secret places.

She gasped, letting her head fall against his arm. She felt surrounded, enveloped in his steely embrace. His size and strength combined into a mesmerizing power that demanded her submission.

Simon's mouth trailed fire across her neck before coming to rest on the pulse at the base of her throat. His wet tongue caressed her skin, causing blood to leap under its hot touch. She clutched desperate fingers into the thick wool of his coat, no longer wanting escape, wanting to be swept deeper into the dark madness of his kiss.

But the madness receded a moment later when Simon drew back, easing her gently to her feet. Sophie swallowed a whimper of frustration. He stroked her cheek as if to soothe her, but even in the shadows of the alley she could see a look of masculine satisfaction cross his features.

"I thought so," he murmured, his voice a husky growl that set her skin tingling once more.

Sophie shook her head, trying to banish the wooly feeling from her brain. She had completely lost the thread of their conversation, although she knew she should still be angry with him for something.

She opened her mouth, but no words came out.

"Never mind, sweetheart." Simon's hand settled at the base of her spine, nudging her gently toward the street. "Let's get you home before anyone misses you, or there will be the devil to pay for this night's work."

Sophie allowed him to guide her along to the carriage, dimly aware that he still needed a set-down for his imperious and high-handed conduct tonight. But she seemed to have left her wits behind in the alley. And until she found them again, she decided that in this case at least, discretion really was the better part of valor.

* * *

"Lady Jane and Miss Stanton are in the drawing room, my lord. I will announce you," Yates said.

Simon draped his coat over the butler's outstretched arms and dropped his hat and gloves on the ornate side table inside the front door of his aunts' townhouse. "I'll announce myself."

His mood had only improved slightly since last night. Finding Sophie down in the stews had been the shock of his life. He didn't know what had tempted him more—the idea of shaking her until her teeth rattled for disobeying him, or shoving her skirts up and taking her right there in the carriage. Neither course of action had been remotely acceptable, so he had wedged himself into the opposite corner of the coach and done his best to ignore her on the short ride back to St. James's Square.

That hadn't been easy, since she had nattered on endlessly about her two misbegotten street urchins. He had momentarily silenced her by planting a fierce kiss on her lips. Even so, Sophie had managed to wheedle from him a promise to discuss the fate of the children first thing in the morning. But the sweet taste of her mouth had made the concession worth it, and that had surprised the hell out of him too.

He smiled as he strode down the hall to the back of the house, recalling Sophie's reaction to his kiss. To all his kisses. She melted like wax in his arms, and he had no doubt she would eagerly accept his proposal once he made a formal and proper declaration. He really couldn't blame her for refusing to give him an answer last night. After all, a slum alley was hardly the place to propose to any woman, much less a sheltered miss like Sophie.

The door to the drawing room stood ajar. The sound of Aunt Jane's old harpsichord, the tones faded but true, drifted into the hallway. Simon slowed to a halt, knowing what would come next—Sophie's shimmering soprano, picking out the melody of one of the old country ballads so beloved by his aunts.

He stopped and leaned against the doorframe to listen to the voice he had heard so often as a youth, but had almost forgotten with the passage of years. The pure, lilting sound resonated in his bones, awakening deep memories. His eyes drifted shut as he remembered the lad he had been. A lad who loved music and played the pianoforte for a funny little girl wearing spectacles, who sang with the voice of an angel. He had ceased playing the instrument a long time ago, but back then he had enjoyed the music almost as much as Sophie.

The song ended, but the delicate vibrations of Sophie's voice lingered in the air. Then Aunt Jane laughed, and Simon jolted free of the music's spell.

His dark mood rushed back. Both the lad and those simpler times had departed years ago, and he had no wish for either to return.

When he pushed the door open, he saw Sophie beside his aunt at the harpsichord, looking sweetly youthful in a gauzy yellow gown, spectacles perched on the end of her nose as she examined pieces of music. Her head jerked up at the sound of his footfall, eyes widening as they met his. She cast her gaze back to the music. One slender hand fluttered up to touch a cheek turned rosy with heat.

Aunt Jane rose from the instrument and extended her hand. "Simon, dear boy. We didn't expect you until tea."

He bowed over her hand, pressing a gentle kiss on her soft, wrinkled skin.

"Good morning, Aunt Jane. I hope I don't inconvenience you."

"Not at all. You've missed Eleanor, though. She's gone to the baths for a treatment, poor dear. Her chest is very troublesome these days."

"I'm sorry to hear that. I had hoped for a better report this morning."

"I'm sure the waters will do her a world of good. They

usually do, when she can be compelled to take them." She waved her hand vaguely toward a gilded ebony chair in front of a settee. "Please sit, my dear. I'll ring for tea."

"Thank you, but no. I won't trouble you. I've come this morning to talk with Sophie."

"Indeed?" Aunt Jane's eyes searched his face, and then flickered over Sophie's blushing countenance. A smile touched her lips. "What have you done now, Sophia? Simon looks very stern this morning."

Sophie narrowed her eyes at him in silent warning.

"I can't imagine, my lady," she replied in a carefully bland voice.

"Well, Simon, I'll see you tonight at Lady Penfield's, I'm sure. Good-bye, my dear." His aunt offered him a perfumed cheek before she rustled over to the door. "Sophia, we can leave for the Pump Room after you've had your little chat."

The door closed quietly behind her. Sophie continued to stare at the music on the harpsichord, apparently doing her best to pretend he wasn't in the room.

"You don't have to ignore me, Puck," he said. "I'm not here to reprimand you."

"Lucky me," she grumbled, jumping up from the instrument. She skirted around him and took a seat in a high-back chair set against the wall, as far away from him as she could get.

His unorthodox proposal last night had clearly failed to impress her.

"Sophie, I want to apologize for my behavior last night. My proposal to you was exceedingly clumsy, and you have every right to expect more from me. I had fully intended to call on you yesterday, but I was unavoidably detained most of the day on business. I called last night, but you'd already left for the theater."

She looked at him. "Is that *all* you're apologizing for?"

He frowned. "What else would I apologize for?"

"You weren't exactly helpful with Becky and Toby last night. Not only did you scare them, you refused to even let me tell you about their situation. You couldn't have been more arrogant or dismissive."

His temper spiked. How the hell did she find the nerve to reprimand *him* for last night's foolish escapade?

"You really don't want to know how unpleasant I can be, but if you ever go back to Avon Street, you will have the misfortune to find out."

She popped out of her chair and stalked across the room. A slender finger jabbed into his chest as she glared up at him.

"I know just how unpleasant you can be, I assure you. And callous, too! Those children need my help, and I'm going to give it to them, whether you want me to or not."

He swallowed a scathing retort, reminding himself that he had come to propose to her, not pick a fight. "I'm not being callous, just realistic. I have no doubt their life is difficult, especially since their mother died, but they do have a father and a roof over their heads. Their situation is not desperate."

She crossed her arms over her chest and stared into his face.

"Sophie, what could you possibly expect? That I would waltz into the blasted place and demand their father take better care of them? Too foolish by half, my girl, if you think that will do any good. In fact, you just might get them thrown onto the parish, and from there to the workhouse. Hardly the result you're looking for, I'm sure."

She looked blank for a moment, but then her anger drained away. She wandered over to a heavily cushioned divan, sumptuously covered in gold silk, and sighed wearily as she sank down onto the plump cushions.

Simon's throat tightened as he noted the grey smudges under her beautiful eyes. Her complexion was pale and drawn, and she looked as if she hadn't slept well in days. Why hadn't he noticed that before?

"Sophie . . ."

When she shook her head at him, he went to join her on the divan. He tipped a finger under her chin and made her look into his eyes.

"Very well, Puck. Tell me what troubles you so about these children."

She did, her voice stumbling over words he loathed hearing on her innocent lips. The story sickened him, and he knew what she told him could very well be true. It was certainly a common practice in London brothels to offer virgins—or girls claiming to be virgins—to the highest bidder.

"But the girl denied it, did she not?"

"Yes, but she's trying to protect her brother from their father's wrath. Who knows what he would do to them if they tried to escape."

"Perhaps the boy misunderstood what he heard. He's young." At least Simon hoped so, both for the girl's sake and for Sophie's. Either way, there was little he could do to rectify the situation. No one would care about yet another girl sold into prostitution.

"I don't think Toby misunderstood anything." Her voice held a familiar stubborn note.

"Even if this tale is true—which it may very well be," he added as she took an angry breath, "there is little we can do about it. The father would simply deny it, and what magistrate would not accept his word? You have done what you can, Puck, and you must let it go. The girl does not wish for your help."

Her bow-shaped mouth set into a mutinous line.

"You are not to go back down there. I mean it." Simon allowed the implied threat to color his voice.

He couldn't believe it when she rolled her eyes at him.

"Sophie," he growled.

"That reminds me," she interjected. "How did you happen to find me last night? What exactly were you doing in that part of town?"

Damn. He had been hoping she'd forget that question.

"After I called here last night, I ran into Nigel Dash in Milsom Street. I joined him for a few hands of cards at a private club in St. James's Parade." Sophie didn't need to know he'd been too restless and irritated—strangely so, in his opinion—to sit at the gaming table for more than a half hour.

She wrinkled her dainty nose at him. "A hell, you mean."

He sighed. "No, I mean a club. And I'll thank you to keep such damned impertinent comments to yourself."

"Simon! Such language."

She squared her shoulders in what he knew to be mock outrage. He couldn't help giving the minx a reluctant grin, and a sweet dimple flashed back at him.

"But you still haven't answered my question," she persisted. "How did you get to Avon Street from St. James's Parade?"

He hesitated, but realized he might as well tell her the truth. She would pester him till he did, and he made it a point never to lie to her. Well, almost never.

"I wanted to walk by the workhouse. It . . . disturbed me that you had been there without me to support you." He still couldn't bear the thought of his little elf in that pesthole without him there to protect her. He knew his explanation sounded absurd, but some inner compulsion had driven him to Avon Street to see the place for himself.

"Oh," she breathed. Her eyes grew round and misty as they searched his face.

"Imagine my surprise, then, when I saw Aunt Eleanor's carriage parked in front of a public house on the worst street in Bath. James and John were most disconcerted to be found in such a compromising situation, I assure you," he added.

She had the grace to look guilty. "You won't say anything to Lady Eleanor, will you? I really didn't give them a choice."

"No, I won't say anything, and yes, I can believe you gave them no choice." He reached over and took her hands in his. "Sophie, there is something else we must settle between us today, as you well know."

She blushed and cast her gaze down at their conjoined hands.

"I know I made a hash of it last night, but I assure you that my intentions are genuine. Sophia, it would be my greatest honor if you would allow me to care for you, and to call you my wife."

She studied him with round, solemn eyes. "Is that all you want to do? Take care of me?"

He laced his fingers between hers, not quite sure of her mood.

"Well, someone has to keep you out of trouble, Puck."

The look of hurt that flashed across her features surprised him. Simon felt another stab of frustration. For some reason today, every word out of his mouth seemed to go sideways.

"Sweetheart, I'm joking. I care for you a great deal, and I believe we are well suited to each other."

"I know," she responded softly. "I 'don't make a fuss.'"

"You don't make a fuss about silly things, but there's more to it than that." The hurt look on her face had eased, but he still didn't like the wariness in her eyes. "We know each other—we understand each other, Sophie. The St. James family and the Stanton family have been attached by the bonds of friendship for a very long time, going back five generations, at least. Our families would be very pleased by this union, and you would relieve your mother and Robert of a great deal of worry."

"That's not a good enough reason for us to get married," she said, her voice catching in her throat.

He thought it was, as were the other reasons he wished to marry her. But comparing her worth to a seam of coal or a wool mill was hardly an effective way to support his case, and he couldn't seem to find the right words to express how he felt about her. Perhaps because he was so unsure of that, himself.

He moved closer, sliding one arm along the back of the divan, and behind her shoulders. He leaned down and brushed his mouth across her plush lips. Those lips trembled beneath his, and his heart responded with an unfamiliar stab of tenderness.

"No," he said, drawing back so he could study her face, "perhaps not. But surely you realize after all these years how much I care for you. You are my family, my responsibility, and have been for a long time."

He repressed a grimace as the memory of Sophie's tumble into the lake flashed through his mind. She needed him, for so many things. "And I know you've been lonely since Robert and Annabel married. You need never be alone again."

When she jumped in her seat, he knew he had hit the mark full on. How could she think he wouldn't notice how much she missed her brother? And what would it take to get her to say yes? His elf was proving unexpectedly resistant.

"I swear on my life I will always cherish and honor you, and honor our marriage. You will never want for anything again, and I promise that I will always protect you." He clasped her cold hands in a firm grip, silently willing her to say yes.

She raised her solemn eyes to his, and for an insane moment Simon imagined she gazed straight into his soul. He resisted a sudden impulse to stand and move away from her.

"All right." Her voice was uncharacteristically soft and uncertain.

Simon found himself wanting to hold his breath. "Do you mean yes?"

She sighed. "Yes, I'll marry you."

Triumph surged through him, accompanied by a substantial measure of relief. He told himself that it simply resulted from the understandable desire to have the issue settled to his satisfaction. "Thank you, sweetheart. You won't regret it, I promise."

Her mouth lifted in a wry smile. "I'll hold you to that."

"Be sure of it. I'll talk to Robert and my aunts, write to your mother and grandfather, and see to the announcements. I'd like to put it in the *Bath Chronicle*." He dropped her hands, extracted his pocketbook, and made a notation to direct Soames to write to the paper. A choking noise interrupted him.

Sophie stared at his face, her lips pursed in a dismayed oval. His jaw clenched. He should have known it wouldn't be this easy.

"Now what?"

"Do we have to tell anybody yet? This is all so sudden and unexpected. I really would like a few days to grow used to the idea before I have to talk to anyone about it."

"Sophie—"

"It's just that I would like to keep it between us for a time." She gently smoothed down the front of his waistcoat. "Wouldn't that be nice? Just the two of us, and nobody else to share it with? You know how people will gossip once they find out."

She stretched up and pressed a small kiss on his chin. He grimaced, knowing full well he was being managed.

"Fine. We'll keep it to ourselves for now. But I'll decide when to talk to Robert and my aunts."

"Of course. Whatever you say." Her lips curved into a tiny, satisfied smile, as she cautiously allowed herself to relax into the circle of his arms.

Simon had to repress a laugh as she snuggled against him. Of course she would try to manipulate him. After all, it was in her nature to do so, and he was happy to indulge her if he could. A few days to themselves wouldn't make a difference—in fact, he rather relished the idea—and he could still tell Russell about their betrothal.

Besides, Sophie would learn soon enough that when it came to manipulation, he had mastered the game long ago.

Chapter Nine

What in heaven's name had she done?

Sophie gazed at her reflection in the pier glass of her dressing table. She didn't look like Bath's latest version of the village idiot, but her actions suggested otherwise. Why had she agreed so readily to Simon's marriage proposal this morning? Every instinct within her had whispered—nay, shrieked—out a warning. He had been too determined, too . . . purposeful. Simon would never marry her simply because of some old-fashioned, ridiculous sense of duty to their families. Would he?

No. She knew Simon. Something else was going on, but whatever it was still eluded her and she needed time to puzzle it out—away from him. Every time he touched her, or looked at her with that hot gleam in his eyes, she felt as if she would faint—just like some idiotic heroine in one of Mrs. Radcliffe's dreary novels. And, blast the man, he knew it, and had no compunctions about using her feelings to manipulate her, just as he had today.

She winced as she recalled her own naiveté. Of course she should have expected his proposal the minute he had taken her in his arms and kissed her. Everyone knew Simon would rather shoot himself than create a scandal, and toying with the affections of an unmarried girl was scandalous behavior indeed—even more so under his exacting code of conduct.

"There, miss, you look pretty as a picture. I'm sure all the fine gentlemen at Lady Penfield's party will be falling all over themselves to dance with you," said Sally, Lady Jane's maid. The young woman smiled with satisfaction as she inserted the last pin into Sophie's new coiffure.

"Thank you, Sally." Sophie inspected her image. The maid had arranged her thick mass of auburn curls into an artfully disheveled twist, with strands of tiny crystal beads woven throughout to catch the light. A few tendrils drifted in silky disarray around her neck and shoulders. "You've done a splendid job."

"You have lovely hair, Miss Stanton, if I do say so myself. If only you would remove your spectacles. Not that you don't look almost perfect, even with them on," Sally added hastily.

Sophie wrinkled her nose. The last thing she needed was to spend another night stumbling around a ballroom or unintentionally snubbing her friends. In any event, Simon didn't seem to care whether she wore her spectacles or not, so she might as well keep them on.

She rose from the dressing table, making another check of her new cambric gown in the cheval glass set against her bedroom wall. The delicate fabric, in a pale shade of buttercup yellow, swirled around her slight figure. An emerald-colored sash wrapped softly beneath her breasts and fell in fluttering ribbons to the hem of her skirts. The dress, as her modiste had promised, was the height of fashion, and gave her an elegance she so often lacked. Her grandmother's diamond earrings also added a hint of sophistication, something she obviously needed now that she might become a countess any day.

Her stomach lurched at the thought. She took a steadying

breath, then turned to collect her pale yellow gloves and velvet cloak from Sally. She might look almost perfect, but she felt tired as a pair of old boots and dreaded another evening of loud conversation in overheated rooms. Even worse, she would have to face Simon and pretend that nothing earth shattering had just happened between them. How she hoped to accomplish that miracle, Sophie had not the slightest idea.

She hurried down the stairs to join Lady Jane. Lady Eleanor hated evening parties, and had already retired to her bed-chamber.

"Besides," Lady Eleanor had bellowed at dinner, "Eugenia Penfield is the greatest bore in Bath, and that's saying some-thing. I can't stand all that caterwauling from the violins at her balls. No, thank you. I shall have a cozy evening at home and take myself off to an early bed."

Lady Jane, comfortably settled in the carriage, smiled as Sophie climbed in. "I know it's foolish to take the coach since we are only going to the Crescent. But it's so chilly in the evenings that I can't abide the thought of a chair." She arched her brows as she ran a discerning eye over Sophie. "My good-ness, you look especially lovely this evening, my dear. You're wearing your grandmother's diamonds. This must be a more special evening than I anticipated."

"Oh, you . . . you are too kind, my lady." Sophie hoped the shadows in the coach hid the blush creeping up her neck. Did Lady Jane already know Simon had made an offer? If he had broken his promise to keep silent, she would strangle him before the evening was out.

After only a few minutes, the vehicle rumbled to a stop in front of Lady Penfield's majestic townhouse in the Crescent. James handed Lady Jane and then Sophie onto the pavement, the wind from the heights snatching at their hoods and whip-ping their cloaks around their bodies. They hurried up the short walk of the house into the small but elegant entrance hall. Lady Penfield and her husband stood at the top of a polished oak staircase, waiting to greet their guests.

"Lady Jane, Miss Stanton, how delightful! The weather is so dreadful tonight. I vow the wind is enough to send me into a decline. I told my dear Penfield that my nerves are continually shredded by the howling tempests up here on the Crescent." Lady Penfield, a tiny woman wearing an enormous red silk turban, tittered merrily, apparently delighted by the state of her nerves. "It will likely be the death of me, but the aggravating man refuses to listen. He would insist that we take a house up here instead of down in Laura Place. For the life of me I can't imagine why."

"If I may remind you, my dear," huffed the portly and obviously corseted Earl of Penfield, "you were the one who insisted we rent in the Upper Town. Over my objections, I might add."

"Oh, nonsense. I said no such thing," her ladyship giggled. "Do go in, my dears. The music will be starting any moment. Miss Stanton, you look lovely tonight, although why you will insist on wearing your spectacles is something I cannot imagine. Perhaps I should talk to your mother about it the next time I see her. You are going into your fourth Season, you know. We don't want you moldering away on the shelf now, do we?"

"Thank you, your ladyship." Sophie's teeth already ached from clenching her jaw, and the evening had barely started.

"You mustn't mind her," whispered Lady Jane. "She has no children of her own, and so must fuss over everyone else's."

Her godmother swept her into the ballroom, sparing the need for more conversation with their hostess. Perhaps if she were careful, Sophie could avoid Lady Penfield for the rest of the evening. If only she could avoid everyone else at the same time.

Mr. Puddleford emerged from behind a screen of potted plants where he had obviously been lying in wait. "Miss

Stanton, I've been wondering when you would grace us with your presence. I have been most eager to procure your hand for the first dance."

"Oh, Mr. Puddleford." Sophie dredged up a weak smile. She glanced about the spacious room as the violins scraped out the first notes of "Lady of Pleasure." Where was Simon when she needed him?

Lady Jane waved her away. "Go ahead. I see Mrs. Hughes across the room. I haven't spoken to her in an age."

Sophie resigned herself to the inevitable. Placing her hand in Mr. Puddleford's, she allowed him to lead her into the set.

He beamed as they made their way through the intricate figures of the dance, clearly delighted to be in her company. She sighed when he squeezed her hand as they moved down the line. Poor Mr. Puddleford was such a nice man. Not ill-looking, and he worshipped the ground she walked on in his own absent-minded way. Why couldn't she have fallen in love with him instead of Simon?

As they made the turn at the bottom of the room, Sophie looked at her partner's round, good-natured face and knew she could never go through life with a name like Mrs. Puddleford.

She was a shallow creature indeed.

After what seemed an age, the set came to an end. As Mr. Puddleford bowed over her hand, she furtively scanned the room, hoping to see either Simon or her brother.

"Miss Stanton, perhaps I could persuade you to step out onto the terrace with me. I'm sure you must be hot after your delightfully graceful exertions on the dance floor. There is something most particular—"

"Look! My brother and his wife. Come, Mr. Puddleford. I'm sure Annabel will have some pressing questions about her orchids." Ignoring his spluttering objections, she stuck her arm in the crook of his elbow and pulled him across the dance floor.

"Hallo, sis. Looking in prime twig tonight." Robert grinned at her before turning his attention to her escort. "Puddleford. Can't seem to go anywhere without running into you these days. Extraordinary."

Robert imperiously inspected the older man through his quizzing glass, doing his best imitation of a protective older brother. Sophie bit her lower lip to keep from laughing. Her brother must be taking lessons from Simon in the art of aristocratic bad manners.

Mr. Puddleford glanced uneasily from Sophie to Robert, shuffling his feet as if his dancing shoes had just shrunk a size.

"Mr. Puddleford. How nice to see you again." Annabel shot a warning glance at Robert while extending her hand to the widower.

"The pleasure is mine, dear lady." Mr. Puddleford bowed solemnly over her hand.

"The next set is forming, and I so long to dance. Robert refuses—it is so aggravating—and I see all the other men are engaged. Won't you take pity on me?" When Annabel turned on her full battery of charm, no man—not even one bent on proposing marriage to another woman—could refuse her.

"Delighted, of course." He gallantly offered Annabel his arm. With a lingering glance over his shoulder at Sophie, Mr. Puddleford allowed himself to be pulled into the set.

"Ain't she magnificent, Soph?" The smile returned to Robert's face as he followed his wife's progress down the room. "She certainly pulled your bacon out of the fire, old girl."

Sophie finally let her laughter bubble out. "You are fortunate, Robert. I truly don't think you deserve her."

"I don't."

At the earnest, almost reverent tone of his voice, Sophie's amusement faded. Simon would never feel that way about her.

Almost as if her thoughts had conjured him up, Simon

strolled through the double doors of the ballroom. Clinging gracefully to his arm, attired in a shimmering, cream-colored silk dress that clung—just barely—to her ample bosom, was Lady Randolph. Sophie blinked in disbelief. Only Lady Randolph would have the nerve to wear a color normally reserved for debutantes, and use it so well to magnify her astonishing sensuality.

Heads turned all over the room as Simon escorted the countess through the crowd. Many of the men wore expressions of avid appreciation and curiosity, while more than one matron's countenance froze into lines of open disapproval. The unmarried ladies stared greedily at Simon, most of them not bothering to mask their envious resentment of the woman on his arm.

Sophie struggled to keep her fists from clenching into her skirts. Her chest grew tight with the effort to contain the hatred for Lady Randolph that pulsed through every vein in her body. She could hardly breathe, and for one moment she wondered if she might hate Simon too.

"That woman is a menace," muttered Robert as he glared at the countess. "I swear I'll never speak to Simon again if he marries her. I really thought he'd given her up."

"But I thought . . ." Sophie broke off when her voice croaked.

Her brother cast her a guilty look, clearly having forgotten her presence beside him.

"Nothing, Soph. Spoke out of turn," he said hastily. "Don't listen to me."

She gripped his arm, wrinkling the rich burgundy fabric of his sleeve between her fingers.

"Tell me." She stared Robert right in the face. He flushed the color of old brick.

"Annabel would have my hide if I discussed such a thing with you."

"Robert, I've been out much longer than Annabel," she

said through clenched teeth. "I need to know. Are Simon and Lady Randolph . . . are they still having an affair? All the gossips said it was over months ago."

Her brother eyed her with a doubtful expression, then looked at Simon and Lady Randolph as they chatted with Lord Penfield. The countess stood on tiptoe to murmur something in Simon's ear. He tilted his head to listen, a brief smile touching his lips.

"Doesn't look like it's over to me," Robert said gloomily.

Sophie closed her eyes as the floor pitched beneath her feet. She took several deep breaths, wondering if she was the only person in the room whose ears were suddenly filled with a loud buzz.

"Sophie!" Her brother's sharp voice recalled her to her surroundings. "What's wrong? I've never seen you look like this." His usual cheerful drawl was laced with worry.

She forced herself to speak past the lump in her throat. "Robert, why do you dislike Lady Randolph so much?"

He grimaced. "She uses people, without a care how it affects them. I can't explain it, but I swear when she talks to me I can feel the ice dripping down my back. She's like that crazy Italian woman from that dusty old history you made me read. You know which one I'm talking about."

"Lucrezia Borgia?" Sophie blinked, astonished that her sweet-natured brother would compare Lady Randolph to such a monstrous woman. "Surely you can't be serious?"

"That's the one. You don't know, Soph, and I can't tell you some of the things I've heard. Not idle gossip, either, but from someone . . ." He cut himself off, then gave her a sharp look. "Just take my word for it. Stay away from her. And if Simon knows what's good for him, he'll stay away from her too."

* * *

"Oh, Mr. Dash! You do say the most amusing things." Sophie swiped another glass of champagne from a passing waiter.

"Don't I just." Nigel Dash eyed the glass in her hand. "Miss Stanton, don't mean to throw water on your head, but don't you think you've had enough champagne?"

"Absolutely not." Sophie took a healthy gulp from the delicate crystal goblet. The bubbles didn't tickle her nose nearly as much as they did two glasses ago. In fact, she was quite beginning to like champagne.

Almost as much as she liked Nigel Dash. She'd always been fond of him, but until just an hour ago she'd never noticed how attractive he could be. When she peered at him over the top of her spectacles, he really looked quite handsome. Perhaps if she drank another glass of champagne he might become almost as handsome as Simon.

Sophie gazed around the crowded ballroom, humming a little tune under her breath. For a night that had begun so poorly it had turned out rather well, especially after she decided to ignore Simon. She had danced every dance, and flirted with so many men she couldn't even remember some of their names. Even better, her behavior had obviously infuriated Simon, although she didn't really give a fig about that. Her supposed fiancé stood across the opposite side of the dance floor, scowling at her and everyone else, and generally looking as bad-tempered as a gouty old spinster.

As she took another sip of Lord Penfield's excellent champagne, Sophie contemplated sticking her tongue out at His Royal Imperiousness, the starched-up Earl of Trask. Now *that* would give the old biddies something to gossip about. Besides Lady Randolph's plunging décolletage, that is.

She had almost convinced herself to do it when she heard the first bars of the waltz. Spinning on her heel—which made her head swim—she grabbed Nigel's sleeve.

"The orchestra is playing a waltz. Isn't that marvelous? Mr. Dash, please ask me to dance."

"Charmed, I'm sure, Miss Stanton." Nigel plucked the champagne goblet from her hand. "But I've a feeling someone else has plans for you at the moment."

She frowned at him. How dare he take her champagne from her?

"What plans? Lady Jane went home an hour ago. Robert and Annabel will be taking me to St. James's Square in their carriage." She peered around the room, looking for her brother and his wife. Not surprisingly, Robert had taken Annabel onto the dance floor.

She sighed. He never missed an opportunity to waltz with Annabel, no matter how unfashionable it was to dance with one's wife.

"What did you do with my champagne?" she groused.

"I think you've had quite enough to drink tonight, Sophie." Simon's voice fell with a menacing growl on her ears.

She suppressed a shiver and spun around to face him.

Must remember not to turn so quickly.

"Simon." She fixed a smile on her face, staggering against him. "How delightful. Are you done frightening everyone on the other side of the room? Mr. Dash, would you be so kind as to give me back my goblet? I'm feeling rather flushed from the heat."

Simon glowered at Nigel, who bowed and slipped away through the crowd. Taking her champagne with him.

"Coward," she muttered.

Simon must have caught her remark, for his lips pulled back over his teeth, rather like the feral dog she saw in the street just the other day.

"Oh, good Lord," she huffed, "I suppose you're going to

deliver me another lecture. You can be such a bore sometimes, Simon."

He grasped her elbow and began to maneuver her through the room toward the door. "Get ready to be bored, then. But not here. I'm taking you home."

"What if I don't want to go home?" As his big hand tightened around her arm, a reckless exuberance raced through her body.

"You'll go home if I have to toss you over my shoulder and carry you." His face told her the threat was not an idle one.

"Very well," she grumbled, craning her neck to look at a passing waiter who carried a large tray of champagne goblets. "But I must say good night to Robert and Annabel. They were supposed to take me home."

"I've already spoken to your brother."

"You've thought of everything, haven't you?" she said in a snippy voice. How thrilling that she could sound as nasty as Lady Randolph so often did.

Oh, good Lord. Speak of the devil.

Sophie suddenly caught sight of the countess talking to Mr. Puddleford, of all people. Lady Randolph gently waved an enormous white fan in front of her equally enormous white bosom. Mr. Puddleford's wide eyes seemed riveted by the spectacle of so much exposed flesh. Perhaps Sophie should make a detour from Simon's absurd rush to the door and warn the naïve widower of the terrible danger he faced.

Just then Lady Randolph looked directly at her and smiled, a smile so contemptuous that Sophie's fingers itched to slap her. Sophie glanced up at Simon. He had obviously seen that look as well, for a dark flush suddenly glazed his cheekbones.

She looked back at Lady Randolph as the viperous witch slid her hand over Mr. Puddleford's arm, causing the poor man to visibly gulp. Something must be done, and done immediately.

Thrusting her bosom up as high as she could, Sophie caught Mr. Puddleford's eye and winked. The widower gasped and dropped his wine goblet, sending it crashing to the floor. Sophie heard Simon literally grind his teeth. She gave his arm a little squeeze and smiled to herself as he unceremoniously dragged her from the ballroom.

Chapter Ten

It took only a few minutes, thank goodness, for the hackney to carry them to St. James's Square. Simon looked ready to throttle her. Not that Sophie cared about that, although it was a tad uncomfortable wedged up against his unyielding body while he was in such a nasty temper. Anger radiated from him, filling the space of the coach with the crackling energy of an approaching storm. It was a miracle, really, that he didn't set her garments on fire with his fiery glare.

He took her arm in a firm grip as he handed her down from the coach. She should probably be nervous, but the thundering scowl stamped on his features only made her want to giggle. Just like she had giggled when he had hauled her from Lady Penfield's ballroom under the scandalized gazes of half of Bath.

"I still think it very rude that we didn't say good-bye to Lord Penfield," she said. Her words sounded oddly slurred, as if her mouth couldn't keep up with her brain. "He looked quite taken aback when we rushed by him without a single word. I so wanted to thank him for serving such delicious champagne." She sighed as she thought of all those lovely goblets of sparkling nectar being consumed without her.

"Your drinking days are over," Simon growled as he towed her up the steps of the townhouse.

"How dare you—" Sophie broke off her tirade when the door swung open and Yates stood back to admit them.

"Good evening, my lord, Miss Stanton. I hope you enjoyed the ball at Lady Penfield's."

"We certainly did." Sophie smiled at the dignified older man. How odd she had never noticed before that Yates had quite a lot of hair growing out of his ears. "The ball was splendid, it truly was. Until his lordship," she directed a scowl at Simon, "decided we had to leave. Quite before anyone else, I might add."

Yates cast a startled glance at Simon's thunderous countenance. His eyes popped wide for an instant before his usual mask of schooled indifference slipped back into place.

"I'm glad to hear it, miss. Would you like some tea in the drawing room? Lady Jane has already gone to bed, but I can have a tray brought up immediately."

By this time Simon had shrugged out of his greatcoat and pulled Sophie's cloak from her shoulders. He tossed the garments to the butler.

"No tea, Yates. That will be all." He grabbed her hand. "See to it that we are not disturbed." He herded Sophie up the stairs to the gold drawing room. She twisted to see Yates staring after them, his mouth hanging open in astonishment.

She repressed another giggle. Not that she had much breath left over to laugh with. Simon had been rushing her about ever since he ordered her home from Lady Penfield's. It was beginning to make her head spin in the strangest way.

After pulling her into the drawing room, Simon closed the door with carefully restrained force.

"What are you snickering about now?" he demanded. His handsome features were set in lines as grim as she had ever seen. She stared at him as he deftly twisted the key in the door.

"Why are you locking the door, Simon?"

"I don't want to be disturbed." His face still looked stern, but the gleam in his hawklike gaze as it focused on her sent ripples of sensation dancing across her skin.

"Have you ever noticed Yates has hair in his ears?" Not that she actually wanted to discuss the butler's ears, but she needed something to distract herself from those predatory eyes.

Simon muttered a few words she didn't catch. No doubt one of his typically unflattering comments about her.

Turning her back on him, Sophie began to wind her way in slow circles around the old-fashioned pieces of furniture scattered about the room. Light from the lamp set on a pedestal table barely penetrated the shadows. As she drifted by Lady Jane's harp standing next to the pianoforte, she trailed one hand across its strings. Ghostly echoes of long-ago music drifted through the air.

Simon muttered again and walked over to the fireplace, crouched down, and set a spark to the logs that had been laid in the grate for the morning. He straightened and then leaned his arm along the gilt-edged mantelpiece. A brooding expression marked the fierce angles of his utterly masculine face as he followed her progress around the room.

Sophie decided to ignore him. She still felt captured by that exuberant recklessness, and dancing around the room kept her from flying apart into a thousand shimmering pieces.

"Just how drunk are you, by the way?" Simon drawled in a polite voice. "I only ask because I want to know if it's worth attempting a coherent discussion with you."

Sophie spun on her heel and glared at him. "I'm not drunk at all, you insufferable beast. For once I decided to have some fun, and not sit in a corner and wait for you or any other man to notice me. Not that you were likely to pay any attention to me in the first place, what with Lady Randolph draped all over you like a . . . like a paphian!"

She winced. Yelling made her temples throb.

"Sophie, what the hell is the matter with you tonight? I ask you to marry me, and the next thing I know you're inhaling champagne and flirting with every rake in Bath. No doubt the scandalmongers will be dining out on your antics for the next two weeks."

"I'm sure I don't care what a lot of vulgar mushrooms say about me," retorted Sophie. "And you shouldn't care either."

"I care a great deal about the conduct of the next Countess of Trask, and how that conduct reflects upon me." His eyebrows arched over his patrician nose. He resembled nothing so much as a statue of a Roman senator, if a statue could ever look to be in a towering rage.

"Well, perhaps I don't want to be the Countess of Trask. Perhaps I don't want to marry you after all." The words fell from her lips before she could stop them.

Silence descended between them, one so charged with menace that Sophie couldn't suppress a shiver. Simon stepped toward her.

"That decision has been made, Sophia."

His voice was soft, but the hint of steel clashing on rock made the breath catch in her throat. How dare he try to intimidate her?

"I can still change my mind."

He took another step forward. "You will not cry off, Sophie. I forbid it."

Simon's brawny physique loomed large in the shadows cast by the fire, his hooded eyes barely concealing the ice in his midnight gaze. But ice could burn flesh and spirit almost as much as flame.

All that restrained menace sent tingling sensations racing down her spine—the same kind of shivers that happened whenever Simon kissed her. She sucked in a breath, suddenly craving the feel of his mouth on her lips and his hands on her body.

She was about to ask Simon to kiss her when he planted his hands on his lean hips, and shook his head in disgust. "I should have known better than to let you talk me into keeping our engagement a secret. If you think you can go about acting like a foolish chit you must be out of your mind."

The delicious feeling in the pit of her stomach evaporated. "If you can flirt with Lady Randolph after you've asked me to marry you, then I can flirt with whomever I want." She flounced back across the room and threw herself onto the settee.

"What the deuce are you talking about? I was not flirting with Bathsheba, I mean, with Lady Randolph." Tugging impatiently at his cravat, he jerked it from his neck as if it were strangling him. He followed her to the settee, stopping at its foot to tower over her.

Sophie lay back against the cushions, dangling her foot over the edge, swinging it back and forth.

"You were. I saw you. She was draped all over you like—"

"I know. A paphian. Where you pick up such language is beyond me. I shall have to take a good look at your reading material—"

She sat bolt upright and glared at him. He glared right back.

"—and your friends, when we're married. Once more, I was not flirting with Lady Randolph. Bathsheba is merely an old friend. We've known each other for years, and I have always enjoyed her company. She is one of the leaders of the ton, and you know it. I fail to see why you dislike her so much."

"And have you always been 'just friends'?" Sophie threw her head back to gaze up into his face. She could feel her hair starting to come loose from its knot, the tendrils escaping down around her shoulders. "And are you still 'just friends'? You looked quite cozy to me, and to everyone else at Lady Penfield's, I dare say."

His lips compressed into a hard line. "Whatever my history may have been with Lady Randolph—which is none of your business, by the way—there is nothing between us now. I give you my word."

She gave a snort, recalling all too vividly the triumphant smile Lady Randolph had sent her way—and the embarrassed flush that had stained Simon's cheeks. She leaned back against the plump cushions and studied his grim expression.

"You're such a hypocrite, Simon. You're as dictatorial and snobbish as your grandfather, who, I swear, was the most insufferable man to ever set foot in the House of Lords. No one could ever live up to his standards, especially after your cousin Sebastian died. He made your life a misery; do you remember?"

Simon turned as still as a marble statue. Except for his eyes. They blazed with a fury that made her wonder if she *had* lost her mind to provoke him so thoroughly.

"And just like your grandfather," she plunged on, driven by a terrible mix of emotions she couldn't begin to explain, "you do whatever you want, whenever you want. And, apparently, your ridiculously correct code of conduct doesn't pre . . . pre . . ." For some reason her tongue felt thick and clumsy. ". . . preclude a flirtation with your former mistress, despite our engagement!"

Those imperious eyebrows of his ticked up another notch. The anger began to fade from his countenance, replaced by a familiar look of irritation.

"May I remind you," Simon intoned in a patronizing voice, "that you were the one who wanted to keep our engagement a secret? What the devil do you want? Bathsheba Randolph arrived at Lady Penfield's at the same time as I did. I gave her my arm to escort her into the room. What would you have me do? Be rude to her?"

"Yes." Sophie lurched to her feet. Simon grabbed her by the elbows to steady her. "I would like you to be very rude to her."

"Well, I won't. And stop acting like a silly girl," he exclaimed, giving her a slight shake.

He used to shake her like that when she had misbehaved as a child. Really, he couldn't possibly be more arrogant.

"You know what I think?" she retorted. "I think you should marry Bathsheba." She heard the reckless anger in her voice. Felt it thrumming under her skin.

Simon's dark brows practically shot up into his hairline.

"You suit each other so well, after all. You're both selfish and arrogant, and think only of yourselves. Yes, that's the best solution for everyone. You marry Lady Randolph, and I'll do exactly what I want. And that doesn't involve you telling me how to live my life." She flung that last bit at him, but her heart hammered so violently she thought it would burst from her chest.

His big hands circled her arms, strong fingers flexing into the shivering flesh below her puffed sleeves. The rest of him remained motionless, except for one muscle that pulsed in a jaw carved from granite.

As she stared into eyes as black and hot as pitch, she had to force down a pathetic squeak that threatened to escape from her throat. What had she done? Simon always kept an iron grip on his temper, but had she finally pushed him too far?

They stared at each other for what seemed an eternity. She couldn't move a muscle, couldn't even bat an eyelash. All she could do was gaze helplessly into features that looked, at this moment, as if they belonged to a demon sent to drag her to the depths of hell.

Then his lips parted, and a soft breath whispered across her cheeks.

"You don't mean that, do you?"

She couldn't move, mesmerized by the heat in his eyes, a heat that glowed not only with anger, but with another flame she was beginning to recognize. His hands tightened around her arms, and he lifted her up on her toes. His warm mouth brushed her ear. Every part of her body began to tremble.

"Answer me, love. Do you really want me to marry Bathsheba?" His voice was soft and compelling.

"N . . . no." She cringed at the breathless quaver in her voice. But the idea of Simon in Lady Randolph's arms . . . it would kill her.

A laugh rumbled in his chest. She felt the vibrations deep within her own body.

"Good. I assure you I have no desire to marry anyone but you." Slowly, his mouth descended to hers, and Sophie gave herself up to the velvet madness, opening to him with a desperation she had never felt before.

He murmured soft, indistinguishable words against her lips as he eased her back down on her feet. Every inch of him burned against her, and the rigid length of his masculinity nudged her belly. At the feel of *that*, of him pressed into her, her legs began to shake with an exquisite weakness. She wrapped her arms around his neck and pressed back, loving the feel of her smaller limbs enclosed in his powerful embrace.

Simon ran his tongue between the edges of her lips, silently urging her to open for him. She sighed, and welcomed the hot champagne taste of him as he plundered her mouth. His tongue stroked deep inside, then retreated to lick her lips before sliding back in once more. She whimpered, her head falling back under his sensual onslaught.

The tiny sound that escaped her seemed to gentle his touch. One hand slid up her back, forming a sheltering cradle for her body. He pulled her closer, and her nipples contracted into buds as they pressed into the brocade of his waistcoat. The thin layers of her gown and her chemise were as nothing against the firm contours of his broad chest. She felt his tension, the flex of his muscles, the rise and fall of his breath.

He kissed her, his mouth consuming her with a fierce passion, and Sophie's own breathing turned into a stuttering gasp. She trembled as unfamiliar, delicious sensations compelled her to dig her fingers into his shoulders. Simon deepened the kiss, molding her to his will. She clutched at him, tasting the residue of his anger, feeling it in the iron of his hands. But his fury had transformed into something else, into a searing masculine possession. Her instincts screamed at her to surrender, to melt into his greedy embrace. Swept under by a strong, sweet current of longing, Sophie gave in to his demand, even though she knew his convulsive grip would leave more than one mark on her softer flesh.

For a moment more his grasp on her became almost painful, but then he pulled his mouth away and eased his embrace.

"Simon!" Even to her own ears, her protest sounded petulant.

"My God." His mouth looked tight, as if he was in pain. "What are you doing to me?"

"Kissing you?" she ventured, not sure what she had done wrong. It had all felt so wonderful, and she was sure he thought so too. She tried to read his expression, wondering if she had misunderstood what he wanted.

He set her at arm's length, although his hands rested on her shoulders.

"Did I do something wrong?" Sophie forced herself not to squirm under his now wary gaze. She was a woman grown, after all, and he was her fiancé—at least for the moment. But his watchful silence was beginning to annoy her.

"Simon, if you're not going to kiss me, then tell me what's bothering you. If I'm not doing it right I'd like to know."

His laugh sounded guttural. "Believe me, you're doing it exactly right. I desire you in every way a man desires a woman, but I cannot take advantage of you like this. It would be outside the bounds of all propriety."

"But I want you to take advantage of me, really I do." She blinked as the words escaped her mouth, appalled she was begging him to make love to her. But, after all, he had started it.

A grim smile touched the corners of his mouth. "You should be careful what you ask for. You just might get it."

"And you shouldn't start things you don't intend to finish, Simon. It's really quite rude."

His smile grew into something genuine. "I thought you wanted me to be rude."

"Not to me." The delicious melting feeling between her legs had started to fade. She wriggled closer, inadvertently pressing her hips against the bulge in his trousers. That caused an interesting change to the lines of his countenance.

"Kiss me again, Simon," she coaxed. "I do so love it when you kiss me."

"Later." His voice was so rough the melting feeling in her legs came rushing back. "We need to discuss what's happening between us, and what it will mean to you."

"I know exactly what's happening. You're making love to me."

He surprised her with a rough bark of laughter. "Not yet, but I will be if we keep this up."

She slid her arms around his neck, and stretched up on her tippy-toes to plant a kiss against the faint bristle of his chin. "Well, please get on with it and stop wasting time."

He paused for several long moments, staring at her through narrowed eyes. His handsome face grave, it seemed as if he struggled with some weighty decision.

"Are you sure, Sophie? Once we do this, you will be mine, irrevocably. I'll never let you go."

"Oh, yes, Simon. I'm very sure. Very sure, indeed."

Actually, she wasn't. Wasn't sure she should marry him, given that he probably didn't love her. But she was certain beyond all doubt that she wanted him to finish what he had started a few moments ago. It was foolish beyond all measuring, but for tonight, at least, she wanted to believe that Simon truly belonged to her. And it might be the only chance she ever got.

He pressed a kiss to her forehead. "All right, love. I'll give you what you seem to want. This is against my better judgment, but perhaps it's the wisest course of action, after all."

Her mouth gaped open. Where did he find the nerve to lecture her at a moment like this? "Simon, why must you always be so difficult? I ask you to do one little thing, and you . . ."

He pressed his hand over her mouth. "Sophia, I've been waiting for this for quite some time. You're going to be quiet now, and do as I say."

She grabbed his hand and pulled it away. "Really? You've been waiting for this? Why didn't you ever tell me?"

He growled at her again, and then smothered her lips in a ferocious kiss. But even as Sophie melted into his arms, she had the definite impression that he intended to silence as well as seduce her.

His strategy was working.

Chapter Eleven

Sophie inhaled, pulling in the scent of sandalwood and Simon as he worked to remove her gown. His deft fingers searched out ribbons, laces, and tapes, tugging and untying, even as he trailed damp kisses across her cheeks and down her throat. His touch seared her flesh, causing a shuddering heat to race down her belly and through her legs.

"Sophie." His breath raised prickles on the sensitive skin beneath her ear. She forced herself to drag open heavy eyelids, though she didn't remember closing them in the first place.

The drawing room refused to come into focus. Velvety shadows made the atmosphere seem murky, the furniture transformed into fantastic, oddly distorted shapes. She blinked into Simon's face—mere inches from her own—his hard-edged features thrown into stark relief by the uneven light cast from the flames in the hearth.

Simon had removed her spectacles. When had that happened? She felt defenseless, more exposed without them on her face than she felt standing before him without her gown.

A teasing smile played around the corners of his mouth as his eyes lingered over her body. "You'll be more comfortable if you lie on the settee."

"Oh, yes, of course." Sophie winced at the squeak in her voice. She sounded like a demented squirrel.

Simon didn't seem to notice. His eyes continued their downward drift to a point just at the top of her legs. She followed his gaze, finally registering the fact that she now wore only her chemise. The flickering glow of the fire reduced the linen to transparency. She gulped, her throat gone suddenly dry, as Simon's fingers brushed over her chest and stomach, skimming down to the dusky triangle of hair visible through the delicate fabric.

"You're so pretty." His voice had dropped to a deep rasp. And surely the brimstone in those dark eyes would burn a hole in her chemise at any moment.

Her legs trembled and refused to hold her up any longer, so she collapsed slowly onto the overstuffed cushions of the settee. Even as she nestled back into the silky fabric, she couldn't help devouring Simon with a greedy gaze. She took in the flame-gilded outline of his lean hips, his broad chest, and his massive shoulders. He exuded a formidable masculinity as he shrugged out of his formfitting tailcoat, which he then tossed onto a wingback chair. Sitting down beside her, he went to work on the buttons of his waistcoat.

"Sophie?" His gravelly voice held a curious note of hesitancy.

"Yes?" She couldn't resist reaching over to stroke his sinewy forearm. Heat seeped through his finely woven shirt, the muscles beneath the fabric as hard as a blade tempered in the flames of a forge.

"How much do you know about, ah, marital relations?"

She snatched her hand back. "Simon! What a question to ask at a time like this."

A laugh that sounded more like a groan escaped from his lips. "It seems like the perfect time to ask. I don't want to frighten you, Puck, or rush you into anything. You're such an innocent thing."

Sophie edged toward the other end of the settee, suddenly very conscious of the puckered tips of her breasts, clearly visible under her filmy chemise. She crossed her arms over her chest and frowned. Why did he always have to destroy every romantic moment that occurred between them—especially when they were as rare as hen's teeth?

"I'm not that innocent. I did grow up in the country, after all. I spent just as much time around horses and other breeding animals as you did. It doesn't really seem all that complicated."

He shook his head in silent reprimand, even as his hands curled around her wrists to coax her arms away from her chest. One index finger traced the soft swell of her breast until it stroked across her veiled nipple. A piercing ache shot from the tip of his finger to the dark cove between her legs.

"You're talking about mechanics, nothing more." The delicious rumble of his voice penetrated every part of her body. "What do you actually know about lovemaking between a man and a woman? Do you have any idea of what I intend to do to your sweet body? Trust me, Sophie, I can make you lose your mind with pleasure."

His daring words set all her nerve endings aflame. His big hand closed around her breast, stroking and kneading the compliant flesh until the nipple pearled against his palm.

"I . . . I know that Robert and Annabel always seem to be happy first thing in the morning." The more he stroked, the more her eyelids drooped.

"Would you like to feel that way, my love?" His hands were on both breasts now, rolling beaded nipples between his fingers until they were throbbing points of exquisite sensitivity.

Sophie could only moan in reply. His hands moved over

her body, silently urging that she lift her hips as he pulled the chemise over her head in a rustling slide of cool linen.

"Open your eyes again, sweetheart."

She slowly obeyed him, although it took a few moments for her passion-dazed vision to focus on his face. His angled cheekbones were flushed, and his mouth had narrowed into a thin but beautifully carved line.

She shivered, suddenly aware that Simon had withdrawn his warm hands from her body to clench them in tight fists against his powerful thighs. His thick hair was disheveled, as if he had run his fingers through it, and his eyes gleamed with an intoxicating combination of laughter and desire.

That look made her sigh with pleasure, and she lifted a hand to caress the edges of his enticing mouth. He caught it, pressing his lips against her palm. His breath scorched the sensitive flesh. She could feel her nipples contract even more, though he only touched her hand.

"God, you're beautiful, Sophie. Like sugar and cream. I never would have believed what you were hiding under all those prim little gowns."

His greedy eyes consumed her. She blushed from head to toe with the realization that she sat before him completely naked, while he had only removed his coat and cravat. Her senses were jolted into a painful state of awareness— awareness of her own vulnerability and his dominating sensuality as he loomed over her.

But she didn't fear him, or have any desire to cover herself. Instead, her heart pounded as his eyes raked over her body grown rosy and damp with excitement. She relished his hot gaze and the way his other hand twitched against his leg, as if he could barely keep it from her body.

The situation was depraved, of course, and not something she could ever—not even in her wildest dreams—have imagined. For just tonight, though, she wasn't plain old Sophie

Stanton, but a bewitching and seductive woman who would claim whatever she wanted.

And what she wanted was Simon.

She felt a dreamy smile touch her lips as she watched him, entranced by the dark flush on his cheeks, the rapid rise and fall of his breathing. His eyes narrowed on her breasts, and his look became hard and possessive.

"Touch me, Sophie," he rasped.

She blinked at the unexpected command. "Where?"

"Anywhere. Just touch me."

She reached trembling fingers to his chest, parting the top of his shirt before beginning to fumble with the laces. Under her hand beat the hard rhythm of his heart.

She obviously took too long for his liking. With an impatient hiss of breath, Simon brushed her fingers away and yanked the garment over his head.

Sophie swallowed a choking breath at the sight of his naked chest and shoulders, corded with muscle and bronzed to a golden sheen by fire and lamplight. She shyly traced one hand over his ribs. It was like touching the sleek sides of a blooded stallion, all hard flesh and grace. Her fingers delved into the fine pelt of dark hair that covered his chest and flat stomach, and arrowed down under his waistband.

He was magnificent. A champion, and so much more powerful than she. But despite all that power, that overwhelming masculinity, his skin twitched and his muscles jumped wherever her fingers explored him.

"Enough," he groaned. He eased her onto the plump cushions, wedging her against the back of the settee as he came down beside her. The cool silk upholstery slid against her skin, contrasting with the heat that poured from his torso. A spicy masculine scent enveloped her. For a dizzying moment it reminded her of cool autumn nights, and the rustling secrets of an ancient forest.

But those images fled her mind as his lips covered hers and only sensation remained. His teeth nipped at the edges of her mouth. Then he stroked deep, his hot tongue claiming her so sweetly that the flesh between her thighs grew soft and damp. While his tongue explored, his hand drifted down her neck to cup her right breast between long fingers.

Those knowing fingers tugged on her nipple, pulling it into a throbbing bud. Sophie broke away from his mouth on a gasp, arching her spine in surprise. The cushioned back of the settee pushed her against him as she involuntarily pressed the aching peaks of her breasts into the hair covering his chest.

"Do you like that, little one?" His midnight eyes narrowed with predatory intensity.

"Yes," she managed to squeak, although a tiny, rational part of her mind realized the question was likely rhetorical.

A husky laugh was her only answer.

A moment later he moved down her body and fastened the wet slide of his mouth on her nipple. Electric tingles streaked across her skin. She wriggled beneath him, struggling to relieve a bewildering sensation of emptiness deep within.

She ached for him, and she sensed that Simon knew how much control he had over her body. As she whimpered in his arms, he played at her breasts. Sucking, stroking, tugging on the distended little nubs of flesh until she felt frantic with the waves of pleasure that seemed to ripple out from her very core.

Suddenly he released her. The coolness of the air on her damp nipples made them contract with painful intensity. Simon loomed over her, his powerful figure a shadowy outline in the light cast by the fire.

"Why . . . why did you stop? Please don't stop now." She barely recognized the pleading husk of her own voice.

She saw the glint of his teeth as he smiled, but he remained silent. He gently pushed her down on the cushions before wrapping one arm around her shoulders, cuddling her against his chest, his touch both tender and full of strength. Never before had Sophie felt so protected and yet so impossibly vulnerable.

But then his leg intruded between her thighs, pushing into her soft, secret flesh. Contractions throbbed deep within her womb. She gasped, overwhelmed by the astonishing pleasure of fine cloth over muscle brushing against her cleft. But before she could even absorb how delicious it felt, Simon pulled his leg away and shifted onto his side. He reached down, cupping her mound in his hand, his fingers delving deep into her tangle of curls.

Sophie bit off a cry, shrinking back from the startling intimacy of his touch. His hand stilled. She stared into his eyes. They burned with a restless flame that even she—inexperienced as she was—recognized as an all-consuming hunger. She couldn't utter a word.

Simon nuzzled her cheek with lips that seemed both ravenous and tender. "Gently, my sweet," he murmured in a rough but somehow soothing voice. "I won't hurt you, I promise. I could never hurt you, Sophie."

"But, it does hurt, doesn't it?" Now that the moment was upon her, she felt both her courage and her desire begin to wither.

His clever fingers moved again, stroking her soft folds. The gentle motion centered itself on the plump bud hidden deep within the cove of her thighs. As he continued to circle, the throbbing ache began to build once more, and she could feel honey-slick moisture dampening her skin and his hand. She buried her face, flushed with a bashful heat, into his shoulder.

"Yes, love, it will hurt a bit," he whispered in her ear. "Well, actually, it might hurt quite a lot, but only for a moment. Then all will be pleasure, I promise you."

His fingers slid over her flesh, dipping inside the entrance to her body before returning to tease the tender peak of her sex. She raised her hips in a silent plea, no longer caring about the pain that was to come. She became a creature of spiraling need—a need only Simon could gratify.

He caressed her, layering the pleasure until she floated in a midnight world of shadows and Simon. Everything ordinary faded away. Only he remained. His hands on her body, his mouth on hers, his possessive lovemaking that flung her to the edge of a precipice.

She knew any moment she would fall off that precipice and shatter into a thousand little pieces.

Sophie reached up and grabbed his head, yanking him into a hard kiss. An unbearable yearning tightened every muscle in her body as she devoured his sinful mouth with the pent-up force of all her years of loving him.

Simon's hand left her body as he broke their kiss. He tugged at the fall of his trousers then moved on top of her, crushing her into the cushions. He scissored her thighs open, and she felt the broad head of his shaft nudging against the entrance to her body.

"Ready, sweetheart?" His voice held a rough tenderness.

To just say *yes* wasn't enough. She answered by planting a passionate kiss on his lips as she clung to his neck. He flexed his hips, kissing her deeply as he penetrated her flesh. Pressure, then pain, began to build. Sophie dug her fingernails into his muscles, refusing to cry out at the slow but relentless invasion. He flexed once more. A searing pain lanced her deep inside.

But after only a few moments the burn of his penetration faded into insignificance, subsumed by the incredible feeling of his hard length inside her yielding, moisture-drenched sheath. She felt claimed by his masculinity—sublimely delicate and feminine in his powerful embrace.

It was wicked. It was frightening. It was the most exciting thing to ever happen to her.

She licked her parched lips and struggled to find her voice.

"I had no idea it would feel like this . . . that I would feel so much," she breathed.

Simon stared down at her, looking momentarily stunned. "I should bloody well hope not," he growled, before lowering his head to capture her mouth once more.

Chapter Twelve

God, she felt good.

Simon clenched his teeth, struggling to maintain his self-control as he savored the feel of Sophie's velvet-soft body underneath him. If he didn't get hold of himself right now he would climax like an untried Etonian tumbling a dairy maid in a barn.

She had surprised him, his little sprite, but not in the way he would have expected. Of course Sophie adored him, and of course she willingly relinquished her virginity as soon as he claimed it. But what had shaken him was the discovery of her sensual nature, now grown ripe and his for the taking. Her eager response to his lovemaking had surprised him, setting her well apart from the jaded pleasure-seekers he had once taken to his bed. No woman had pushed him closer to the limits of his control—or made him feel so . . . well, he couldn't seem to put a name to it.

She wriggled beneath him, silently demanding his attention. He flexed, and pushed his cock even farther into her supple flesh as his tongue explored the depths of her mouth. She moaned, sinking deeper into the ridiculously overstuffed cushions of the settee as he pressed into her.

Pulling his mouth from hers, he slowed the pulsing stroke of his hips. He sucked in a shuddering breath and looked down at the fey creature reclining on the pillows beneath him. Her skin glowed with a damp flush, and her hair curled in unruly locks of silk and russet around her pretty face.

Sophie's eyes snapped open. He could see the pupils dilate as she struggled to focus her vision. She stared back at him, her emerald-flecked gaze filled with so much raw emotion that Simon had to repress the urge to flinch.

"Simon?"

Her voice, catching on an unfamiliar sultry note, slid across his senses like a heavy velvet scarf. His cock pulsed inside her sheath. But even though they were locked in the most intimate of embraces, closer than they had ever been, Simon could still hear hesitation in her voice. His heart contracted with a tug of unexpected tenderness as a shadow of anxiety rippled across her features.

He slipped his arms around her shoulders and pulled her up to his chest. Her soft breasts pressed against him, teasing him with their ripeness. He wanted to go slowly, wanted her body to have time to adapt to him, but he couldn't help giving her a hard nudge. That drew another moan from her lips as her eyelids drooped shut again.

An amazing impulse to laugh rustled through him as he watched Sophie's lips curve up in a dreamy smile. Her slender legs wrapped themselves around his hips and she tilted her bottom up, unconsciously opening herself more fully to his body's invasion.

He stroked again into the syrupy heat. God, he wanted to taste her—to consume her tender flesh until she cried out for him to stop.

But it was too soon to partake in those headier games of love. He would awaken Sophie, slowly and carefully, to the sensual delights that were opening before them.

Denied the taste of her body, he indulged himself with the champagne-tinged flavor of her mouth, sucking in her sweet essence. She responded eagerly, stroking her tongue between his lips as her slender fingers danced over his back and shoulders. He had to fight the urge to push into her with a punishing rhythm.

Good God, she made him feel like a savage.

"You have no idea how much you tempt me." He licked the corner of her mouth. "You're just like a little pastry, fresh out of the baker's oven."

Her eyes widened in shock. She pinched him hard on the bicep.

"Don't tease me, Simon. I'm not a child anymore."

That remark did make him laugh.

"No, you're not, Puck, although I'm still getting used to that fact."

"Don't call me Puck, especially not now," she said. Her scowl was adorable.

Simon nipped her lower lip. "I'll call you whatever I want. After all, I should have some compensation for always pulling you out of trouble."

She gave him another hard pinch on the arm.

"Ah, you'll be sorry for that, Sophie. I have you right where I want you." He slid his hands down to her bottom, pulling her up and crushing her against his groin. She moaned as he began to stroke into her—steady, powerful, relentless.

He reached a hand up into her hair, thrusting his fingers through the thick mass, gently pulling her head back to give himself access to the sleekness of her white throat. Strands of crystal beads slipped from her curls to fall with a glittering sparkle to the carpet. Auburn hair cascaded over yellow pillows like a river of flame.

She glistened in the firelight, a rare pearl polished to a high gleam.

"Simon!" She whimpered again as he maintained the driving pulse within her.

The sound of her voice, the writhing of her soft, scented limbs, drove him wild. All the demons from the deepest pits of hell wouldn't have been able to hold him back any longer. He plunged into her—high and hard—and she arched up to meet him, matching his stroke with perfect accord.

An insatiable hunger gripped him, compelling him to go even deeper, to claim every part of her.

He hooked her left leg over his arm, opening her completely to his fierce thrust. Sophie threw her head back and gave a strangled cry—a low, keening sound of ecstasy. Her slick body throbbed around him as he surrendered to his climax, smothering his face in the soft cushions of the settee to muffle his own shout. He poured himself into her, and for one disorienting moment it seemed as if his flesh, his very spirit, had fused with hers.

The moment passed, overridden by an intensely physical rush of satisfaction that he had so thoroughly taken the woman lying beneath him.

Eventually, his breathing slowed from an uneven shudder to a more normal rhythm. Simon eased Sophie onto the cushions but remained between her legs, reluctant to pull himself from the clasp of her warm body. In fact, he had no intention of ending their interlude any time soon—despite the late hour and their scandalous use of his aunts' drawing room. After she'd rested a bit, he might try introducing her to some variations on the theme, after all.

He blew out a contented breath and nuzzled the soft skin beneath her ear. Sophie had yet to say a word—unusual for her. She was likely stunned by her first sexual release.

That, or the effects of the champagne were catching up to her.

She stirred beneath him, her bottom wriggling in an altogether delightful way. His cock twitched with a renewed

sense of interest. He grinned, planting a wet kiss on her neck.
Sophie had a great deal of potential in the bedchamber, and
he intended to take every opportunity to develop her burgeon-
ing talent. It was certainly the most enjoyable way he could
think of to keep her occupied and out of trouble.

He lifted his head to study the girl he had known for almost
a lifetime. A rosy blush stained her clear cheeks, and her eyelids fluttered madly, as if she were struggling to awaken from
a dream. She looked sweet, vulnerable, and very young. Simon
felt the familiar urge to protect her swell within him, along with
a rush of emotion so powerful it made every muscle in his body
tighten around her. With a jolt, he realized that what he felt was
an overwhelming need to possess her.

To claim her as his woman.

He let that wash through him. Sophie belonged to him now.
He wasn't capable of loving her as she wanted to be loved,
but she had given herself to him, and he would allow nothing
to come between them. Not his former lover's jealous machi-
nations, nor even Sophie's foolish notions about saving the
world. From now on, her life would revolve around him and
the family they would create together. He would see to that.

Sophie's quivering eyelids lifted. Simon leaned down to
kiss her swollen mouth, but she jerked her head back, staring at him with a look of . . . well, of horror.

He stared back. No, not horror. Outrage. Sheer, unadul-
terated outrage. She glared at him as if he had just tossed a
litter of kittens into a lake, after kicking an elderly vicar in the
seat of his pants.

Christ.

He had seen that look before, and it meant a thundercloud
was roiling just over his head. Before he could say anything,
Sophie's pretty pink lips curled up into a snarl. She laid a
hand flat on his chest and shoved.

"Simon, move."

Her voice held a chill brittle enough to shatter every pier glass in the house.

"Please get off me now," she continued from between clenched teeth, "or else I'll have to push you to the floor."

He repressed a groan as he felt a dull ache begin to throb along the back of his neck. What the hell was wrong with her now? And what would it take, exactly, to bring the frustrating little minx under control once and for all?

If Sophie hadn't been trying to will away the worst headache in the kingdom, she would have burst into laughter at the expression of stupefied amazement on Simon's face. But her temples were gripped in a band of throbbing pain, and she thought her head might blow apart if she moved any more than necessary. Either that or she would cast up her accounts all over Lady Eleanor's yellow silk settee.

Even worse, she might get sick on Simon, who still lay with her in a sweaty tangle of naked arms and legs. She had to get him off before her stomach embarrassed them both.

Sophie shoved him again, but she might as well have been trying to topple one of the monoliths of Stonehenge. Swallowing hard against another wave of nausea, she tried to ignore the fact that her mouth tasted foul as the bottom of a dust bin.

"Please," she managed to croak. "I must sit up."

He stared at her, not with the possessive sensuality that had made her insides turn to soft custard, but with a scowl that suggested he'd rather argue than make love to her.

Not that she could blame him. She couldn't believe it herself that such a magical episode had gone so tragically awry. Until a few minutes ago, everything had been perfect. Simon's lovemaking had been thrilling. His mouth, his hands, his body moving in hers, had swept her into a place of so many astonishing sensations that she thought she might lose her grasp on reality. But just seconds after that raging tide of pleasure had washed through her limbs, she felt as if someone had smacked her on the head with a large book—the collected works of Shakespeare at the very least.

"What the devil is wrong with you?" Simon's voice lanced through her brain.

She closed her eyes against a gripping pain that squeezed her eyeballs. "I think I might be sick."

He muttered under his breath as he shifted against her. His big body lifted away, and the cool air of the drawing room enveloped her, obliterating the heat of his masculine essence. She shivered.

"This is what happens when you drink four goblets of champagne." His voice was now as dry as anything she had quaffed at Lady Penfield's. "Come, Sophie, up with you now."

Gentle hands slid under her back as Simon easily lifted her into a sitting position. Sophie cautiously opened her eyes. The room spun like a dervish, forcing her to gulp to keep her stomach where it belonged.

"My glasses." Even to her own ears her voice sounded annoyingly weak. If she hadn't felt so wretched she would have kicked herself for succumbing to an episode of what must be the vapors.

"Not yet, Puck. Put your head down for a spell. I'd ring for smelling salts, but I think we've shocked Yates enough for one evening." His low voice purred with amusement.

"Very funny," Sophie mumbled as he pressed her head down onto her knees.

He rubbed her back with a soothing hand, then carefully brushed tangled hair away from her damp brow. Sophie took several deep breaths. That combined with his gentle touch seemed to bring her rebellious insides under some semblance of control.

"Does this help, sweetheart?" His fingers delved beneath her hair to massage the back of her neck.

She sighed gratefully. "Yes, thank you."

"Good, because we need to talk."

"What about?" she murmured, relaxing into the mesmerizing stroke of his powerful hands.

"I'm going to post the notice of our engagement in the papers, and set a date for our wedding. After tonight, I see no other choice."

"Hell's bells." Sophie tried to sit up, but Simon kept a restraining hand planted at the base of her spine, forcing her to direct her words to the floor. "I don't know why you're in such a rush. And I can't believe you want to talk about this while I'm feeling so . . . so . . ."

"Top-heavy? Jug-bitten? Disguised?"

"Unwell," she ground out. It was difficult to register an offended dignity with one's head between one's knees.

Simon began to snicker. Clearly the blasted man didn't have a romantic—or sympathetic—bone in his body.

"Let me up," she insisted, pushing against his hand.

He choked back another laugh and helped her sit up, resting her against the back of the settee. Simon retrieved her glasses from the nearby ebony table and propped them onto her nose.

"Better?" His face was grave, but his voice held a hint of laughter.

Although the edges of the room still revolved in an alarming fashion, Sophie's vision came into focus on the man lounging next to her. With the dying fire cutting shadows across his rippling muscles, Simon could have passed for a statue of a Greek warrior come to life. She considered climbing into his lap and pressing kisses onto his tempting mouth, but regretfully decided that her stomach and head wouldn't cooperate with another bout of strenuous activity.

"Yes, thank you. Much better," she sighed.

He reached over and threaded a hand through the wreck of her coiffure. Strong fingers rubbed the aching surface of her scalp. Her eyelids closed as the needlelike pain in her temples began to fade.

"Sophie, we do need to talk about setting a date."

Her eyelids snapped open. She twisted in her seat to look at him, wincing at the stabbing jolt to the back of her neck. Simon's dark gaze was devoid of any expression except, perhaps, one of wariness.

"Why are you so insistent we set a date? I've agreed to our engagement. This"—she waved her hand in a vague circle, as if to encompass the monumental event that had just occurred between them—"this doesn't change that. I still need time to get used to the idea of our marriage." And to the idea that she would soon be legally and morally subject to her husband's wishes, even if that husband was Simon. "And you promised," she added.

"I know, but we've run out of time," he replied in a cool voice. "I have urgent business in London and can't afford to delay my return to the city any longer. And you need to order your bridal clothes and begin planning for the wedding."

She jerked upright in her seat. *Leave Bath?* She couldn't. She had a chance to help Becky and Toby, no matter what the blasted Earl of Trask might have to say about it. He may have forgotten them, but she hadn't.

Well, maybe for a little while, but that wouldn't happen again.

Simon frowned as she edged away from him. His hard eyes, glittering like coal, swept over her, then he rose with athletic grace from the settee. Turning his back—he really did have a magnificent set of shoulders—he grabbed his shirt from the chair where he had tossed it and began to turn out the sleeves.

Sophie yanked her attention from the bronzed sinews of his back and neck, determined to refocus on the conversation.

"Why must we rush back to town? You never said anything about this important business before tonight. I'm not ready to leave Bath. And I'm not ready to announce our engagement, either."

He didn't even look at her, pulling his shirt over his head instead. A shivery sense of anxiety crept up her spine. Was he avoiding her question? Simon never did that. The man didn't know how to be anything but blunt, at least with her.

His head emerged from the folds of his shirt. He threw a hooded glance her way before turning to search for the rest of his clothes scattered about the room.

"Fine. If you don't want to return to the city, then we can be married here. I'll still need to go up to London to discuss the settlements with your mother and your grandfather. Your family, I'm sure, will be happy to travel to Bath. I assume you'll want your mother to be here when you get married," he finished sarcastically.

He *had* avoided her question. Why wouldn't he explain why they had to get married in such a rush?

Sophie gaped at him. He was holding something back, something important. Every instinct she possessed confirmed it. The idea that he had obviously decided to lie to her about it made her naked flesh crawl with goose bumps.

She shook her head, wishing desperately she could obliterate the woolly clouds from her brain. What should she do? Simon had retreated behind the imperious facade that would deflect any attempts to pry the truth from him. But she couldn't marry him until she knew what he was hiding from her. Especially—and she could barely stand to think about this—if it had something to do with Lady Randolph.

Simon took her silence for acquiescence, for he extracted his pocketbook and a pencil from his tailcoat and began to make notes.

"I'll notify the local parish tomorrow, so the banns can be

posted Sunday. We can be married in three weeks." He paused
for a moment as he frowned at his notebook, then resumed his
rapid scribbling. "You can order your wedding clothes here.
Aunt Eleanor and Aunt Jane can help you. It's not London, but
surely there are some respectable modistes in Bath who can
provide you with what you need. I expect you to begin shop-
ping tomorrow, so there will be no pointless delays. Have the
shopkeepers send the bills to me."

An acrid taste of panic flooded her mouth. Why in God's
name was he pushing so hard? And why wouldn't he even
look at her?

"Simon, stop." Sophie put as much authority into the command as she could.

He glanced up, a smile lifting the edges of his mouth as his
gaze drifted over her naked body. Sophie could feel the hot
rush of blood staining her cheeks. She grabbed her chemise
from the heap of clothing on the floor and yanked the flimsy
garment over her head.

They stared at each other for a long moment. The smile on
Simon's lips faded, the lines of his face hardening until it resembled that Greek statue once again. *No happy bridegroom
this*, she thought with a sinking heart.

"Now what?" His tone was now positively grim.

Sophie steeled herself to ask the question she had sworn
she never would—or at least not yet. But his behavior demanded she seek the truth. The man who had made passionate love to her had disappeared, replaced by the arrogant earl
who rarely deigned to show emotion. She didn't trust that
man, and right now she had a great deal of difficulty imag-
ining herself married to him.

"Simon." Her voice caught. She swallowed and tried again.
"Simon, do you love me?"

He had looked away to tuck his pocketbook into the folds
of his coat, but her question made him jerk around in surprise.

"What the hell kind of question is that?" His black eyes narrowed to slits. "Sophie, have you gone completely mad?"

She stood her ground. "Well, do you?"

He sighed, buttoned up his brocaded waistcoat, and then shrugged into his formfitting tailcoat. A weighted silence filled the room, blending with the shadows around them. Her heart gave a sickening thump as she realized he was buying time to formulate an answer.

He finally looked at her. "I've loved you ever since you were a little girl. Why do you think I pay so much attention to you?"

She almost choked. Paid attention to her? Brotherly scolds and reprimands were his idea of paying attention to her?

"Well, that's very sweet of you." She could hear the grumble in her voice. "But that's not what I'm talking about. Are you *in love* with me, Simon?"

His dark brows snapped together like a trap. "What's the difference?"

Her heart squeezed another painful thump against her breastbone. Simon had, as usual, identified the exact nature of the problem, even though he probably didn't realize it. He cared for her, but he had clearly fortified himself against the tempestuous emotions that swept through her every time she came within a hundred feet of him. How could she ever hope to have any control in their marriage—even self-control—if he refused to grant her any part of his true self?

"Sophie?" He studied her with narrow intensity, as if she were some exotic creature in a menagerie.

She blew out a tight breath and rose to her feet. Her head ached a great deal too much to think her way through the problem tonight. Well, more than one problem, since she couldn't shake the disturbing notion that he had lied to her about something.

Her throat constricted with unshed tears, but she forced herself to speak past them. "I'd rather not talk any more tonight. You'd better go before Yates or one of the other servants discovers what we've been doing in here."

A brief grin slashed across Simon's dark visage. "I expect the old codger has a fairly good idea of what's transpired."

"For heaven's sake, don't joke about it," Sophie hissed as she grabbed his arm and began to drag him across the drawing room. The thought of discovery made her stomach pitch like the deck of a fishing boat in a storm.

"Very well, I'll go," he grumbled as he let her tow him to the door. "But tomorrow we will set a date for our wedding. I won't take no for an answer."

She wrenched open the door, stepping aside to let him pass. He walked through and turned, obviously intending to continue their argument, but Sophie slammed the door in his face and twisted the key in the lock. The solid panels of the mahogany door muffled the sound of his oath. After a few moments she heard him stalk toward the front of the townhouse, his heavy footsteps echoing loudly with his disapproval.

She sagged against the coolness of the polished doorframe, her heart pounding so rapidly in her throat she could hardly breathe. Making love with him had been the worst mistake of her life. He had taken her innocence, claimed her for his own, and would continue to insist on marriage as soon as possible. His honor, and the demands of society would allow for nothing less.

But she wasn't ready to marry him. And she might never be if he kept acting the way he had tonight. Something was terribly wrong, and she needed the time to find out what it was.

Somehow, she had to find a way to turn back the clock.

Chapter Thirteen

The coming of the dawn didn't weaken Sophie's resolve, or lessen her sense that Simon had lied to her. Well, he could bluster away till Armageddon, but she had no intention of being pushed into a hasty marriage. And she certainly wouldn't leave Bath until she saw Toby and Becky again, and assured herself of their safety.

Given his way, Simon would ruthlessly carry her back to her mother's house in Mayfair, then head straight to Grosvenor Square and to Grandfather Stanton, who would agree to anything Simon asked for. In less than a month, Sophie would find herself trussed and delivered like a Christmas goose to her impatient bridegroom, who would then serve her up to the ton on a gold-leafed platter.

And trussed up like a Christmas goose was exactly how she was beginning to feel, in spite of Simon's declarations and lovemaking. He had never before shown any inclination to marry her, though both their grandfathers and his aunts had often voiced the hope that "the stubborn lad would come to his senses and marry the poor girl."

Sophie still winced whenever she recalled the long-suffering look on Simon's face as he deflected the labored jests about founding a new family dynasty. He had never laughed or made a joke in return, which had made the whole thing worse. If only he hadn't taken it so seriously, as if marrying her was the most horrifying idea he could imagine. She had put up with it for years and for some demented reason had loved him anyway, though she had always known he would rather set sail for India on a broken-down raft than take her as his wife.

But now, for some reason, he wanted her. And if last night was any indication, wanted her with an alarming, if flattering, intensity. She had slept barely a wink after she had climbed into bed, jerked from sleep by disturbing dreams of Simon's mouth on her lips, his hands on her breasts, his—

"Sophia Stanton, you're turning as red as a beet. Are you coming down with a fever?"

Sophie jumped inches off the carriage squabs as awareness of her surroundings came flooding back. How humiliating to be thinking of *that* while driving through the streets of Bath with Simon's Aunt Eleanor. As if trying to hide the marks on her neck left by his voracious kisses hadn't been bad enough.

"I . . . I don't think so, ma'am," she scrambled. "Although I may have eaten something last night that disagreed with me."

Lady Eleanor's dark skirts rustled their disapproval. "How like Lady Penfield to serve bad refreshments. I remember one of her routs in London when she served lobster patties that smelled like a goat pen. I, of course, had the sense not to eat them, and I directed everyone that night to avoid them as well. But Mrs. Groton insisted on sampling them—a decision, I assure you, she came to regret."

The feathers on the old woman's bonnet quivered with righteous indignation, leaving no doubt of the severe agonies inflicted by the lobster patties.

"There were no seafood patties last night, my dear ma'am."

"Regardless, I insist you take a glass of the waters today. It's just the thing for bilious complaints."

Sophie grimaced. Better to eat one of Lady Penfield's suspect patties than choke back yet another glass of the vile healing waters of Bath.

The family carriage rolled to a stop in front of the imposing portico and columns of the Pump Room. James lowered the step and handed Lady Eleanor to the pavement. Sophie jumped to the ground, waving aside the footman's offer of assistance. The old woman grumbled under her breath, but declined to scold, leaning heavily on Sophie's arm as she trudged into the Pump Room.

The magnificent Tompion clock had just struck noon. Elegant ladies and soberly clad gentlemen crowded the room to sip the waters and gossip about the previous evening's parties. The musicians, in their usual place in the west apse, provided a tuneful back note to the cheerful, discordant chatter that rose and fell in waves.

Lady Eleanor and Sophie made their way to the top of the room, nodding to acquaintances but not stopping until they reached a few chairs set back against the wall. After settling the old woman into her seat, Sophie fetched a glass of water from the fountain attendant.

Lady Eleanor frowned, taking the glass. "Where is your water?"

"Oh, I seem to have forgotten it," Sophie replied absently as she scanned the crush of people. She both hoped and dreaded that Simon would come to the Pump Room this morning. After last night's soul-shattering encounter, she should obviously speak to him in private, but she was dead certain he would respond with outrage when she announced her intention to put off their wedding. Better to spring it on him in a public place, where he'd be less likely to attempt intimidation.

Or worse, try to kiss her into submission. Which, she had to admit, had a much better chance of working on her than intimidation.

"Sophia, stop craning your neck like a stork."

"Yes, ma'am."

Sophie stretched up a bit further—it really was inconvenient being so short—but couldn't spy Simon anywhere. She let her gaze drift over the crowd, relaxing as she encountered nothing more than a few disapproving stares from the usual assortment of bombazine dragons. No doubt her behavior at Lady Penfield's had occasioned a few choice tidbits of gossip this morning.

Despite her fluttering nerves, Sophie couldn't help snickering as she imagined the ton's reaction to her engagement to Simon, and what it would mean for her. No one would dare snub the Countess of Trask. Perhaps there were some advantages to becoming his bride after all—aside from the obvious ones he had shown her last night.

A moment later her laughter died when her eyes encountered the one person in Bath she least wanted to see, especially this morning.

Lady Randolph headed toward their corner of the room, her lush body wrapped in wine-colored silk that made her auburn curls glow like flame. As usual, she had a handsome escort by her side, looking as if he, too, wished to wrap himself around her voluptuous body in the same clingy way as the fabric of her gown. Sophie didn't recognize the man, but he seemed somehow familiar.

Oh well, at least it's not Simon doing the clinging.

Her headache from last night, still lurking behind her eyeballs, returned full force under Lady Randolph's malicious gaze. Why couldn't the blasted woman just leave her alone?

"My dear Lady Eleanor, Miss Stanton, how delightful to meet you this morning," purred the countess. "Why, Miss Stanton, I had no expectations of seeing you at all."

"There's no explaining your expectations, Lady Randolph,"

replied Lady Eleanor, her voice frosty. "Why shouldn't Sophia be out and about today?"

"She seemed most unwell last night at Lady Penfield's ball. Perhaps it was something she drank."

Lady Randolph's escort laughed, earning him a hard-eyed stare from Lady Eleanor.

"More like something she ate," barked the old woman. "And who might this jackanapes be? You could remember your manners, Countess, and properly introduce him."

The other woman's eyes narrowed, but she maintained her cream-pot smile. Sophie wished that, just once, the sophisticated widow would lose her poise in front of an audience.

"Allow me to present Mr. Watley. He's been in Bath for only a few days, which might explain why you haven't seen him."

"My lady. Miss Stanton."

Mr. Watley gave a graceful, correct bow and returned his gaze to Sophie. He seemed fascinated by her, and with a sickening flash she realized she had seen him before. He was the man outside the theater. The man who had watched her with avid curiosity as she helped Toby inside Lady Eleanor's carriage.

Sophie sucked in a breath through her teeth. If Lady Eleanor found out about that particular escapade, there would be the devil to pay for both Sophie and the servants who had escorted her that night. She prayed Mr. Watley had the sense to keep what he saw to himself.

"Charmed, I'm sure," intoned Lady Eleanor, obviously not charmed in the least.

Lady Randolph turned back to Sophie. "I do hope you are feeling better today, Miss Stanton. How unfortunate that Simon had to take you home last night. He was greatly missed, I can assure you."

"I'm fine, your ladyship. Thank you for inquiring," she ground out.

Mr. Watley didn't bother to hide his knowing smirk.

"My nephew knows his responsibility when he sees it," Lady Eleanor intoned. "He has been taking care of my god-child since she was a girl."

Sophie refused to let her eyeballs roll up to the ceiling. Is that how everyone saw her relationship to Simon—simply as one of responsibility?

The malicious gleam returned to Lady Randolph's eyes. "I've always thought Simon was very good with children. He's so noble and self-sacrificing to all his family."

"You needn't tell me my nephew's good qualities, Bathsheba. I know them very well," snapped Lady Eleanor as she struggled to her feet. "Sophia, give me your arm. I'd like to stroll around the room a bit."

Sophie dropped a short curtsy, casting a glance at the countess and her escort. Their expressions were rigid in the face of Lady Eleanor's blatant snub, but Mr. Watley quickly recovered and executed a faultless bow. The old woman ignored him as she moved away with stately grace.

Sophie choked back a laugh. "Ma'am, that was splendidly done," she murmured in her godmother's ear.

"Never could abide the woman, even if she is supposedly good ton. I swear, her antics sent her husband to an early grave, even if he did accidentally kill himself in a carriage race."

Sophie frowned. "What do you mean?"

"Randolph was mad for her, from the very beginning. She didn't give a stitch for him—married him for his money. Oh, the girl was always discreet. Never embarrassed him in public, although she often cut very close to the line. But there were rumors that quite a few men besides Randolph shared her bed. Poor silly fellow couldn't stand it. If he hadn't cracked his curricle on the road to Brighton, he would have drowned himself in a barrel of brandy."

Sophie's jaw went slack. Lady Eleanor had never spoken so frankly to her before—at least not about something so scandalous.

The old woman cast an impatient glance. "Don't give me that look, miss. I know you understand me. You're not a simpering schoolgirl anymore, not that you ever were. I want you to stay far away from that woman. For all her fine airs she is a bad piece of business, and for some reason she seems to have taken an extreme dislike to you."

Sophie gave her head a small shake. It never ceased to amaze her that her godmother, who rarely left the house, observed a great deal more than one could ever imagine.

Lady Eleanor expelled a sigh. "I never could understand Simon's fascination with Bathsheba. Madness to go anywhere near the viperous creature. I do hope he has learned his lesson."

Sophie caught her foot on the ruffled trim of her hem, but managed to catch herself.

"Pay attention, Sophia," rapped out Lady Eleanor. "We'll both end up in a heap on the floor thanks to your clumsiness."

Muttering an apology, Sophie took a firm grip of Lady Eleanor's arm and walked slowly on.

Did everyone know Simon and Lady Randolph had been lovers? And did everyone think they still were? He had assured her last night that he and the widow were now merely friends, but why did Sophie find that so difficult to accept? All her instincts clamored that Simon was holding something back. She would find out what it was if she had to tie him to a chair and pummel it out of him.

"Ah, and there's the great man himself," grumped Lady Eleanor, gazing toward the front of the Pump Room. "I wondered when he would make an appearance."

Sophie's heart banged against her ribs. All the dark magic of last night's memories came rushing back as she watched Simon prowl toward them through the company. She tried to swallow, but her mouth and throat were suddenly parched. The potent combination of longing and frustration that flooded through her every time she saw him would surely drive her to Bedlam, in short order.

He moved with a long, easy stride, nodding to friends but never pausing until he stood before them. His eyes gleamed as he openly—and thoroughly—inspected Sophie from tip to toe. A hot rush of blood seemed to flush every part of her skin in response. She couldn't help scowling at her own ridiculous reaction to his possessive gaze.

Her forbidding expression apparently failed to deter him, because his eyes sparkled with laughter. He smiled as he bent over his aunt's gloved hand.

"Good afternoon, my lady. I'm pleased to see you looking so well."

Although clearly irritated with her nephew, Lady Eleanor couldn't keep her lips from twitching into an answering grin. As usual, Simon's smile could charm the devil out of the doldrums.

"Well, my boy, how are you? I had thought to see you before this, but I suppose you had business this morning, as you always do."

"Alas, yes. Believe me, I would much rather spend the morning with you and Sophie than in the company of two ill-tempered bankers and my slave-driver of a secretary."

"Simon, you spend too much time with those vulgar city men," said his aunt. "You know how your grandfather felt about such things. Family and land—those are what matter, not these newfangled schemes that occupy all your time. I've hardly seen you since you've come to Bath."

Simon's face grew remote as he listened to the familiar and aggravating family refrain. Sophie had heard those disapproving remarks often enough over the years when visiting the St. James's estate, and had seen the tight-lipped bitterness on Simon's face when the old earl had lectured him about his determination to seek a life of study at Cambridge. She had felt the pain he experienced as her own every time his grandfather pulled him further away from the life he truly desired.

But Simon had buried his disappointment years ago beneath a mask of careful indifference. At least Sophie thought it was a mask, although she had to admit she sometimes didn't recognize the boy she had loved in the man he had become.

"Forgive me, dear aunt." Simon's voice was level and polite. "My business should be concluded in a few days, and then I promise to spend more time with you."

Sophie frowned. Why was Simon lying again? He had every intention of returning to London as soon as possible.

She opened her mouth to question him, but he smoothly cut her off.

"Aunt Eleanor, would you mind if I stole Sophie away for a few minutes? I have something most particular I wish to say to her."

Sophie almost choked when the old woman winked at her nephew. Simon looked startled, but then sudden laughter eased the hard set of his features.

"By all means, my dear," Lady Eleanor said affably. "I see Davinia Lethbridge sitting by the musicians. I haven't spoken to her in an age. Take all the time you want."

Before Sophie could object, Simon tucked her hand in the crook of his arm and began to lead her away.

"Simon, did you say something to your aunts about our engagement?" Sophie hissed from behind the false smile she plastered on her lips.

"Of course I haven't, Goose. I gave you my word. But you know what the old gal is like—she has desired marriage between us ever since you put up your hair and let down your skirts. She'll take any opportunity to throw us together."

"Really, Simon. Don't call Lady Eleanor an old gal—it's very rude."

He laughed and steered her to one of the inset windows on the opposite side of the room. Although still in full view of the crowd, the alcove provided some privacy. It was, Sophie realized, the perfect setting to deliver her sure-to-be-unwelcome message. All could see, but none could overhear. Simon wouldn't dare lose his temper in front of half of Bath.

She ordered the butterflies in her stomach to cease their fluttering, took a deep breath, and turned to face him.

The speech she'd practiced so carefully withered under Simon's hot gaze. The cheerful chaos of the Pump Room faded as she tumbled into the dark well of his eyes, returning to that place of magic and sensation that had ensnared them both last night.

His big hand brushed the fine velvet of the pelisse covering her back, sending a hard, wracking shudder down her spine. Dear Lord. How was she ever to say what she must say? Even a roomful of gossips—many of whom were eyeing them with great interest—couldn't keep her from melting into a pool of honey under the warmth of his touch.

"How are you feeling today, my sweet?" His husky voice rumbled through every limb of her body. It was all she could do not to close her eyes and lean into the hand that lingered at the base of her spine. "I hope you have recovered from last night. You seemed a tad out of sorts when you so graciously bowed me out of the room."

She snapped her head back and glared at him. Trust Simon to ruin the moment—again. The teasing light in his eyes stiffened her resolve.

"Whatever can you be talking about? I had a perfectly pleasant evening last night, and I feel most well today."

He snorted. "Sophie, you had more than a pleasant evening last night, if you recall. It's now time to pay the piper. Although there's no doubt I took advantage of you in my aunt's drawing room, of all places, I have no intention of apologizing. In fact, I would do it again. You belong to me now, sweetheart, and you may as well admit it. The sooner we announce our betrothal and set a date for our wedding, the better."

She did her best to appear both innocent and bewildered— a challenging task, since his blunt words had set the butterflies pinwheeling in her stomach once again.

"Simon, I've already told you that I have no intention of announcing our betrothal. At least not yet. You promised you would give me time to adjust to the change in circumstances, and I intend to hold you to that promise."

His brows arched up in exaggerated surprise. "Let me remind you, Puck, there's been quite a substantial change in the circumstances, as you so delicately put it. You gave yourself to me last night—rather enthusiastically as I recall— and that changes everything. It's now imperative we get married with no delay."

Sophie took a deep breath and stepped off the cliff.

"Simon," she gasped with feigned outrage. "Have you lost your mind? There has been nothing in my behavior that would modify our agreement one whit."

For a harrowing moment he seemed slack-jawed with shock. But that didn't last. The lines of his face set like stone with an alarming rapidity that made her question the sanity of her plan.

"Sophie," he ground out, "what are you playing at? You slept with me last night. You came apart in my arms. I know you didn't imbibe enough champagne to forget that very interesting event."

She drew herself up to her full height. Just level with his

chin, she forced herself to ignore the unmistakable warning signaled by the compression of his lips.

"After you brought me home last night, I went straight to bed," she said primly. "I don't know how you could say otherwise."

He closed his eyes. Now he looked like a basilisk. A very angry basilisk. She let her gaze dart around the room, wanting to look anywhere but at Simon's furious countenance.

Her eyes suddenly fell upon Lady Randolph. The countess was observing them, a canny smile playing around the edges of her crimson-tinted lips.

Sophie jerked her attention back to Simon. His eyes were open now. As hard as flint, they regarded her with suspicion.

"Why are you doing this, Sophie? What do you want from me?"

"I want you to respect our agreement, Simon. I have no desire to leave Bath at this time, nor am I ready to announce our betrothal to the world."

His voice rumbled down to a low growl. "So you hope to gain my compliance by pretending that nothing happened in the drawing room last night? That your naked body didn't shiver in climax beneath mine?"

She gasped, his rough language sending a quivering thrill straight to the still-tender flesh between her thighs. Sophie mentally grabbed for the slipping traces of her resolve, blurting out the first thing that came into her head.

"You must be thinking of someone else, my lord. Your former mistress, perhaps?"

His sudden stillness was so alarming that her stomach pitched to her knees with the awful conviction that not even a crowd of gossips in the Pump Room could prevent him from exploding with anger.

But Simon had formidable self-control. Even as unnerved

as she was, Sophie couldn't help but admire his restraint. God only knew she didn't deserve it.

He blinked a few times, looked quickly around the room, then settled his features into a mask of polite boredom. Only the coal furnace smoldering in his dark eyes indicated the magnitude of his struggle within.

"My dear girl." His quiet voice warned of impending doom. "I will not be manipulated. I suggest you learn that lesson immediately. Things will go poorly for you if you don't."

Her own temper, repressed until now by her agitation, flared at his threat.

"I've had enough of this insulting conversation, my lord. Please take me back to Lady Eleanor. I'm quite sure she's ready to return home."

The angled planes of his handsome face turned hard as quartz, but he nodded his head in acquiescence. She suspected he didn't trust himself to keep his temper under control much longer. Thank God his abhorrence of scenes spared her the need to play out her ridiculous but necessary charade one second more.

As Simon escorted her back to his aunt, Sophie's eyes were once more irresistibly drawn to Lady Randolph, standing only a short distance away with Mr. Watley. An exultant smile shaped the edges of the widow's beautiful mouth, and her crystalline gaze glittered with a malignant triumph she made no effort to contain.

Chapter Fourteen

What the hell had just happened?

Simon stared at his fiancée's slim figure, rigid with indignation, as she escorted Aunt Eleanor from the Pump Room. If he didn't know better he could have sworn someone had just yanked his brains from his skull, shaken them about like a terrier shakes a rat, and then reinserted them upside down. His teeth were so tightly clenched it just might take a chisel to pry them apart.

He had been absolutely certain of her last night, assuming her anxious reaction to their lovemaking—and his insistence they set a date for their marriage—had been due to the unusual amount of champagne she had consumed earlier at the ball. She was an innocent, and their physical intimacies were bound to upset her, even though she had clearly enjoyed them in the moment. Hell, the spectacular sex had stunned *him*, and he had lost any pretensions to innocence long ago.

In fact, he had been so sure of her that after he met with his bankers this morning, he instructed Soames to draw up the contracts for the new mills in Yorkshire. Simon had planned on leaving Bath this afternoon to meet with Jedediah Russell at his offices in Bristol, and complete negotiations before the canny factory owner could be tempted by any other offers.

But, as usual, Sophie had thrown a spanner into the works. Russell would never agree to anything unless he knew his potential partner had unrestricted access to a sufficient coal supply. In his latest missive to Soames, Russell had made it clear that he wanted proof, not promises. The announcement in the *Bath Chronicle* of the betrothal of Miss Sophia Stanton to the Earl of Trask had been intended to provide that assurance.

Jerking to awareness of the sideways glances and curious stares of the other patrons in the Pump Room, Simon repressed a groan. More than a few scandalmongers had witnessed his argument with Sophie, but he had been so amazed by her lunatic attempts to manipulate him that he had been hard put to control his anger. Every ounce of his willpower had been press-ganged into fighting the urge to shake the little baggage. Well, if Sophie thought she could outmaneuver him, she would soon learn a surprising lesson.

He spun on his heel, barely avoiding a crash into a lush little package wrapped in burgundy silk. Simon bit back the foul curse that sprang to his lips.

"Good day, my lord."

The scent of Bathsheba's expensive French perfume wafted up his nostrils. He suppressed the impulse to sneeze.

Odd. That seductive scent, and Bathsheba's practiced sexuality, had always made his cock twitch with lust. But for the first time it occurred to him that his former mistress seemed . . . unwholesome.

"Lady Randolph."

"You seem in a great hurry, Simon." Bathsheba's voice dropped to a low, amused tone. "Are you charging off to play nursemaid to Sophie again? I understand how loyal you are to anyone you consider family, but that impertinent child is a scandal waiting to happen. She is apparently unable to go about in public without causing a scene."

The back of his neck prickled. Bathsheba might sound amused, but his instincts—finely honed by years of fighting with ruthless men of trade—had suddenly run up a battle ensign.

"I wasn't aware that Sophie had caused any scenes," he said in a cool voice.

Bathsheba's charming smile vanished, her impeccable self-control slipping as her expression turned petulant.

"Really, I wonder how you can be so tolerant of that dreary little bluestocking. You spend so much time with her, one would suppose you were courting the girl."

He fixed her with a steady gaze until she flinched. Her cheeks paled as she stared at him with a look of growing horror.

"Simon . . ."

"Good day, my lady." He gave her a short bow, but ignored her grasping hand as he turned and strode to the door of the Pump Room.

Damn.

As if things weren't bad enough, now he had to contend with his former mistress making thinly veiled threats against his fiancée. What in God's name had gotten into Bathsheba? Surely she couldn't be hankering after their old liaison? Rumor had it she had already taken Watley as her current lover, so why the jealous display? It defied all sense, but his instincts clamored too loudly to ignore. Puck was now his to protect, and he would do whatever it took to keep her safe.

He strode out the door into the crisp fall air, heading past the imposing abbey toward the Avon River and Pulteney Bridge. It took but a few minutes at a quick pace to reach Robert and Annabel's fashionable townhouse in Laura Place.

The footman who answered his knock informed him that

both Mr. and Mrs. Stanton were at home. Intensely aware of the difficulties that lay before him, Simon bit back yet another curse as he followed the livery-clad servant up the stairs to the drawing room. Robert would be furious, of course, but the lad could be managed. Annabel was another matter entirely. She might be young, but she had a will of iron, and he had little doubt she would heartily disapprove of his plans for Sophie.

"The Earl of Trask," announced the footman.

Simon cast a glance around the small but well-appointed drawing room. Annabel and Robert sat side by side on a sofa next to the window. The midday sun streamed through the glass, bathing the couple in a cheerful glow and picking out bright strands of honey-colored hair in Annabel's locks. Robert had a book facedown in his lap, ignoring it in favor of assisting his pretty wife, who seemed to be struggling with a particularly recalcitrant piece of embroidery.

The air of contentment in the room was palpable and, given Simon's current mood, annoying.

"Simon, old fellow," Robert exclaimed as he jumped to his feet. "Never expected to have you come calling in the middle of the day. Didn't you mention last night that you might be going out of town? Some urgent business to attend to, wasn't it?"

Simon's mood went from grey to black.

"Yes, but I've had to put off my plans until I wrap up a few loose threads here in Bath. I hope to leave town by the end of the day."

"I'm sorry to hear that, my lord. We had hoped to see you tonight at dinner with your aunts," said Annabel.

Simon froze. She gave him one of her sweetest smiles and stretched out her hand. Shaking off his paralysis, he moved over to the sofa to acknowledge her greeting.

"The misfortune is mine, Mrs. Stanton," he replied, bowing over her slender fingers. "I, too, looked forward to seeing you."

"I know your aunts will miss you very much. Lady Eleanor is so rarely well enough to entertain. How unfortunate you can't delay your journey by a day."

Simon inwardly winced at the delicate but well-placed jab. Annabel was almost as relentless as Sophie when it came to nagging him about his duty to his aunts.

"Now, Bella," admonished Robert indulgently, "no need to scold. I'm sure Lady Eleanor has rung a massive peal over him already. It ain't like any man would ever want to go looking to disappoint the old battle—"

Annabel's eyes flashed a warning.

"Old girl," Robert amended hastily. "Unless he had to. You'd never hear the end of it. Ain't that right, Simon?"

Simon cleared his throat and gave a terse nod. *Hell.* He'd forgotten that his aunts would be hosting a small dinner party tonight. He resisted the urge to pull out his pocketbook and pencil, instead making a mental note to send formal regrets over to St. James's Square this afternoon.

Along with a large arrangement of Aunt Eleanor's favorite roses.

Annabel put away her embroidery. "Robert, shall we ring for tea? Or would you rather a port or a sherry, my lord?"

"Thank you, but no. I've come to see Robert on a matter of business. You'll forgive me, Mrs. Stanton, if I ask you to excuse us for a few minutes."

Robert's brows shot up into his hairline—understandable given that Simon made it a point never to discuss business with family or friends, save one or two exceptions. Robert was not one of those exceptions.

Oddly enough, Annabel didn't seem at all put out by his request. She gazed at him and then nodded, as if some particular question had just been answered.

"Of course, my lord. I look forward to seeing you again

when you return to Bath." She dropped him a quick curtsy, her eyes sparkling with something that looked suspiciously like laughter.

Simon waited until she had left the room before speaking. "Please sit, Robert. I've something very important to discuss with you."

The boy looked puzzled, but resumed his seat. Simon lowered himself into a delicate and remarkably uncomfortable Sheraton chair.

"Robert, I've come to ask your permission for Sophie's hand in marriage. I realize that approaching your mother and grandfather would be more appropriate, but I hope to expedite matters by speaking to you first."

Joy transformed the young man's wary features in an instant. He leapt to his feet.

"Capital, old fellow! Annabel was certain that's why you'd come to Bath. I thought she was talking flummery, but she'll be overjoyed to know she was right."

"Unfortunately, your congratulations are premature," Simon responded dryly. "While I appreciate your support, a few difficulties with your sister appear to have surfaced."

Robert looked at him blankly for a moment, but then sighed and sat back down. "Why does it not surprise me to hear that? Have you already asked her to marry you?"

"Yes. She accepted my proposal, although in what might be considered a less than graceful fashion."

Robert started to laugh, but hastily smothered his chuckles when Simon glared at him.

"I'm sorry to hear that, old man."

"In addition, she asked that we keep our betrothal secret, at least for the time being. Sophie apparently thinks she needs time to adjust to the notion of becoming my wife."

Robert frowned. "I don't like the idea of a secret betrothal.

She shouldn't be keeping it from her family, and neither should you."

Simon blinked. "Of course not. I tried to explain that very point to Sophie, but she wouldn't listen."

Robert eyed him. His guarded expression made him appear older than his years. "It ain't like Sophie to be so skittish, and everyone knows she's been mooning after you ever since . . . well, since forever. But she's been on the shelf for years now. Practically an ape leader, in fact."

Simon throttled back a sharp retort. Sophie had been out for several Seasons, but to think of her as an old maid was absurd.

"Perhaps she does need a little time to adjust to the idea," Robert mused. "After all, as Countess of Trask she'll be one of the most powerful leaders of the ton. That will be a change for her, especially since the old girl's more used to being on the receiving end of the dragon's breath, not being one of the dragons herself."

"Robert, I would be grateful if you would stop referring to Sophie as an *old girl*."

Robert ignored him. "I suppose that as long as Mamma and I know about the engagement, you can give her the time she needs to get used to the idea of marriage." His frown disappeared, replaced by a smile that made him look remarkably like Sophie.

"Unfortunately, time has run out. It's imperative that Sophie and I announce our betrothal immediately. I would like to post the banns this Sunday and marry in three weeks' time."

"Why the rush, Simon? Doesn't seem very sporting of you if Sophie isn't ready to do that."

Simon repressed a stab of something that felt uncomfortably like chagrin. "Because Sophie and I have been intimate, Robert. I certainly hope I don't have to explain to you what that means."

"What?" Robert roared—actually roared—and bounded to his feet. Simon had never once heard the lad raise his voice, but he should have expected it. Anytime Sophie was involved, things were bound to go to hell in a handcart.

"Calm down, Robert. Let me explain. You can take me out into the garden later and pound me into a bloody pulp, but right now we have to solve this problem and get Sophie to agree to marry me."

The boy glared at him, but subsided into his seat. He looked angrier than Simon had ever seen him. "Don't think I wouldn't, Simon, even though you outweigh me by two stone. That's my sister we're talking about, not some . . . well, you know exactly what I mean. She ain't one of your light-o'-loves, after all."

Simon felt a dull heat creep up from under his collar. "I know, Robert, and I sincerely apologize. The fault is entirely mine. You can believe I will do everything I must to make it right. Sophie is an innocent, and I ask you not to think less of her."

Robert grumbled something unflattering, but finally relented. "Of course I don't think any less of Sophie. But as for her being innocent of any wrongdoing, I saw how badly she was behaving last night, which is when I suppose, well . . . when *it* happened. Wanted to take her home myself, but Annabel wouldn't let me. Why the blasted girl decided to kick over the traces now is beyond me. God only knows what Mamma will have to say about this."

"I think it best we keep the details from your mother."

Robert eyed him uncertainly. "Well, given what happened between the two of you, why is Sophie dragging her feet? I would think she'd have the sense to realize that time is of the essence. Good God, if anyone found out, her reputation would be in tatters."

Simon hesitated. "I'm beginning to suspect she's not quite

sure of me. Or, rather, not quite sure why I asked her to marry me."

"Why *did* you ask her to marry you?" Robert blurted out. "Until yesterday, I was afraid you were going to marry that . . . I mean, I thought you were considering asking Lady Randolph to be your wife."

"Robert." Simon leaned forward in his chair, which creaked ominously beneath his weight. "There is nothing between Lady Randolph and myself. Sophie need never worry about that, or anything like it. I give you my word."

Robert gave a tiny nod, but his gaze remained wary. "You still haven't answered my question. Why are you marrying her?"

Simon had been debating with himself for the last hour how much to reveal to Robert. It was bad enough keeping secrets from Sophie, even though he did it to spare her feelings. But it didn't seem honorable to withhold the reasons from her older brother.

"My reasons are twofold," he began. As he explained the intricacies of his negotiations with Russell, a cloud of gloom settled over Robert's countenance. Simon felt the sting of guilt, but he pushed it away. Robert knew as well as anyone that marriages in the aristocracy were made to strengthen families and estates, not satisfy emotional whims. Still, he should reassure the boy.

"But that's not the only reason I want to marry Sophie," he said, meeting Robert's troubled gaze with a steady one of his own. "You know how fond I am of her. Nothing would make me happier than to care for her as she deserves to be cared for. I promise you she will be happy with me, and will never want for anything I can give her."

Robert shook his head, looking even gloomier. Simon forced himself to remain silent, surprised by how much he needed the boy to believe him.

"Fond, eh? I hope you didn't say that to her."

Simon flexed his fingers on the spindly arm of the chair. There were days when Robert tried his patience almost as much as Sophie did.

"Robert, you know as well as I that Sophie has an unfortunate knack for getting into a great deal of trouble. I suspect that will only get worse over time. Did you know she went to the workhouse in Avon Street looking for the boy who stole her reticule?"

Robert's eyes bugged out of their sockets. He started to sputter with outrage, but Simon cut him off.

"That's just the beginning. I won't bore you with the details. Suffice it to say that your sister is in desperate need of a husband to control her more wayward impulses. You know it, your mother knows it, and your grandparents know it, too."

"But—"

"I cherish Sophie. I always have, and I always will. She needs me, and you can't doubt that she loves me. Ours will be a happy marriage, and it will put an end to the restlessness that seems to have come over her. She can't be allowed to dwindle into an old maid. I simply won't allow it, and neither should you." Simon heard the determination in his own voice, realizing with a shock how much he meant it. He couldn't bear the thought of Sophie growing old, unhappy and alone.

Robert deflated as if someone had pricked him with a needle. "Blast you, of course you're right. And Annabel would seem to agree with you. But if you hurt her, Simon, in any way, I swear I'll kill you. I mean it."

Simon nodded. "I know. Sophie will be happy, Robert. I promise you."

Robert straightened up and tugged on the edges of his waistcoat. He looked at him with an air of expectancy, slipping easily into the familiar habit of relying on Simon to provide the answers to life's most vexing questions.

"Well, old man, I hope you have a plan, because Lord knows Sophie doesn't listen to me. Never has."

"I do have a plan. But we must—and I emphasize this, Robert—we must keep it from both Sophie and Annabel. Although my plan is entirely necessary, it's not something either of them will like."

Gloom settled over Robert's features once more. "Then why do I have the feeling I'm not going to like it either?"

Chapter Fifteen

Lord, what had she done now?

Sophie expelled a weary sigh. Lady Langton stared at her from behind a stack of novels, her rabbitlike nose twitching with scandalized excitement. Sophie had noticed a similar reaction from several other people she had encountered since she left the townhouse in St. James's Square immediately after breakfast.

She forced herself not to glare back at the plump baroness, shifting her attention to the impressive collection of history books in Mr. Barratt's circulating library on Bond Street. But the finely tooled markings on the leather spines faded into a gilded blur as her thoughts traveled once more to the cause of her troubles.

Simon.

Her stomach lurched south at the thought of her absent fiancé. He had sent a note two days ago informing her that he was leaving town on business but would return to Bath as soon as he could. Her first reaction had been outrage at his cavalier dismissal of both her and his aunts, who had expected him for dinner that evening. That surge of emotion had been followed by a guilty wash of relief. She wasn't ready to face him. Not yet. Not after how outrageously she had treated him in the Pump Room.

She squeezed her eyes shut in a vain attempt to block the images of that scene from her mind. But nothing could diminish the discomfort with her ploy to keep Simon at bay, or with his slack-jawed and then furious response to her refusal to acknowledge their earth-shattering intimacies.

Intimacies that had left their mark on her body and her soul. Intimacies that no sane woman would try to deny.

Her cheeks flamed with heat as she recalled the intoxicating strength of his muscular body, and how it had felt when he had pushed himself inside her. Her legs still grew weak at the memory. It meant she'd spent the last two days tottering around like an old lady, since their encounter on Lady Eleanor's settee was all she could seem to think about.

Every waking moment.

And every sleeping moment too. Dreams of Simon's hands stroking her skin and his mouth devouring her made her jerk awake each night, twisted in the sheets, her body drenched in sweat.

She clapped shut the *History of the Battle of Carthage* and shoved it back into its spot on the shelf. Enough was enough. She had spent more time thinking about Simon than he deserved. His disregard for her wishes had forced her into a distressing course of action, but it had been necessary. The sooner he learned he couldn't bully her, the better. If Simon wanted to marry her, he must learn to treat her with consideration and respect, not order her about as if she were a child.

Ignoring the stares of Lady Langton, who seemed entranced by her presence in the shop, Sophie continued her fruitless perusal of Mr. Barratt's shelves. Instead of wasting time thinking about Simon or looking at books, she should be devising a plan to help Toby and Becky. After all, they were the reason she had insisted on staying in town.

But how in heaven's name could she assist them? Simon had forbidden her to return to their father's tavern, and Becky had flatly refused her offer of help. Perhaps if she could discover the name of the children's aunt and where she lived in London, she could somehow find a way to get them there. But she would need someone to help her acquire that information, and the only person who might be able to do that— besides Simon—was Reverend Crawford.

Yes, he would do.

Nodding to herself with satisfaction, Sophie spun on her heel to head for the door. She gasped, jerking back to avoid a crash with a woman dressed in a red velvet pelisse and enveloped in a cloud of expensive perfume.

Lady Randolph had apparently appeared out of thin air, her fern-colored eyes smoldering with ill will.

"Good morning, Miss Stanton." Her ladyship's voice held enough venom to poison a small town.

Sophie righted herself and shoved her poke bonnet out of her eyes. "Good morning, Lady Randolph. How . . . er . . . pleasant to see you."

The woman's eyes shot flaming arrows at her.

"It must be a pleasant morning for you, my dear. Allow me to offer my congratulations on your most advantageous match. I'm sure Simon is pleased to be adding to his holdings in the north. He has been looking to buy land in Yorkshire for quite the longest time, and your dowry will no doubt provide him with what he has been searching for."

The air rushed from Sophie's lungs in an enormous whoosh. Time ground to a halt as she stared into Lady Randolph's perfect, rigid features.

"What are you talking about?" she finally blurted out.

The anger in Lady Randolph's eyes leached away as another equally unpleasant emotion took its place. The image of a barn cat about to leap on a mouse flashed through Sophie's brain.

"Why, your betrothal to Simon, Miss Stanton." A chilling smile touched the edges of the countess's red-tinted mouth. "I read the notice only this morning in the *Bath Chronicle*." Lady Randolph raised her arm to display a crumpled newspaper that she held in her sleekly gloved hand.

Sophie snatched the paper and rustled through the pages until she found the notice. Starkly laid out in black and white for the world to see was an announcement of the betrothal of Miss Sophia Stanton to the Earl of Trask.

"Of course, the ladies of the ton will surely regret the loss of so fine a man to the obligations of matrimony." Lady Randolph's silken voice seemed to come from far away.

Sophie blinked rapidly, then raised her eyes to encounter a gaze oozing with malice. A feeling of doom began to penetrate the shock that held her nailed to the floorboards. Suddenly, the whispered titters between Lady Langton and another woman in the library took on new meaning, as did a loud snort of laughter from a man on the other side of the room.

"But Simon is a man who rarely disappoints a woman, if I do say so myself," continued Lady Randolph. "I'm sure you'll soon learn to share him with the rest of us."

Sophie took a breath and met her rival's lethal gaze head-on.

"I'm sure I have no idea what you're talking about, my lady," she said. "I have several other errands to attend to. Good day to you."

She dropped the paper at Lady Randolph's feet as she stepped around her to pass through the door into Bond Street. It took every ounce of willpower to keep her spine stiff and her pace even as she passed the windows of Mr. Barratt's library. Her heart thundered in her chest, and her skin tingled with what she imagined were the avid gazes of people in the street.

Now everything was clear. The curious stares this morning. The whispers and the poorly concealed laughter. Simon had betrayed her. He had taken their secret and divulged it to the entire ton. He had laid bare his lack of trust, revealing how little respect he had for her.

And he had exposed her to a woman he knew despised her, and who quite possibly was still his mistress.

As Bond led into Milsom Street, she quickened her pace, her racing, angry heart driving her hard up the hill. By the time she reached the Circus, her pulse was beating drumlike through her limbs. If she hadn't been so breathless, she would have hiked up her skirts and run the rest of the way home.

A few minutes later she arrived in St. James's Square, flushed with exertion and panting with a fury that squeezed her chest. She pounded the knocker against the door, shifting from foot to foot until the footman let her in.

Yates emerged from a door at the back of the hall. "Good morning, miss."

Sophie yanked at the ribbons of her bonnet, desperate to relieve the pressure of the silk bands from under her chin. Fighting an odd feeling that threatened to overwhelm her, she ripped the hat from her head and thrust it at the butler.

"Has Lady Eleanor come down from her room?"

"Yes, miss. Her ladyship is in the gold drawing room with morning callers."

Sophie took a deep breath, hoping to calm her galloping heartbeat. "Who is here?"

"Lord Trask, and Mr. and Mrs. Stanton."

Robert. Thank God she didn't have to face Simon alone. Her brother, at least, would stand by her.

Sophie stood for a moment in the hall, willing her heart to slow and her limbs to cease trembling. She would need her wits about her to confront Simon. It would be appallingly difficult, given that she would have to explain to the others why she had wished to keep their engagement a secret from everyone, including their own families.

"Very good, Yates. I'll join them."

She marched up the stairs behind the butler. He tapped on the door and announced her before stepping aside to let her pass by into the brightly lit room. She blinked hard and adjusted her glasses, trying to focus her eyes after the dim light of the hall.

After a few seconds the dancing motes in her vision disappeared, and the figures of her family settled into their familiar shapes. Robert and Annabel sat together on the settee. Lady Eleanor was ensconced in her favourite wingback chair, and Lady Jane stood just behind her, one slender hand resting on her sister's shoulder. Warm October sunlight streamed through the windows, touching all their faces with a warm, comfortable glow.

All except one—a figure that stood backlit against the window, broad-shouldered, brutally masculine in its outline and almost menacing in its stillness.

Simon.

Lady Eleanor turned in her chair, her piercing eyes locking on Sophie.

"There you are. Please to come over and stand before me."

She resisted the impulse to move, raising her chin as she stared back at her godmother. "I thank you, ma'am, but I'm quite comfortable where I am."

The dark figure by the window shifted. Simon stepped forward, his handsome features thrown into relief now that he had stepped away from the shafting sunlight. Sophie's heart sank at the self-contained, even remote, expression on his face. Did he have no idea what he'd done to her?

"My dear, why don't you sit down?" His voice was gentle, but she heard the note of command.

"Thank you, no." Her words seemed to be scraping over broken stones as they fought their way out of her parched mouth.

He sighed. "My love, I simply wish us to talk. Your family wishes to talk to us, as well."

The brittle control inside her chest shattered. "How dare you call me that? How could you do this to me, Simon? You betrayed my trust. You've humiliated me before my friends and family. I'll never forgive you."

His dark brows shot up, and his cool reserve vanished in an instant. "Sophie, there's no need to resort to childish threats."

Robert shook his head. "That tears it," he muttered, shifting his gaze away in an obvious attempt to avoid her eye.

Sophie hesitated, unnerved by her brother's refusal to look at her. And was that a glare Annabel gave him? She never looked at Robert like that.

"Sophie." Simon's deep voice jerked her attention away from her family.

"What?" Even to her own ears, her voice sounded sullen.

His gaze turned flinty. "Don't be rude, my dear. It doesn't become you."

Her temper flared. "Why shouldn't I be rude? You're the one who said I was childish. Perhaps you'd like to lock me in my room without any supper."

A muscle pulsed in his jaw. He took another step forward.

"Enough, Simon." Lady Eleanor's voice rapped through the room. "Sophia, please come over here right now."

There was no point in disobeying. She cast another furious glance at Simon before moving to stand in front of her godmother. Her muscles ached from the mad dash home and the strain of holding herself so rigidly.

"Now, goddaughter, perhaps you would like to explain why you insisted on keeping your engagement to my nephew a secret? Surely there is no shame in a betrothal to the Earl of Trask?"

"My reasons are my business, Lady Eleanor," she said, suddenly deciding she didn't need to explain herself to anyone. "Simon promised to respect those reasons. Since he broke his promise, I see no reason to tell anyone else."

"Sophia Stanton, how dare you speak to me in such an impertinent fashion? What would your dear mother say?" huffed Lady Eleanor. Lady Jane stirred from her motionless stance behind her sister and directed a warning frown at Sophie.

"Come on, Soph. No need to get all starchy. Tell me what the problem is," Robert interjected in a wheedling tone. "Maybe I can help."

Sophie whipped around. If she didn't know better, she would think her brother was hiding something. She hadn't seen him looking this guilty since the time he accidentally smashed her glass unicorn when he was twelve years old.

"The problem, Robert, is that my *betrothed*," she invested the word with as much sarcasm as she could muster, "seems to think I'm a child he can order about willy-nilly. He has no respect for me, nor does he trust my judgment. That doesn't bode well for a marriage."

"Perhaps I would trust you more if you acted like a sensible woman instead of a petulant child," Simon retorted.

"And perhaps I would trust *you* if you wouldn't lie about why you really want to get married, or lie about your mistress." The words flew past her lips before she could stop them.

A silence so thick she could almost feel it on her skin fell on the room. Lady Eleanor gaped at her, struck dumb, probably for the first time in her life.

"Sophia." Simon's voice dropped almost to a whisper, but the menacing growl was more disturbing than a shout. Sophie turned away from her godmother to meet his obsidian gaze, shivering at the dark warning that struck her like a blow. "We talked about this."

For a long moment they stared at each other. Sophie felt the struggle between their wills on a soul-deep level—a struggle as dangerous, as powerful, and as intensely intimate as their lovemaking had been. Simon's eyes flared with a different kind of heat as a flush crawled up her neck.

The image of Lady Randolph's beautiful, spiteful face leapt into her mind. Did Simon look at the countess the way he was looking at her right now?

Sophie shook free of her paralysis. "Do you know how I found out about the announcement in the paper?"

He frowned, the wary look returning to his face. "I came to see you right after breakfast, but you had—"

"The countess," she blurted out. "Countess Randolph told me. In Barratt's. In front of everyone."

His dark eyes filled with pity and regret. Bile rose in her throat at the sight, and she knew in that moment everything she feared was true.

"Sophie." His voice was unbearably gentle.

"How could you tell your mistress, Simon? How could you tell your mistress before you told me? Did you plan this with her?"

She could hear a shocked gasp coming from Lady Jane.

"That's enough, Sophia Stanton," Lady Eleanor barked. "If I didn't know better, I would think you had gone mad. What Simon does with other women is his business, not yours. You are not to ask of such things."

"Aunt Eleanor, would you—"

Lady Eleanor cut Simon off. "Be quiet. You and Sophia have made a herculean mess of this situation, which I am now obligated to clean up. I will not have either the St. James name or the Stanton name dragged through the muck."

She directed a stern gaze at Sophie. "Sophia, you should be grateful that Simon has asked for your hand in marriage. Both families have desired this for years, and both will benefit greatly from the union. General Stanton and Simon's grandfather planned this marriage while you were still in the cradle, as you well know, and you will bring honor to all of us by this match."

Lady Eleanor's words fell like a death blow upon Sophie's heart. How could she have imagined Simon might actually love her?

"Thank you for your help, Aunt Eleanor," Simon interjected in a dry voice. "I'm sure Sophie understands everything now."

Sophie pivoted on her heel to gaze at him. "Why do you want to marry me, Simon? Tell the truth."

He winced. She was stunned to see a dull red creep across his cheekbones.

"Puck, it might be better if we talk about this alone."

She couldn't bear his gentle tone or his endearments. "Why should we speak alone? After all, we're not building a family, we're building a dynasty. Why shouldn't the whole family be part of this discussion? This is a business matter, isn't it? It's my dowry you want, not me."

Something flashed across his face. If she hadn't been looking straight at him she would have missed it, since his usual reserved expression fell back into place instantly.

"Don't be ridiculous. I've already told you why I want to marry you."

She felt the walls of her carefully constructed world come tumbling down. She knew now they had been built on shoddy, self-indulgent stories she had told herself since she was a little girl—foolish, romantic lies.

"I won't do it." She choked on the words. "I will not be a pawn. I will not be a sacrifice on the altar of your ambitions."

He jerked back as if she had slapped him.

"Sophie, for God's sake." He shoved his hand through his thick hair in a gesture of frustration.

"Really, Sophia, you are most dramatic." Lady Eleanor had

obviously decided to launch back into the fray. "It's time you gave up your sentimental notions about life. You could learn from the example of your fiancé. Simon relinquished that kind of foolishness years ago to do his duty by his family."

Sophie could actually hear Simon grind his teeth. He looked like he wanted to throttle every person in the room, including her.

"Sophie." Robert sounded desperate.

She slowly turned to look at him. He had been so quiet these last few minutes she had almost forgotten he was in the room. Why wasn't her brother coming to her aid?

"Robert, you understand, don't you? I won't settle for less than what you and Annabel have. I can't." Sophie felt moisture trickle down her cheeks. She rubbed it away with an impatient hand—she had no time to waste on tears.

"Of course you can't, dearest." Annabel's voice quivered with emotion. "Nor should you."

Robert rolled his eyes at his wife before returning his gaze to Sophie.

"You won't be settling for anything, sis. You'll be the Countess of Trask." Her brother was pleading with her now. "We did this for your own good, Soph. Can't you see that? You can't rattle around forever like an old tabby. Besides—"

Don't! Don't say it. She waited for the blade to fall.

"Besides," continued her brother, "you love Simon. Everybody knows that."

Sophie dimly heard Simon utter a curse. Finally, the enormity of her family's betrayal swept through her veins like a tide driven by a winter storm. Blinking back a few useless tears, she turned her back on Robert and made her way to the door. She stopped when she came level with Simon.

"I'd rather be a spinster for the rest of my days than married to a man who cares more for his estates and for his mistress than he cares for me." Sophie looked up and met Simon's pitch-black eyes. They blazed with an emotion she couldn't begin to understand. His hand convulsed as if he might reach for her, but instead he clamped his arm back to his side.

"My lord, I thank you for the honor of your proposal, but I consider our engagement to be at an end."

Chapter Sixteen

Sophie gulped several times, waiting for the choking feeling in her throat to subside before staggering over to a rosewood chair against the wall. Fleeing to her bedroom may have been the coward's way out, but the look of pity on Simon's face had made her stomach churn with nausea. She'd had to get out of the drawing room, and quickly.

Slumping down into the brocaded seat, she let her bleary gaze wander about the room. She took in the pretty Chinese wallpaper and the beautiful Chippendale bed with its carved, pagoda-style canopy. She had always felt like a princess whenever she snuggled beneath the bed's quilted silk and fine linens, staring up at the ornate mahogany canopy as she weaved happy daydreams about her future.

But that happiness had withered today in the stark light of Simon's and her family's betrayal. Her daydreams had been burned away, and nothing would ever be the same.

A quiet knock sounded at her door, but she couldn't bring herself to answer. Why couldn't they just leave her alone?

A moment later the door swung open.

"May Annabel and I come in?" asked Lady Jane.

She nodded, not yet able to find her voice.

The older woman swiftly crossed the room and dropped to her knees beside the chair, enveloping her in a lavender-tinged embrace.

"Come, darling. All is not as bleak as it seems." She stroked a cool, soft hand across Sophie's face.

"Goodness, you're so pale. I won't permit you to worry yourself into a decline, my love. Simon and Robert have acted very improperly, but I'm sure all will come out right in the end." Lady Jane gave her an encouraging smile.

The burn in Sophie's throat grew worse. How could they all be so blind?

"I won't marry him, my lady. Even if he is your nephew. Even if everyone wants me to. I just can't." That sickening pressure squeezed her windpipe once more, reducing her words to a croak.

Annabel plumped down on the floor in a swirl of peach-colored cambric. She took Sophie's cold hands between her own and began to chafe the warmth back into them.

"Of course you mustn't, darling. Not if you don't want to. No one can make you do anything." A scowl settled over her delicate features, making her look almost fierce. "Simon and Robert acted most disgracefully, and I promise you that your brother will know exactly how unacceptable his behaviour is by the end of the day."

If she hadn't felt so awful, Sophie would have laughed at the severe tone in her sister-in-law's voice. Annabel was several years younger than her husband, but she could make him quake in his hessians. Of course, she wouldn't stay mad at Robert for long. As soon as he gave her one of his mooncalf looks of adoration, she would forgive him.

Simon would never love her like that, and she would likely spend the rest of her days ramming her heart against the barricade he had built around his emotions.

A shiver skated down her spine as she foresaw an uncertain

future as the Countess of Trask. That part of loving Simon had always troubled her—that part she had never wished for. Now the role seemed an even greater burden. If she married him, she would become the chatelaine of several noble estates, a leading hostess of the ton, and likely a mother—but never the cherished wife of the man she had the misfortune to love to distraction. So many obligations, and for what?

She looked into Annabel's solemn face. "You understand, Belle, don't you? Why I had to say no? It's not me that he wants, it's my dowry. That's all he cares about."

Annabel nodded. "I agree that announcing your betrothal without your permission was foolish and arrogant, and I hope you box his ears for it. But he did it to protect you, Sophie, because he cares for you so much."

"The way he cares for Lady Randolph?" she retorted.

"Sophie," Lady Jane broke in. "I would swear on my life that Simon is not conducting an affair with that woman."

A pulse of anger shot through her chest. "You weren't in the bookstore, my lady. I was. I can assure you—"

Her godmother cut her off with a chop of her hand. "I can't speak for his previous behaviour, but I'm certain whatever happened between my nephew and Lady Randolph is at an end, and has been for quite some time. You mustn't allow that to influence your decision. Only your feelings for Simon—and his for you—should be of relevance in this situation."

Annabel leaned on the arm of the rosewood chair. She stared earnestly into Sophie's eyes.

"Lady Jane is right. Robert would never have agreed to the proposal if he thought Simon was not finished with Lady Randolph. I'm certain of it."

Sophie's mouth gaped open as she absorbed that bit of information. "Simon asked my brother's permission to marry me? You mean Robert knew about the announcement in the *Chronicle* even before this morning?"

Annabel began to look annoyed. "Yes, it was very bad of
them. We're agreed upon that. But when Robert admitted to
me this morning what he had done, I questioned him closely.
I'm certain, as is Robert, that Simon wants to marry you pri-
marily for the right reasons—because he feels deeply for you,
and wants to care for you."

Sophie couldn't help but notice Annabel had avoided
saying he loved her. The knowledge twisted like a rusty blade
in her gut.

"Oh, yes, I'm sure he cares a great deal for me. According
to Lady Randolph, he cares a great deal for the estate in Yorkshire that Grandpapa added to my dowry this year." Sophie
no longer cared if she sounded as bitter as she felt.

Lady Jane made an impatient sound and rose to her feet.
"Sophia Stanton, Lady Randolph is a manipulative bitch."

Annabel's rosebud mouth dropped open with shock at the
unexpected profanity. Sophie knew just how she felt. She
doubted anyone had ever heard Lady Jane utter a vulgar word
in her entire life.

"My lady—" Sophie had to choke back a laugh that was
partly a sob.

"No, really, Sophie," her godmother ruthlessly interrupted
her. "Only a fool would allow her future to be determined by
one who bears her such ill will. And I know you're not a fool."

"No," Sophie muttered, pressing her fingertips to her throbbing temples. "My future will be determined by a man who only
sees me as a commodity that will enrich his financial empire."

Lady Jane closed her eyes, seeming to withdraw into herself for a long moment. When she opened them again, her
godmother's normally mild gaze filled with sadness. The
older woman seemed to be wrestling with some kind of
painful question.

"I know that's not true, my dear," Lady Jane said. "Simon

loves you. Surely you haven't forgotten how he cared for you after your father died?"

The knife twisted again. Sophie half expected to look down and see blood flowing from a wound in her abdomen.

Her father's unexpected death from a fever had nearly destroyed her entire family. Her mother had succumbed to a spell of profound melancholy that lasted for months. Robert had tried to console both mother and sister, but he had been little more than a boy himself. And in all too short a time Grandpapa Stanton—grief-stricken at the loss of his only son—had sent Robert back to school, deeming that a return to normal life was the best course of action for his new heir.

After her brother's departure Sophie had tumbled into a bewildered panic, wandering the empty, black-shrouded rooms of their townhouse, finding comfort only in the arms of her grandmamma, Lady Stanton.

And in Simon's arms, as well.

He had come down often from Cambridge during those bleak months, enveloping her in fierce hugs before whisking her away in his curricle for long rides outside the city. He spent hours with her, allowing her to hold the reins while he told one silly story after another in an effort to make her laugh. In his company, she could forget the terrifying void her father's death had created deep within her. Simon had drawn her back to the world of the living. He had eased her pain and tempered the fear of death that haunted her childish dreams. He had made her feel safe again.

"Ah . . . you do remember."

Lady Jane's murmur broke into her thoughts. Sophie pushed the image of that strong but affectionate young man as far from her mind as she could. She stood, slipped around Annabel, and began to pace the room. Her godmother's steady gaze followed her.

"Yes, I remember," Sophie replied, her voice brittle and

much too high. "But he's changed, and I don't think he can go back." She had never thought she'd feel anything equal to the wrenching loss of her father, but Simon's act of betrayal threatened to pitch her headlong into that place of raw vulnerability once again.

Lady Jane nodded. "He's a man, with a man's responsibilities. But I believe that, deep down, he is the same as he always was. He's been caring for you almost since the day you were born. You must remember—"

"No!" Sophie jerked to a halt in front of a window that looked out over the small garden, faded to the color of burnt almond now that the chill of autumn had arrived. "I don't want to remember anymore. There's no point. I have to make my decisions based on how he treats me now."

"Memory is the receptacle of life, dear child. Without it, we are nothing." Lady Jane's voice was full of compassion.

Sophie gripped the polished wood of the window frame, resisting the gentle pull of her godmother's words. "I will not allow myself to love a man who treats me with so little respect . . . who treats me as if I were a child, unable to make decisions for herself."

She heard the defiant note in her voice, but she didn't care. Sophie couldn't marry a man who thought so little of her, no matter what her family wanted.

Lady Jane sighed, and Annabel slumped down on the floor once more, leaning against the chair leg in weary resignation.

"And I thought Simon was stubborn," Annabel said with a huffy little growl.

Sophie shrugged. An awkward silence fell over the room, but she felt no compunction to break it. Eventually, her godmother joined her at the window as she stared out into the lifeless garden.

"Sophie, did you know I was once engaged to be married?"

Sophie blinked, surprised by the revelation.

"Richard was the most wonderful man in the world. It was many years ago, of course," her godmother said in a soft voice. "I was nineteen, and was thought to be one of the prettiest girls out on the town that Season. He was the second son of a viscount. I met him here, in Bath, where his father had sent him to take the waters. Richard was quite frail, you see, and had been ever since he was a little boy. He suffered greatly—"

Lady Jane broke off. Sophie forced herself to remain motionless, to not say a word or ask a question.

"But he had the heart and soul of a lion, and he loved me passionately," the older woman continued. "He was determined to marry me, though his doctors were quite certain he wouldn't live to see five and twenty. His father feared for him, but he saw how much we loved each other and didn't stand in the way of our betrothal. I always thought he hoped our marriage would give Richard something to live for."

A gentle melancholy descended on Lady Jane's features, as if the old sorrow had been filtered through a cool October mist.

"What happened?" Sophie whispered, her heart already breaking with the answer.

"He died one week before our wedding," she replied as a bittersweet smile touched her mouth. "He passed in his sleep, a few hours after a small dinner party to celebrate our betrothal. He was so happy that night, and I have always been grateful that he left this world with a heart full of love and contentment."

"Oh, my lady, I'm so sorry." Sophie's chest ached with the weight of her godmother's old sorrow, which somehow seemed bound up with her own.

Lady Jane ignored her, lost in her memories. "Eleanor wanted us to leave Bath, but I couldn't. Though I was surrounded by reminders of him everywhere—at church, in the Assembly Rooms, where we used to walk together in the Orange Grove—I couldn't leave. I was too afraid I would forget his dear face, his precious voice, if I didn't have the images of our time together all around me."

She looked at Sophie, her eyes blazing with stark intensity.

"Did you think this was the life I wished for, Sophie? A spinster's life? Without children to love, or a husband to cherish me? Did you think this was the life that Eleanor wanted? She gave up everything for me. And here we are—two lonely old women who cling to each other for comfort."

"But you were young." Annabel's voice cracked with emotion. "Surely there were other suitors who courted you. Why did you never marry?"

Lady Jane glanced at Annabel, her misty blue eyes dark with pain.

"There was only ever him for me, my dear. I think you know how that feels, don't you?"

Annabel nodded.

Lady Jane looked back at Sophie, her gaze no longer gentle. Her expression grew stern.

"As there is only one man for you, Sophie, and you know it. I've seen how you look at Simon. How you are with him. He's the only one in the world for you, and if you relinquish him you'll surely end up like me."

A bolt of panic streaked through her, but Sophie refused to concede defeat. "What's wrong with being like you? You're happy, aren't you?"

"I've learned to be happy, yes. But I've never felt joy again."

Sophie pushed against the old grief and sorrow. Her godmother's loss had been tragic, but her betrothed had loved her with all his heart. What could Simon give her but a life of small and ordinary misery, unchanged from day to day?

"Joy hurts," she whispered, feeling as brittle as Venetian glass.

"Life hurts, my dear," replied Lady Jane in a suddenly brisk voice. "That was a lesson you were forced to learn at a very young age. I'm sorry to say there is another difficult lesson you must learn today. One of self-discipline."

The older woman turned Sophie by the shoulders to look at her. Her mouth compressed into a surprisingly stern line.

"Eleanor was correct. Scandal would surely result from the sudden dissolution of your engagement to Simon. If you won't think of yourself, then you must think of your family. You will not break your engagement to my nephew, at least not immediately. If, after a respectable period of time, you cannot bring yourself to marry him, then you will act as you see fit. Until such time, I expect you to behave with dignity and consideration, both to Simon and to the rest of us."

Annabel scrambled up from the floor and hurried over to join them.

"Sophie, dearest, please give Simon another chance. I'm sure he never meant to hurt you—he's just a silly man. They don't really know how to behave properly. After all, look at Robert."

Her sister-in-law's winsome smile pierced the angry shield Sophie had erected around her heart.

"I know Simon cares for you above all others," Annabel said, laying her small hand on Sophie's arm. "Let him prove it to you."

Sophie looked miserably at her godmother. Lady Jane hesitated, then delivered the final thrust of the blade.

"Think of your mother, my dear. And the general."

Sophie's resistance collapsed. Her mother and grandfather would be devastated by her rejection of Simon, and by the resultant scandal. As much as she wanted to, she knew it was pointless to resist the combined efforts and the anxious concern of the Stanton and the St. James families. No matter what her relatives might think, she had as keen an appreciation for the families' reputations as they did. She didn't fear scandal—like Simon did—but she wouldn't court it, either.

Sophie bowed her head in silent submission, though she

knew her heart would never recover from the blow. Despite what Annabel said, Simon would never be the man she needed. He would never be the man she had fallen in love with all those years ago. She'd been a fool, a blind, sentimental fool, to believe he was.

As Sophie followed her godmother and Annabel from the room, she vowed she would never be a fool again.

Chapter Seventeen

Simon paid off the hackney driver, hunching his shoulders against the rain that hissed down in ash-colored streamers to the broken cobblestones. Ice water dripped from his hat and seeped under the collar of his greatcoat.

Avon Street was a hellhole at the best of times, but on a wet October day it had to be one of the grimmest corners of the kingdom.

Almost as grim as his mood.

The chill that leached through his coat failed to cool the heat of his anger—anger with his blasted relations, but mostly with himself for mishandling such a delicate situation. Posting the betrothal notice in the *Chronicle* had been a colossal mistake, but what else could he have done to bring Sophie under control?

That question had plagued him from the moment she stormed out of Aunt Eleanor's drawing room until now, when he found himself standing outside The Silver Oak. Given how devastated she had been—he still winced when he recalled the look of anguish in her eyes that even her spectacles couldn't hide—he counted himself lucky she was still his fiancée.

He'd spent the longest hour of his life waiting in the drawing room after Aunt Jane and Annabel followed Sophie upstairs to her bedroom. Aunt Eleanor had delivered a scathing lecture on the idiocy of men in general and of Simon and Robert in particular. After a short-lived attempt to defend himself, Robert had subsided into a miserable silence, relieving his wounded pride by casting resentful glares across the room at his coconspirator.

Simon hadn't bothered to respond to his aunt's accusations. After all, she was correct.

After an eon, Aunt Jane had finally returned with the news that Sophie had agreed to honor their engagement. His relief had been short-lived. Aunt Jane had tartly added that Sophie's acquiescence had everything to do with her wish to avoid a scandal, and not with a desire to marry Simon.

Shrugging off his lingering guilt over the morning's events, Simon stepped under the sheltering porch of the tavern. He pulled off his sodden beaver hat, flicked the water from the brim, and absently put it back on his head.

The problem, of course, was that Sophie no longer trusted him. Her irrational female brain had convinced her he was still involved with Bathsheba. How Sophie could ever imagine he would treat her so dishonorably was beyond his comprehension.

He reached for the door of the tavern, guilt bleeding through him once more as he thought of the pain she had made no effort to conceal. Yes, dammit, he wanted her dowry. But he wanted her, too—every soft, sweet inch of her. His need to claim her in the most elemental way possible was fast becoming a compulsion that threatened to consume every logical thought in his brain. How Puck had managed to blow all his careful formulations to smithereens was something he still couldn't fathom. Well, if she needed proof that he cared for her then prove it he would, and in a way she couldn't possibly deny.

He pushed through the battered oak door into the foul-smelling tavern. Even though the street had been dark and dreary, the light was so poor he had to strain to make out the shapes before him. A small fire emitted greasy smoke from a dirty hearth. Cheap tallow candles and a few battered lanterns provided a fitful glow that struggled to reach into the dank corners.

In the late afternoon, the tavern was half full of dockworkers seeking shelter from the rain and warmth from a dram of blue ruin. The sound of rough voices and harsh laughter faded as the men turned, one by one, to study him.

Simon ignored the wary inspection as he threaded his way between the tables and benches to the rough-hewn bar at the opposite side of the room. He deliberately dropped his wet hat on the scarred wood of the bar, brushing the rain from his shoulders before meeting the eyes of the barkeep. He knew Taylor by sight, and he looked every inch as ugly as his reputation.

Taylor was a big man, broad-featured with an openly hostile gaze. Simon frowned, taking in his fine wool coat, expertly tied cravat, and large, pearl-headed stickpin nestling in folds of crisp linen. Toby and Becky had been dressed in near-rags, but from his clothes it was clear the owner of The Silver Oak had another source of income besides the meager wages of the local dockhands.

He returned Taylor's hostile regard with a steady silence, allowing a brief smile to lift the corners of his mouth. A charged minute ticked by as the two men stared at each other. Finally, Taylor snorted in disdain and reached for a glass under the bar.

"What'll it be, guv? Fancy a bit of daffy to chase away the cold?"

"I'll take a pint of heavy wet." Simon extracted a coin from inside his coat and tossed it onto the bar.

Taylor pocketed the coin with a massive fist before turning away to pour a tankard of cloudy-looking stout. He slammed the pint down on the counter, allowing the liquid to slosh onto the bar.

"Quality don't usually do their drinking at The Silver Oak, guv. At least not so early in the day. Lost your way?"

Simon tossed back a large swallow of the bitter liquid before answering. "I have business with you, Taylor."

"Do tell," he sneered, lips curling back from a surprisingly good set of teeth. "And who might you be that you have business with Jem Taylor?"

"I'm the Earl of Trask."

Taylor's brows shot up as his sneer slid into a crafty grin. "Ah! Pleased to meet you, my lord. Everyone in Bath knows of the Earl of Trask. Never thought to see you in my humble little tavern, though. How can I be of service?"

Before Simon could answer, a door next to the bar swung open, and Becky emerged, carefully balancing steaming bowls of food on a heavy-looking tray. He watched as she served the men, her slender form moving between tables with an unconscious yet seductive grace. She was only a child, but her beauty drew forth lewd comments and foul leers in her wake. Becky tried to ignore them, but her stiff shoulders and tight face gave away her distress as she hurried to complete her tasks.

He bit back a curse. No wonder Sophie wanted to rescue her. Right now Simon would have enjoyed nothing more than to beat every man in the room into a bloody pulp. Something about Becky—her innocence, perhaps—reminded him of Sophie at that age, and the thought of Puck subjected to such degradation made him want to punch something.

As Becky walked past, her tray now loaded with empty glasses, she looked up and met his eyes. She gasped and jerked to a halt, the tray wobbling in her hands, the glasses beginning a precipitous slide toward the floor. Simon grabbed the tray and steadied it.

"Careful, child." He smiled at her, plucking the tray from her trembling hands and placing it on the bar.

Becky stared at him with huge eyes, seemingly struck dumb with terror. Simon turned back to the bar, hoping his apparent indifference would calm the girl and prevent suspicion on her father's part.

But as he caught the calculating look on Taylor's face, he knew he'd failed. He practically growled, lamenting his lack of discipline. He had planned only to make a general inquiry about Toby's well-being, in the guise of a charitable man who had been dismayed by the boy's wretched condition. The last thing he intended was to signal a particular interest in either child, for that could very well bring the father's wrath down upon their heads.

Simon slid his half-empty tankard across the bar and raised a bored eyebrow at Taylor. Becky reached a stealthy hand for her tray and began to creep past him toward the kitchen door.

"Stop." The father growled the command at his daughter. She froze, then slowly turned around.

"M'lord. I'd like you to meet my daughter," Taylor said.

Simon moved languidly to face the girl, resting his elbow on the bar, schooling his face to indifference.

Becky gripped the tray with shaking hands, and even in the dim light of the tavern Simon could see the smoothness of her face turn ashen.

"Becky, this here is the Earl of Trask. Make a proper curtsy to his lordship, now. Just like your ma taught you."

Becky placed the tray on the bar, took her grimy skirt in her hands, and made a graceful curtsy. Thick black hair curled around her face, trailing down to gently curving breasts as she bowed forward. Her loose-fitting shirt gaped open, revealing creamy, perfect skin. Every man in the tavern was riveted by the sight, and Simon damn well couldn't blame them. He had never seen a girl as beautiful or as terrifyingly vulnerable as Becky.

"Say hello to his lordship." Evil intent breathed through Taylor's quiet order.

Becky rose from her curtsy and fastened wide pleading eyes on Simon. "Good day, your lordship."

"Child." He kept his voice bored and remote, but he knew he had already lost the battle.

Her father gave a jerk of the hand. "All right, girl. Back to the kitchen with you."

Becky snatched her tray and fled to safety.

"She's a right beauty, that one. Takes after her ma." There was a strange, fierce pride in Taylor's voice as he gazed after his daughter's retreating figure. "She'll do well by me, I'll see to that."

The nape of Simon's neck prickled at the tone of ruthless greed in the man's voice. When Sophie had told him that Taylor wanted to sell his daughter to the highest bidder, he had dismissed it as a tale cut from whole cloth—a story invented by a frightened boy to extract money from a soft-hearted lady. He no longer doubted a single word.

"About that business of yours, m'lord," said Taylor. "Maybe I can guess what you be lookin' for in The Silver Oak."

"I doubt it."

The other man grinned, clearly undeterred by Simon's deliberately arrogant manner. Taylor leaned across the bar and spoke in a confiding voice.

"Everyone knows your reputation with the ladies, m'lord."

"Careful, Taylor."

The man shrugged. "Bath is a small town. There be no secrets here. And it's no secret that you keep only the best. My Becky is the greatest beauty this town has seen in years, and she ain't no trollop, neither. Her ma saw to that. She'll be worth every penny to the lucky man who spreads her thighs."

Simon dropped his hand off the bar and clenched it into a fist. There was little about the world that surprised him anymore, but Taylor's callous dissection of his daughter's future would shock the most hardened jade.

Mistaking his silence for acquiescence, Taylor forged ahead.

"And, she's a virgin. I've seen to that, m'lord. Aye, he'll be a lucky man who takes his pleasure with her the first time. And I'm suspecting you might be that man, your lordship. For the right price."

Simon expelled a hard breath. A slaughtering fury swept through him, every muscle in his body hardening in preparation for a fight. In that moment, he wanted nothing more than to kill the man, if only the law wouldn't hang him for it. But it wouldn't help Becky and Toby. Without a father, their fate would likely be even worse.

That murderous intention must have been writ large on Simon's face, for Taylor jerked back, knocking over the tankard of stout. He stepped away from the bar.

"What do you want from me?" he snarled.

Simon rested a leather-gloved fist on the bar.

"I want you to listen to me. And do not dare to question or doubt what I say."

Taylor began to grope for something under the bar, but paused when Simon narrowed his eyes at him.

"Try it and you're a dead man." He gave Taylor his most lethal smile. "In fact, try anything and you're a dead man. That includes your plans for your daughter. She has my interest now, and if word ever reaches me that you've harmed her, I won't bother to go to the magistrate. And if you try to prostitute her, I'll close the Oak down in a heartbeat. As you say, the girl deserves better."

Taylor's face had turned a bruised-looking shade of purple. He was snorting like a wounded boar, but he didn't reply to Simon's threat. He didn't have to—Simon knew exactly what he was thinking.

"Yes, I know," he continued. "You would like to kill me.

That would be unwise, however, since my servants know exactly where I am. Heed my words, Taylor. I'll be watching."

He retrieved his hat from the bar, turned on his heel, and made his way leisurely to the door. Silence followed in his wake. Silence, and a sullen resentment, more telling and more deadly than any shout of anger.

He stepped outside and turned his face to the rain that sleeted down in icy prickles. After the noxious atmosphere of the tavern, even the soot-filled air of Avon Street seemed clean by comparison.

"My lord." A breathy whisper reached his ears. He recognized the voice instantly. *Toby*.

The boy tugged at his forelock before flitting into the dank alley past The Silver Oak. Casting a quick glance around, Simon strode after him.

Toby crouched behind a pile of filth and old crates, all but hidden by the shadows of the looming walls on either side of the alley. He beckoned Simon closer.

"You didn't tell, my lord, did you?" The lad's voice was thin with fear.

He reached out and gently rubbed some dirt from Toby's cheek. The boy flinched. Simon clenched his teeth against the urge to return to the tavern and give Taylor the beating he deserved. That kind of impulse, however, would serve no purpose. The man had a legal right to his children, and unless Simon could prove some grievous harm there was little he could do to protect them.

He extracted a guinea from his pocket and wrapped the boy's dirty little paw around it. Toby's eyes grew almost as round as the coin.

"Toby, I'm staying in lodgings in Milsom Street." Simon gave him the address. "If ever you need me, if ever your sister needs me, go there. Ask for me, or for my secretary, Mr. Soames. I will tell the porter to be on the lookout for you."

Toby inhaled a wavering breath and met his gaze. A look of cautious trust crept into his pale blue eyes and he bobbed his head in agreement.

He touched the boy's cheek once more, then spun on his heel and stalked from the alley. As he turned his face into the cleansing rain, he ruefully acknowledged that Sophie had been right again.

Chapter Eighteen

Sophie leaned back in her chair, enjoying the spectacle of Robert defending himself to his irate wife.

"Blast it, Annabel, why would I want to dance with Lady Hume?" he exclaimed, casting a furtive look at the rotund baroness as she stomped around her crowded drawing room.

Annabel gave him a steely-eyed glare. "Because she is your hostess and one of your mother's oldest friends."

If Sophie hadn't been so angry with Robert, she would have laughed out loud at the hangdog expression on his face. But since she was still furious with him, she hoped Annabel would make him dance with every bilious old woman in Bath. And hoped his feet got thoroughly trod upon in the process.

"She'll natter on forever about her beastly grandchildren," he implored. "The woman is a menace, Belle. Honestly."

Annabel simply narrowed her eyes. Robert made one last desperate appeal. "Besides, you know her breath is like the inside of an old boot. It's enough to drive a fellow to Bedlam."

His wife responded with an impatient tap of her foot, the silver beadwork on her slipper reflecting the light from the nearby sconce.

"Oh, all right." Robert glared at Sophie. "I hope you know this is your fault, sis."

She repressed the urge to stick her tongue out, instead giving her brother a sugary-sweet smile. He muttered a few choice words about sisters before stomping off to meet his doom.

"Finally," breathed Annabel. "I thought he would never leave. He's been trying to explain away his outrageous behaviour all day, and I just won't have it."

She leaned forward on the edge of her chair and inspected Sophie's face. "How are you feeling, dearest?"

They sat in relative obscurity in the far corner of Sir Geoffrey Hume's elegant, Chinese-inspired drawing room. Most of the other guests had bunched together at the opposite end of the room, outside the double doors of the adjoining saloon, where a small orchestra played country dances and the occasional waltz.

Invitations to Sir Geoffrey's private balls were highly coveted in Bath. His champagne was excellent, the food superb, and the company refined. Sophie would have enjoyed visiting the sumptuously decorated townhouse in Sydney Place if her world hadn't come crashing down earlier in the day.

She gave a slight grimace. "I'll survive, Belle, I promise."

Annabel heaved a sigh. "It's so lowering to realize men can be such idiots. I thought better of Robert—and of Simon. Perhaps it's best not to expect too much of them. That way one is bound not to be so disappointed." She smiled encouragement at Sophie, as if her madcap logic actually made sense.

Sophie rolled her eyes at her.

Annabel sighed again. "I know. I wish I could say something that would make this horrible day go away."

"Well, you can't," Sophie replied.

It was all she could do to get the words past the lump in her throat. Annabel's sympathy somehow made everything seem worse. Her sister-in-law only meant to help, but Sophie was sick to death of thinking about Simon and the farce of her engagement. It was bad enough that she had to drag herself out to parties, worse that she had to accept the astonished congratulations that came with her altered state, and worse yet that she had to pretend to be happy about it. Even her teeth ached from the false smile she had plastered on her face all evening.

Sir Geoffrey sauntered up, the aging beau dressed impeccably as always. He executed a faultless bow despite his creaking corset. "Mrs. Stanton, may I have the honor of the next dance? Miss Stanton, I wouldn't think of asking you to stand up for this set. No doubt you will want to wait until your fiancé arrives, eh?"

Despite the twinkle of genuine benevolence in Sir Geoffrey's eyes, Sophie could barely resist the impulse to box his ears. It wasn't his fault. The person who deserved a good, hard slap still hadn't arrived. How typical of Simon to keep her waiting, even after such a dreadful day as this.

Annabel hesitated, loath to leave Sophie but unwilling to offend their host.

"Go ahead, Belle." She conjured another smile. "I'm happy for the opportunity to have a rest before Simon arrives."

"I'll be back as soon as I can," Annabel whispered as she took Sir Geoffrey's hand.

Sophie eased her numb bottom to the edge of the pretty but hard beechwood chair, wondering how long she would have to wait before Simon bothered to show up. Once he did, she would make him take her home. Not that she wanted to be alone with him, but even that was preferable to an evening spent like an exotic insect under a magnifying glass.

The minutes ticked by as she watched the dancers through the double doors to the saloon. Engagement to the Earl of Trask seemed to have resulted in a strange combination of avid curiosity and precipitous abandonment. Even her middle-aged bachelors had been driven away by the news of her impending marriage

She twisted her favourite diamond bangle around her gloved wrist. Simon had sent a terse note promising to meet her in good time tonight, but he hadn't made much of an effort so far. Was this a glimpse into her future? Always waiting for a man who cared more for everything else in his life than he did for her?

Maybe, she reflected with a sickening pang, he didn't think she was worth the bother. She couldn't decide which was worse—hoping Simon would grow bored with her and leave her alone, or fearing he had never really cared for her in the first place.

A pleasant male voice jerked her out of her gloomy reverie. "Ah, Miss Stanton. Why so glum? Surely no creature as lovely as you has cause to look so forlorn?"

Her stomach did a sickening flop. Where had Mr. Watley come from? She stiffened. More to the point, where was Lady Randolph?

"I find myself wondering where all your suitors are," Mr. Watley murmured as he arranged his limbs in the vacant chair beside her. He smoothed a nonexistent wrinkle from his superfine tailcoat, then gave her a charming smile. "Surely they haven't been frightened off by the prospect of your wedded state? Respectable men are such fools, don't you find, Miss Stanton?"

Sophie couldn't think how to respond. Was he flirting with her? Handsome men never flirted with her. She laughed uncertainly, not wishing to appear rude.

"I'm sorry, Mr. Watley. I only know respectable men."

His pale blue eyes glittered. "We shall see what we can do to change that, lovely lady."

He *was* flirting with her. But why would he bother? The latest on-dit had him attached to Lady Randolph, and they had certainly seemed friendly the other day in the Pump Room. Could his flirtatious behaviour be yet another attempt by the countess to humiliate her in front of half of Bath?

Her chest grew tight. As if today hadn't already been bad enough.

She pretended to be Lady Eleanor, forcing herself to sound majestic. "I'm surprised to see you alone, Mr. Watley. Or is Lady Randolph in the other room?"

He arched his brows, looking genuinely surprised.

"No, Miss Stanton. I am alone. Her ladyship has other engagements tonight," he said, giving the words a faint, bitter taint.

The muscles of her neck and shoulders pulled into hard knots. What did he mean by *other engagements*? Could Simon be with Lady Randolph right now? Surely he wouldn't do that to her—not after today.

She shook away the gruesome thought.

"Her loss is my gain," she said, affecting a bright tone.

He unleashed a charming smile. "My sentiments exactly, Miss Stanton." His voice dropped to a low purr. "I say, don't you find the atmosphere stifling in here?"

Now that she thought about it, it was rather stuffy. She nodded cautiously.

"I'm told Sir Geoffrey has a lovely conservatory—small, but elegant, and with some rare species of plants," said Mr. Watley. "Perhaps I could tempt you into a brief stroll? I'm sure it will be worth the effort. His fuchsias are rumored to be some of the rarest in England."

Sophie hesitated, not quite trusting the man's motives. She glanced at the ormolu clock on the ebony sideboard. Almost ten thirty. And still no Simon.

"Come, my dear. What can be the harm? All we need do is step through the library, and there we are. Don't be nervous," he added with an outrageous wink. "I already know at least one of your secrets, and I have not betrayed you.

Surely you can trust me to keep my counsel on something as harmless as a stroll amongst the greenery?"

A bland smile played around the corners of his mouth. He looked harmless. A voice inside her whispered not to trust him, but it was true he hadn't revealed what he'd seen that night outside the theater. The night she'd taken Toby into Lady Eleanor's carriage. The night Simon had proposed to her.

Simon. The memory of their kiss in the alley brought a hot flush to her cheeks. Where the devil was he, anyway? He should have been here ages ago.

"I really should wait for my fiancé, sir," she replied.

Mr. Watley's smile grew knowing. "It would appear his lordship has other amusements this evening. Why should you not have a few of your own? Surely you don't desire to sit against the wall all evening with the spinsters and widows, do you?"

His gentle taunt wormed its way past her defences. What could be the harm? It wasn't as if they would be leaving the house, or going out into the gardens. Not on such a cold night. And the muscles in her neck *had* twisted into an impossibly hard little knot, which would no doubt lead to a headache. Perhaps a nice, relaxing turn in the conservatory would do her good. If Simon deigned to appear while she was strolling with Mr. Watley, well, so much the better.

She silenced the warning voice in her head and rose from her chair. With a gently triumphant smile, Mr. Watley extended his arm. As far as Sophie could tell, no one saw them leave the room and go across the hall to the library, which was unfortunate given her growing desire to avenge herself on Simon.

They crossed the shadowed library to a pair of double doors leading to the conservatory. She paused as they crossed the threshold, her eyes widening with genuine delight.

Sir Geoffrey's conservatory was a compact but elegantly designed half-dome of metal and glass with a tessellated floor of black and white tile. Pots and tubs of varying sizes—some made of stone and others of polished wood—had been packed into every corner of the room, all filled to overflowing with exotic flowers and plants. Oriental fuchsias nestled alongside chrysanthemums, camellias, and geraniums. An orange tree in a stone pot stood in the center of the room, a dozen pieces of ripe fruit hanging from its well-tended branches.

"How beautiful." For a moment she forgot her anger at the world. "Mr. Watley, thank you for bringing me here."

"I am overjoyed you are pleased," he replied, escorting her to a wooden bench next to the orange tree. "But nothing in this room compares to your astonishing beauty."

Now *that* was a bit much.

She peered at him, her spectacles slightly misted by the moist air of the conservatory. Men like Mr. Watley could spout flowery compliments as easily as they breathed. After all, flattery was a dandy's stock in trade. But he did seem to be gazing at her intently, with a gleam in his eyes that made her shift uneasily on the hard bench. Perhaps allowing him to bring her to this secluded place had been a little unwise.

Her discomfort soon faded, replaced by boredom as Mr. Watley kept up a relentless stream of compliments about her hair, her gown, her figure—really, that was getting a bit warm—and, finally, her graceful deportment. When he compared her to one of the gráces of classical antiquity, she could barely stifle a giggle. No one had ever called her graceful before, not even the middle-aged widowers.

Mr. Watley clearly didn't sense her growing restlessness. In fact, he had moved closer on the bench, close enough for Sophie to discern the extra padding in the shoulders of his formfitting coat. An image of Simon's massive shoulders—naked and corded with muscle—leapt into her mind, causing a strange weakness in all her limbs. Compared to that of her erstwhile fiancé, Mr. Watley's physique was that of a youthful stripling.

Sophie blinked as her companion's thigh brushed up

against her gown. She was about to suggest they return to the drawing room when he grabbed her arms and planted an alarmingly enthusiastic kiss on her lips.

No man but Simon had ever kissed her like that before— and Simon's kisses were altogether in a different category. For a stunned moment she allowed her curiosity to run away with her. Emboldened by her acquiescence, Mr. Watley gripped her tightly and tried to slip his tongue between her lips.

A sour taste of revulsion surged in her throat. She choked and pushed against his chest, her gloved hands slipping against the silk front of his waistcoat.

She wrenched her mouth free. "Mr. Watley! I insist you take me back to the drawing room immediately."

The dandy's fingers dug into the soft flesh above her elbow-length gloves. His eyes glinted with a lecherous ardour. "You needn't play coy with me, sweet Sophia. We both know why you let me to bring you in here."

He bent and tried to reach her lips once more. Sophie dodged, banging the top of her head against his chin. He cursed, grabbing for the nape of her neck, his other hand pawing at her waist.

Panic bolted along her nerves. She swiped at his arm, teetering over the back of the bench. No one had seen them come in here. No one would come to her rescue. Should she scream?

She righted herself, pushing at Mr. Watley with all her strength. He gasped out a strangled cry and toppled sideways—straight into the orange tree which, along with Mr. Watley, went crashing to the tiled floor.

Sophie jumped up and raced for the door, leaving the hapless dandy in a tangle of broken tree limbs, shattered pottery, and a small pile of dirt. A lone orange dangled over his head, as if someone had carefully placed it there. A second later the fruit dropped from the limb and bounced off Mr. Watley's forehead. He whimpered.

"I suggest we keep this unfortunate incident to ourselves, Mr. Watley." Her breath came in a pant, but she strove for a dignified tone. "You may know my secret, but if my fiancé ever discovered your . . . your impertinence, things would go very badly for you indeed."

A string of curses met her threat. She spun on her heel and fled through the library. Slipping into the hallway, she gave a silent prayer of thanks that it was deserted. Then she took a deep breath, forced her trembling limbs to steady themselves, pulled her wrinkled gloves taut above her elbows, and prepared to return to the drawing room.

A deep voice pierced the quiet. "Sophie."

She almost jumped out of her kid slippers. Simon strode down the hallway, a velvet cloak flung over his arm. He looked stern. Panic once more whipped her heart into a mad gallop.

"You're flushed. What's wrong?" he said as he came up to her.

Even as she tried to calm her thundering heartbeat, she plastered a bright smile on her face. "Nothing. I'm just surprised to see you."

His eyes narrowed under suspicious brows. "Why? I told you I would meet you here tonight."

"Well, ah, it was getting so late I was beginning to think you weren't coming."

"Sophie, when I say I'm going to do something, I do it."

She bit back the retort that sprang to her lips. The arrogant earl needed a set-down, but this was not the time to get into an argument. She had to get him away from the library door before Mr. Watley put in an appearance.

Simon gave her a thorough look. The nostrils of his patrician nose flared as if he could sniff out her lies. She tried not to squirm under his inspection.

"What are you doing out here?" he demanded.

"I had to visit the retiring room. Not that you needed to know," she huffed, feigning indignation.

When he opened his mouth, she cut him off in an attempt to forestall any more questions. "Why don't you escort me to the saloon? Truly, Simon, I've been longing to dance with you all evening."

His eyebrows shot up. She winced inwardly. Considering how their last conversation had ended, she may have over-played her hand. He hesitated, but obviously decided to let her deranged suggestion go unchallenged.

"As much as I would like to dance with you, my dear, it's getting late. It's time for us to leave."

She noticed for the first time that it was her burgundy cloak draped over his arm. As much as she wanted to be gone, she hadn't actually thought about the consequences of being alone with Simon. The very idea made her wish she was back in the conservatory with Mr. Watley. At least she could manage *him.*

"I suppose you're right. But I must tell Annabel we're leaving, and say good night to Sir Geoffrey and Lady Hume."

"I've already done so." He draped the heavy cloak over her shoulders and tied the tasseled cord under her chin.

The feel of his warm fingers brushing her skin made her gulp. She raised her eyes, scanning his features for any kind of reaction. He looked cool and remote—the mask of the im-perious lord having slipped once more into place.

Weariness descended on her like a shroud. "I'm ready to go home, Simon."

He hesitated and the mask slipped. "Not home. Not just yet. We need to talk in private."

Her breath caught in her throat. Not more talking. Why couldn't he leave her alone? "I don't think that's a very good idea. I'm really very tired."

His eyes, dark as midnight in the shadowed hall, gave nothing away. "I'm sure you are, Puck. But it must be done.

We must resolve the questions that stand between us, for both our sakes."

She moistened her lips, acutely aware of him as he loomed over her. He looked so handsome, so . . . so masculine in his severe tailcoat and dazzling white cravat. He even smelled wonderful. The faint scent of sandalwood and leather teased her with memories of the glorious night when she had surrendered . . . well, thrown herself at him, if she were to be honest about it.

Doubt twisted within her like a Gordian knot. He wanted her to trust him again. She could actually *feel* him willing her to trust him—could see it in the flaring intensity of his gaze.

How could she, when she didn't even trust herself?

He stroked a thumb over the sensitive skin of her neck. She had to stifle the whimper of longing that rose to her lips.

"I never meant to hurt you, Sophie. You know that. Let me explain what happened."

His sinfully seductive voice slid over her, overcoming all her resistance. She nodded weakly, hating how easily he could persuade her.

Simon took her arm and led her from the house to the waiting carriage.

"Where are we going?" she whispered.

"To my lodgings in Milsom Street."

Her anxiety spiked again. *Alone with Simon. In his private apartments. Late at night.*

Her rational mind—and propriety—demanded she refuse him. But if that incident in the conservatory had taught her anything, it was that Aunt Jane had been correct. Simon was the only man she would ever love. She had to find out if he could return that love, even a bit, and if he regretted treating her as he had. For them to have any chance of a life together—if only as the friends they once had been—she needed to know.

It took only minutes to reach his lodgings. She barely had

time to catch her breath before he was ushering her into his apartment, untying her cloak and tossing it over the arm of a square-backed chair. He moved silently to a heavy mahogany table covered in ledgers and correspondence and turned up the lamp that had been left there. The soft light glowed, highlighting the hard planes of his face.

Sophie's heart gave an extra, painful beat. Something akin to despair crept through her as she studied his rugged features. Would she ever truly know him? Ever pierce the shield he had erected around his heart? He knew everything about her, but these last few days had left her feeling she no longer understood anything about him.

He steered her with a gentle hand to a leather club chair beside the table. She perched on the edge of the seat, watching him uncertainly. To her surprise, after discarding his greatcoat and gloves, he knelt on the floor before her. He took her hands and began to strip the gloves from her arms. Tiny shivers danced up her spine.

"Sophie, I owe you an apology." He didn't look at her, keeping his attention on the task of easing the butter-soft kid from her fingers. "What I did was wrong, and I never would have done it if I hadn't been convinced there was no other way."

He finally looked up and gave her a rueful smile. "You have a rare talent for driving me insane, Puck, and that little scene you put on in the Pump Room forced me past the limits of my endurance."

Sophie couldn't repress a stab of guilt. "Simon . . ."

"No, the fault was mine. I should never have let you talk me into making love to you that night. I knew it was a mistake."

Irritation quickly replaced guilt. "Well, it might have been a mistake, but not for the reasons you think."

He ignored the peevish note in her voice. Instead, he took both her gloves and dropped them to the floor. Raising one of her cold hands to his lips, he pressed a burning kiss into her palm. The tiny shivers racing up her spine turned into a jolting shudder.

He returned her hand to her lap, keeping his on top of it. When he spoke, his voice was quiet and self-contained, but he kept his gaze fastened on their clasped hands. "My behaviour was less than honorable, Sophie. I knew full well I was pushing you, and I regret that. But I did it to protect you. You don't realize how vulnerable you are. There are those who would hurt you if they could, and it's my duty to keep you safe."

She sighed, frustrated that he wouldn't meet her gaze. "But don't you see? That's the problem. I'm not a child anymore, and I'm not that innocent. I need you to respect me, not order me about as if I were still in the schoolroom."

That brought his head up. "Believe me, Sophie. I do recognize you're no longer a schoolgirl. Fully recognize it."

A sly grin transformed his expression as his eyes raked over her body. Despite her irritation, she felt an answering heat.

"But you're not tutored in the unhappy ways of the world," he continued, "and I hope you never are."

She opened her mouth to object, but he placed a long finger across her lips.

"Sophie, hush. Let me apologize."

Subsiding into her chair with a grumble, she decided it was best to ignore the smile lingering around the corners of his mouth. After all, he could hardly enjoy this. Simon rarely apologized to anyone.

His amused expression faded, replaced by a serious, direct gaze. "I acted the fool when I should have been patient and understanding. I won't make the same mistake twice, I assure you. I won't lie to you again, and I will never break a promise, either."

Sophie tried to resist the urge to capitulate, but she could feel her heart turning traitor. As she gazed into his eyes, she knew he spoke the truth—at least as he understood it. She yearned to accept his apology, but it felt too much like surrender. What control of her life, her emotions, would she have if she gave in to him?

"I don't know, Simon." Her voice held a humiliating quaver. "When Lady Randolph . . ."

He cut her off, shaking his head. "No. She means nothing to me, Puck, and never will again. I give you my word of honor. You are the only woman in my life."

Sophie gazed wretchedly back at him. She loved him so much she sometimes felt there was no room inside for herself. But how did he actually feel about her? It was all very well to apologize, but he would never be true to her. Not true in his heart, the way she was to him.

Simon rose with a masculine grace, pulling her up with him. He took her face between his hands and brushed his mouth softly against her lips. She trembled, every part of her yearning to feel his arms around her once more. To give herself to him. But once married, she would forever be weighed down by her need to win his love.

"I care for you more than anyone, Puck," he murmured, trailing a string of tender kisses across her cheek. "Nothing will ever mean more to me than having you as my wife. That I promise."

Her resistance crumbled. She choked back a whimper and lifted her face to his. His lips captured hers in a hot, devouring kiss, his arms lashing her against his hard chest.

But as Sophie yielded to him, surrendering to her own love and weakness, something deep within whispered a warning. Simon still hadn't said he loved her, and she was beginning to believe he never would.

Chapter Nineteen

Triumph surged through Simon's veins. And, he ruefully acknowledged as he explored Sophie's honey-sweet mouth, a feeling of relief she had capitulated so completely.

He slid one hand down to her hip, easing her softness into his already full-blown erection. It had taken but a moment for him to turn as hard as a pike—ready to pull off her clothes, spread her legs, and plunder the heat of her tempting body. He throttled back the impulse. She needed reassurance, not ravenous lovemaking.

When she had asked him about Bathsheba, her finely drawn features etched with anxiety, he had almost taken her then. But her eyes, brimming with vulnerability behind her gold-rimmed spectacles, had held him back. She required tenderness and understanding, and he would give her those in full measure.

Sophie trembled in his arms even as she returned his kiss with a shy enthusiasm that threatened to break his self-control. He softened his mouth against her lips, hoping to soothe her, but little tremors coursed unabated through her limbs. He set her away from him just as she tried to clutch at his shoulders.

"Are you cold, my love?" He stroked her tumbled curls

back from her pale face. They felt like velvet ribbons twining around his fingers.

"A little." She gave him a wavering smile.

He dropped a kiss on her plush mouth and eased her down into the club chair.

"Rest for a minute, Puck. I'll get you something warm to drink."

Simon crossed to the marble chimneypiece and stirred the banked fire to a roaring flame. He glanced back at Sophie. She perched on the edge of her seat, peering anxiously at him as she followed his every move. He paused, struck by the pure lines of her elflike face, and the abundance of her wild auburn hair. What a fool he had been, blind to her all these years.

Her unique beauty would belong only to him, he vowed as he strode through the connecting door to his bedroom. Sweet and funny, Sophie had a heart more generous than a man could imagine. He would see to it that she never had cause to mistrust him again.

He shrugged out of his coat and waistcoat and untied his cravat, tossing them onto a ladderback chair by the door. As he grabbed a decanter of brandy from the top of his wardrobe, he glanced at the richly upholstered canopy bed standing in the center of the room. He couldn't help grinning as he thought of all the sensual pleasures he would be sharing with Sophie in that bed very soon.

Simon strode back to the drawing room and paused in the doorway. He gripped the crystal decanter in a tight fist, cursing silently at the scene that met his eyes.

His ever-curious fiancée stood before the large worktable holding a rustling piece of parchment in her trembling hand. He knew exactly what it was. He knew from the stunned, almost blank look on her face. She held a survey of the Stanton estate in Yorkshire—the one that demarcated the proposed sites for his future coal mines.

Frustration with his carelessness rolled through him.

"Ah, Sophie, I wanted to talk to you about that." He moved cautiously to the end of the table, placing the heavy decanter well out of her reach. It wouldn't be the first time Sophie had resorted to physical measures to express her frustration with him, and he had the childhood scars to prove it.

She looked at him, her eyes filled with a volatile combination of vulnerability and resentment.

"This is what you wanted all along, isn't it?" Her voice held a flat, almost toneless quality.

He weighed his words carefully. If he didn't get the next few minutes right—explaining everything to her with as much honesty as he could—their life together would be over before it had begun. He had to make her realize how much this meant to him.

"Yes, I want that land. I won't pretend it doesn't matter. It does. Very much. And I won't pretend it wasn't a factor in my decision to marry you. But it wasn't the only reason. If it was, I would tell you, I swear it. I would never force this marriage on you, and I won't force it now. After listening to me, if you wish to end our engagement, I will accept your decision and will make our families accept it, as well."

He paused, trying to gauge her reaction. "But this is important, Sophie, so I ask you to give me a fair hearing. I promised I would never lie to you again, and I won't. Believe that, and trust me."

Her eyes widened at the pleading note in his voice. Hell, he couldn't blame her. It shocked him too. She stared at him, clearly suspicious. For a moment, he thought she would refuse to hear him out. Instead, she dipped her head in cautious agreement.

He moved around the table to join her. Gently plucking the parchment from her hand, he spread it out flat on the table.

"As you can see this is a survey of your lands in the north, lands which I believe hold the key to a prosperous future—for our family and for the people of Yorkshire. I know it sounds odd, Sophie, but you can be a part of something much more important than our own petty, everyday concerns."

She crossed her arms and gave an unladylike snort. "Like the success of our marriage?" she retorted.

Considering what she was capable of, that was a fairly mild rejoinder. He took a deep breath and forged ahead.

"See here, and here," he said, pointing to the projected sites for the mines. "An engineer from the Royal Society is dead certain your lands are rich with coal, Sophie. As am I."

"Coal," she whispered, staring down at the parchment. "You're marrying me for my coal." The pain of disillusionment laced her voice and struck him to the quick.

"I'm marrying you for more than that," he said, forcing back an unfamiliar sense of panic. "The most important reason is that I can't imagine spending my life with anyone but you. You are the only woman in the world for me. That I swear on my grandfather's life."

Sophie's gaze flew up to meet his. Her pretty mouth quivered as she blinked back a shimmer of tears. More than anyone, she would know how seriously he took such a vow. After all, he had given up everything to accede to the old man's autocratic demands.

He stood quietly, waiting for a sign—for any indication she might believe him. Endless seconds ticked past as her questioning eyes searched his face. Finally, she returned her attention to the parchment.

"Continue," she said. Her voice was clipped, but held a touch more warmth than it had a few minutes ago. And, if he wasn't mistaken, a reluctant curiosity.

Repressing a sigh of relief, he shrugged the tightness from his shoulders before looking back to the survey.

"What do you know about the textile industry, Sophie—the wool trade, in particular?"

She wrinkled her forehead, looking thoughtful. "As much as most, I suppose. It's the lifeblood of the nation, is it not?"

"And has been for decades. The war greatly enhanced England's dominance of the trade. Our naval blockades of enemy ports throttled their industries and gave us command of both the materials and the means of production."

He hesitated. "Does this make sense to you?"

Her brows snapped together in a scowl. "I'm not an idiot, Simon. I do read the papers, remember?"

He bit his lip to keep from smiling. "Of course, my sweet. Forgive me for ever doubting you."

"Please get on with it," she said with an impatient wave.

"The development of new machinery and advances in mill design has made it possible to produce finished products at a much greater rate. These products are the foundation of our trade with foreign markets. And those markets are vast and their appetites insatiable. In order to feed them, we must expand. We must build bigger mills, and we must power those mills."

The wounded look in her eyes had disappeared, replaced with a growing interest. The tension in his gut began to ease.

"Do you know how the mills are powered, Sophie?"

"Steam, I would think."

"That's right, steam. And do you know how we power the steam engines?"

She narrowed her eyes. "Coal."

"Correct, my dear. And the Stanton lands in Yorkshire are exceedingly rich in coal."

One hand fluttered up to cover her mouth as she stared at the documents strewn across the table. Remorse washed through him for the pain he was causing her, but he had gone too far to turn back now. He had to trust her to make the right decision.

She dropped her hand. Her eyes, glittering with angry challenge, met his. "Who will build these mills? You?"

"No. There is a man in Bristol, a factory owner, who seeks a partner to build mills in the north. But he requires assurance of a steady supply of coal before he will agree to the contract. Coal from Stanton lands will provide that assurance, Sophie."

She blinked owlishly from behind her spectacles, and then sighed. "And how is this supposed to make me feel better, Simon? We seem to be right back to where we were this morning. All is business for you, including me."

"I would never deny how important my trading concerns are to me. Or how much I want to succeed." His grandfather would spin in his grave to hear such a statement, but the old earl had not lived to see the times now before them, the end of the traditional ways of living.

"There are other considerations, however, considerations that should weigh on the mind of every man of business or wealth in this country." He set the survey aside and reached for a pile of architectural drawings. "I want you to look at these, Sophie. These are the designs for the new mills I will build with my partner. They would employ hundreds of men. Perhaps, in time, thousands."

She bent her head over the papers. Her slender hands slowly traced the lines and figures of the drawings as she inspected his plans.

"Over the long years of the war, many men have given their lives for England," he continued. "Many more have now returned home from the Continent—to wives and children, to families they must support. But they have no work. These mills could be part of the answer. They would provide work for decommissioned soldiers and help stave off the discord that threatens England's peace. Legions of men without work could lead to dire consequences for all of us. The French learned that lesson years ago."

Her delicate eyebrows arched upward. "I didn't know you were concerned about such things, Simon. After the way you reacted about the workhouse . . ."

"That was about you, not about what you saw there."

Her expression was troubled, her eyes full of doubt. "Do you really think it's possible to help these men?"

He rubbed a hand against the back of his aching neck. "I believe it is possible, sweetheart, and I'd like to try. We can't let these men return home to nothing. There's going to be the devil to pay for all of us if we don't provide some proper means of employment."

She regarded him with solemn eyes, as if waiting for something more. He made one last effort to convince her.

"Sophie, I know how you long to help those less fortunate, but can't find the way to do it. If you consent to be my wife, you'll be a woman of power and influence, married to one of the wealthiest men in the land. There is much you could do to change things—much we could do together. Your life could have true purpose, beyond the foolish whimsies of the ton. And," he reached out and traced the soft curve of her neck, "you would make me a very happy man."

One of her hands rose up to touch his fingers where they stroked her skin, but then she dropped it back to the table.

He tried an encouraging smile. "Think of all the children you could save if you had access to my fortune."

That brought the scowl back to her face. "I ought to murder you for keeping this from me. But I suppose your stupid male logic told you it was best not to hurt me with the truth, didn't it?"

He spread his hands in silent apology.

She eyed him balefully. "You're a beast, Simon, and an idiot. You know that, don't you?"

The last bit of tension leached from his body. "I depend upon you to tell me that whenever you think it necessary, my sweet."

She blew out an exasperated breath.

"All right, Simon. I understand what you wish to accomplish. I know you'll never love me as much as I love you, but I suppose there's no help for that. It's not in your nature."

He blinked. It was the first time she had ever admitted to loving him, and the force of it shot through his chest like a cannonball.

"But you're a good man," she continued, blithely unaware of the impact of her words. "I've always known that, even when you're being a complete ass. No doubt we'll drive each other to Bedlam, but I promise I'll do my best to be a good wife and a good countess. After all," she finished morosely, "it's what everyone seems to want."

He moved quickly, pulling her into a fierce embrace.

"I hope it's what you want as well, love," he said, holding her against his chest.

"Don't be a looby, Simon. You know it is," she mumbled into his shirt. "Everyone knows."

He smiled at her disgruntled tone, relishing the enticing feel of her lithe body in his arms. They held each other for several moments, offering and receiving comfort, until she stirred restlessly.

"I just wish there was something we could do for Toby and Becky," she said.

He brushed her curls back from her face. "Well, as to that . . . maybe I already have."

She jerked her head back. "What did you do, Simon?"

He smiled, arching one brow.

"Tell me." She pinched his arm.

He laughed. "Very well, little demon, but only because I fear the damage you'll otherwise inflict upon me."

He drew her to the club chair and settled her on his lap. Leaving out the more revolting details, he related the events that had occurred at The Silver Oak. She listened breathlessly, interrupting only once to ask a question. Her expressive face reflected the rapid shift in her emotions as she absorbed his story.

"Oh, Simon." She wriggled excitedly, setting off an interesting reaction in the region of his groin. "I wish I had been there to see it! I wish I could go down there and beat that horrid man myself."

He seized her face in his hands, forcing her to sit still. "Sophie, if you ever dare to go to The Silver Oak, I swear I'll—"

"Oh, pish. Stop lecturing. I'm forgiving you for being so nasty to me. In fact, I'm so proud of you I could burst."

She threw her arms around his neck and mashed her lips to his mouth. But before he could deepen the kiss, she pulled back and gazed at him with eyes as beautiful as Russian amber.

"I love you, Simon St. James, I love you so much. And I always will."

He laughed and drew her back into a triumphant embrace. The ground had been rough and the going heavy, but his plans were finally coming to fruition. No more obstacles stood in his way.

Sophie would be irrecoverably his, and soon.

Simon might be an idiot, but Sophie knew she was a fool. One who apparently never learned her lesson. He had deliberately used her as a pawn in his business affairs, and still she couldn't help throwing herself into his arms. Part of her wished she had the fortitude to box his ears and walk right out of his life, but that was beyond her capabilities.

Simon cradled her in his lap, his arms locked in a possessive embrace. His tongue slipped past her lips and surged into the depths of her mouth, eagerly taking what she so cravenly offered. As she sank into the luscious delirium brought forth by his kiss, her embattled wits admitted she no longer had the strength to fight him. She wanted him too much, and when he touched her *that* way, his long fingers trailing up her stomach to her breasts, it felt as if he had set a torch to her body.

When he pulled his mouth from hers, she gasped, struggling to reclaim at least some small measure of sanity. Was this a mistake? Should she allow him to make love to her again? She feared being vulnerable once more—prey to the storm of emotions that held her in a merciless grip. But he had apologized, and most sincerely. Of that she was certain.

More importantly, he had finally admitted he cared for her more than any person in his life. She could have wished for a more passionate declaration, but Sophie understood him well enough to know how difficult it had been for him to reveal even that much.

As if he could sense her momentary withdrawal, Simon seized her attention by sucking on and then nipping her lower lip. She pulled in a breath, shivering at the curious thrill invoked by his aggression.

"Pay attention, my love," he said as he gently removed her glasses and set them on the worktable. "You'll wound me if I suspect you're bored."

Sophie couldn't hold back a nervous giggle. "Then I suggest you try harder to keep me from getting bored."

He swooped down and took her lips in an achingly short kiss that still left her gasping for breath.

"I'll see what I can do to amuse you." His voice was heavy with sensual promise.

She sighed as his hands moved to cup her breasts. He tweaked her nipples, caressing the hard tips until it seemed she would go mad with pleasure.

She moaned and arched her back, weak with the delicious sensations that racked her body. He shifted to wrap his arm securely about her, forcing her to lie still against his massive chest. His hot breath fanned her cheek as he continued to stroke her tingling breasts through the thin silk of her gown. Every time he fingered her nipples—gently tugging on them to the edge of pain—insidious warmth flowed through her veins and pooled between her legs.

Though impulse dictated she shut her eyes, concentrating only on the sensations he evoked within her, Sophie forced herself to focus on her lover. Her desire to watch him at play was wicked, but she couldn't help it. In any event, Simon didn't seem to find her behaviour scandalous, at least not in this particular instance.

He studied her body, his expression rapt as he untied her tapes and laces with swift, knowing fingers. In less time than it took to think about it, he had pulled her gown and chemise down, exposing her breasts to his gaze. She panted, and the soft globes quivered, the nipples flushing to a dusky rose.

A sharp hiss escaped from between Simon's clenched teeth. The hard planes of his face and his stern jaw made him look like a conquerer of old, a warrior about to claim a long-sought prize. It was feudal, really, but the idea of her as his prize made her squirm with impatient excitement.

"Sophie." His voice sounded strangled by a combination of laughter and desire. She couldn't help but squeak when he moved a warm hand back to possessively claim a breast. "Let's move into the bedroom, shall we?"

"Why?" She stretched to follow the movement of his clever fingers as they stroked and massaged her sensitized flesh. "It's so cozy in here, by the fire."

Besides, she didn't want him to stop touching her, not even for a second. Nothing had ever felt as delicious as Simon's calloused hands on the softest parts of her. It was as if she were floating on a cloud of warmth—a warmth that made her weak with desire. The idea of standing on her own two feet seemed impossible.

"You wish me to make love to you in a chair?"

"Why not?" She gave a voluptuous sigh, mesmerized by the kneading motion of his fingers. "You made love to me on a sofa."

His laugh sounded more like a feral growl. "You're a damned peculiar girl, Sophia Stanton, and I'm grateful for it."

She wriggled her bottom on his aggressive erection. "Why, Lord Trask, you do know how to flatter a girl."

"I'll show you flattery."

She shivered at the erotic threat in his voice.

To her surprise he stood, bringing her to her feet with him. She staggered and would have collapsed to the floor if not for his strong grip. Before she could voice her irritation, he stripped the clothes from her body, leaving her stockings, garters, and shoes intact. He pressed her back into the club chair. She jumped at the feel of the soft, cool leather making contact with her naked bottom and thighs.

"Simon! What are you doing?"

He gave a low, wicked laugh. "Flattering you."

She gasped as he took her nerveless legs and draped them over the broad arms of the chair. Her thighs were spread wide, her most secret parts exposed before him.

"Simon!" Sophie tried to pull her legs down onto the seat, but his unyielding hands held her firmly in place.

"Stay still." He invested the words with all the authority of a command. She gulped, stunned by the ferocity marking his features.

"Really, this is outrageous," she protested weakly.

"You're the one who wanted flattery. Well, I'm going to flatter you in the best way I know how."

As he had just a short time ago, Simon dropped to his knees in front of her chair. But she hadn't been naked then, totally exposed to his gaze, vulnerable in a way that was intimate, unnerving, and exciting.

He stroked his hard, masculine hands up the pale flesh of her thighs.

"Look at yourself, Sophie," he whispered. "Look at how beautiful you are. So sweet, so damned innocent."

She looked down at her smooth belly. At the nest of downy curls at the juncture of her thighs spread wide. At Simon kneeling between her legs, his brawny body—clad only in black trousers and a white linen shirt—making her seem all the more dainty and feminine in comparison. The startling contrast, the fevered images of what he would do to her, made her damp flesh turn to hot honey in anticipation.

"The only thing that's outrageous is how much I want to taste you," he muttered, his voice thick.

"T . . . taste me?" What did he mean by that?

He slipped his hands under her bottom, titled her pelvis, and bent to push his mouth through the soft curls at the entrance of her body. She jerked as if she had been struck by a bolt of lightning. His only response was to pin her to the chair and deepen his lascivious kiss.

Sophie writhed in his grip as he sucked her most tender flesh. Rapturous sensations rocketed through every limb. As he laved her cleft, performing a wicked dance with his tongue, the sensations coalesced into an aching fullness deep within her womb. It was so much stronger than the night he had first made love to her that she didn't think she could bear it.

"Simon," she pleaded, breathless and needy.

He ignored her, using his tongue, his lips, and even his teeth to catapult her onto a plane of delicious agony that threatened to overwhelm the few wits she had left. Just as she was about to beg him to stop—completely undone by the sight of him between her legs, the feel of his voracious mouth on her body—he eased one finger into her sheath and gently sucked her aching bud between his lips.

She cried out as her bottom lifted off the chair. He followed, his hands grasping the softness of her cheeks, his mouth still fastened on her sex. Contractions tightened and then released within her womb, and he seemed to absorb it all as she writhed against him.

Eventually, the spasms subsided into a long shudder, and then into a gentle throb. She came back to herself, to an awareness of her damp flesh on slippery leather, to the cool absence where Simon's mouth had been. She lifted heavy eyelids to find him sitting back on his heels, hands resting on his muscular thighs. Sophie had no difficulty reading the look of rampant male satisfaction on his handsome features.

She could barely think, but she had to find a way to wipe that detestably smug and knowing expression from his face. As usual, he beat her to it.

"I told you I knew how to flatter a lady."

Chapter Twenty

Sophie made a grab for her spectacles, wincing as she peeled her damp thighs from the leather cushions of the club chair.

"Allow me." Simon came to his feet in one fluid movement. He plucked the spectacles from the table, carefully balanced them on her nose, and adjusted the spindly metal frames around her ears.

"Is that better, Puck?"

He grinned, still smug and full of himself, but looking so big and handsome that she had to repress an addle-brained sigh of appreciation.

She forced a glower, working hard to put on a snit. "Oh, do give over, Simon. It wasn't that good."

His eyebrows shot up. "That sounds like a challenge to me."

He swooped down and pulled her off the leather seat, ignoring her yelp of protest.

"That hurt," she grumbled, rubbing her tingling bottom.

He laughed and swept her into his arms. When she shoved against his chest, he responded by clamping her against a body as unyielding as stone.

"Put me down," she squealed, kicking a little as she put up

a token struggle. Her dancing slippers fell unheeded to the floor as he strode through the open doorway of his bedroom.

"Your fault." He carried her to a luxuriously appointed bed in the centre of the room. "I never could resist a challenge."

He tossed her lightly onto the overstuffed mattress. She choked back a nervous giggle as she struggled into a sitting position. She had barely recovered from his first bout of outrageous lovemaking, but the gleam in his eyes suggested the episode in the chair was simply the beginning. As he yanked off his linen shirt, ripping it in his haste, she wondered if she had the fortitude for his sexual attentions—especially on a nightly basis—for the rest of her life.

That thought stole her breath. A quivering weakness crept through her limbs. Simon threw his shirt to the floor and refocused his gaze—dark as pitch and just as hot—back on her. He rested a hand on one of the bedposts and took his time giving her a leisurely but scorching inspection. She could practically feel her flesh sizzling as his eyes moved over her.

Sophie glanced down at herself and realized with an odd little jolt that she still wore her garters and stockings. Those few scraps of silk and blue knotted ribbons accentuated her shocking lack of modesty and her vulnerability under his burning gaze.

Her eyes flew to his, and she blinked. The sophisticated earl, disciplined to a fault, had disappeared, replaced by a man in the grip of a primitive lust. A battle-hardened warrior, an invader. And there was little doubt he was about to claim his prize.

Her body flamed from her scalp to her feet. She ducked her head, hiding her face behind her disheveled hair. It was one thing for Simon to make love to her, even in a chair, but that look made her decidedly nervous. She started to slither backward, intent on climbing under the brocaded satin coverlet as quickly as she could.

His laugh low and wicked, he shot out one hand to grip her ankle.

"Don't move," he ordered. She froze, her limbs responding instinctively to his seductive command. He moved round the bed, lighting a branch of candles set on a small side table. A soft light flared.

Her skin tingled as she realized that every part of her was ruthlessly exposed. "Simon, what are you about?"

"I want to see all of you." He kicked off his shoes and rapidly removed the rest of his clothing, his eyes never leaving her body.

"But you already saw me in the other room."

He came down heavily onto the bed and pulled her into his arms, wrapping his hard-muscled body around hers.

"I want to watch your face when you take me in—all of me," he growled.

"Simon!" The room spun for a few seconds as she stared into the ravenous gaze of a stranger. She shivered, her nerves humming with a raw mixture of trepidation and excitement.

His eyes met hers. "Don't hide from me, Sophie. Ever."

It was all she could do to nod her head.

He rewarded her with a tender brush of his firm lips against her mouth. The last whispers of her resistance faded, replaced by a ravenous need to appease him—emotionally, sexually, in every way she could. All that mattered was pleasing him and, in doing so, pleasing herself.

"Good girl." A ghost of a smile touched his mouth, but then he was moving over her, blanketing her body with his primal heat.

She reached to pull him down into a kiss, but he slid away. His lips trailed fire down her neck and across her shoulders. She shifted beneath him, relishing the feel of his coarse night beard rasping over her smooth flesh.

He hadn't even reached her breasts before her nipples, already sensitized by his play in the other room, puckered into burning peaks. She moaned her eagerness, urging him to kiss the tight points. But he seemed content to slowly lick his way around them, nuzzling her ribs, tasting the insides of her elbows, nibbling at the undersides of her breasts—everywhere but where she most longed to feel his tongue. She thrust against him, pushing her pelvis into the erection that lay heavy between her thighs.

He lifted his head. "What do you want, Sophie?" His voice was hoarse.

"You know," she whimpered.

His eyes glittered. "Yes, I think I do."

He settled more firmly between her thighs, just touching her sex with the tip of his erection.

"Please," she moaned, wriggling beneath him.

"As you wish, my lady."

His mouth fastened on her nipple. The hungry sweep of his tongue, his teeth scraping across the beading tip, was sweet agony. She grasped his head, fisting her hands into his thick hair. His mouth worked one breast, then the other. Pleasure unfurled within her like a bright, spangled ribbon.

He gave one last heavy suckle and pulled away. Sophie groaned, feeling the tug deep in her womb. She widened her legs, silently urging him to take her, desperate to feel him inside.

His lips parted in a fierce smile, and he surged into her with one powerful stroke. She gasped, stunned by the depth of his penetration. Her racing pulse throbbed in her throat, her belly, even deep in her sex where she clenched around him.

"Oh, my lord," she moaned, arching up against his chest. Her pearled nipples rubbed against hard muscle, and the erotic ache in her core spun even tighter.

"That's right, Sophie. I am your lord—you belong to me," he rasped in a voice as rough as distant thunder.

She shivered deliciously, but didn't reply, too swept up in the slide of his body. He was big, and he stretched her just to the point of pain, but she didn't care. Nothing mattered but to feel the strain of his hard muscles against her softer flesh, to know that he possessed her so thoroughly.

His predatory gaze bored into her, but his touch was achingly tender. His rhythm slowed as he explored her cheek and neck with hot, open-mouthed kisses.

She inched her fingers up his arm to his broad shoulder. Her hand looked small and slender resting on the corded muscles that ran from neck to bicep. She sighed, unable to contain the bliss that surged through her limbs with a voluptuous weight.

"Mmmm . . . you make me feel . . ." She caught her breath as he rocked into her with a slow stroke.

"Tell me how I make you feel, my sweet."

"Safe," she blurted out, tumbling into the mesmerizing pull of his coal-black eyes. It defied all logic, given how unsure she was of him, but *safe* was the only word that fit.

"You *are* safe," he murmured. "No one harms what is mine."

His voice held that note of arrogant possession that always annoyed her, but in this particular instance it reduced her to a state of exquisite surrender. Boneless, she sank into the soft mattress.

"Yes," Simon murmured. "Give yourself to me, my angel."

He pushed his shaft even deeper, thrusting her legs wide with urgent hands. She moaned, arching her back as the tip of his sex pressed against her womb.

He gasped, suddenly pulling out of her and coming up on his knees.

Dazed, she lifted her head, surprised by the unexpected withdrawal. Had she done something wrong?

"W-what's the matter?"

"It's not enough." He moved quickly, slipping his hands under her body and flipping her onto her stomach. She squeaked, too dazed and weak to resist. Besides, all she wanted was for him to finish what he started, no matter how he did it. She would go mad if he didn't.

Big hands pushed her knees wide.

"I want everything, Sophie," he growled, moving between her legs. "I want it all."

God, she was an insanely tempting little morsel—so fresh and sweet, like a delicate ice to cleanse his jaded palate. Simon clenched his teeth against the need to plunder Sophie's body so thoroughly that she would never again forget to whom she belonged. He took a huge breath, refocusing his senses on the enticing picture she made, sprawled amongst the rumpled bed linens.

Her flushed bottom wriggled invitingly beneath him, an invitation to sin he wouldn't refuse. He grabbed a pillow and shoved it under her belly. After a brief assessment, he lifted her and tugged another pillow beneath her hips.

"Simon," she protested, trying to push up on her elbows.

"No, love." He pressed his hand into the small of her back and gently held her in place. With his other hand he stroked the firm globes of her pretty ass, and then trailed his fingers down between her thighs. The sensual contrast between his strength and her delicacy made his erection throb with an almost painful ache.

Simon tilted her pelvis and spread her legs wide. Her pink, glistening cleft was fully exposed. The temptation to plunge back into its hot embrace was overwhelming.

But he held himself back, knowing that by prolonging the agony his release would be that much the sweeter. He brushed his fingers over her silky flesh, tickling soft lips already drenched by his previous attentions.

She choked back a groan and turned her face into the linens. "Oh, Simon. This is torture."

"For me as well, darling. The sweetest torture I've ever known."

He tormented her with his fingers, relishing the sight of his cock resting between her pale thighs. Lust rode him with a hard spur, and he was dying for the moment when he would penetrate her sheath with one hard thrust. But Sophie this way—writhing with sensual abandon beneath him—was just too good to pass up.

Twice he brought her to the brink of climax with his teasing fingers. The third time he used his erection to stroke against her aroused bud, once more pulling back just before she found her release. By then she was sobbing with frustrated desire, but still he held back. He would allow no doubt to exist in Sophie's mind that she was his, and that only he could bring her to ecstasy.

She wriggled backward in a vain attempt to impale herself on his shaft. He pulled away with a strangled laugh.

"Simon," she wailed in frustration.

He couldn't hold back any longer. Tilting her hips even higher off the pillows, he drove into her melting flesh, seating himself to the base of his shaft. Sophie cried out as she climaxed, gripping him with a throbbing heat. She pushed up on her elbows and thrust against him, rotating her pelvis against his groin.

Simon clenched a fist in her thick mass of hair and gently pulled her head back and up. She twisted around, seeking his kiss, sucking his tongue into her mouth.

The primal urge to mate drove their mouths apart. He fell into a pounding rhythm as Sophie writhed beneath him. The scent of her sweet musk, the feel of her skin, the sound of her husky moans, flooded his senses with a furious heat. Her swollen flesh clamped around him in another set of tight spasms, triggering his own burning climb to release. He finally exploded, crying out a hoarse shout as he poured himself into her with a wrenching completion.

An eternity later he collapsed on top of her, utterly spent, dazed by what had surely been the best orgasm of his life. She panted beneath him, all satin and sweat-drenched skin.

He tried to collect himself enough to roll off her, but he

simply didn't have the willpower to pull out from her sheath. In fact, if he had his way, he'd spend the rest of the night—hell, the rest of his life—right where he was. Buried deep inside the most alluring woman he'd ever encountered.

That thought jolted him back to a stunned awareness. Sex with Sophie was astoundingly different, and he was beginning to realize she might be the one woman he could never get enough of.

That wasn't a good development.

"Simon, I can't breathe."

A sharp little elbow dug into his side. He reluctantly pulled out of her and rolled onto his back, bringing her with him. Settling her into the crook of his arm, he reached out with his other hand and pulled the coverlet over their rapidly cooling bodies. Sophie snuffled her contentment into his ribs as she snuggled against him. Her hand trailed along his thigh and brushed his groin. Unbelievably, his flaccid staff twitched with renewed interest.

Not good at all.

He craned his neck to look at the bundle of trouble that lay so peacefully in his arms. How had this happened? How the hell had she wormed her way past all his defenses, to the point where he could no longer imagine life without her? As usual, she refused to stay where he wanted her, both literally and figuratively. Given her propensity for mayhem and his newly discovered weakness for her, she would likely cause him no end of chaos and scandal.

Even more alarming was the nature of his rapidly growing obsession with her. It was all very well for Sophie to be in love with him—after all, she had been mad about him for years. Certainly he would always cherish and protect her, but she could never mean so much to him that he would lose control of her, or of himself. If Sophie ever recognized how easily she could distract him, she would run him ragged.

With the best of intentions, of course. She was no Bathsheba, nor even remotely like most other women of the ton. But if she were allowed to kick over the traces, he would spend the rest of his life pursuing her through workhouses, gin mills, and God knows where else her demented tilting at windmills would take her.

No. He was not a man to be controlled by a woman, not even Sophie. The sooner she realized that, the better.

She stirred in his arms, twisting around to face him, her head coming to rest on his chest. Big eyes gazed up at him, filled with so much trust and happiness that his heart compressed with a bittersweet shock.

"Oh, Simon, I do love you so much."

He swallowed the impulse to respond in kind, instead dropping a kiss in the riotous tangle of curls on top of her head. She rubbed her cheek against his chest and sighed dramatically.

He knew that sound. Best to ignore it, since it was usually a prelude to something he was sure to dislike.

Another minute or two passed in blessed silence. Simon gradually relaxed, unable to resist the comfortable drowsiness weighing down his eyelids. Perhaps he would rest for a few moments before taking Sophie again. After all, the night was still young.

His eyelids snapped open when she dug her toes into his calf and sighed again, this time so forcefully she stirred the hairs on his chest. He stared at the ceiling and repressed the urge to curse. Might as well get it over with, whatever *it* was.

"What's wrong, Sophie?" he asked, trying to be patient.

She ducked her head under his arm and avoided his eyes, a sure sign of impending doom.

"I wish there was something more we could do for Becky and Toby. I'm concerned their father will hurt them, despite the fact you warned him not to."

The bedclothes muffled her words, but genuine worry filtered through her voice. He gave her a reassuring hug.

"Taylor knows I mean business, Puck. He won't dare cross me. Besides, I made it clear to Toby that he should come for me at the first sign of trouble."

She looked up, anxiety casting an unwelcome shadow over her pretty face. He hated that she worried so much.

"But Toby is so afraid of his father, and he doesn't really know you." She hesitated. "He does know me, though. Perhaps if I were to go see him . . ."

She broke off with a startled squeak as he rolled over, pinning her beneath him. Round eyes grew even rounder as he captured her face between his hands.

"Sophie." He could barely get the words out past his clenched teeth. "If you ever, ever go down to the stews again, there will be the devil to pay, I promise you. I'll see to it that you won't be able to sit down for a week."

She opened her mouth, preparing to launch into a tirade. He smothered her lips with a punishing kiss, ignoring her pathetic attempts to push him off. Thrusting his tongue between her lips, he ruthlessly explored her until she began to moan with a reluctant pleasure.

He broke off, noting with satisfaction her disoriented expression.

"I mean it," he said softly. "Stay away from The Silver Oak."

Her slender brows snapped together as irritation obliterated her dazed response to his kiss.

So much for that strategy.

"Don't threaten me, Simon. I'm not a girl who has yet to let down her skirts. I'll do whatever I think is right and just to protect those children. Besides," she added, tipping up her chin in defiance, "it's not like you can stop me."

He sighed and shifted onto his elbows. Would they have an

argument every time they had sex? Life with Sophie was looking more complicated by the second.

"Not unless I lock you up in the root cellar," he admitted. "But I do expect you to exercise some common sense. Taylor is a dangerous man, and The Silver Oak is the worst kind of flash house. You will be the death of me if I have to constantly worry you will slip off to see those children."

She gave him a searching look, the angry glitter in her eyes beginning to fade. After a moment she stretched up to give him a gentle kiss.

"I understand you want to keep me safe, Simon, but those children need more protection than I do. Please let me," she pleaded.

He forced himself to stiffen his resolve. She would have to learn obedience to his wishes starting now, or she *would* be the death of him.

"I'm your husband, Sophie, or I will be in a few weeks—"

She narrowed her eyes at that.

"—and I insist you obey me in this. I give you my word that all will be well. I will see to Becky and Toby's welfare, both now and after we leave Bath. You must learn to trust me, my love."

She softened beneath him. "Of course I trust you, but the children know me better. And you can be rather intimidating, you know. In fact, I wouldn't be surprised if you frightened the poor boy when you spoke to him today."

He lowered his head. "I didn't frighten him, and you are not to go down there," he growled, injecting as much menace into his voice as he could.

She rolled her eyes. "That's exactly what I'm talking about. Now I'm sure you scared him to death."

"Sophie—"

"Oh, all right. I promise I won't ever go down there without you. Is that satisfactory?"

It was obvious from her exasperated look that she was only

humoring him. But since he had no intention of ever taking her down to The Silver Oak, he supposed the grudging capitulation would have to do.

"I have your word on it?" he demanded, annoyed with himself that he even had to ask.

She rolled her eyes again. "Of course, silly. I promise."

He forced himself to smile, even though long years of dealing with Sophie told him that her promise was halfhearted at best. But a moment later she wrapped her arms around his neck, arching up to brush pink, kiss-swollen lips against his mouth. The hard points of her nipples pressed into his chest, sending a hot rush of blood directly to his groin. He groaned and pushed her heavily into the bedding, deciding that any further conversation about Toby and Becky could wait for another time.

It took but a few minutes to make her ready for him. Simon eased into her soft, delicious body, giving himself up to the luxury of her enveloping heat. But before he relinquished all hold on rational thought, he recalled one other piece of business that had to be settled between them. And since sex apparently made Sophie compliant—or as close to it as she ever would be—he decided to strike while the iron was hot.

"Sophie," he murmured, dropping gentle kisses on her cheek. "I want to post the banns so we can be married by the end of the month."

She sighed, arching her spine as he withdrew to the entrance of her tight sheath. When she didn't answer right away, he pulled himself from the saturated flesh in a slow, teasing slide. She thrashed her head against the pillows, moaning in frustration.

"Sophie . . ." he coaxed.

"Whatever you want," she whimpered. "Just don't stop."

He plunged back into her, casting off all restraint, wanting and needing it as much as she did. As he spiraled toward physical oblivion, he exulted in the satisfaction that he finally had Sophie right where he wanted her.

Chapter Twenty-One

The dreary October rains had finally ceased, and clear, fine weather had blown in. The Bath company seemed to be out in force this afternoon, hurrying to the shops or taking leisurely strolls to the Pump Room. Simon drew the crisp fall air deep into his lungs, relishing an uncommon feeling of contentment as he strode up Bond Street to the jeweler's.

Sophie was his. The very notion still made him shake his head in disbelief, but by Christmas they would be man and wife, and she would be safely ensconced at Kendlerood House, his family's ancient manor in Lincolnshire. He imagined Puck as chatelaine of his estates, comfortably settling into her role as lady of the manor. He grinned. Perhaps she would even be pregnant by Christmas. They had certainly made a good start on that project over the last few days.

The thought of Sophie grown soft and round with his baby was surprisingly enticing, and not just because she would provide him with an heir. Unlike most men he knew, Simon liked children and looked forward to fatherhood. Sons and daughters—and he wanted two or three of each—would have the added benefit of keeping his mischievous elf busy and out of trouble. When she had her own babies to care for, she wouldn't have the time to rummage through workhouses and taverns looking for lost sheep and hopeless causes.

But it was more than that. Children would make Sophie happy. Since her first Season, she had watched her friends and cousins marry and start families of their own. Then Robert and Annabel had wed, and her fears that she would dwindle to the status of a maiden aunt had become obvious, at least to him. Simon couldn't repress a twinge of guilt over that, since he *was* partly to blame. After all, if she hadn't been in love with him, she likely would have married long ago.

But Sophie's wish for a family of her own would be granted, and the sooner they started, the better. Her well-being was now linked to his in a most elemental way, as last night had shown with stunning force. That truth made him hellishly uncomfortable, but it could no longer be denied. Responsibility for her happiness now rested with him.

Simon dodged a pair of chattering matrons as he stepped into Bassnett's, the most prestigious jeweler in Bath. The clerk behind the counter in the empty store looked up to greet him with a smile.

"Good afternoon, sir. How may I assist you?"

"My secretary, Mr. Soames, dropped a ring off last week for cleaning and repair. I understand it's ready."

The man looked puzzled for a moment, then his brow cleared.

"Ah, yes! The antique poesy ring. A beautiful piece, Lord Trask. I was expecting Mr. Soames to pick it up later today. I'll step into the back room and wrap it for you."

"I'd like to see it first."

"Of course, my lord."

With an apologetic smile, the clerk disappeared through a doorway at the back of the shop. Simon removed his gloves and tossed them onto the counter. He supposed he should have allowed Soames to run this errand, but he wanted to see for himself that his grandmother's poesy ring had been properly cleaned and the dent marring its surface repaired to his satisfaction.

The ring had been in the family since the time of William and Mary. One of his ancestors had given it to his wife on their wedding day, and it had been passed down from father to son ever since. It had last been worn by his grandmother and had remained untouched, along with the other family jewels, since her death fifteen years ago. Though much too old-fashioned for his taste, he knew his fiancée would be touched by its mawkish sentiment and thrilled to receive it as a betrothal gift.

The clerk returned a few moments later with the piece resting on a velvet-covered tray. Simon plucked it up for a critical inspection.

The simple gold band had been polished to a high gleam. The goldsmith who had worked on it knew his business, for no trace of repair marked either the surface of the ring or the inscription on the inside of the band. He held it up to the light and read the engraved words: *As true to thee as thou to me.*

Sophie would love it.

Nodding his approval, Simon handed the ring back. He would have preferred to see a diamond or an emerald on her hand, but he could give her a more appropriate token of his esteem later on, perhaps for her birthday. Or on the birth of their first child.

The shop bell jangled. Simon had his back to the door, but when the heavy scent of jasmine and roses wafted up his nostrils, he knew exactly who had entered.

He bit back a groan and turned around. Bathsheba stood before him, clad in an elegant, formfitting carriage dress. She was astoundingly beautiful, and as hard and lethal as a steel blade. Only a year ago he had willingly gone to her bed at the slightest opportunity, but now he couldn't understand how he had ever preferred her to Sophie.

For a long moment they stared at each other like boxers in the ring. When the corner of her mouth kicked up in a questioning smile, he forced himself to make a polite bow.

"Lady Randolph."

Her eyes glittered with satisfaction at his small concession.

"Good morning, my lord. I was surprised to pass by and see you in here. Are you choosing a gift for your fiancée? I remember well the many times you did so for me."

She raised a graceful hand to push back a lock of hair curling down from under the brim of her stylish hat. The deliberate gesture displayed the emerald bracelet on her wrist—the one he had given her when he broke off their affair.

The clerk cast a swift glance from her face to Simon's and disappeared into the back room.

"What do you want, Bathsheba?"

"Simply to talk. We used to talk all the time, don't you remember?"

Simon didn't bother to answer. She gave him a veiled look and strolled over to one of the glass cases, tapping a gloved finger over a tray of enamelled snuff boxes. Another clerk hurried over to pull the tray out for her inspection. Simon silently cursed. How long did it take to wrap up one small ring?

"I was sorry not to see you at Sir Geoffrey's salon last night, but I was otherwise engaged," said Bathsheba. "And so, apparently, was Sophie."

Simon had to force himself not to clench his fists. He knew he should spin on his heel and walk out the door, but something held him in place.

"Cut line, Bathsheba. What is it you wish to say?"

She turned away from the case. Her eyes rounded, faux innocence and treachery all wrapped up in one tempting package.

"I only wish to give you a warning. As one of your dearest friends, I feel it is my obligation to do so."

The other clerk threw him a startled glance, and Simon

jerked his head in a silent command. The man glided through
the door to join his compatriot in the back room.

"Alone at last, dear Simon."

"Whatever it is, Bathsheba, get it over with."

"So cold," she sighed. "How times have changed."

"Bathsheba—"

She smiled, her face a porcelain mask of malicious intent.
"Of course, you're impatient to find out about dear little
Sophie. I'm sorry to say that your fiancée has been behaving
recklessly again. She had quite a charming private interlude
with Mr. Watley last night—in Sir Geoffrey's greenhouse. I
won't bore you with the details, but suffice it to say that she
seems to care little for her own reputation." She paused dramatically. "Or so I'm told."

He fought the desire to grab Bathsheba and shake her until
the teeth rattled in her head.

"Who told you that?"

She gazed back at him, the picture of serene loveliness.
"Mr. Watley, of course."

The sour taste of anger flooded his mouth. How could
Sophie have been so naïve? And why the hell could she never
stay out of trouble?

He took a step forward until he loomed over Bathsheba.
She suddenly looked uneasy. Though she didn't move, she
seemed to shrink away from him.

Simon kept his voice low and even. "I would suggest, Lady
Randolph, that you tell Mr. Watley to have a care. I will not
tolerate gossip about my future wife."

She drew herself up, eyes widening even further in mock
alarm. He had to give her credit for her quick recovery.

"Of course not. How could you even think it? Mr. Watley
is the most discreet man I know, I can assure you."

"He'd better be, if he knows what's good for him."

He grabbed his gloves off the counter, then pivoted on his

heel and brushed past her. Soames could pick up the blasted
ring tomorrow.

He pushed through the door and into the street, his whole
body tightening with fury. Sophie had lied to him. Her eva-
sive, flustered behaviour last night and her ready agreement
to leave with him now made perfect sense. She must have just
come from the greenhouse and her pathetic assignation with
Watley. Obviously she had wanted to make him jealous. But
why then had she pretended nothing had happened? What had
Watley done to her that she made such an effort to conceal it?
If he had touched even one hair on her head, Simon would
strangle the bastard and throw his lifeless body in the Avon.

He stalked up the crowded street, barely aware of his surroundings. If Sophie had wanted to make him jealous, it had
worked. It simmered through his veins, raw and maddening,
scorching him with an infuriating sense of helplessness. No
matter what he did, he couldn't seem to bring her under control. He couldn't even control his own blasted emotions,
much less her.

Bathsheba, damn her, was right about one thing. Sophie
was a scandal waiting to happen, at the point when he could
least afford the distraction. His future partner, Russell, had
traveled up from Bristol and was staying at The Pelican on
Walcot Street, where Simon would join him for dinner and a
discussion about the new mills. The last thing he needed was
damaging gossip that could threaten either his or Sophie's
reputation. Russell was a high stickler, if there ever was one.
At the first hint of scandal or setback to their proposed partnership, the cautious factory owner would have no compunction about finding another investor. Simon had to squash
whatever problems Sophie's ruinous behaviour had caused,
and without delay.

A quick glance at his pocket watch confirmed he was late
for an appointment with his bankers. This time he did curse,

castigating himself for allowing this mess to develop. Since his grandfather's death, he had vowed that no one would control the course of his life again. That had been the driving force behind all his actions, and now his bitter ex-mistress and his goose-cap of a fiancée threatened to turn everything on its head. His carefully constructed plans—everything he had worked for these past several months—were about to go up in smoke, all because Sophie didn't have the good sense to keep out of the way of someone like Watley. Simon had known all along she had the potential to bring chaos into his life, but hadn't thought it would happen even before he could get his ring on her finger.

He couldn't do much about Bathsheba, but he could damn well do something about Sophie.

Chapter Twenty-Two

Sophie yawned as she glanced over at the gilt timepiece on the mantel in Lady Eleanor's drawing room. Almost ten o'clock. As much as she was enjoying *Guy Mannering*, she'd been nodding over the same three pages for the past hour and was beginning to think longingly of her bed. Lady Eleanor, as usual, had retired early. Lady Jane had gone to a party and would not return before midnight. Sophie had only her book for company until Simon came to call.

She smiled, letting her thoughts drift back to the previous night. No wonder she could barely keep her eyes open. Simon had made love to her three times—not including the thrilling incident in the club chair—before he had finally taken her home in his carriage just before dawn. Her thighs ached, her back hurt, her female parts were so tender she could barely sit, and she couldn't wait until he took her back to bed and did it all over again. Thank goodness she would soon be with him every night, with his strong arms wrapped around her and his sinful mouth covering her body with kisses. She wondered if she was turning into a lightskirt, because just thinking about it made her stomach jump with delicious anticipation.

The clock bonged out ten chimes. She sighed and put down

the book, too distracted by thoughts of Simon to concentrate. He should be arriving soon, according to the note he'd sent her earlier in the day.

Sophie extracted his terse missive from the pages of her book. It wasn't exactly a love note but, then again, Simon wasn't the kind of man to express himself in flowery phrases. Still, the words, written in his bold copperplate hand, seemed cold, even distant. He asked her to remain at home until he called, which he would do as soon as he finished dinner with Mr. Russell. It was phrased more like a command than a request, though, as if she had done something to annoy him.

She chewed her lip, trying to ignore the niggle of doubt gnawing away at her. He certainly hadn't been cold the last time she had seen him, no matter what his note suggested. Perhaps he was tired as well, but that didn't seem likely. Simon had the constitution of a bull, as he had amply demonstrated last night.

She shrugged and stuck the note back between the pages of her book. Simon would always be Simon, and that meant she would have to accept his foibles along with his virtues. He could certainly be immensely irritating at times, but he was a good man. He cared for his family and friends and always tried to do right by them. God knows, he had always been by her side—her faithful protector—whenever she needed him.

Besides, his note wasn't the only letter she had to think about. This afternoon, the post had brought thick envelopes from her mother and her grandparents with congratulations on her unexpected betrothal.

Actually, her mother and grandmother hadn't seemed very surprised by the news, expressing their pleasure with quiet happiness and words of gentle advice. Her grandfather, on the other hand, hadn't been able to contain his joy. Grandpapa Stanton had been so excited that he had splattered ink blotches all over the crosshatched lines of the parchment.

She smiled wryly. For once, she had made everyone in her family happy. The truly amazing thing was that she had managed to make herself happy, too.

A quiet scratch sounded against the door panels. She blinked. Had she missed Simon's knock on the front door?

"Enter." She rose, smoothing down her skirts.

James the footman bowed his way into the room. "Sorry to disturb you, miss. I didn't know what else to do," the young man said, his face a study in dismay.

"What's wrong, James?"

He hesitated. Sophie's heart skipped a beat. Had something happened to Simon?

"It's that boy, miss. Toby. The one from The Silver Oak."

"What about him?"

"He's in the kitchen. I didn't want to bother you, him having caused so much trouble and all, and not wanting to disturb Lady Eleanor . . ." He cast a nervous glance over his shoulder. "But the boy insisted. He's well nigh worked himself to a frenzy, and I didn't know what else to do."

Sophie moved for the door. If Toby had worked up the nerve to track her down in St. James's Square, something must be very wrong.

She rushed down the stairs to the basement with James close on her heels. Moments later she skidded to a halt on the paved stones of the kitchen floor. Toby huddled in a chair by the big, open hearth. Mary, the kitchen maid, bent over him, trying to console the boy as he choked back hysterical sobs.

"Thank God, miss," Mary said with obvious relief. "The poor boy can barely speak."

Sophie dropped to her knees in front of Toby. He stared at her with terror-filled eyes as he struggled to bring his sobs under control. His face was smudged with soot and tears, and his mouth quivered.

"Miss . . ." he gasped.

She took his grimy hands in a firm clasp. "It's all right, Toby. Whatever it is, I'll help you."

"It's B-Becky, miss. My pa and Mrs. Delacourt are going to sell her off tonight."

The breath seized in Sophie's lungs. "When?"

"Men are already in The Silver Oak, waiting for it. My pa has locked Becky in the storeroom. I couldn't get her out! I ran to find Lord Trask, but he weren't at his lodgings, and the porter wouldn't tell me where he went."

He burst into tears again.

"Miss." James's voice held a note of warning. "If Lady Eleanor wakes up and hears the boy . . ."

Sophie nodded. "Toby, we'll stop your father, I promise. But you must be quiet. Becky needs your help, and so do I."

She rubbed his scrawny back through his tattered shirt, her heart aching with pity and fear. They had to find a way to save the girl, but how? She had promised Simon she wouldn't interfere, but what choice did she have? There could be little doubt that whoever purchased Becky in this disgusting transaction would rape her soon thereafter. She had to act immediately if she had any chance of saving the girl from a terrible fate.

"Toby, can I get into The Silver Oak without being seen?"

James groaned behind her.

Toby fought to bring his sobs under control. "Yes, miss. I left the back door off the alley unlocked. My pa shouldn't notice at this time of night. You goes in from the back alley, and the storeroom is the first door. On the left."

Sophie glanced up at Mary, who stood anxiously clutching her apron. "Mary, you and Toby must go and find Lord Trask. Tell him to meet James and me at The Silver Oak."

"For God's sake, Miss Sophie," James burst out. "Lord Trask will have my head if I take you back to that hellhole."

She ignored him and concentrated on the alarmed-looking maid. "I know you're frightened, Mary, but we have no choice.

Lord Trask is dining tonight at The Pelican on Walcot Street. Go there immediately, and tell him I sent you."

Sophie rummaged in the slit of her gown for her coin purse, extracting half a guinea. "Take this. Fetch a hackney at the end of the street."

Mary cast a glance at James, who gave her a curt nod. Toby jumped off his chair and wrapped his arms around Sophie's waist.

"I'll find his lordship, miss. You can bet on it."

He grabbed Mary's hand and headed for the door, dragging the reluctant maid with him.

Sophie plucked a grey worsted cloak from a hook on the wall by the pantry and threw it over her shoulders as she turned for the door.

"Miss," James said in a warning voice.

"James, we must leave now if we're to save this girl."

"And how are we to do that, miss? John Coachman and the groom can't help us. They're with Lady Jane at Sydney Place. How are we to even get into this storeroom? And what if the back door is locked, after all?"

"I don't know, James, but I'll think of something." She rushed out to the hallway, the footman scrambling after her.

They went through the servant's entrance into the street. The cold night was ominously dark under a moonless sky. Shivering, Sophie pulled the cloak tightly around her body and hurried toward Upper Church Street. They should be able to find a hackney there.

"What if Lord Trask doesn't get there in time?"

"Don't worry, James. Lord Trask will come."

"Aye, and he'll kill me if anything happens to you, miss."

"Then I'll just have to see that I don't get hurt."

A string of curses erupted from her companion's mouth. She had to bite back a startled laugh. The situation must be dire, indeed, for James to lose his impeccable self-control.

"Think of the scandal, Miss Sophie, if anyone should ever find out you went to The Silver Oak. We should go to The Pelican first, instead. His lordship—"

"Enough, James," Sophie snapped. "The Pelican is in the opposite direction, and we can't afford to waste time. A child's life is at stake. His lordship would not give a hoot about scandal under these circumstances, I can assure you."

At least I hope he wouldn't.

Sophie chided herself for that thought. Simon would never worry about gossip at a time like this. Yes, he might be angry she placed herself in danger, but he would understand she had no choice. Even though it meant she had to break her promise to him.

She gave her head an impatient shake. She couldn't worry about such considerations. Not now. Not with Becky in danger. If they failed to reach her in time—

Thrusting ugly images of rape from her mind, she lengthened her stride. She had no choice. Simon would see that.

Spying a hackney just up the street, Sophie touched James's arm and urged him forward. He glared at her, but hailed the driver. A few moments later they were jammed against each other in the damp hackney, enduring a bone-jarring ride to Lower Town. The footman muttered profanity under his breath the entire way.

"Oh, do be quiet, James," she growled.

"You'll be the death of me, Miss Sophie. If not by his lordship's hand, then by Lady Eleanor's."

A pang of remorse shot through her as she took his hand and jumped down from the carriage. Her godmother would be furious if she ever found out, and James and Mary might take the brunt of that fury. Well, she would have to worry about that later too. Besides, with a little luck, they might all be back in St. James's Square within the hour.

The hackney had dropped them off well past The Silver

Oak. She pulled the scratchy wool hood over her face, picking her way past heaps of reeking garbage as she followed James to the alley. They passed a small group of well-dressed bucks, obviously drunk and looking for trouble. One of them reached for her cloak.

"Looking for some home brewed, guv?" James's voice was low and threatening as he shoved Sophie behind him.

The man gave a raucous laugh, but let them be, weaving down the street after his friends.

"Thank you, James."

He snorted. "I expect we'll see a deal more trouble before the night's out."

She flitted in his wake into the dank alley running behind the alehouse. She could barely see. The only light filtered through the one, soot-covered window at the back of the building.

James crept up to the door that led into the tavern. He looked back at Sophie. "Are you sure, miss?" he whispered.

She reached past him and gripped the handle. The door opened easily under her fingers. James shook his head and stepped in front of her, slipping into the dim passage. She followed and carefully shut the door.

The light was almost as bad in the hallway as it had been in the alley. In the gloom she could just make out several casks set against the walls, and an open door farther up the passage that led to the kitchen. The smell of rank meat and stale beer assaulted her nostrils. She had to swallow to keep the gorge from rising in her throat.

James hissed as a barmaid exited from the kitchen, loaded down with a large tray of steaming bowls. He and Sophie shrank against the wall, but the serving girl didn't look their way as she pushed through a swinging door at the opposite end of the passage. The sound of aggressive male voices drifted back as the door swung on its hinges.

Those were the men who would bid for Becky as if she were horseflesh.

After a few agonized moments of waiting to see if the serving girl would return, they slid along the wall to the door of the storage room. She groped past James to find the handle. Locked.

Blast. Of course it would be too much to expect that Taylor would have left the key in the lock.

"Break it down," she whispered to James.

He stared at her, his face set and grim, then nodded. He lashed out with his leg, kicking his foot into the handle. The door vibrated and groaned, but didn't yield. He kicked the lock twice more before the door flew open with a crash. She winced at the noise, praying that the commotion in the ale room and the kitchen would be loud enough to cover their actions.

James pulled her into the storeroom and wrestled the broken door shut.

A lamp on an overturned crate lit the small room, crammed to the ceiling with casks of ale and boxes. Sophie blinked and peered into a box open on the floor. It overflowed with silk handkerchiefs, scraps of fine-looking lace, enamelled snuff boxes—all manner of expensive trinkets. In addition to all his other sins, Taylor was obviously a thief.

A muffled squeak drew their attention.

James hurried to a dark corner of the room, and Sophie rushed to follow. Becky sat on a pile of sacks in the corner, gagged with a piece of cloth. Her wrists were tied with rope, and she was dressed only in a thin cotton shift. Sophie dropped to her knees.

The girl's sapphire blue eyes were almost black, her pupils dilated with terror. Sophie yanked the saliva-drenched gag from her mouth.

Becky inhaled and broke into a rasping cough.

"James, stand by the door and watch for Taylor." Sophie

went to work on the ropes. "Try to sit still, Becky. I'll have you free in a minute."

The girl did her best, but trembled so badly Sophie couldn't get a decent grip on the knots. The rope was thick and coarse, and the fibers scraped against her fingers.

"Hurry, miss. My pa will be back any minute." The girl's terror infected Sophie, making her fingers clumsy and slow.

"James," she called softly. "I can't untie these ropes."

The footman hurried over and dropped to one knee. He brushed Sophie's hands aside and began pulling on the knots.

"Hurry, hurry," sobbed Becky.

Sophie didn't hear the creak of the door and the scrape of a boot until it was too late. As Becky looked up with a startled gasp, a massive fist crashed down and caught James in the temple. The footman collapsed in a heap on the floor.

Sophie cried out as a swarthy man—demonic-looking in the fitful light—yanked her up from the floorboards. Cruel fingers bit deep into her arms, lifting her until her feet dangled off the floor.

"Pa, don't hurt the lady," Becky wailed.

"Shut your yap, girl," he snarled.

Sophie gazed into Taylor's mud-colored eyes. Her breath seized in her lungs. If Simon didn't arrive in short order, she would soon be dead. Or worse.

Panic gave her strength, and she struggled to free herself from his punishing hold.

"Let me down immediately," she gasped, fighting to keep her voice strong. "You'll be sorry if you don't."

Fear squeezed her heart as Taylor responded to her futile command with a taunting laugh.

"And who might you be, little lady? Come to steal my Becky right out from under my nose, are you? Who sent you? Mrs. Cummings? That cow had her chance, but I wasn't good enough for her fancy house. So she tries to steal my girl for her own customers."

He shook her so hard Sophie's teeth chattered.

"I have n-no idea what you're talking about," she stuttered.

"Not likely."

"She don't, Pa. I promise." Becky gazed at Sophie, her eyes dead with despair. "Ma Cummings keeps a brothel on Little Corn Street. Pa tried to sell me to her, but she refused."

"Aye, she did. Too young, she said Becky was. Called me a pig for trying to get what I deserved. Now I know what her game was. Steal her away from me."

A pulse of fury rippled through Sophie's body. "You're mad," she snarled into Taylor's ugly face. "Put me down and let me take your daughter from this place, or I'll see you swing from the gallows!"

The big man lashed a blow across her face. Pain exploded through her skull. She struggled for breath, too stunned to cry out as sparks danced before her vision.

"Pa!" shrieked Becky.

"What's happening in here?"

Sophie tried to squint through the starbursts to see who had entered the room, but Taylor's blow had knocked her glasses askew. He gave her another shake and dropped her to the floor. She fell hard on her bottom, groaning as pain lanced up her spine.

"Jem, what are you doing?" The stern voice came from a woman who moved quickly to Taylor's side.

Sophie righted her glasses and peered at a woman both handsome and genteel looking, clad in a black, well-cut dress. Her glistening brown hair was pulled into a smooth chignon, and she had a sensible, calm-looking countenance.

Thank God. Surely, this lady would help them.

"Please, ma'am." Sophie crawled over to put her arms around a trembling Becky. "I've come to take this girl away from here. Her father is about to sell her to one of those men out there. He must be stopped."

The woman arched her plucked brows and perused Sophie. Then she let out a husky peal of laughter.

"Oh, miss," moaned Becky. "That's Mrs. Delacourt. She's the abbess who's going to sell me."

Sophie met the woman's amused, callous gaze. A horrified chill began to seep through her veins.

Oh, God. If Simon didn't arrive soon they were done for.

"What is your name, my dear?" Mrs. Delacourt asked in a voice as pleasant as if they had encountered each other in the Pump Room.

"Sophie Stanton," she managed to croak out.

"Well, Miss Stanton, I don't know why you"—she glanced down at James's body—"and your friend want our Becky—"

"She's one of Cummings's girls," interrupted Taylor.

Mrs. Delacourt frowned. "No. I know all her girls. And this one doesn't have the look about her. Too innocent."

"I'm here to take Becky from this vile place," Sophie said in sharp voice. "My fiancé is the Earl of Trask. He will be here at any moment to rescue me. I would strongly suggest you let us go before that happens."

Mrs. Delacourt looked incredulous. "Surely, my dear, you don't expect us to believe *that* Banbury tale. No respectable woman would ever set foot in The Silver Oak—much less sneak in through the back door. What kind of lord would allow his fiancée to run around town like a common trollop?"

"Clara."

Sophie's attention snapped back to Taylor. Amazingly, the color had leached from his ruddy face.

"What now?" Mrs. Delacourt snapped.

"The little bitch might be telling the truth."

Mrs. Delacourt went very still.

"Trask was in here yesterday." Taylor's eyes shifted away

from the madam's sharp gaze. "He warned me not to hurt Becky. That's why I thought we should go on with the auction right away. Get it over with before he came back."

A vein pulsed in the woman's forehead. "And you're telling me this *now*?" She reached down and flicked aside Sophie's grey cloak, running an expert eye over the blue cambric gown that lay beneath. Dismay cut a harsh track across her face.

"Lord Trask is on his way this moment." Sophie couldn't keep a small note of triumph from her voice.

Mrs. Delacourt's eyes narrowed to calculating slits as she studied Sophie's face. For a moment she seemed to waver, but then a cunning smile pulled up the corners of her mouth.

"I doubt it. You may be his fiancée, but I don't believe he'd permit you to come down here with only a . . . well, a servant, by the looks of him. I suspect his lordship doesn't even know you're here. Still, you're quite the little problem, aren't you?"

Sophie ignored the swell of fear in her belly. "I assure you—"

"Shut your gob," snarled Taylor. He looked at Mrs. Delacourt. "What do we do with them?"

"Kill them," she replied in a dispassionate voice.

Sophie felt the floor drop out from under her.

Taylor yelped. "Have you gone daft, woman? She's quality!"

"My point exactly. She'll bring us down, Jem. Look what you've done to her face."

All at once, Sophie became aware of a dull throb below her cheekbone. She touched her face, wincing at the stab of pain. When she pulled her hand away it was sticky with blood.

"You've assaulted a lady, Jem. I've no intention of ending up on a transport ship, or swinging from the gallows. I've worked too hard to escape this pesthole, and I won't let an interfering chit stop me now. You've got to kill them and dump the bodies. With luck, they'll think the pretty thing has run off with her footman." She laughed. "She certainly wouldn't be the first lady to do so."

Taylor's eyes rolled in panic. "But what if Trask comes looking for her at The Oak?"

Mrs. Delacourt flushed scarlet with rage. "And what can we do, Jem? Let them go? We're done here in Bath, and you know it. The new magistrate has been sniffing around The Oak for weeks. We've made enough to start over somewhere else, especially after tonight. Becky's sure to fetch us a handsome price."

Taylor looked surly, but finally relented with a grunt and a nod.

"Good." The madam reached down and grabbed Becky by the shoulders. "I'll take care of this. You get rid of them."

"No!" the girl shrieked, clinging to Sophie.

Rage jolted Sophie's heart into a roaring gallop, flooding her with a desperate strength. She kicked Mrs. Delacourt while trying to maintain her hold on Becky. Her foot connected with the madam's shin. Mrs. Delacourt staggered back with a scream of outraged pain.

"That's enough." Taylor grabbed Sophie by the hair, dragging her backward across the rough floorboards, away from Becky's clutching hands. Her eyes flooded with water as pain lanced through her scalp, like he was ripping out every hair on her head.

She blinked a few times, trying to clear her vision. By the time she could see again, Mrs. Delacourt had dragged the sobbing girl from the room, slamming the door behind her. A horrid silence fell over the storeroom, broken only by Taylor's harsh breathing. Sophie raised her eyes to meet her captor's feral gaze.

He looked like a wild boar, right down to the white foam leaking from the corners of his mouth. Taylor peeled back his thick, wet lips in a travesty of a smile. It was the most terrifying thing she had ever seen.

"Now, girl, I think we have enough time to spread your pretty thighs before I kill you."

His gaze flickered to her legs. Sophie looked down and saw that her dress and chemise had bunched up around her knees. She struggled to yank them down, scrambling away from the beefy hands that grasped at her.

"You've ruined everything," he rasped. "Now I'll take what I'm owed for my troubles. My cock will be the last thing you feel before you die."

Sophie slammed up against the wall. Taylor laughed and stalked toward her. She cast a wild glance at James, still motionless in the opposite corner. He would be dead soon too.

Oh God, Simon—where are you?

She swallowed a hysterical sob as Taylor loomed over her. His hand moved to the fall of his breeches, and he started to flick open the buttons. As he worked to free himself, revulsion surged in a burning tide through her veins. It couldn't end like this. She couldn't give up. Not without a fight.

Sophie exploded off the floor, flinging herself past Taylor's legs. He grunted in surprise. She didn't look back as she scrambled to her feet and ran for the door. As her fingers touched the handle his meaty hand grabbed her neck, yanking her away from the door. She screamed, her breath rushing out from her lungs in an agonizing shriek.

"Shut up, you bitch!"

Taylor spun her around, seizing her shoulders in an iron grip. His features purple with rage, he looked like a devil from the depths of hell. Sophie struggled wildly in his grasp and shrieked again.

He struck her on the side of the head, knocking her to the floor. She collapsed, stunned by the pain, unable to move or even make a sound.

Taylor kicked her legs apart. Flinging himself down on her, his massive body squeezed out what little breath remained in her lungs. His clumsy hands began to fumble with her skirts.

She tried to push him off, but a nightmarish lethargy gripped her limbs. Black threads snaked across her vision. Panic began to fade, but something worse replaced it—a dull certainty that she would never see Simon or her family again.

A loud crash penetrated her leaden misery. Suddenly, Taylor's body seemed to fly through the air. As it thudded to the floor she gave a huge gasp, coughing as her chest felt the freedom from his weight. After a moment, her vision cleared, and she saw a man standing over her.

Simon. Looking like an avenging angel.

"Sophie, are you all right?" His voice was glacial, but his dark eyes burned with rage.

She managed a nod.

Simon looked over at Taylor, who was moaning into the floorboards. A cold smile touched the edges of her fiancé's lips.

"And now, you bastard, I'm going to kill you."

Chapter Twenty-Three

Simon launched across the room and hurtled into Taylor just as the big man pulled himself to his knees.

Sophie struggled into a sitting position, sucking deep pulls of breath into her straining lungs. Without her spectacles, and in the dim, flickering light, she could barely see. She began to grope for the gold frames, trying to ignore the sounds of the pitched battle behind her.

There! Her spectacles had fetched up against a crate. She grabbed them and shoved the battered frames onto her nose, scrambling to her feet as a tremendous crash rocked the storeroom.

She spun around. Simon and Taylor were rolling on the floor, knocking over boxes and casks as they landed punishing blows on each other. A cask flew against the wall and splintered, spilling a cascade of ale over the rough floorboards. Both men slipped in the frothing liquid, neither able to find enough purchase to get to his feet.

They grappled, and, even though Taylor was the bigger man, Simon managed to pin him to the ground. But the brute wrenched an arm free and drove a huge fist toward Simon's head. Sophie gave a strangled cry as Simon jerked back with a grunt, evading what would have been a devastating blow. Locked together, they rolled into the crate holding the oil lamp, sending it teetering over the edge of the makeshift table. Sophie lunged and grabbed it before it crashed to the floor.

With the killing grace of a predator, Simon surged up into a fighter's crouch. As Taylor came up to his knees, Simon smashed his fist into the man's face. The blow connected with a sickening crunch, snapping the big man's head back. Blood sprayed from his shattered nose.

Desperate to help but uncertain how, Sophie hovered close as Simon rained more ferocious punches on Taylor's face and body. Cursing, the big man lashed out, connecting once or twice. But Simon might as well have been carved from a slab of marble for all the effect Taylor's blows had. He quickly reduced Taylor to a cowering, blood-spattered mass, his broad back pressed to the wall as he covered his face and pleaded in a slurred voice for Simon to stop.

Sophie realized with a sickening jolt that Simon had every intention of beating the man to death. She had to stop him. Taylor deserved to die, but God knows what would happen to Simon if he killed him. He might even end up on trial for murder.

She dumped the lamp on a crate and skidded over the slippery floor to his side.

"Simon!" she cried, grabbing his arm. He flicked her off as if she were nothing more than a fly. He slammed his fist into Taylor's jaw, and the man crumpled to the floor. Simon pounced on his prostrate body and cocked his arm again. But before he could unleash another blow, Sophie grasped his shoulders and hauled back with all her might.

"Simon, no! Please stop. He didn't hurt me."

Blind with rage, he tried to shake her loose again, but she clung to him, pleading for him to stop, begging him to listen.

Finally, his arm froze, his body trembling with the effort to contain his fury. After an agonizing eternity he lowered his fist.

Sophie glanced at Taylor, who lay unconscious on the floor. She cautiously loosened her clutch on Simon's shoulders and stepped away, ready to throw herself on him again if necessary. A final shudder rippled across his back, and he rose, turning slowly to face her. Their gazes met, and she gasped.

His stark features were drawn into a tight mask, but his eyes held a mix of raw emotions—rage, fear, and something else. Something wild and elusive. It seemed as if a veil had been ripped aside and the man she thought she knew—cool, calculating, and always in control—had vanished forever. It frightened her, but the desperate intensity she read in his gaze also filled her with an earth-shattering joy.

"I thought you were dead. I thought he had killed you." His voice was so low and harsh she barely recognized it.

"I thought you wouldn't come in time," she quavered, attempting a smile.

He moved then, pulling her into an embrace so fierce that her ribs felt smashed into her lungs. She could barely breathe, but she didn't care.

"I'll always come for you, Sophie. Never doubt it."

His voice shook, and she broke into a sobbing laugh as she buried her face into his smooth waistcoat.

"I should have known," she whispered as she snuggled against him. Of course he had reached her in time. He always did.

He let out a steady stream of low curses as he crushed her in his arms. She ignored them, letting the terror and shock of the last hour flow away as she inhaled the scent of healthy male and spilled beer. She sank against him, seeking his warmth, relishing the feel of his powerful body enveloping her.

After a few minutes he gently pushed her away, holding her at arm's length as he gave her a rapid but thorough inspection.

The black anger in his deep-set eyes had begun to fade, although heat flared when his gaze fell on the cut on her cheek.

"Are you sure he didn't hurt you?"

"My face is sore, but I'm otherwise unharmed."

He nodded, but his eyes narrowed, his expression turning cool and opaque. Sophie blinked at the sudden change. It felt as if he had slammed a door in her face.

"Why did you disobey me, Sophie?" His voice turned as hard as his eyes.

She stared at him, bewildered by the stern, almost judgmental look on his face.

"Simon, I'll explain everything when we get home, but we must find Becky. That horrible woman took her away."

"Becky is fine. Soames and Russell have her safe in the ale room."

"Oh, thank God." She sagged against him, weak with relief. "You'd better check on poor James. Taylor hit him very hard."

Simon made an impatient sound as he released her. She shivered, missing his warmth the instant he let her go.

He stalked over to James and crouched down on the floor beside him, gently turning the footman's bruised face to the light. "How long has he been out?"

She opened her mouth to answer when a tall, spare-looking man, dressed plainly in black, strode into the room. He cast an assessing glance over her before looking at Simon. "My lord, do you need assistance?"

"Thank you, no, Russell. Taylor has been disposed of."

Russell's mouth twitched as he perused the barkeeper splayed on the floor. "So I see. You should know that your man has sent the boy to fetch the watch. In the meantime, we have locked the woman away until the law arrives."

James moaned and began to stir. Sophie expelled a sigh of relief. The poor fellow had been down for so long she had begun to fear he would never wake up.

Russell switched his gaze to Sophie and gave her a brief nod. "You are Miss Stanton, I presume." His voice sounded heavy with disapproval.

"Yes, I am," she said, wondering at his tone. She curtsied, suddenly aware of how dishevelled and dirty she must look. "Thank you for coming to my aid, sir."

She gave him a grateful smile, but to no effect. He studied her with a somber expression on his long face before turning his back on her.

Her smile wavered. After everything she had been through tonight, his rudeness shouldn't have stung, but it did. Her cheeks grew hot as an all-too-familiar sense of humiliation crept through her.

"Russell, I'd be grateful if you would ask Soames to step back to the storeroom," Simon said over his shoulder. "I promise you won't have to remain in this vile place much longer."

"Of course, my lord. I'll wait in the ale room for the watchman."

He brushed past Sophie on his way out the door. She stared after him, astounded by his behaviour.

"Simon, why was Mr. Russell so rude to me?"

He gave her a searing look. "Hell, Sophie, the man's a Methodist. Can you imagine how he feels coming into this disgusting pit? I had to ask him to help rescue my betrothed from a pair of thieving whoremongers. God knows what he must think of me—and of you."

By now, Simon had helped James struggle into a sitting position. The footman's skin was tinged an odd shade of pea green and one side of his face had swelled up with an ugly bruise, but he seemed to be coming to his senses. He swayed as Simon hauled him to his feet. Sophie rushed over to lend support, and they helped him sit on an overturned crate.

James stifled a groan, then fixed an anxious gaze on Sophie. "Miss, are you all right?"

"Yes, James, you needn't worry. Everything will be fine."

Simon muttered something under his breath, shaking his head.

"Lord Trask," James ventured, looking as if he were about to face the executioner, "I beg you to forgive me for allowing this to happen, but"—he glanced up at Sophie—"I didn't think I had a choice."

"I'm sure you didn't, James," Simon replied, casting a dark look her way.

She bristled at his expression, but reminded herself that Simon must still be grappling with the residue of shock and anger. She bit back the retort that sprang to her lips, determined to retain the last shreds of her patience.

"You're not to worry about a thing, James," she said, patting the footman on the shoulder. "I'll speak to Lady Eleanor myself. Everything will be—"

Simon cut her off. "You'll do nothing of the sort, Sophie. In fact, from now on I expect you to button your lip and let me handle this. You're in enough trouble as it is. There is nothing you could do or say that would help James or anyone else."

She froze, her cheeks flushing with a sudden heat. Before she could respond to Simon's outrageous comments, Russell and Soames walked into the room. Soames's eyes, full of concern, came to rest on her.

"Miss Stanton, I'm very glad to see you unharmed."

She gave him a grateful smile. At least one person in the room still retained full possession of his manners.

"Lord Trask," he said, "Mr. Russell will take James home in the hackney. I think it might be best if they were to leave now, while the watchman is busy and before the constable arrives." He gave Simon a knowing look.

Simon nodded brusquely. "Can you stand, James?"

"Aye, my lord. Don't worry about me." The footman grimaced as Russell helped him to his feet.

"Russell," Simon said, extending his hand, "I can't thank you enough. You have my enduring gratitude."

Russell took Simon's hand in a brief clasp before helping James from the room.

"My lord," continued Soames. "There is no reason for you and Miss Stanton to remain. I'll finish up here. And I'll make certain that neither the watchman nor the constable mentions Miss Stanton's name in the report to the justice. With a little luck, we'll prevent anyone from knowing she was here. At least officially."

Sophie was about to ask how he could manage that, but the look on Simon's face made her swallow the question.

"I'll see you at my lodgings when you're finished," Simon replied.

"As you wish, my lord. I would also suggest you and Miss Stanton leave by way of the alley. The other hackney is still waiting down the street."

"Christ! Thank you for stating the obvious, Soames. Of course I'm going to take her out through the alley."

Sophie winced at Simon's sarcastic tone. His relief at seeing her more or less unhurt had obviously evaporated, replaced by an exceedingly ugly mood. Simon in a temper was never a good thing—for anyone.

Soames ignored his employer's retort with commendable dignity.

"I'll bid you good night, Miss Stanton. I hope you suffer no ill effects from your ordeal."

"Thank you, sir. For all your help."

Soames left and, except for Taylor, still unconscious on the floor, they were alone. The intense quiet was sudden and unnerving.

Simon's eyes began to narrow again, and a muscle in his jaw started twitching. She repressed a sigh. The only thing she wished for right now was to go home, take a bath, and crawl into bed. It would appear, however, that she would have to endure a dressing-down from Simon first. Best to try and head it off before it commenced.

"Well, Simon," she said, giving him a placating smile, "all's well that ends well."

He stared at her, disbelief writ large on his face.

"If you believe that, Sophie, then you are an idiot—someone who can't be trusted to tell the truth to the man she claims to love, or to keep herself out of trouble."

Shock slammed through her. "'Claims to love'? What are you talking about?"

"Do you have any idea how big a problem you've caused?" he shot back, ignoring her question. His anger flared up like smoldering embers bursting into flame. "You promised you wouldn't come back here without me. By breaking that promise, you betrayed my trust and deliberately put yourself in danger. You could've been killed."

"But I wasn't. Toby and Mary found you in time—"

"Barely," he snapped. "They spent precious minutes in the kitchen at The Pelican arguing with a fool of a waiter who refused to let them in. You should be eternally grateful that Toby had the wits to break free and run through the inn looking for me. Can you imagine the commotion that caused? Who might have seen him? And I don't even want to describe Russell's reaction when a dirty little street urchin broke into our dining room."

Sophie fought to choke back her rising anger. "Simon, any person would have done what I did. When a child's life—"

He cut in. "Any person? Who among our acquaintances would allow themselves to be drawn into something like this, Sophie? Most people I know would be appalled by your behavior."

"I don't care about most people," she retorted. "I only care about you—that you would think and feel as I do about—"

He interrupted her with a short, bitter laugh. "If thinking like you requires me to be naïve and foolish, then I thank God I'm nothing like you."

She flinched, but he ruthlessly carried on.

"After tonight, God knows why I still want to marry you. You'll cause me nothing but trouble. For some strange reason, however, I do. But you need to understand, Sophie, that our lives will be led on my terms, and my terms alone."

"Simon, you must understand. I couldn't wait. I had to try to save Becky," she pleaded, shocked by how desperate she sounded. How could Simon treat her like this? How could he fail to see she had made a life-and-death decision?

His sensual mouth thinned into a hard line. "You should have sent for me and remained at home instead of racing down here like an impetuous fool. You put James's life in danger as well as your own."

"There wasn't time. I had no choice." She caught her breath at the wave of pain squeezing her heart.

"I'm dismayed you believe that. It's now painfully clear to me you are lacking in judgment and, if allowed to, you'll go through life causing nothing but gossip and scandal. I've already had to deflect the rumors about your foolish interlude with Watley last night."

"What?" she gasped.

"And now this." He stalked up to her, his eyes narrowed into furious slits. She took a hasty step back to the wall.

"Hear me well, Sophie. From now on, unless you are accompanied by me or one of your relations, you will only leave the house when attended by a footman of my choosing. He will report to me, and I will know what you are doing every minute of every day. And if you don't learn to behave yourself, I swear I'll move you to Kendlerood Manor, and there you'll remain until you acquire some common sense."

His words tore into her with blistering force. She wanted to run, to be anywhere but here, but she commanded herself to meet his relentless gaze.

"Simon, I won't let you tell me how to lead my life. You don't have the right."

His eyes flashed. "I do, and I will. I swear, Sophie, you will obey me, or I'll lock you up and throw away the key."

Her mind seized, and she jerked back, banging her head smartly against the wall. But the pain of that small blow paled against the anguish invading her heart. Her spirit sank under a chilling weight. How could Simon treat her with such contempt, especially after what she and the children had suffered tonight?

"Jesus, Sophie!" He pulled her away from the wall and into his arms.

She struggled fruitlessly in his grip before letting herself go limp.

"Let me go," she whispered.

He closed his eyes for a moment as a look of self-disgust twisted his features. "God, Sophie. I didn't mean that. You know I would never do anything to hurt you." He reluctantly released her before shoving a hand through his dark, tumbled hair.

"Never mind, Simon." She pulled the wool cloak around her body, shivering with a cold that cut into her bones. "I'm very tired. Please take me home."

"I'm sorry, Puck. It's just that I have to . . . I need to keep you safe. I'm afraid you'll be harmed if you don't let me take care of you."

She couldn't stand to listen anymore, or look at the harsh regret stamped on his features. Turning away, she flipped the hood of her cloak over her ragged topknot and slipped out the door. He sighed as he followed her down the passageway.

Simon reached past her to open the door to the alley. She hurried out, rushing to stay ahead of him. He stalked close on her heels as they turned into Avon Street toward the hackney that waited a few steps away. The street was busy with late-night revellers. Sophie ducked her head to avoid the stares of men on their way to one of the many taverns or gaming hells in Lower Town.

As she waited for Simon to open the door of the carriage, a gust of wind snatched away the hood of her cloak, exposing her face. Simon gave a smothered curse and yanked the rough material back into place. A moment later he bundled her into the hackney, vaulting in after her.

He banged on the roof, and they jolted to a start over the rough cobblestones. The silence between them throbbed in her ears, echoing the painful thudding of her heart. Sophie stared into the darkness, and into the empty future that stretched before her.

How could she do it? How could she marry a man who valued his reputation above all else, including her love?

Chapter Twenty-Four

"Sophie, dear, are you sure you don't want me to stay home?" Lady Jane stood in the doorway of the back parlor, a frown of gentle concern on her face.

After choking down a piece of dry toast at breakfast, Sophie had retreated there, seeking refuge in the cheerful clutter of her godmother's light-filled retreat. A cozy fire crackled in the Rumford grate, but even the warmth of its flames failed to penetrate the chill that had taken hold of her body. She resisted the urge to huddle deeper into the overstuffed armchair she had dragged up to the fire, instead wrapping her wool shawl tightly around her shoulders.

"No thank you, my lady. I'm fine." She conjured up a smile, hoping to assuage Lady Jane's anxiety.

Her godmother's frown deepened. Apparently her smile looked as unconvincing as it felt.

"My love, I think it best I send a note around to Dr. Miller. You look most unwell."

Lady Eleanor pushed her sister aside and stumped into the room, garbed in a sturdy pelisse and prepared for an expedition to the baths. "Oh, do leave the girl alone, Jane. The last thing she needs is a pair of old women fussing about. Peace and quiet, and a snuggle with Simon. That'll set her to rights."

Sophie allowed her latest needlework disaster to drop into her lap, unable to speak past the sudden constriction in her throat. Lady Jane's kindness and Lady Eleanor's remarkable forbearance had been her only comfort since Simon had brought her home from The Silver Oak last night. She had expected to be pelted with questions and reprimands when she ventured down to breakfast, but the opposite had occurred. Lady Jane had quietly brought her a cup of strong tea, and Lady Eleanor had only made one grumbling remark about the cut on her cheek. True, the old woman had glared at James when he came in with a plate of kippers—he had insisted on serving, despite a truly impressive black eye—but Lady Eleanor had only snapped at him twice, which was nothing short of a miracle.

Sophie cleared her throat and tried again. "Lady Eleanor—"

"Never mind, child," she interrupted. "You don't have to say a word. Best you stay at home for a few days until those bruises fade. We'll say you've caught a cold. There have been a shocking number of chest ailments this Season, so no one will be surprised. In fact, I can't believe I haven't been brought to bed with one myself."

Sophie smiled gratefully at her older godmother, whose gaunt features were shadowed by a concern her gruff manner failed to conceal.

Lady Eleanor took Sophie's chin in a soft grasp and turned her face toward the clear morning light streaming through the window. She tsked as she studied the marks on her cheek.

"Crushed strawberries—that's what you need for these bruises. I'll have James fetch some from the market. Of course, he needs them more than you do, given the beating he took. But he should count himself fortunate I haven't thrown him out into the street. The very sight of him is enough to give me a spasm."

Lady Jane huffed out a quiet breath of laughter. "Oh, Eleanor, you would do no such thing. And where in heaven's name is he to find strawberries at this time of year? A cool compress and Denmark lotion is the best thing for Sophie's complexion. I'll have Sally bring them up right away."

"I'm sure if James looked hard enough he could find strawberries. That's the least he can do to make up for his bad behaviour," retorted Lady Eleanor as she pulled on her gloves. "Sophie, you tell that nevvie of mine that I expect to see him at dinner tonight. I have quite a deal I wish to say to him, and I won't take no for an answer."

The old woman swept from the room. Lady Jane gave Sophie a swift, lavender-scented kiss before hurrying out after her sister.

Sophie settled back into her chair, grateful to be alone. As much as she loved her godmothers and cherished their kindness, she needed time to ponder her situation. Her thoughts had been spinning in a maddening whirl ever since she awoke from a troubled sleep early this morning. Simon would arrive soon, and she still hadn't any idea how to respond to the bewildering accusations he had thrown at her last night.

The muscles of her chest constricted as she recalled with painful clarity his bitter words. They had torn like birdshot through her heart, and she had been tempted to end their betrothal on the spot. If not for the fact that he had seemed to instantly regret his behaviour, she would have done so.

Once Simon had bundled her safely into the hack, Sophie found herself finally responding to the full horrors of the evening. She had started to tremble with a violence that shook her limbs. Simon had pulled her into his arms, murmuring soft endearments until she gave up her resistance and collapsed against his brawny chest. The whole ride home she had silently berated herself for her being so weak, but she couldn't find the strength to reject the security of his powerful embrace.

They had reached St. James's Square to find the entire house lit to the attic and in an uproar. Lady Jane had arrived home only a few minutes earlier, just as Mr. Russell was hauling James out of the other hack. Lady Eleanor, awakened by the commotion, stood at the first floor landing and demanded in a booming voice to know what was happening. Ignoring all of them, Simon had picked Sophie up and carried her to bed.

"Sleep, love," he had murmured, dropping a gentle kiss on her brow. "We'll talk tomorrow."

He drove everyone from the room but Sally. The maid had silently helped Sophie wash and undress before she crawled like a shivering animal into bed, the thick velvet coverlet a welcome weight on her exhausted limbs.

She had slept—albeit uneasily—but now she had to face the day and all that lay before her. The hollow feeling in the pit of her stomach was a sign she could no longer ignore. As horrific as Taylor's assault had been, her fiancé's words were truly devastating. Simon didn't trust her. He didn't understand her. And, in spite of his affectionate behaviour in the carriage on the way home, he obviously didn't love her.

With a sigh, she stopped pretending to work and threw her embroidery into the basket by the armchair. She got up and moved to the window overlooking the garden, resting her sore cheek against the soothing chill of the glass pane.

The question that had plagued her for hours returned with a vengeance. How could she marry Simon? She would have to give up her freedom, even her will, forever placing herself in thrall to his commands. The worst, of course, was that she still loved him so desperately. She couldn't remember a time when he didn't mean the world to her, when he wasn't woven into the fabric of her days, her very life.

But the way he had treated her last night made her stomach

churn with something close to fury. Did he really think so little of her? And if he did, how could they have any chance of happiness together? At the first sign of trouble, Simon would roll her up and ship her north to his estates, while he remained in the city to pursue his business and whatever other pleasures he might seek, including . . .

Her mind rejected the image of Simon and Lady Randolph together. Even in her anger she believed him when he said their affair was finished. And she knew in her heart Simon would be faithful to her once . . . *if* they were married. But it would be a marriage to crush the heart and deaden the spirit, since it would be founded only on a sense of obligation to her and loyalty to their families. Love would not enter into Simon's cold calculation of how their lives would unfold.

Or would it?

Sophie let out a little growl and began to pace the room, more frustrated than she could ever remember. Simon *had* to feel more for her than just a sense of obligation. After all, he had always been there when she needed him. Always. At every crisis in her life—whether pulling her from a lake, or driving her about for hours to stop her from weeping for her father— he had been there by her side. Never abandoning her. Never failing to rescue her, just as he had done last night. Didn't she at least owe him the chance to explain himself?

She paced from wall to wall, trying to understand Simon, trying to find a way to forgive him. A hopeful voice in her head, the one that always refused to give up on him, insisted he had flown into a rage because he loved her and wanted to keep her safe.

To be fair, Sophie acknowledged with a grimace, she had been rash last night. She probably should have fetched Simon from The Pelican first, instead of rushing to The Silver Oak. His masculine logic would see that as the appropriate course of action. Truth be told, if she had done so, the situation might have been resolved much less dramatically.

That didn't excuse his outrageous behaviour, of course, and God knew she didn't want to spend the rest of her life at daggers drawn every time they disagreed. Or exiled to Kendlerood Manor whenever he lost his temper with her—especially since that seemed to be a daily occurrence.

She sighed, still no closer to an answer. The only thing to do was have it out with him and hope he hadn't meant those awful threats. If he had, then no matter how much it would rip her heart to shreds, no matter how much it distressed her family, there would be no marriage.

Nodding with satisfaction, she headed for the door. It might be a good idea, after all, to apply a cold compress to her cheek and dust some rice powder over the bruise. No point in looking like a battered pugilist when Simon came to call.

A distant knock sounded on the front door. *Blast.* Simon already. She hurried over to her godmother's writing table with its inset pier glass and tucked in a few errant locks that had spiralled down from her topknot. Sadly, nothing could be done to improve her complexion.

There was a light tap on the door.

"Enter." Sophie plastered a bright smile on her face.

James stepped in, alone. The grim expression on his puffy face startled her.

"What's wrong, James?"

"You have a visitor, miss. I told the lady you weren't taking callers, but she insisted I announce her." His scowl deepened. "She's refusing to leave until I do."

"Who is it?"

"Lady Randolph, miss."

She sank down into a hard Windsor chair by the door. *As if this morning weren't bad enough.*

James looked grim as death. "Miss, she said it was

about last night. What happened at . . . she said you would
want to know."

The brittle cold in her bones suddenly turned icy. What
should she do? If Simon arrived and discovered her with
Lady Randolph, he would be furious. This was what he had
feared—that someone would find out about the incident
at The Oak and spread it all over Bath. And from Bath to
London, and throughout the rest of their acquaintance. The
ton was little better than a country village when it came to
gossip, and it would take only a few days before the rumors—
greatly exaggerated, no doubt—reached the ears of her
mother and grandparents.

Her mind skating on the verge of panic, Sophie fought back
the urge to order James to evict the woman from the house.
No doubt Simon would wish her to do so, and then turn the
problem over to him to solve. But he was such a bull in a china
shop she felt certain he would only make things worse.

She took a deep breath, trying to steady her nerves. The
countess had not gone looking for Simon. She had come to
see her. The consequences of ignoring her could be disastrous. Sophie had to find out what the blasted woman wanted
and do whatever she could to appease her. And she had to do
it fast, before her fiancé appeared on the doorstep.

She rose to her feet. Smoothing down the crumpled skirts
of her plain round gown, she inwardly cursed the fact that she
had paid so little attention to her toilet this morning. The
thought of confronting her sworn enemy while looking like a
common drab made her stomach hurt. "Show her in."

"Miss . . ."

"Now."

He bowed and left the room. A few seconds later, she heard
the light step of dainty heels tapping on the floorboards.

"Miss Stanton, here is Lady Randolph."

Sophie dropped a curtsy, swallowing a desperate need to

cough. Between the heaviness of Lady Randolph's jasmine-scented fragrance and her own sense of rising anxiety, she could swear her throat was starting to close.

The countess gazed at her, a secret smile playing around the corners of her tinted mouth. She stared thoughtfully at Sophie for a few moments longer, then one of her delicate eyebrows arched up, as if to ask a question.

"You and your footman appear to have been in a brawl, Miss Stanton. I vow. You seem to lead the most interesting life."

Sophie led her to one of the old-fashioned Sheraton chairs so beloved by her godmothers, feeling as stiff and awkward as a schoolgirl. The countess floated over and perched gracefully on the edge of her seat, her draperies pooling in a saffron wave of silk and sarcenet around her tiny feet. Even in this raw, damp climate, she wore only the lightest and most fashionable of designs.

"My goodness," said the countess, casting an amused glance around the cluttered parlor. "What a quaint little room. So perfect for a household of spinsters."

Sophie felt her face harden. "What do you want, my lady?"

"Ah, straight to the point. Very good. No wonder Simon likes you—you have something of his bluntness about you." She smiled. "Not a very attractive quality in a wife, however."

Something nasty crawled up Sophie's spine. When most women smiled, their faces tended to soften. Not Lady Randolph's. Her smiles were so chilling, so devoid of emotion, they could have turned Medusa into a statue.

"I have no wish to play games with you, Lady Randolph. My fiancé will be arriving shortly, and he will be most displeased to find you are here."

The woman's smoky green eyes darted about the room before coming to rest on Sophie. *Now, that's odd.* For a moment she could have sworn the countess looked vulnerable, perhaps even frightened.

Sophie peered at her, wishing she could clean her glasses, but the moment had passed. That cold, killing smile was firmly back in place.

"Very well, Miss Stanton. I will cut bait. You were seen last night exiting The Silver Oak, a well-known flash house and purveyor of unmentionable activities. A friend of mine happened to be passing in Avon Street and noticed quite a commotion. Imagine his surprise to see you dragged out of a dark alley by your fiancé, looking for all the world as if you had just been tumbled in a hayloft. My friend saw your footman, as well. James, isn't it? He appeared to be tumbling about in the same hayloft. Or rather, to have been thrown out—perhaps by an irate lover." Her throaty voice was laced with malicious amusement.

Sophie's hands clenched into fists. "Who told you that?"

"That hardly matters. More to the point, my friend is quite a rattle. He came straight to me, and only when I begged him to hold his tongue—as a special favor to me, you understand—was I able to stem the tide of gossip. For now."

Sophie had read many books about India, and about the snake charmers who mesmerized their captive prey with a transfixing gaze. She felt like one of those hapless creatures right now, trapped by one who held all the power. "What do you want?"

Lady Randolph tilted her head, inspecting her with an almost sympathetic gaze. "You're not right for him, you know. He needs someone more sophisticated. A wife who is able to see to his comforts."

She smiled that cream-pot smile of hers, and Sophie wanted nothing more than to strike her right across her perfect face.

"And be the kind of hostess a man of his prominence deserves. You're little more than a chit, my dear, and an awkward one at that. You can't seem to keep yourself out of trouble, either. Can you imagine the uproar in the ton if it were known that the granddaughter of General Stanton visited taverns with her footman?"

Sophie clenched her jaw, rage and despair warring for dominance in her heart. "No one would believe you," she retorted. "And I may be an awkward chit, but you're a bitch."

Lady Randolph looked stunned, but then she laughed— a bitter sound that hurt the ears.

"You're right, my dear. An adventuress, some would call me. I respect your courage in confronting me, Miss Stanton, but not enough to change my mind. The ton *will* believe the rumors or, at least, enough of them to cause a scandal. Your reputation is precarious as it is. It wouldn't take much to sink it completely." She paused delicately. "We both know how much Simon would hate that."

She came gracefully to her feet in a rustle of silk. For a moment, she looked at her reflection in the pier glass on the writing table and seemed to preen.

"Really, my child," she said, her tone oddly kind, "you know you're not the wife for Simon. You will only bring unhappiness on him and your family if you persist in this foolish engagement."

"Maybe I'm not," Sophie blurted out. "But you're not the wife for him, either. Simon's a good man. He would come to despise you, if he doesn't already."

Something like anguish flickered in Lady Randolph's eyes. Her tightly gloved hand fluttered up to cover her heart.

"No." Her voice sounded high and thin. She cleared her throat and began again. "No. We understand each other. We're alike, he and I. He's simply forgotten that for a little while. I'll make him remember."

She moved quickly to the door, without her usual ease. "My friend will keep his counsel if I tell him to. You have one day, Miss Stanton, to make your decision. By tomorrow, I will expect a note informing me that you have broken your engagement. If you do not"—she gave a shrug—"I can't answer for the consequences. But I can certainly imagine how Simon will feel about the gossip. And as for General Stanton, perhaps the less said the better."

Sophie tried to swallow the ball of pain that had lodged itself in her throat. She watched in despair as Lady Randolph reached for the door.

"Why are you doing this to us?"

The countess froze, her hand suspended above the knob. She slowly turned to look at Sophie. Her eyes were strangely weary, and the skin over her delicate features seemed as brittle as dry parchment.

"Because I must." Her voice sounded as hollow as an empty well. "I'm sorry, my dear. It's for the best—for all of us. I understand Simon. I'll make him happy, I promise."

Sophie frowned, struggling to understand the change in the other woman's manner.

But a moment later the hard mask fell back into place. A cynical smile once more tugged at the corners of Lady Randolph's lush mouth. "Don't bother to get up, Miss Stanton, or ring the bell. I'll show myself out."

The door closed quietly behind her.

Sophie had no idea how long she sat there, staring blindly down at her lap. Simon would never marry Lady Randolph. If only one fact could penetrate the buzzing in her head, it was that. But he would never marry Sophie, either. Or if he did, he would regret it for the rest of his life.

The countess would make good on her threat. Even though many would not believe the more salacious elements of the tale, there was enough that was true. And, apparently, there were enough witnesses to verify she had been seen at The Silver Oak in very compromising circumstances. The scandal would be the biggest the ton had seen in years.

Simon would never forgive her. That he blamed her already

for last night's debacle was clear, and this would prove his point beyond all doubt. She had been halfway to forgiving him for his behaviour toward her, but now there was no question of that. She must drive him away, and make sure he understood she meant it. Their marriage could never survive the fatal taint of such heinous gossip, and he was too proud to bear it without his honor suffering a tremendous blow. Obligation would dictate he wed her, but there would be little affection and, in time, resentment would take its place.

Simon might even come to hate her. She couldn't bear that. Better to be alone, with her few tattered shreds of dignity, than to be trapped in the sterility of a loveless marriage.

She stood and went to the door. He would be coming soon, and she must get herself ready. Not that it really mattered how she looked, she thought blearily. After all, she had already lost him. Finally, and forever.

Chapter Twenty-Five

The bells of St. Michael's tolled out the noon hour as Simon hurried along Brock Street, cursing the time he'd wasted in yet another drawn-out meeting with Russell. He'd fully intended to call on Sophie first thing this morning, but had been forced to spend the past two hours convincing his erstwhile business partner there would be no repercussions from last night's debacle.

It hadn't been easy. Russell had been mortally offended by the incident. Soames, however, had outdone himself, explaining to the irate businessman what he had done to squelch potential gossip. The resourceful secretary had managed to convince the constable—with a little help from Simon's purse—that it was James, and only James, who had befriended Toby and Becky and tried to help them.

Now that Taylor and his female accomplice were in custody, and the children already gone to their aunt in London, Simon had good reason to believe a scandal could be avoided. No one else had seen Sophie at the tavern, and he had every intention of getting her the hell out of Bath as quickly as possible. Since Becky and Toby had been satisfactorily dealt with, she couldn't possibly have any more objections to leaving this godforsaken town. At least he hoped not.

A shout brought him back to his surroundings. He leaped back as a coach rounded the corner at Upper Church Street, lumbering by just a few inches from his booted feet. The driver cursed and shook his hand as the vehicle drove past.

Simon grimaced, annoyed by his own carelessness. He was so distracted by Sophie's troubles he could barely think straight, much less walk down the street without getting run over by a carriage.

Every minute in Russell's company this morning had been torture. More than once Simon had been tempted to excuse himself. Bedeviled by worry for Puck, he had wanted nothing more than to see for himself she was truly unharmed. Only the knowledge the factory owner would have bolted if Simon abandoned the meeting had kept him in his chair and away from her.

And, he admitted ruefully, his impatience also stemmed from a nagging concern about how she might respond to him after last night. He had been a brute, lashing out at her with mindless anger. But when he saw her flat on her back on that storeroom floor, with Taylor's filthy hands groping under her skirts, rage had extinguished all rational thought. Thinking about it still made his gut churn, and part of him wished Sophie hadn't stopped him. He would gladly have killed Taylor for what he had done to her and never suffered a moment's regret.

He halted in front of his aunts' townhouse in St. James's Square, forcing himself to take a slow, steadying breath. *Bloody hell.* His hands were shaking. How had he let events slip so thoroughly out of control? Ever since he proposed to Sophie his life had been a series of chaotic episodes, each one bringing him closer to disaster. The sooner he had her riveted to his side, the better.

He knocked, and Yates opened the door.

"How are things today, Yates?" he asked, handing the morose-looking butler his hat and gloves.

"As well as could be expected, my lord. Lady Eleanor and Lady Jane are at the baths, and Miss Stanton is in the drawing room."

"I'll show myself up." Simon took the steps two at a time, then quietly let himself into the drawing room.

Sophie had curled up on the settee, wrapped in a heavy white shawl and fast asleep. He trod lightly over the thick carpet to her side.

Deep in slumber, she looked exhausted and pale, with dark circles standing out like smudges under her eyes. As he took in the purpling bruise on her right cheek, the muscles in his upper body clenched tight as a fist.

He must have made a noise, because she stirred in her sleep and rolled onto her back. Her topknot came undone, and her hair fell against the pillows in a stream of living amber. The gentle swell of her breasts—creamy above the lace trim of her bodice—rose and fell in a soft rhythm. He felt the familiar tightening in his loins, this time combined with an overpowering urge to sweep her into his arms and carry her away, never to let her out of his sight.

He sighed. She looked as fragile as a buttercup, yet her delicate exterior hid a strong will and a warrior's temperament. Her actions last night had been foolish beyond measure, but he could never doubt her courage. Or the fact that she was no longer a child, despite his harsh accusations. What she had done displayed a selfless generosity that was beyond him— an active sympathy for two wretched, impoverished children who had no one to look to but a sheltered young woman. And she had not hesitated for an instant to help them.

He bowed his head and accepted his fate. Sophie would never change, and she would run him ragged, but last night had finally shown him that he couldn't live without her.

Kneeling on the floor beside her, he brushed the hair away from her face.

"It's time to wake up, sweetheart." He dropped a kiss on her plush mouth.

"Simon," she murmured, still half asleep. One small hand clasped the lapel of his coat as she returned his kiss.

He nuzzled her, enjoying the sweet, drowsy taste of her mouth, then pulled back. "Yes, love. I'm here."

Her eyes flew open, wide and startled behind the lenses of her spectacles. She jerked away and scrambled to the other end of the settee, pulling herself into a sitting position. Her expression grew wary.

He smiled, trying to ease her concern. She likely thought he still was angry with her. He reached out to stroke her face, but she dodged his hand.

His smile began to feel forced. "I'm sorry to wake you, Puck. I'm sure you're very tired. I had a meeting with Russell this morning, and couldn't get away."

"Now there's a surprise." She grimaced and rubbed her right temple.

"Do you have the headache?" He tried to touch her face again, but she pushed his hand away and stood up.

He sighed and rose to his feet. She obviously wasn't going to make it easy for him. Might as well get it over with.

"Sophie, I owe you an apology. I said things to you in the heat of the moment last night that I deeply regret. I hope you can find it in your heart to forgive me."

She snorted. "That's all you ever do, Simon. Apologize after you've ripped me to shreds. I'm sorry, but I don't want to live my life never knowing when the next attack will occur."

He tamped down his irritation. "Don't you think you're being overly dramatic?"

"No, I don't. You're always mad at me—"

"Always, Sophie? Even when we're in bed together?"

She scowled as a blush crept over her delicate cheekbones. "Last night was a perfect example. I tried to explain, but you wouldn't listen. After all I'd been through, your first response was to threaten to send me away—or lock me up. I won't have it, I tell you. So you might as well take yourself off right now, *Lord Trask*, and leave me alone."

She was flushed and breathless, her eyes bright with a combination of anger and unshed tears. And her hands shook as she gripped the fabric of her skirt. Every instinct he possessed suddenly tingled into awareness.

"I know, love. I'm sorry," he said, watching her carefully. "I would never do such a thing. You surely must know that. The shock of seeing you like that . . . well, let's just say it unhinged me."

She gave a little pant, looking more distressed by the minute. What in blazes was wrong with her? Why would she find his apology so upsetting?

"Sophie, surely you understand the danger you put yourself in. Not to mention what would happen to your reputation if anyone—"

"Hang my reputation," she snapped. "It's not my reputation you're worried about, it's yours. You're obsessed with your reputation and your business. You don't care a whit about me."

"Don't be a nod-nock," he retorted as his irritation flared. "Of course I care about you. I'd have to, to apologize after you acted so foolishly last night. Why can't you behave like a sensible woman and be content with the life you have?"

He wanted to recall the words as soon as they were out of his mouth. Sure enough, her eyes popped wide with outrage.

He sighed. "Sophie—"

"No! I've had enough, Simon. You're not my father or my brother. You have no right to tell me how to lead my life. I don't want to marry you. Now go away and leave me alone."

"Oh, for God's sake, Puck. What's the matter with you? I've apologized, haven't I? Tell me what's really bothering you."

He took a step forward, looming over her. She scuttled

around behind the settee, as wary as a hunted rabbit. Despite his anger, she looked so unhappy it was all he could do not to seize her and fold her securely into his arms.

"You don't love me, that's what the matter is," she blurted out. "I won't marry a man who doesn't love me. Now please leave me alone." Her voice had climbed into a shrill, unfamiliar register.

He stood nailed to the floor, shocked by the intensity of her emotions, stunned by her desperate desire to be rid of him. Surely she couldn't mean it? Not Sophie.

"You don't love me," she repeated when he didn't answer. "Not the way I need to be loved."

What was wrong with him? Why couldn't he seem to move or say a word? All he could manage was to gaze at her as she stood there, hugging her body as if she feared she would fly into a thousand pieces at any moment. He took in her slim figure, her elfin face—so alive with feeling—and tried to imagine life without Sophie. It would be calm and orderly, businesslike and productive. Devoid of feeling and empty as hell.

"I do love you." His entire body vibrated with the impact of those four simple words. "I've always loved you. And I always will."

He gave a dazed laugh. For the first time in his life, he had no idea what to say or do next. It was as if someone had put him in a blazing forge, softened him up, and then pounded him back into shape. Except it was a new shape, and everything about his world had changed.

She stared back, her complexion bleached as white as her wool shawl, her full mouth quivering, as if she held back sobs.

"You do?" she finally managed to choke out.

He moved around the settee to stand before her. "As unbelievable as you may think it, I do."

She tilted her head back to look at him, her eyes full of

vulnerability and hope, her soft mouth parting in surprise. His body instinctively answered her fragile, utterly feminine response with a pulse of heat and a raw surge of something that felt like joy.

Then she blinked, and the emotion drained from her face. Her pupils seemed to contract until all the light went out of her eyes.

"Like your grandfather loved your grandmother, Simon? Not even shedding a tear when she died. Is that how you love me?"

He heard a low, ugly noise, and realized that it came from his throat. She ignored it and kept on in a harsh voice he no longer recognized.

"I don't believe you. You're just like your grandfather, Simon. Cold and unfeeling. You'll say anything to get what you want. And what you want is my land, not me. The man I loved no longer exists. He died years ago. I'd rather spend the rest of my days as a lonely spinster than be married to you."

She moved toward the door, her slender back a rigid line underneath the gauzy fabric of her dress. "You can stay and explain to your aunts, if you want," she said, not bothering to turn around. "I'm going to my room."

As he watched her walk away, anger sliced through his gut and boiled in his chest. How dare she compare him to his grandfather? She, who knew better than anyone what the old man had been like. What the hell had gotten into her?

As for walking away . . . Sophie belonged to him, and no one could ever change that. Not even her. And she was naïve to think she could ever escape him.

Sophie could barely breathe as she walked to the door. She had accused him of the worst thing she could think of. Watching the love in his eyes transform into shock, then anger had sliced her heart into ribbons. Her harsh words had levelled him, and Simon would never forgive her.

It was for the best. Lady Randolph's words popped into her head, making her want to scream with the injustice of it all. She had to get out of the drawing room. Before despair overtook her, and before Simon recovered from his stunned paralysis. His anger would surely erupt any moment.

As her fingers reached for the brass knob, she heard him move in a hard rush. He pushed her flat against the wall, his chest a granitelike barrier along her spine. The impact of that masculine heat and strength sent a throbbing pulse of fear and longing coursing through her veins.

He twisted the key in the lock, blocking her escape.

"Let me go," she gasped, struggling in the hard cradle of his upper body.

He didn't give an inch. His brawny arms encircled her in an unbreakable grip as he pressed his fully rampant erection into the swell of her bottom.

"You think me cold, Sophie?" His voice was a fierce growl against the nape of her neck.

She ground her teeth, unable to repress a shiver of excitement.

"The last thing I am around you is cold." His tongue darted hot and wet into her ear. "As you're about to find out."

One big hand moved up to capture her breast. His long fingers delved beneath the edge of her bodice, finding a nipple, squeezing it into an aching point.

"Go to hell." Her voice was more plea than taunt as she tried to repress the arousal surging through her body.

"I probably will, but we're going to go up in flames together first."

He sucked the tender skin of her neck, licking and biting his way down to the top of her shoulder. His fingers worked at her breast, bringing a release of moisture between her legs.

How could she let him do this? How could *she* do this? She should scream—tell him he was hurting her, do something to make him stop. Letting him love her would only make things worse when she had to reject him again.

Her heart beat frantically against her ribs. God, she wanted him so much. Every part of her body responded to him, yearned for him. Prepared itself for the sweet invasion that made her shake with anticipation.

His questing mouth slid back up her neck to her jaw, leaving a trail of shivers in its wake. He nuzzled her cheek with a tenderness that unravelled her resistance.

She groaned and dropped her head onto his shoulder, giving up everything to him. If only for this brief moment, she wouldn't deny him what they both craved.

He murmured husky words of satisfaction as he pulled his hand from her bodice and brought it between her thighs. Cupping her sex through the thin layers of clothing, he pulled her back against his bulging erection. She bit her lip and groaned, tipping her pelvis into his caressing hand. Suddenly, she was ravenous with the need to feel him inside her.

"Simon," she moaned.

Urgent hands pulled up her skirts. She whimpered with relief as his calloused fingertips found the throbbing bud of her sex. He played with the hot flesh, holding her fast as she squirmed against his chest.

She was already slick—she could feel it as his fingers circled and stroked. The ache in her core intensified as he alternately cupped and flicked the hard peak.

"God, Sophie, you're going to drive me insane," he moaned as he rubbed his face against her neck.

She shivered, relishing the bristling feel of his skin. He flattened her against the wall, his body an iron cage behind her. Her nipples, pushed tight against her bodice, tingled with painful intensity. She arched back against him in an effort to relieve the ache.

As she did, he pushed a finger deep into her sheath. Sophie bit back a cry and went up on her toes. He inserted another finger and pumped gently, building the sensation in a slow, hot surge.

She pressed her hands against the cool plaster of the wall, pushing back as he played with her. The feel of him behind her—his body grown hard with passion—made her feel weak and hot with desire. If he didn't come inside her soon, she would go up in a flaming puff of smoke.

"Simon," she panted. "Please. Now."

"Yes, love. Now." His voice shook with desire.

His hand slipped away, and she could feel him tear at the fall of his breeches. A moment later his hands were back on her, pushing the fabric of her gown and chemise up around her waist. His fingers spread wide on her hip bones, taking a firm grip before lifting her off the floor. The tip of his erection probed her wet flesh, and with one sharp movement he surged into her heat.

She cried out, pushing against the wall with a desperate strength as he worked her body up and down his thick shaft. Each hard thrust rubbed against the most sensitive part of her sex, bringing her closer to climax. He brought his lips to her ear, his breath a scorching pant. His entire body strained in need for a release as urgent as hers. She sobbed, overcome with the force of her love and the devastating certainty this would be their last time together.

He let her toes hit the floor as he pushed back into her with another aggressive thrust, his erection rubbing hard against her throbbing nub. She cried out, flinging her arms wide against the wall as she climaxed. A moment later he followed, pulsing in her slick heat. Her body convulsed around him once more, and she collapsed, utterly spent. If not for the muscular arms locked so securely around her, she would have slid down the wall to the floor.

After a few dazed moments, he steadied her and carefully pulled out. She winced, the tender flesh between her thighs aching from his lovemaking, and the emptiness that followed his withdrawal.

But that pain was as nothing compared to the shame crawling along her nerves. How could she have given in to him like this? Behaving so disgracefully in broad daylight, especially after she had rejected him. Lady Randolph had nothing on her.

The contempt he must feel for her made her cringe, and she wanted to creep into a deep, dark cave and never come out.

"Sophie . . ."

"Don't. Don't say a word." She winced at the self-loathing in her voice as she cut him off.

With trembling hands, she smoothed her dress and re-arranged her bodice. When he tried to help, she pushed him away and fumbled for the lock of the door, refusing to meet his eyes.

"Sweetheart, don't be ashamed," he said. "You can't say no to me any more than I can say no to you."

His voice held a hint of masculine arrogance. He reached out a hand to cup her cheek. She swatted at it, her face burning with mortification.

"Just go away, Simon. I don't want to talk about it, and I don't want to see you again. It's over."

She heard him make an impatient noise and, out of the corner of her eye, saw him quickly button up the fall of his breeches. As she fumbled once more to open the door, he grabbed her by the shoulders and spun her around.

Their gazes locked. His was dark and merciless.

"This isn't over, Sophie. It will never be over."

He lifted her right out of her slippers and planted a smother-ing kiss on her lips. Before she could respond he released her and wrenched open the door, striding out without a glance at her.

Sophie staggered to a cane chair next to the window and collapsed onto the seat. A choking laugh forced its way from her throat as she dropped her head into her hands. He would always see the world—and her—as something to bend to his will. But not this time, and for her, never again.

Their life together was over before it began, and the sooner he learned that lesson the better.

Chapter Twenty-Six

Simon couldn't find words ugly enough to describe his mood. His thoughts had been racketing through his brain like a shuttle on a loom since the moment he stormed out of his aunts' townhouse. He had mentally replayed his fight with Sophie a dozen times as he sought to make sense of her odd and frustrating behaviour. At the end of a long day, he felt not a whit closer to ascertaining the root of the problem. Worse still, he couldn't shake the feeling that she was in trouble and needed him.

Sophie still loved him—of that he was certain. She wouldn't have surrendered in that blaze of passion if she didn't. Not Puck. She was innocence and honesty personified, and incapable of hiding her true feelings.

The heated images of her slender body splayed up against the wall, melting like honey under his rough caresses, drove him away from his desk. She had met his lovemaking with a sweet intensity, but he had acted the brute with her, once again. No wonder she wouldn't speak to him. He had obviously gone stark raving mad, at least when it came to her.

He dropped into the leather club chair by his desk—the very one she had sprawled in so sensuously the other night.

Everything he saw or touched reminded him of Sophie. Life without her was fast becoming intolerable, and now he didn't have the faintest clue how to get her back. He hadn't felt this helpless since the day his grandfather ordered him home from Cambridge all those years ago.

A knock pounded on the front door of his lodgings. He sighed, rubbing the aching muscles in the back of his neck. With any luck, the caller would be visiting another lodger. The last thing he needed was an evening of idle chitchat with one of his Bath acquaintances.

A tap sounded on the door to his apartments. He blew out a soft curse as he rose to answer it.

"You have a visitor, m'lord," said the porter. He paused portentously. "A lady."

"Who is it?"

"She wouldn't say, m'lord. And she's wearing a veil."

Sophie. Thank God she'd finally come to her senses. "Show her up."

He tugged his cravat, easing the pressure of the starched linen. If he hadn't been so bloody thankful she was going to relent, he would have been tempted to throttle her for putting him through such misery.

A petite woman, dressed in a grey velvet pelisse and swathed in a black veil, stepped into the room. French perfume assailed his nostrils, twisting his insides with frustration and disappointment.

Bathsheba threw back her veil. Her face was composed, but her eyes glittered with a hectic, almost wild, excitement.

"What the hell are you doing here, Bathsheba?"

She glided over to the club chair, pulling off her gloves as she sank gracefully down onto the leather seat. Simon had to clench his fists against his sides to stop himself from yanking her from the chair.

"Do sit down, Simon. You'll give me a crick in my neck."

He remained standing. "Whatever it is, get on with it."

Her lips turned down in a seductive, practiced pout. "So cold. I suppose it's only to be expected after what happened today." She paused, as if waiting for him to respond.

Christ. He was sick of her manipulation. How could he have ever preferred her to Sophie?

"All right, I'll bite. What happened today?"

She looked genuinely startled. "Oh. I've come to offer my condolences. I understand your betrothal to Miss Stanton has come to an end. I'm not surprised, of course. It was a colossal mistake, and I'm so grateful you've come to your senses."

Her words hit him with the force of a blow. "Who told you that?"

"I have my sources."

"Your sources are wrong. My engagement to Sophie stands."

"But I got a note—" She cut off the words on a slight hiss.

He strode over and pulled her from the chair. She gasped, eyes going wide, but didn't struggle to break free.

"Who sent you the note?"

Bathsheba's eyes shifted away. Anger rose, tight and fierce in his chest, as the morning's events suddenly began to make sense.

"Sophie," he rasped. "Why would she write to you?"

She swallowed, as if her throat had suddenly gone dry. "A piece of information reached my ears this morning. A very damaging piece of information. I knew Miss Stanton would want to know."

Simon let her go so abruptly that she dropped back into the club chair. But she didn't stay there, instead rising to follow him to the window.

"Simon, I did this for you. Sophie will bring you nothing but gossip and scandal. The poor thing can't help it—she simply has no discipline. But what she's done now . . . everything that came before pales in comparison."

He stared blindly into the street below, fighting back the tempest of fury that threatened to cloud his brain. Who had seen them last night? Had someone followed him down to The Silver Oak? He'd been so careful to shield Sophie from—

Watley.

He had been at The Pelican last night with a noisy group of young bucks. Simon had been tempted to challenge the bastard on the spot for the liberties he'd taken with Sophie, but Russell had been waiting.

"What did Watley tell you?"

He felt, rather than saw, her start. She hid her emotions well, but her reaction told him he'd guessed correctly.

"That Miss Stanton was seen at The Silver Oak tavern with one of Lady Eleanor's footmen. Consorting with thieves and prostitutes. And that you dragged her away," she answered in a quiet voice.

"No one will believe it," he said hoarsely. Neither of them had to say what *it* was. Her meaning was perfectly clear.

"Simon, the ton will attack a woman for daring to walk past White's in the middle of the day. What do you think they'll do to Sophie if word of this gets out? They may not believe everything, but they'll believe enough. Her reputation already hangs by a thread after her antics these last few weeks. Do you want to ruin her for good? If you truly care, you'll do what you must to protect her."

A wheedling tone crept into her voice. "But I can help you. Let me talk to Watley. I'm sure I can convince him to hold his tongue."

"And what must I give in exchange for your help?"

A small hand crept up his sleeve. Through the haze of his anger, he noticed her fingernails were bitten to the quick.

"I want you to come back to me, Simon. I want you to marry me. You've forgotten how good we were together, but I can remind you. We were made for ĕach other . . . you'll see." Her voice dropped to a seductive whisper. "Let me show you."

A shudder coursed through his body. He shook her arm off and moved to the other side of his desk.

"You're mad, Bathsheba. I'll never marry you. And I *will* marry Sophie."

Something much like panic distorted her beautiful features. But after a moment her iron will reasserted itself.

"Are you willing to face that kind of scandal? All for that ridiculous chit? I always believed you had more sense than that. What will your aunts say?" Her treacherous gaze narrowed, sharp with speculation. "And what of General Stanton? How do you think he'll feel when he discovers you refused to quell the gossip about his granddaughter?"

He took a step forward. "Do not try to blackmail me, Bathsheba. Things will go very badly for you if you do."

Her eyes flared with anger, but underneath it lurked fear. The emotions poured from her petite frame, boiling through the air like a swarm of furious bees.

"Don't reject me, Simon. I vow you'll regret it for the rest of your life. And so will Sophie."

He stared at her, dumbfounded and full of helpless rage. Bathsheba had him by the throat, and she knew it.

Chapter Twenty-Seven

It had been five days since Lady Randolph walked into the parlor at St. James's Square and blown Sophie's life to smithereens. That, and the encounter with Simon, had been earth-shatteringly awful, but it had seemed then that things couldn't get worse. Clearly the worst was just getting started.

Lady Eleanor swept into the drawing room, a startling sight in a puce-colored dress and a gigantic matching turban.

"No long faces, Sophia," she boomed. "I won't have it. We'll march in, heads high, and the devil take the lot of them."

"A few long faces are certainly in order, Eleanor," chided Lady Jane as she retied the sash on Sophie's gown. "After what the poor child's suffered these last few days, I can't imagine why you're forcing her to go through with this charade."

They fell silent. The tempest had broken over their heads, as swift and deadly as a winter storm at sea. Lady Randolph had not kept her promise. A few days ago, word of Sophie's adventures at The Silver Oak had begun filtering throughout the Bath company. The gossip had accelerated with lightning speed— totally inaccurate, of course, and surprisingly vicious— and nothing her godmothers said to their friends made any difference. They, too, were affected, as morning visits and dinner invitations dwindled to a trickle.

Even worse, Simon wasn't there to defend them. He had departed from Bath the day Sophie broke their engagement, with no indication when he would return.

Lady Eleanor cleared her throat. "We're going because Stantons don't run and hide, that's why."

"This Stanton would be happy to run and hide, rather than suffer death by ton," muttered Sophie.

She'd resisted her godmother's plan to attend the ball at the Assembly Rooms this evening, knowing it would only provide more fodder for the gossips. Aunt Eleanor had been implacable, however, insisting that family honor dictated no other course. Sophie had finally given in. Her godmother would likely drag her there by her topknot if she didn't fall into line.

"Besides," added the old woman, "Robert and Annabel are going. We can't leave them to face all this rot without our support. You've got to do it for the family, Sophia. You've done nothing to be ashamed of—unless you count your sentimental notions about life as shameful, which I certainly don't. Face down the old cats one last time, then you can leave for your grandfather's estate with a clear conscience."

"I know. It's just that—" Sophie broke off, swallowing the lump that had taken up permanent residence in her throat.

"Oh, Sophie." Lady Jane gave her a quick hug.

Lady Eleanor watched them with a sad wisdom. They all knew what Sophie's future was likely to be, and the loneliness she would have to bear. Without even a sister to grow old with.

"You're a brave girl, Sophia, and I'm sorry you have to go through this. If only you had thought to wake me that night, I could have done something to help you. I wish I could have dealt with that poltroon and his doxy myself!"

Sophie choked out a laugh at the idea of Lady Eleanor

storming The Silver Oak. Now that would've given the gossips something to talk about.

"That's more like it." Lady Eleanor smiled. "No more moping from either of you. Not tonight, anyway. Let's be on our way—we don't want to keep our audience waiting."

Lady Jane gave a delicate snort. "Heaven forfend."

All too soon, the carriage deposited them at the Assembly Rooms. They disposed of their cloaks, shook out their skirts, and prepared to head into the fray.

"Courage, my love." Lady Jane tucked her hand into Sophie's elbow. "This time tomorrow you'll be far away from here."

Away from everyone she loved, exiled by her own choice to General Stanton's most northern estate. Robert and Annabel were following in a few days, but Sophie likely wouldn't see her mother and grandparents for several weeks, if not longer. And Simon—she had no idea when she would see him again.

She blinked hard, trying to push his image from her mind. If she thought of him now, or how he must have reacted to the news of the scandal, she would turn tail and run. He would never forgive her. How could he? Losing the coal from her estates would be bad enough, but losing his reputation over something as tawdry as this—

"Ready, my dear?" Lady Eleanor's question interrupted Sophie's downward spiral.

With her godmothers flanking her, she squared her shoulders and headed into the Octagon Room. The crowd parted, giving them just enough space to move unimpeded to the opposite, less crowded end of the room. Lady Eleanor bestowed an imperial nod on the occasional acquaintance, but otherwise ignored the smirks and grins, the whispers and cutting remarks that followed in their wake. Sophie marched grimly forward, every part of her skin flushed with a maddening heat.

Just ahead, she spied Mr. Puddleford talking to one of the Heathcote sisters. She breathed a sigh of gratitude. He would acknowledge her, of course. There had been many a rout or party where no one would talk to the poor man but her.

"Good evening, Mr. Puddleford." She gave him her best smile. "How nice to see you again."

"I . . . I . . ." The pudgy little man rolled his eyes in panic in the direction of his companion.

"Come away, Mr. Puddleford." Louisa Heathcote's shrill voice rose above the crowd. "The company in this part of the room is intolerable. Not at all respectable."

A pomaded fop behind Louisa tittered and repeated the remark to another man. It would only take moments for the ill-mannered rebuff to sweep the room.

"Come along, dear," murmured Lady Jane. "I see Robert and Annabel at the top of the room."

Sophie's vision blurred, but she forced her feet to move. A scorching mix of emotions burned away at her, like vinegar on an open wound. Rage that anyone would insult her godmothers, and a sickening shame that she had brought this trouble down upon her family.

She blinked away her tears, furious that she felt like crying. She had helped save Toby and Becky and would do it again, if she had to. Louisa Heathcote and the lot of them could go to the devil, for all she cared.

"Sophie, darling." Annabel's gentle voice and warm hug brought her back to herself.

"Here, sis." Robert appeared at his wife's shoulder. "I managed to snabble some chairs for us. You look like you could do with a rest. In fact," he said, peering at her face, "you look done to a cow's thumb."

"I'm fine," Sophie automatically responded, as she had done so many times in the last few days.

"Of course you are." Her sister-in-law patted her hand. "You just need to be gone from this horrid place. We all do."

As they settled into their chairs, Annabel launched into a

grimly cheerful recounting of her correspondence with various family and friends. Sophie smiled vaguely and pretended to listen. But, as happened whenever she had nothing to occupy her mind, all she could think of was Simon.

God, she missed him. With an ache that burrowed into her very bones. The pain of the last few days would have been little more than a fleabite if he were still by her side, protecting her as he had done for so many years. But now . . . now she had no choice but to go on without him. Perhaps the ache would eventually fade, and life might return to something that resembled normal. Eventually.

If only she didn't feel so lonely. As lonely as that terrible time after the death of her father.

She grimaced, irritated with her mawkish self-pity. She had made a decision to protect her family, and she had held to her end of the bargain. As far as Sophie was concerned, Lady Randolph carried the blame for all of this. Unfortunately, the countess wouldn't be the one to suffer.

"Oh, good God," muttered Robert from the chair beside her.

"What is it?"

"Over there." Her brother, looking as if he had just swallowed a bad oyster, pointed toward the archway leading into the room.

Sophie craned her neck, trying to see over the throng. "There does seem to be quite a commotion, doesn't there? And it's not even one that we caused."

"Don't bet on it," he said morosely.

"General Stanton and Lady Stanton," announced the master of ceremonies into the sudden hush that had fallen over the room.

Sophie came to her feet, as did Annabel and Robert. Perspiration misted the back of her neck as she watched the dignified old couple make a slow progress through the crowd. What in heaven's name were they doing here?

Her stomach lurched. For a moment, she feared she might

cast up her accounts in front of half the population of Bath. She bit back a hysterical giggle at the absurdity of the image, and forced herself to take a deep breath as her grandparents approached.

Annabel gave a swift curtsy before launching herself into Lady Stanton's arms. "Grandmamma, Grandpapa, I'm so happy to see you."

Robert cleared his throat and gave his grandfather a nervous smile. "Good evening, sir." His voice sounded considerably higher than its normal pitch.

General Stanton glared back at him. "Well, grandson, will you also tell me how happy you are to see me? Spare me your canards."

Robert blanched. The general leaned in closer, until they were nose to nose.

"Good lord, my boy! What are you about letting your sister get into so much trouble? You're supposed to be protecting her. And because you didn't do your duty, your grandmamma and I had to pull ourselves away from our own comfortable hearth, and come to this godforsaken place and consort with the worst set of vulgar mushrooms I've seen in years."

"Really, sir, you know as well as I—ouch!" Robert scowled at Annabel, who gave him a look of wide-eyed innocence.

General Stanton switched his gaze to Sophie, his features as stern as a gothic saint.

"Well, miss? What do you have to say for yourself?"

The silence in the room thrummed in her ears. It seemed the entire world waited for her answer. She dropped into a deep curtsy, held it for several moments, then rose to her feet.

"Good evening, Grandfather." She met his narrowed gaze with as much composure as she could muster. "It's wonderful to see you looking so well."

His thin mouth twitched, and then he gave a gruff laugh. "That's my girl. Come and give your old grandpapa a hug."

She stared at him, not quite sure her ears were working as they should. He pulled her into his arms. It took all her discipline not to burst into tears as he gave her a rough hug.

"There now, miss. You've all made a mull of things, as usual, but your grandpapa will set it right." He glared at their eager, jostling audience. "And anyone who doesn't think I have the power to do so will find it goes very ill for them."

"Yes, my dear, I'm sure they will. But do let Sophie go. You're crushing her gown." Lady Stanton extracted Sophie from his arms and gave her a soft hug.

Sophie returned the embrace, still too dazed to ask any questions. All around them the hubbub had been growing louder by the second, but, once again, a stunned silence fell over the room.

"Now what?" groaned Robert.

"Oh my goodness," squeaked Annabel. "Sophie, look!"

Lady Stanton released her, and Sophie turned to face the room. Her heart took a throbbing leap into her throat when she saw who stood in the archway.

Simon. Looking devastatingly handsome in his flawless black tailcoat and snowy cravat, and radiating so much power and confidence that it reached her from across the room.

He moved swiftly through the crowd, ignoring the murmured comments that followed him like a rippling tide across a wind-scoured beach. He came to a halt before her. Sophie stared into his midnight eyes, breathing so hard that her vision began to blur.

Simon shook his head, a smile playing around his lips. "Sophie, you're fogging up your glasses."

He carefully plucked them from her face, took the lacy handkerchief Annabel offered him, and wiped them clean.

"Thank you," she whispered as he gravely offered them back to her.

"Well, nevvie," groused Lady Eleanor. "It's about time you showed up. We've been having a devil of a time down here."

"Forgive me, aunt. I came back as quickly as I could." He smiled down at Sophie. "I told you I would never abandon you, sweetheart. You know I always keep my promises."

She still couldn't speak. She could only stare into the imperiously aristocratic yet beloved face she thought never to see again.

He tilted his head. "What's the matter, Puck? Cat got your tongue? I'll have to remember to surprise you more often."

Her mouth fell open. "Simon! How can you tease me at a time like this? Don't you—"

"May I have the next dance, Miss Stanton?" He cut her off, unholy amusement dancing in his eyes. "That is, if someone hasn't already claimed your hand. I did see Mr. Puddleford hanging about when I came into the room."

She felt it best to ignore that remark, extending her hand while maintaining a dignified silence. He grinned and led her into the set just forming in the next room.

In truth, Sophie was afraid to open her mouth. She didn't know what would come out—hysterical laughter, tears, or even a scold was likely, and the Stantons and St. Jameses had already provided enough food for the Bath gossips to last a lifetime.

For several minutes they moved through the figures of the dance. Simon ignored everyone but her, his expression relaxed and easy, his eyes smiling and full of love. She could hardly believe it. Where was her imperious earl? How could he not care she had subjected him to the worst kind of innuendo and scandal? She couldn't make sense of it, but the fact that he was here and had convinced her grandfather—the second most scandal-averse man in England—to lend his public support spoke of a love that would trump every obstacle standing in their way.

They came back together, hands and arms intertwined.

"You're not mad at me?" she whispered.

He gave a rueful shake of the head, his dark eyes gleaming like ebony in the glitter of a thousand candles. "No, love. This is my fault. I should have known something was wrong. That you were in trouble. If I hadn't been such a prideful fool, you would have told me."

"Was this—tonight—part of your plan to respond to the scandal?"

"I didn't have a plan, Sophie. I wasn't even sure you would want to see me again, after the way I acted. Your grandmother, though, seemed quite certain you would."

"How did she—never mind. Go on."

He flashed a brief smile. "The one thing I did know was that I had to get to your grandparents before word of the scandal reached them. It was your grandmother's idea to face the gossip head-on. In public, and right where it started. There may be some rumbles for a short time, but when people realize the general and I are behind you, the rumors will die down soon enough. Especially once we're married." He grinned. "Which will be soon, I assure you."

She smiled back, unable to resist the pull of his blatant happiness. The lump in her throat still made it hard to speak, but it lodged there now from joy, not sorrow. There was, however, one thing still troubling her.

"What about Mr. Russell and all your plans?"

He shrugged, truly seeming not to care. "Russell will make his decisions, and I will make mine. You're all I want or need, Sophie. Not wealth or factories, nor Russell and his damned disapproving lectures."

That didn't sound like the Simon she knew. She pointedly raised her eyebrows.

"Well, I do want the factories, and I will find a way to build them," he amended. "But it means nothing without you, my love. And it's taken me much too long to figure that out."

The joy had moved from her throat to flood her entire body. "Really?"

He cast his eyes to the ceiling in amused exasperation. And stopped. Right in the middle of the dance floor. He threw the whole set out of line, and more than one lady shrieked as her partner stumbled into her.

Sophie gasped as Simon went down on one knee.

"What are you doing?"

"Proposing to you," he answered solemnly.

He extracted something from his waistcoat pocket, grasped her trembling hand, and eased a simple gold ring onto her finger.

"Sophie Stanton, I love you, and I want to marry you. And I won't get up off this floor until you agree."

Her face burned with embarrassment, even though her heart soared into the heavens. "Oh, Simon, you fool. Do get up! Everyone's staring."

He looked like he was preparing to stay on his knees all night. "Not until you say yes."

She grabbed his hands and tugged. "I can't believe you're doing this. All right, I'll marry you—just get up. Before everyone thinks you've gone completely mad!"

He laughed and surged to his feet, taking her into his arms and sweeping her down the line.

"Very well, my sweet. God forbid we should cause any gossip."

Epilogue

Kendlerood House
Manor of the Earl of Trask
January 1816

Simon opened the door to the master bedchamber. The longcase clock in the gallery had just chimed out the midnight hour, but Sophie was awake, propped up in bed in a comfortable shamble of pillows and bed linens and wrapped in a thick wool shawl to keep her warm. Her gold spectacles winked in the firelight. Soft, tumbled curls gleamed the color of flame as she bent her head over the pile of documents in her lap. She looked young and innocent, and oh, so serious.

He leaned against the doorframe, watching her, savoring the quiet satisfaction of knowing she was safely in his bed—in his life. For too long he had been a fool. He had made so many mistakes when it came to her, but she had forgiven him and still loved him. It was a miracle he would never forget.

She looked up and smiled a welcome. And, he hoped, an invitation. He had already taken her three times today, but he rather thought they should do it again. When it came to Sophie, he could never get enough.

He strolled over and sat beside her on the bed.

"It's good to have the house to ourselves again, isn't it, Puck?" He took her hand, pressing a kiss into her palm. "I thought that small army of your relatives would never leave."

She rolled her eyes. "Yes, because this house is so cramped we all kept bumping into each other. Simon, I still get lost at least once a week, trying to find my way from one end of this pile to the other."

"Perhaps, but one does grow weary of the bickering between Robert and the general. How Lady Stanton puts up with it is one of life's eternal mysteries. Besides, I like it best when it's just the two of us." He abandoned her palm for the sweet curve of her neck, nibbling his way up to her earlobe.

She giggled and squirmed away from him. "Simon, do stop. I'm trying to work. You've made love to me three times today, already. And it was scandalous of you to insist we do it in the small drawing room in the middle of the day. I almost fainted when I heard the general out in the corridor."

"I thought something else almost made you faint." He followed her across the bed, trying to push the papers from her lap.

"Not now," she said.

He sighed, recognizing her tone.

"What are you doing?" he asked as he settled in next to her, leaning against the headboard of the massive tester bed.

Enthusiasm set off amber sparks in her eyes. "These are the plans for the new hospital for women and children in Bath. Mr. Crawford just sent them, along with a list of those who might be willing to donate funds."

Simon frowned. "Crawford, eh? Writing you again? He seems to take up quite a bit of your time." Time he wanted her to spend with him, not with same damned earnest cleric.

Sophie gave him a stern look over the top of her glasses. "Simon, don't be such a looby."

He grinned, feeling sheepish.

She stroked his chin. "Let me finish reading this letter, then we can talk."

He arranged a few pillows behind his back and relaxed, content, for now, to let her work. But he had every intention of doing something more than talking as soon as she finished.

When Sophie reached for another sheaf of papers, he clasped her wrist, stroking the coral bracelet that encircled it.

"I'm glad you got your bracelet back, Puck." He fingered the delicate beads. "I know how much it means to you."

She went as rigid as a gatepost. His instincts, so attuned to everything about her, woke up. He peered into her face. She looked . . . guilty.

"Sophie, what's wrong?"

"Well, about my bracelet, Simon . . ." Her voice trailed off. She gave him a suspiciously placating smile.

He sighed. "Just tell me now, and get it over with."

She carefully placed the papers to one side and faced him. She looked as if she was confronting a firing squad.

"I didn't tell you the exact truth about the theft. It wasn't my coral bracelet, it was my gold bracelet that was stolen— the Stanton family heirloom. I was taking it to the jeweler's when Toby snatched my reticule. Becky made him return it to me that night I went to the theater." The words came out in a rush, as if she'd been bottling them up for months.

Which she had.

"Why didn't you tell me?"

She winced at his tone of voice.

Damn. He didn't mean to sound so annoyed, but his insides went cold and hollow whenever he thought of the risks she'd taken to recover her bracelet. Now, at least, her seemingly demented behavior in Bath made sense.

"I wanted to," she said, regret coloring her voice. "But I couldn't bear what you and the rest of the family would think of me. You all thought me so careless and scandal-prone. I had to find it before anyone knew it was gone. I'm sorry, but I couldn't tell you."

Behind the glint of her spectacles her eyes held defiance, and more than a hint of the vulnerability that never failed to tug at his heart.

He pulled her into his arms. "Love, you have nothing to apologize for. The fault is mine. If I hadn't been such an ill-tempered prig, you would have trusted me enough to ask for help."

She snuggled against him, a sweet little package of femininity. His rampant desire to protect her—never far from the surface—came up in a rush. As did something else, responding eagerly to the press of her soft breasts and slim hips against his hardening body.

He rolled her onto her back. "But no more secrets, Sophie. I mean it. If I find out you're holding anything back from me I'll have to punish you."

She smiled, a wicked curl of mischief shaping her plush mouth. "And how do you intend to carry out your punishment, my lord?"

"I have many ways, my lady," he growled, tickling her ribs.

She howled with laughter and swatted his hands. Their tussle soon evolved into another kind of play, the best kind of play for adults.

After a time—a very happy time—he eased out of her and lay back, tucking her against his side. She had worn him out, but he still couldn't resist letting his hand drift over her breasts, down her sides, over her smooth belly—

He craned his neck to look down at her body.

"Sophie, is it my imagination or are you getting plump? You did eat quite a lot of sweets over the holidays, as I recall."

She pinched his arm. "Simon, you beast!"

"Ouch. Madam wife, I swear you turn me black and blue." He levered himself over her, nuzzling the scowl from her face with a kiss. "Sophie, I would love you even if you grew to be as large as Jack Spratt's wife."

"No one would ever mistake you for lean, at least down there," she grumbled, wriggling underneath him. Predictably, his staff twitched to life.

He made his way down her body, kissing the gentle swell of her belly. "You're even softer here, and down here, too. I like it." He let his hands wander.

She gasped. "Simon, I have another secret to tell you."

He stilled. "A good or a bad one?"

"I think it's a good one." She hesitated. "I'm with child."

Something popped in his head, and then it filled up with a feeling as fizzy as champagne bubbles. He surged up her body.

"Are you sure?"

She nodded. "Quite sure."

He captured her face in his hands, staring into eyes that gazed back at him with perfect trust and perfect love. He didn't know if his heart could hold so much happiness without bursting, but he had a whole lifetime with Sophie to find out.

"Now," she whispered as she wrapped her arms around his neck. "Isn't that much nicer than a pile of nasty old coal?"

He wanted to laugh, but joy squeezed his throat.

"It's nicer than anything," he managed.

And he meant every word.

About the Author

Vanessa Kelly was born and raised in New Jersey, but eventually migrated north to Canada. She holds a master's Degree from Rutgers University, and went on to attend the Ph.D. program in English Literature at the University of Toronto. Alas, she didn't finish her degree, but she did spend many happy hours studying the works of eighteenth-century British authors and writing about the madness of King George III. She left graduate school to work as a researcher and writer for a large public sector organization. Vanessa now devotes her time to writing historical romance, and hopes that her readers will find her books as much fun to read as they were to write. She currently lives with her husband in Ottawa. You can visit her on the web at www.vanessakellyauthor.com.

More by Bestselling Author
Hannah Howell

__Highland Angel	978-1-4201-0864-4	$6.99US/$8.99CAN
__If He's Sinful	978-1-4201-0461-5	$6.99US/$8.99CAN
__Wild Conquest	978-1-4201-0464-6	$6.99US/$8.99CAN
__If He's Wicked	978-1-4201-0460-8	$6.99US/$8.49CAN
__My Lady Captor	978-0-8217-7430-4	$6.99US/$8.49CAN
__Highland Sinner	978-0-8217-8001-5	$6.99US/$8.49CAN
__Highland Captive	978-0-8217-8003-9	$6.99US/$8.49CAN
__Nature of the Beast	978-1-4201-0435-6	$6.99US/$8.49CAN
__Highland Fire	978-0-8217-7429-8	$6.99US/$8.49CAN
__Silver Flame	978-1-4201-0107-2	$6.99US/$8.49CAN
__Highland Wolf	978-0-8217-8000-8	$6.99US/$9.99CAN
__Highland Wedding	978-0-8217-8002-2	$4.99US/$6.99CAN
__Highland Destiny	978-1-4201-0259-8	$4.99US/$6.99CAN
__Only for You	978-0-8217-8151-7	$6.99US/$8.99CAN
__Highland Promise	978-1-4201-0261-1	$4.99US/$6.99CAN
__Highland Vow	978-1-4201-0260-4	$4.99US/$6.99CAN
__Highland Savage	978-0-8217-7999-6	$6.99US/$9.99CAN
__Beauty and the Beast	978-0-8217-8004-6	$4.99US/$6.99CAN
__Unconquered	978-0-8217-8088-6	$4.99US/$6.99CAN
__Highland Barbarian	978-0-8217-7998-9	$6.99US/$9.99CAN
__Highland Conqueror	978-0-8217-8148-7	$6.99US/$9.99CAN
__Conqueror's Kiss	978-0-8217-8005-3	$4.99US/$6.99CAN
__A Stockingful of Joy	978-1-4201-0018-1	$4.99US/$6.99CAN
__Highland Bride	978-0-8217-7995-8	$4.99US/$6.99CAN
__Highland Lover	978-0-8217-7759-6	$6.99US/$9.99CAN

Available Wherever Books Are Sold!

Check out our website at
http://www.kensingtonbooks.com